Masterpieces

OF

Mystery

Masterpieces
OF
Mystery

The Supersleuths
Revisited

Selected by ELLERY QUEEN

COPYRIGHT NOTICES AND ACKNOWLEDGMENTS

Grateful acknowledgment is hereby made for permission to reprint the following:

The Adventure of the Blue Carbuncle by A. Conan Doyle; reprinted by permission of the copyright proprietor of the A. Conan Doyle works.

The Double Clue by Agatha Christie; reprinted by permission of Dodd, Mead & Company, Inc. from DOUBLE SIN AND OTHER STORIES by Agatha Christie; copyright 1925 by Agatha Christie, copyright renewed 1953 by Agatha Christie Mallowan.

The Dauphin's Doll by Ellery Queen; copyright © 1948, 1951 by Ellery Queen, renewed; reprinted by permission of Scott Meredith Literary Agency, Inc.

The Cop Killer by Rex Stout; from TRIPLE JEOPARDY by Rex Stout; copyright 1951 by Rex Stout; reprinted by permission of The Viking Press.

The Case of the Irate Witness by Erle Stanley Gardner; copyright 1953 by Crowell-Collier Publishing Company; reprinted by permission of Thayer Hobson and Company.

The Most Obstinate Man in Paris by Georges Simenon; copyright 1947 by Georges Simenon; reprinted by permission of the author.

A Man Called Spade by Dashiell Hammett; © 1932 by Crowell Publishing Co., renewal © 1960 by Dashiell Hammett; reprinted by permission of Harold Matson Company, Inc.

The Blast of the Book by G. K. Chesterton; reprinted by permission of Dodd, Mead & Company, Inc. from THE SCANDAL OF FATHER BROWN; copyright 1935 by G. K. Chesterton, copyright renewed 1963 by Oliver Chesterton.

A Matter of Taste by Dorothy L. Sayers; copyright 1928 by Dorothy L. Sayers, renewed; copyright 1956 by Anthony Fleming; reprinted by permission of A. Watkins, Inc.

The Adopted Daughter by Melville Davisson Post; copyright 1918 by D. Appleton & Co., renewed 1946 by the Estate of Melville Davisson Post; reprinted by permission of Robert P. Mills, Ltd.

The Locked Room by John Dickson Carr; copyright 1943 by The American Mercury, Inc., renewed; reprinted by permission of Clarice M. Carr.

The Bearded Lady by Ross Macdonald; copyright 1948 by Kenneth Millar, renewed; reprinted by permission of Harold Ober Associates, Inc.

Murder Under the Mistletoe by Margery Allingham; © 1962 by Davis Publications, Inc.; reprinted by permission of Paul R. Reynolds, Inc.

PHOTOGRAPH CREDITS: pp. 11, 67, 231, 339, The New York Public Library; p. 31, Angus McBean; p. 41, Tracy Photograph (M. Lee), Harvey L. Bilker (F. Dannay); p. 132, François Gonet; p. 167, painting by J. A. McDougall; p. 201, Eileen Darby, Graphic House; p. 246, Radio Times Hulton Picture Library.

CONTENTS

INTRODUCTION

DEAR READER:

On October 14, 1950, George Gallup, Director of the American Institute of Public Opinion, published the results of a nationwide survey on mystery writers—or, as the Institute aptly expressed it, announced the winners in the "Whodunit Derby." To quote from the Gallup Poll report, "all persons who said they read mysteries were asked to volunteer the name of the writer, living or dead, whom they consider tops in the mystery field." Here, in order of their ranking, with the last nine names tied for tenth place, are "the best mystery writers of all time," as of 1950:

1. Erle Stanley Gardner
2. A. Conan Doyle
3. Ellery Queen
4. Edgar Allan Poe
5. Agatha Christie
6. S. S. Van Dine
7. Mary Roberts Rinehart
8. Rex Stout
9. Dashiell Hammett
10. Leslie Charteris
10. G. K. Chesterton
10. Wilkie Collins
10. Mignon G. Eberhart
10. Leslie Ford
10. Craig Rice
10. Sax Rohmer
10. Dorothy L. Sayers
10. Mabel Seeley

Twenty-two years later, on November 13, 1972, the Central American country of Nicaragua issued a commemorative set of

12 postage stamps to celebrate the 50th anniversary of Interpol. Each of the stamps showed a portrait of one of the "12 most famous detectives of fiction." The selection of the top 12 was based on the results of three worldwide polls in which 66 of the foremost mystery critics and mystery editors, 91 of the best mystery writers, and 1090 of the most devoted mystery readers cast ballots. Here is the final ranking of the 18 mystery authors who created "the greatest fictional sleuths of all time," as of 1972:

1. A. Conan Doyle (Sherlock Holmes)
2. Agatha Christie (Hercule Poirot)
3. Ellery Queen (Ellery Queen)
4. Rex Stout (Nero Wolfe)
5. Erle Stanley Gardner (Perry Mason)
6. Earl Derr Biggers (Charlie Chan)
7. Georges Simenon (Inspector Maigret)
8. Edgar Allan Poe (C. Auguste Dupin)
9. Dashiell Hammett (Sam Spade)
10. G. K. Chesterton (Father Brown)
11. Dorothy L. Sayers (Lord Peter Wimsey)
12. Raymond Chandler (Philip Marlowe)
13. John Dickson Carr (Dr. Gideon Fell)
14. Ross Macdonald (Lew Archer)
15. Margery Allingham (Albert Campion)
16. J. J. Marric [John Creasey] (George Gideon)
17. S. S. Van Dine (Philo Vance)
18. Melville Davisson Post (Uncle Abner)

Now, an interesting and provocative question arises, since each list happens to comprise 18 authors' names: How many mystery writers on the first list of the 18 "greatest" survived among the 18 "greatest" of the second list? Analysis of the two lists reveals that while the order of fame changed, no less than 10 mystery writers retained their critical status and reader popularity after the passage of 22 years. Those 10 are Doyle, Christie, Queen, Poe, Gardner, Stout, Chesterton, Hammett, Sayers, and Van Dine. And in the intervening 22 years eight writers rose to worldwide acceptance and prominence—Simenon, Biggers, Chandler, Post, Marric (Creasey), Carr, Macdonald, and Allingham.

Will there be a third poll?—say, another 22 years after the second, in the year 1994. And how many of the first 18 and the second 18 will still be ranked among the greatest mystery writers and fictional detectives of all time, as of 1994? It makes for a fascinating extrapolation. . . .

In the meantime let us revisit 14 of the current supersleuths and again read the adventures and memoirs that probably will continue to delight and excite the mystery fans of 1994—and beyond.

Happy detecting!

ELLERY QUEEN

THE ADVENTURE OF THE BLUE CARBUNCLE

BY A. CONAN DOYLE

Arthur Conan Doyle was born on May 22, 1859, in Edinburgh, Scotland, and received his medical degree from the University of Edinburgh in 1885. Best known for his creation of Sherlock Holmes, the author received only £ 25 for *A Study in Scarlet*, the master detective's first adventure, when it appeared in *Beeton's Christmas Annual* in 1887. Conan Doyle also wrote historical novels, adventure tales, and mysteries not featuring Holmes. He was knighted in 1902 for his work on behalf of the government during the Boer War. In later life, he became avidly interested in spiritualism. He died on July 7, 1930.

MY FRIEND SHERLOCK HOLMES was deeply engrossed with perplexing problems when I called upon him that second morning after Christmas, with the intention of wishing him the compliments of the season. He was lounging upon the sofa in a purple dressing-gown, a pipe-rack within his reach upon the right, and a pile of crumpled morning papers, evidently newly studied, near at hand. Beside the couch was a wooden chair, and on the angle of the back hung a very seedy and disreputable hard-felt hat, much the worse for wear, and cracked in several places. A lens and a forceps lying upon the seat of the chair suggested that the hat had been suspended in this manner for the purpose of examination.

"You are engaged," said I; "perhaps I interrupt you."

"Not at all. I am glad to have a friend with whom I can discuss my results. The matter is a perfectly trivial one"—he jerked his thumb in the direction of the old hat—"but there are points in connection with it which are not entirely devoid of interest and even of instruction."

I seated myself in his armchair and warmed my hands before his crackling fire, for a sharp frost had set in, and the windows were thick with the ice crystals. "I suppose," I remarked, "that, homely as it looks, this thing has some deadly story linked on to it—that it is the clue which will guide you in the solution of some mystery and the punishment of some crime."

"No, no. No crime," said Sherlock Holmes, laughing. "Only one of those whimsical little incidents which will happen when you have four million human beings all jostling each other within the space of a few square miles. Amid the action and reaction of so dense a swarm of humanity, every possible combination of events may be expected to take place, and many a little problem will be presented which may be striking and bizarre without being criminal. We have already had experience of such."

"So much so," I remarked, "that of the last six cases which I have added to my notes, three have been entirely free of any legal crime."

"Precisely. You allude to my attempt to recover the Irene Adler papers, to the singular case of Miss Mary Sutherland, and to the adventure of the man with the twisted lip. Well, I have no doubt that this small matter will fall into the same innocent category. You know Peterson, the commissionaire?"

"Yes."

"It is to him that this trophy belongs."

"It is his hat?"

"No, no; he found it. Its owner is unknown. I beg that you will look upon it not as a battered billycock but as an intellectual problem. And, first, as to how it came here. It arrived upon Christmas morning, in company with a good fat goose, which is, I have no doubt, roasting at this moment in front of Peterson's fire. The facts are these: about four o'clock on Christmas morning, Peterson, who, as you know, is a very honest fellow, was returning from some small jollification and was making his way homeward down Tottenham Court Road. In front of him he saw, in the gaslight, a tallish man, walking with a slight stagger, and carrying a white goose slung over his shoulder. As he reached the corner of Goodge Street, a row broke out between this stranger and a little knot of roughs. One of the latter knocked off the man's hat, on which he raised his stick to defend himself and, swinging it over his head, smashed the shop window behind him. Peterson had rushed forward to protect the stranger from his assailants; but the man, shocked at having broken the window, and seeing an official-looking person in uniform rushing towards him, dropped his goose, took to his heels, and vanished amid the labyrinth of small streets which lie at the back of Tottenham Court Road. The roughs had also fled at the appearance of Peterson, so that he was left in possession of the field of battle, and also of the spoils of victory in the shape of this battered hat and a most unimpeachable Christmas goose."

"Which he restored to their owner?"

"My dear fellow, there lies the problem. It is true that 'For Mrs. Henry Baker' was printed upon a small card which was tied to the bird's left leg, and it is also true that the initials 'H. B.' are legible upon the lining of this hat; but as there are some thousands of Bakers, and some hundreds of Henry Bakers in this city of ours, it is not easy to restore lost property to any one of them."

"What, then, did Peterson do?"

"He brought round both hat and goose to me on Christmas morning, knowing that even the smallest problems are of inter-

13

est to me. The goose we retained until this morning, when there were signs that, in spite of the slight frost, it would be well that it should be eaten without unnecessary delay. Its finder has carried it off, therefore, to fulfill the ultimate destiny of a goose, while I continue to retain the hat of the unknown gentleman who lost his Christmas dinner."

"Did he not advertise?"

"No."

"Then, what clue could you have as to his identity?"

"Only as much as we can deduce."

"From his hat?"

"Precisely."

"But you are joking. What can you gather from this old battered felt?"

"Here is my lens. You know my methods. What can you gather yourself as to the individuality of the man who has worn this article?"

I took the tattered object in my hands and turned it over rather ruefully. It was a very ordinary black hat of the usual round shape, hard and much the worse for wear. The lining had been of red silk, but was a good deal discolored. There was no maker's name; but, as Holmes had remarked, the initials "H. B." were scrawled upon one side. It was pierced in the brim for a hat-securer, but the elastic was missing. For the rest, it was cracked, exceedingly dusty, and spotted in several places, although there seemed to have been some attempt to hide the discolored patches by smearing them with ink.

"I can see nothing," said I, handing it back to my friend.

"On the contrary, Watson, you can see everything. You fail, however, to reason from what you see. You are too timid in drawing your inferences."

"Then, pray tell me what you can infer from this hat?"

He picked it up and gazed at it in the peculiar introspective fashion which was characteristic of him. "It is perhaps less suggestive than it might have been," he remarked, "and yet there are a few inferences which are very distinct, and a few others which represent at least a strong balance of probability. That the man was highly intellectual is of course obvious upon the face of it, and also that he was fairly well-to-do within the last three years, although he has now fallen upon evil days. He had foresight, but has less now than formerly, pointing to a moral retrogression, which, when taken with the decline of his

14

fortunes, seems to indicate some evil influence, probably drink, at work upon him. This may account also for the obvious fact that his wife has ceased to love him."

"My dear Holmes!"

"He has, however, retained some degree of self-respect," he continued, disregarding my remonstrance. "He is a man who leads a sedentary life, goes out little, is out of training entirely, is middle-aged, has grizzled hair which he has cut within the last few days, and which he anoints with lime-cream. These are the more patent facts which are to be deduced from his hat. Also, by the way, that it is extremely improbable that he has gas laid on in his house."

"You are certainly joking, Holmes."

"Not in the least. Is it possible that even now, when I give you these results, you are unable to see how they are attained?"

"I have no doubt that I am very stupid, but I must confess that I am unable to follow you. For example, how did you deduce that this man was intellectual?"

For answer Holmes clapped the hat upon his head. It came right over the forehead and settled upon the bridge of his nose. "It is a question of cubic capacity," said he; "a man with so large a brain must have something in it."

"The decline of his fortunes, then?"

"This hat is three years old. These flat brims curled at the edge came in then. It is a hat of the very best quality. Look at the band of ribbed silk and the excellent lining. If this man could afford to buy so expensive a hat three years ago, and has had no hat since, then he has assuredly gone down in the world."

"Well, that is clear enough, certainly. But how about the foresight and the moral retrogression?"

Sherlock Holmes laughed. "Here is the foresight," said he, putting his finger upon the little disc and loop of the hat-securer. "They are never sold upon hats. If this man ordered one, it is a sign of a certain amount of foresight, since he went out of his way to take this precaution against the wind. But since we see that he has broken the elastic and has not troubled to replace it, it is obvious that he has less foresight now than formerly, which is a distinct proof of a weakening nature. On the other hand, he has endeavored to conceal some of these stains upon the felt by daubing them with ink, which is a sign that he has not entirely lost his self-respect."

"Your reasoning is plausible."

"The further points, that he is middle-aged, that his hair is grizzled, that it has been recently cut, and that he uses lime-cream, are all to be gathered from a close examination of the lower part of the lining. The lens discloses a large number of hair-ends, clean cut by the scissors of the barber. They all appear to be adhesive, and there is a distinct odor of lime-cream. This dust, you will observe, is not the gritty, gray dust of the street but the fluffy brown dust of the house, showing that it has been hung up indoors most of the time; while the marks of moisture upon the inside are proof positive that the wearer perspired very freely, and could, therefore, hardly be in the best of training."

"But his wife—you said that she had ceased to love him."

"This hat has not been brushed for weeks. When I see you, my dear Watson, with a week's accumulation of dust upon your hat, and when your wife allows you to go out in such a state, I shall fear that you also have been unfortunate enough to lose your wife's affection."

"But he might be a bachelor."

"Nay, he was bringing home the goose as a peace-offering to his wife. Remember the card upon the bird's leg."

"You have an answer to everything. But how on earth do you deduce that the gas is not laid on his house?"

"One tallow stain, or even two, might come by chance; but when I see no less than five, I think that there can be little doubt that the individual must be brought into frequent contact with burning tallow—walks upstairs at night probably with his hat in one hand and a guttering candle in the other. Anyhow, he never got tallow-stains from a gas-jet. Are you satisfied?"

"Well, it is very ingenious," said I, laughing; "but since, as you said just now, there has been no crime committed, and no harm done save the loss of a goose, all this seems to be rather a waste of energy."

Sherlock Holmes had opened his mouth to reply, when the door flew open, and Peterson, the commissionaire, rushed into the apartment with flushed cheeks and the face of a man who is dazed with astonishment.

"The goose, Mr. Holmes! The goose, sir!" he gasped.

"Eh? What of it, then? Has it returned to life and flapped off through the kitchen window?" Holmes twisted himself round upon the sofa to get a fairer view of the man's excited face.

16

"See here, sir! See what my wife found in its crop!" He held out his hand and displayed upon the center of the palm a brilliantly scintillating blue stone, rather smaller than a bean in size, but of such purity and radiance that it twinkled like an electric point in the dark hollow of his hand.

Sherlock Holmes sat up with a whistle. "By Jove, Peterson!" said he, "this is treasure trove indeed. I suppose you know what you have got?"

"A diamond, sir? A precious stone? It cuts into glass as though it were putty."

"It's more than a precious stone. It is *the* precious stone."

"Not the Countess of Morcar's blue carbuncle!" I ejaculated.

"Precisely so. I ought to know its size and shape, seeing that I have read the advertisement about it in *The Times* every day lately. It is absolutely unique, and its value can only be conjectured, but the reward offered of one thousand pounds is certainly not within a twentieth part of the market price."

"A thousand pounds! Great Lord of mercy!" The commissionaire plumped down into a chair and stared from one to the other of us.

"That is the reward, and I have reason to know that there are sentimental considerations in the background which would induce the Countess to part with half her fortune if she could but recover the gem."

"It was lost, if I remember aright, at the Hotel Cosmopolitan," I remarked.

"Precisely so, on December twenty-second, just five days ago. John Horner, a plumber, was accused of having abstracted it from the lady's jewel-case. The evidence against him was so strong that the case has been referred to the Assizes. I have some account of the matter here, I believe." He rummaged amid his newspapers, glancing over the dates, until at last he smoothed one out, doubled it over, and read the following paragraph:

Hotel Cosmopolitan Jewel Robbery. John Horner, 26, plumber, was brought up upon the charge of having, upon the 22nd inst., abstracted from the jewel-case of the Countess of Morcar the valuable gem known as the blue carbuncle. James Ryder, upper-attendant at the hotel, gave his evidence to the effect that he had shown Horner up to the dressing-room of the Countess of Morcar upon the day of the robbery in order that he might solder the second bar of the grate, which was loose. He had remained with Horner some little time, but had finally been called away. On returning, he found that Horner had disappeared, that the bureau had been forced open, and that the small morocco casket in which, as it afterward transpired, the Countess was accustomed to keep her jewel, was lying empty upon the dressing-table. Ryder instantly gave the alarm, and Horner was arrested the same evening; but the stone could not be found either upon his person or in his rooms. Catherine Cusack, maid to the Countess, deposed to having heard Ryder's cry of dismay on discovering the robbery, and to having rushed into the room, where she found matters as described by the last witness. Inspector Bradstreet, B division, gave evidence as to the arrest of Horner, who struggled frantically, and protested his innocence in the strongest terms. Evidence of a previous conviction for robbery having been given against the prisoner, the magistrate refused to deal summarily with the offense, but referred it to the Assizes. Horner, who had shown signs of intense emotion during the proceedings, fainted away at the conclusion and was carried out of court.

"Hum! So much for the police court," said Holmes thoughtfully, tossing aside the paper. "The question for us now to solve is the sequence of events leading from a rifled jewel-case at one end to the crop of a goose in Tottenham Court Road at the other. You see, Watson, our little deductions have suddenly assumed a much more important and less innocent aspect. Here is the stone; the stone came from the goose, and the goose came from Mr. Henry Baker, the gentleman with the bad hat and all the other characteristics with which I have bored you. So now we must set ourselves very seriously to finding this gentleman and ascertaining what part he has played in this little mystery. To do this, we must try the simplest means first, and these lie undoubtedly in an advertisement in all the evening papers. If this fails, I shall have recourse to other methods."

"What will you say?"

"Give me a pencil and that slip of paper. Now, then:

Found at the corner of Goodge Street, a goose and a black felt hat. Mr. Henry Baker can have the same by applying at 6:30 this evening at 221B Baker Street.

That is clear and concise."

"Very. But will he see it?"

"Well, he is sure to keep an eye on the papers, since, to a poor man, the loss was a heavy one. He was clearly so scared by his mischance in breaking the window and by the approach of Peterson that he thought of nothing but flight, but since then he must have bitterly regretted the impulse which caused him to drop his bird. Then, again, the introduction of his name will cause him to see it, for everyone who knows him will direct his attention to it. Here you are, Peterson, run down to the advertising agency and have this put in the evening papers."

"In which, sir?"

"Oh, in the *Globe, Star, Pall Mall, St. James's, Evening News Standard, Echo,* and any others that occur to you."

"Very well, sir. And this stone?"

"Ah, yes, I shall keep the stone. Thank you. And, I say, Peterson, just buy a goose on your way back and leave it here with me, for we must have one to give to this gentleman in place of the one which your family is now devouring."

When the commissionaire had gone, Holmes took up the stone and held it against the light. "It's a bonny thing," said he. "Just see how it glints and sparkles. Of course it is a nucleus and focus of crime. Every good stone is. They are the devil's pet baits. In the larger and older jewels every facet may stand for a bloody deed. This stone is not yet twenty years old. It was found in the banks of the Amoy River in southern China and is remarkable in having every characteristic of the carbuncle, save that it is blue in shade instead of ruby red. In spite of its youth, it has already a sinister history. There have been two murders, a vitriol-throwing, a suicide, and several robberies brought about for the sake of this forty-grain weight of crystallized charcoal. Who would think that so pretty a toy would be a purveyor to the gallows and the prison? I'll lock it up in my strong box now and drop a line to the Countess to say that we have it."

"Do you think that this man Horner is innocent?"

"I cannot tell."

"Well, then, do you imagine that this other one, Henry Baker, had anything to do with the matter?"

"It is, I think, much more likely that Henry Baker is an absolutely innocent man, who had no idea that the bird which he was carrying was of considerably more value than if it were made of solid gold. That, however, I shall determine by a very simple test if we have an answer to our advertisement."

19

"And you can do nothing until then?"

"Nothing."

"In that case I shall continue my professional round. But I shall come back in the evening at the hour you have mentioned, for I should very much like to see the solution of so tangled a business."

"Very glad to see you. I dine at seven. There is a woodcock, I believe. By the way, in view of recent occurrences, perhaps I ought to ask Mrs. Hudson to examine its crop."

I had been delayed at a case, and it was a little after half-past six when I found myself in Baker Street once more. As I approached the house I saw a tall man in a Scotch bonnet with a coat which was buttoned up to his chin waiting outside in the bright semicircle which was thrown from the fanlight. Just as I arrived the door was opened, and we were shown up together to Holmes's room.

"Mr. Henry Baker, I believe," said he, rising from his arm-chair and greeting his visitor with the easy air of geniality which he could so readily assume. "Pray take this chair by the fire, Mr. Baker. It is a cold night, and I observe that your circulation is more adapted for summer than for winter. Ah, Watson, you have just come at the right time. Is that your hat, Mr. Baker?"

"Yes, sir, that is undoubtedly my hat."

He was a large man with rounded shoulders, a massive head, and a broad, intelligent face, sloping down to a pointed beard of grizzled brown. A touch of red in nose and cheeks, with a slight tremor of his extended hand, recalled Holmes's surmise as to his habits. His rusty black frock-coat was buttoned right up in front, with the collar turned up, and his lank wrists protruded from his sleeves without a sign of cuff or shirt. He spoke in a slow staccato fashion, choosing his words with care, and gave the impression generally of a man of learning and letters who had had ill-usage at the hands of fortune.

"We have retained these things for some days," said Holmes, "because we expected to see an advertisement from you giving your address. I am at a loss to know now why you did not advertise."

Our visitor gave a rather shamefaced laugh. "Shillings have not been so plentiful with me as they once were," he remarked. "I had no doubt that the gang of roughs who assaulted me had carried off both my hat and the bird. I did not care to spend more money in a hopeless attempt at recovering them."

20

"Very naturally. By the way, about the bird, we were compelled to eat it."

"To eat it!" Our visitor half-rose from his chair in his excitement.

"Yes, it would have been of no use to anyone had we not done so. But I presume that this other goose upon the sideboard, which is about the same weight and perfectly fresh, will answer your purpose equally well?"

"Oh, certainly, certainly," answered Mr. Baker with a sigh of relief.

"Of course, we still have the feathers, legs, crop, and so on of your own bird, so if you wish—"

The man burst into a hearty laugh. "They might be useful to me as relics of my adventure," said he, "but beyond that I can hardly see what use the *disjecta membra* of my late acquaintance are going to be to me. No, sir, I think that, with your permission, I will confine my attentions to the excellent bird which I perceive upon the sideboard."

Sherlock Holmes glanced sharply across at me with a slight shrug of his shoulders.

"There is your hat, then, and there your bird," said he. "By the way, would it bore you to tell me where you got the other one from? I am somewhat of a fowl fancier, and I have seldom seen a better grown goose."

"Certainly, sir," said Baker, who had risen and tucked his newly gained property under his arm. "There are a few of us who frequent the Alpha Inn, near the Museum—we are to be found in the Museum itself during the day, you understand. This year our good host, Windigate by name, instituted a goose club, by which, on consideration of some few pence every week, we were each to receive a bird at Christmas. My pence were duly paid, and the rest is familiar to you. I am much indebted to you, sir, for a Scotch bonnet is fitted neither to my years nor my gravity." With a comical pomposity of manner he bowed solemnly to both of us and strode off upon his way.

"So much for Mr. Henry Baker," said Holmes when he had closed the door behind him. "It is quite certain that he knows nothing whatever about the matter. Are you hungry, Watson?"

"Not particularly."

"Then I suggest that we turn our dinner into a supper and follow up this clue while it is still hot."

"By all means."

It was a bitter night, so we drew on our ulsters and wrapped cravats about our throats. Outside, the stars were shining coldly in a cloudless sky, and the breath of the passers-by blew out into smoke like so many pistol shots. Our footfalls rang out crisply and loudly as we swung through the doctors' quarter, Wimpole Street, Harley Street, and so through Wigmore Street into Oxford Street. In a quarter of an hour we were in Bloomsbury at the Alpha Inn, which is a small public-house at the corner of one of the streets which runs down into Holborn. Holmes pushed open the door of the private bar and ordered two glasses of beer from the ruddy-faced, white-aproned landlord.

"Your beer should be excellent if it is as good as your geese," said he.

"My geese!" The man seemed surprised.

"Yes. I was speaking only half an hour ago to Mr. Henry Baker, who was a member of your goose club."

"Ah! Yes, I see. But you see, sir, them's not *our* geese."

"Indeed! Whose, then?"

"Well, I got the two dozen from a salesman in Covent Garden."

"Indeed? I know some of them. Which was it?"

"Breckinridge is his name."

"Ah! I don't know him. Well, here's your good health, landlord, and prosperity to your house. Good night.

"Now for Mr. Breckinridge," he continued, buttoning up his coat as we came out into the frosty air. "Remember, Watson, that though we have so homely a thing as a goose at one end of this chain, we have at the other a man who will certainly get seven years' penal servitude unless we can establish his innocence. It is possible that our inquiry may but confirm his guilt; but, in any case, we have a line of investigation which has been missed by the police, and which a singular chance has placed in our hands. Let us follow it out to the bitter end. Faces to the south, then!"

We passed across Holborn, down Endell Street, and so through a zigzag of slums to Covent Garden Market. One of the largest stalls bore the name of Breckinridge upon it, and the proprietor, a horsy-looking man, with a sharp face and trim side-whiskers, was helping a boy to put up the shutters.

"Good evening. It's a cold night," said Holmes.

The salesman nodded and shot a questioning glance at my companion.

22

"Sold out of geese, I see," continued Holmes, pointing at the bare slabs of marble.

"Let you have five hundred tomorrow morning," the salesman said.

"That's no good."

"Well, there are some on the stall with the gas-flare."

"Ah, but I was recommended to you."

"Who by?"

"The landlord of the Alpha."

"Oh, yes; I sent him a couple of dozen."

"Fine birds they were, too. Now where did you get them from?"

To my surprise the question provoked a burst of anger from the salesman.

"Now, then, mister," said he, with his head cocked and his arms akimbo, "what are you driving at? Let's have it straight, now."

"It is straight enough. I should like to know who sold you the geese which you supplied to the Alpha."

"Well, then, I shan't tell you."

"Oh, it is a matter of no importance; but I don't know why you should be so warm over such a trifle."

"Warm! You'd be as warm, maybe, if you were as pestered as I am. When I pay good money for a good article there should be an end of the business; but it's 'Where are the geese?' and 'Who did you sell the geese to?' and 'What will you take for the geese?' One would think they were the only geese in the world, to hear the fuss that is made over them."

"Well, I have no connection with any other people who have been making inquiries," said Holmes carelessly. "If you won't tell us the bet is off, that is all. But I'm always ready to back my opinion on a matter of fowls, and I have a fiver on it that the bird I ate is country-bred."

"Well, then, you've lost your fiver, for it's town-bred," snapped the salesman.

"It's nothing of the kind."

"I say it is."

"I don't believe it."

"D'you think you know more about fowls than I, who have handled them ever since I was a nipper? I tell you, all those birds that went to the Alpha were town-bred."

"You'll never persuade me to believe that."

23

"Will you bet, then?"

"It's merely taking your money, for I know that I am right. But I'll have a sovereign on with you, just to teach you not to be obstinate."

The salesman chuckled grimly. "Bring me the books, Bill," said he.

The small boy brought round a small thin volume and a great greasy-backed one, laying them out together beneath the hanging lamp.

"Now, then, Mr. Cocksure," said the salesman, "I thought that I was out of geese, but before I finish you'll find that there is still one left in my shop. You see this little book?"

"Well?"

"That's the list of the folk from whom I buy. D'you see? Well, then, here on this page are the country folk, and the numbers after their names are where their accounts are in the big ledger. Now, then! You see this other page in red ink? Well, that is a list of my town suppliers. Now, look at that third name. Just read it out to me."

"Mrs. Oakshott, 117 Brixton Road—249," read Holmes.

"Quite so. Now turn that up in the ledger."

Holmes turned to the page indicated. "Here you are, 'Mrs. Oakshott, 117 Brixton Road, egg and poultry supplier.'"

"Now, then, what's the last entry?"

"'December 22nd. Twenty-four geese at 7s. 6d.'"

"Quite so. There you are. And underneath?"

"'Sold to Mr. Windigate of the Alpha, at 12s.'"

"What have you to say now?"

Sherlock Holmes looked deeply chagrined. He drew a sovereign from his pocket and threw it down upon the slab, turning away with the air of a man whose disgust is too deep for words. A few yards off he stopped under a lamp-post and laughed in the hearty, noiseless fashion which was peculiar to him.

"When you see a man with whiskers of that cut and the 'Pink 'un' protruding out of his pocket, you can always draw him by a bet," said he. "I daresay that if I had put a hundred pounds down in front of him, that man would not have given me such complete information as was drawn from him by the idea that he was doing me on a wager. Well, Watson, we are, I fancy, nearing the end of our quest, and the only point which remains to be determined is whether we should go on to this Mrs. Oakshott tonight, or whether we should reserve it for tomorrow. It is clear from what that surly fellow said that there are others besides ourselves who are anxious about the matter, and I should—"

His remarks were suddenly cut short by a loud hubbub which broke out from the stall which we had just left. Turning round we saw a little rat-faced fellow standing in the center of the circle of yellow light which was thrown by the swinging lamp, while Breckinridge, the salesman, framed in the door of his stall, was shaking his fists fiercely at the cringing figure.

"I've had enough of you and your geese," he shouted. "I wish you were all at the devil together. If you come pestering me any more with your silly talk I'll set the dog at you. You bring Mrs. Oakshott here and I'll answer her, but what have you to do with it? Did I buy the geese off you?"

"No; but one of them was mine all the same," whined the little man.

"Well, then, ask Mrs. Oakshott for it."

"She told me to ask you."

"Well, you can ask the King of Prooshia, for all I care. I've had enough of it. Get out of this!" He rushed fiercely forward, and the inquirer flitted away into the darkness.

"Ha! This may save us a visit to Brixton Road," whispered Holmes. "Come with me, and we will see what is to be made of this fellow." Striding through the scattered knots of people who lounged round the flaring stalls, my companion speedily overtook the little man and touched him upon the shoulder. He sprang round, and I could see in the gas-light that every vestige of color had been driven from his face.

"Who are you, then? What do you want?" he asked in a quavering voice.

"You will excuse me," said Holmes blandly, "but I could not help overhearing the questions which you put to the salesman just now. I think that I could be of assistance to you."

"You? Who are you? How could you know anything of the matter?"

"My name is Sherlock Holmes. It is my business to know what other people don't know."

"But you can know nothing of this."

"Excuse me, I know everything of it. You are endeavoring to trace some geese which were sold by Mrs. Oakshott, of Brixton Road, to a salesman named Breckinridge, by him in turn to Mr.

25

Windigate, of the Alpha, and by him to his club, of which Mr. Henry Baker is a member."

"Oh, sir, you are the very man whom I have longed to meet," cried the little fellow with outstretched hands and quivering fingers. "I can hardly explain to you how interested I am in this matter."

Sherlock Holmes hailed a four-wheeler which was passing. "In that case we had better discuss it in a cosy room rather than in this wind-swept market-place," said he. "But pray tell me, before we go farther, who it is that I have the pleasure of assisting."

The man hesitated for an instant. "My name is John Robinson," he answered with a sidelong glance.

"No, no; the real name," said Holmes sweetly. "It is always awkward doing business with an alias."

A flush sprang to the white cheeks of the stranger. "Well, then," said he, "my real name is James Ryder."

"Precisely so. Head attendant at the Hotel Cosmopolitan. Pray step into the cab, and I shall soon be able to tell you everything which you would wish to know."

The little man stood glancing from one to the other of us with half-frightened, half-hopeful eyes, as one who is not sure whether he is on the verge of a windfall or of a catastrophe. Then he stepped into the cab, and in half an hour we were back in the sitting-room at Baker Street. Nothing had been said during our drive, but the high, thin breathing of our new companion, and the claspings and unclaspings of his hands, spoke of the nervous tension within him.

"Here we are!" said Holmes cheerily, as we filed into the room. "The fire looks very seasonable in this weather. You look cold, Mr. Ryder. Pray take the basket-chair. I will just put on my slippers before we settle this little matter of yours. Now, then! You want to know what became of those geese?"

"Yes, sir."

"Or rather, I fancy, of that goose. It was one bird, I imagine, in which you were interested—white, with a black bar across the tail."

Ryder quivered with emotion. "Oh, sir," he cried, "can you tell me where it went to?"

"It came here."

"Here?"

"Yes, and a most remarkable bird it proved. I don't wonder

26

that you should take an interest in it. It laid an egg after it was dead—the bonniest, brightest little blue egg that ever was seen. I have it here in my museum."

Our visitor staggered to his feet and clutched the mantelpiece with his right hand. Holmes unlocked his strong-box and held up the blue carbuncle, which shone out like a star, with a cold, brilliant, many-pointed radiance. Ryder stood glaring with a drawn face, uncertain whether to claim or to disown it.

"The game's up, Ryder," said Holmes quietly. "Hold up, man, or you'll be into the fire! Give him an arm back into his chair, Watson. He's not got blood enough to go in for felony with impunity. Give him a dash of brandy. So! Now he looks a little more human. What a shrimp it is, to be sure!"

For a moment he had staggered and nearly fallen, but the brandy brought a tinge of color into his cheeks, and he sat staring at his accuser.

"I have almost every link in my hands, and all the proofs which I could possibly need, so there is little which you need tell me. Still, that little may as well be cleared up to make the case complete. You had heard, Ryder, of this blue stone of the Countess of Morcar's?"

"It was Catherine Cusack who told me of it," said he in a crackling voice.

"I see—her ladyship's waiting-maid. Well, the temptation of sudden wealth so easily acquired was too much for you, as it has been for better men before you; but you were not very scrupulous in the means you used. It seems to me, Ryder, that there is the making of a very pretty villain in you. You knew that this man Horner, the plumber, had been concerned in some such matter before, and that suspicion would rest the more readily upon him. What did you do, then? You made some small job in my lady's room—you and your confederate Cusack—and you managed that he should be the man sent for. Then, when he had left, you rifled the jewel-case, raised the alarm, and had this unfortunate man arrested. You then—"

Ryder threw himself down suddenly upon the rug and clutched at my companion's knees. "For God's sake, have mercy!" he shrieked. "Think of my father! Of my mother! It would break their hearts. I never went wrong before! I never will again. I swear it. I'll swear it on a Bible. Oh, don't bring it into court!"

"Get back into your chair!" said Holmes sternly. "It is very

27

well to cringe and crawl now, but you thought little enough of putting this poor Horner in the dock for a crime of which he knew nothing."

"I will fly, Mr. Holmes. I will leave the country, sir. Then the charge against him will break down."

"Hum! We will talk about that. And now let us hear a true account of the next act. How came the stone into the goose, and how came the goose into the open market? Tell us the truth, for there lies your only hope of safety."

Ryder passed his tongue over his parched lips. "I will tell you it just as it happened, sir," said he. "When Horner had been arrested, it seemed to me that it would be best for me to get away with the stone at once, for I did not know at what moment the police might not take it into their heads to search me and my room. There was no place about the hotel where it would be safe. I went out, as if on some commission, and I made for my sister's house. She had married a man named Oakshott, and lived in Brixton Road, where she fattened fowls for the market. All the way there every man I met seemed to me to be a policeman or a detective; and, for all that it was a cold night, the sweat was pouring down my face before I came to the Brixton Road. My sister asked me what was the matter, and why I was so pale; but I told her that I had been upset by the jewel robbery at the hotel. Then I went into the back yard and smoked a pipe, and wondered what it would be best to do.

"I had a friend once called Maudsley, who went to the bad, and has just been serving his time in Pentonville. One day he had met me, and fell into talk about the ways of thieves, and how they could get rid of what they stole. I knew that he would be true to me, for I knew one or two things about him; so I made up my mind to go right on to Kilburn, where he lived, and take him into my confidence. He would show me how to turn the stone into money. But how to get to him in safety? I thought of the agonies I had gone through in coming from the hotel. I might at any moment be seized and searched, and there would be the stone in my waistcoat pocket. I was leaning against the wall at the time and looking at the geese which were waddling about round my feet, and suddenly an idea came into my head which showed me how I could beat the best detective that ever lived.

"My sister had told me some weeks before that I might have the pick of her geese for a Christmas present, and I knew that she was always as good as her word. I would take my goose now, and in it I would carry my stone to Kilburn. There was a little shed in the yard, and behind this I drove one of the birds—a fine big one, white, with a barred tail. I caught it, and, prying its bill open, I thrust the stone down its throat as far as my finger could reach. The bird gave a gulp, and I felt the stone pass along its gullet and down into its crop. But the creature flapped and struggled, and out came my sister to know what was the matter. As I turned to speak to her the brute broke loose and fluttered off among the others.

" 'Whatever were you doing with that bird, Jem?' says she, looking surprised.

" 'Well,' said I, 'you said you'd give me one for Christmas, and I was feeling which was the fattest.'

" 'Oh,' says she, 'we've set yours aside for you—Jem's bird, we call it. It's the big white one over yonder. There's twenty-six of them, which makes one for you, and one for us, and two dozen for the market.'

" 'Thank you, Maggie,' says I; 'but if it is all the same to you, I'd rather have that one I was handling just now.'

" 'The other is a good three pounds heavier,' said she, 'and we fattened it expressly for you.'

" 'Never mind. I'll have the other, and I'll take it now,' said I.

" 'Oh, just as you like,' said she, a little huffed. 'Which is it you want, then?'

" 'That white one with the barred tail, right in the middle of the flock.'

" 'Oh, very well. Kill it and take it with you.'

"Well, I did what she said, Mr. Holmes, and I carried the bird all the way to Kilburn. I told my pal what I had done, for he was a man that it was easy to tell a thing like that to. He laughed until he choked, and we got a knife and opened the goose. My heart turned to water, for there was no sign of the stone, and I knew that some terrible mistake had occurred. I left the bird, rushed back to my sister's, and hurried into the backyard. There was not a bird to be seen there.

" 'Where are they all, Maggie?' I cried.

" 'Gone to the dealer's, Jem.'

" 'Which dealer's?'

" 'Breckinridge, of Covent Garden.'

" 'But was there another with a barred tail?' I asked, 'the same as the one I chose?'

" 'Yes, Jem; there were two barred-tailed ones, and I could never tell them apart.'

"Well, then, of course I saw it all, and I ran off as hard as my feet would carry me to this man Breckinridge; but he had sold the lot at once, and not one word would he tell me as to where they had gone. You heard him yourselves tonight. Well, he has always answered me like that. My sister thinks that I am going mad. Sometimes I think that I am myself. And now—and now I am myself a branded thief, without ever having touched the wealth for which I sold my character. God help me! God help me!" He burst into convulsive sobbing, with his face buried in his hands.

There was a long silence, broken only by his heavy breathing, and by the measured tapping of Sherlock Holmes's fingertips upon the edge of the table. Then my friend rose and threw open the door.

"Get out!" said he.

"What, sir! Oh, Heaven bless you!"

"No more words. Get out!"

And no more words were needed. There was a rush, a clatter upon the stairs, the bang of a door, and the crisp rattle of running footfalls from the street.

"After all, Watson," said Holmes, reaching up his hand for his clay pipe, "I am not retained by the police to supply their deficiencies. If Horner were in danger it would be another thing; but this fellow will not appear against him, and the case must collapse. I suppose that I am commuting a felony, but it is just possible that I am saving a soul. This fellow will not go wrong again; he is too terribly frightened. Send him to jail now, and you make him a jail-bird for life. Besides, it is the season of forgiveness. Chance has put in our way a most singular and whimsical problem, and its solution is its own reward. If you will have the goodness to touch the bell, Doctor, we will begin another investigation, in which, also, a bird will be the chief feature."

THE DOUBLE CLUE

BY AGATHA CHRISTIE

Agatha Christie was born in Devon, England, on September 15, 1890. Her father, New Yorker Frederick Miller, died when she was a child, and she was raised by her mother, who, along with their neighbor Eden Phillpotts, encouraged her to write. Her first published novel, *The Mysterious Affair at Styles* (1920), introduced Belgian detective Hercule Poirot, who, along with Miss Jane Marple, became one of Christie's most beloved characters. She wrote more than eighty novels, which have been translated into almost every modern language, as well as short stories and plays. She died on January 12, 1976.

"BUT ABOVE EVERYTHING—no publicity," said Mr. Marcus Hardman for perhaps the fourteenth time.

The word *publicity* occurred throughout his conversation with the regularity of a leitmotif. Mr. Hardman was a small man, delicately plump, with exquisitely manicured hands and a plaintive tenor voice. In his way, he was somewhat of a celebrity and the fashionable life was his profession. He was rich, but not remarkably so, and he spent his money zealously in the pursuit of social pleasure. His hobby was collecting. He had the collector's soul. Old lace, old fans, antique jewelry—nothing crude or modern for the man called Marcus Hardman.

Poirot and I, obeying an urgent summons, had arrived to find the little man writhing in an agony of indecision. Under the circumstances, to call in the police was abhorrent to him. On the other hand, not to call them in was to acquiesce in the loss of some of the gems of his collection. He hit upon Poirot as a compromise.

"My rubies, M. Poirot, and the emerald necklace—said to have belonged to Catherine de Medici. Oh, the emerald necklace!"

"If you will recount to me the circumstances of their disappearance?" suggested Poirot gently.

"I am endeavoring to do so. Yesterday afternoon I had a little tea party—quite an informal affair, some half a dozen people or so. I have given one or two of·them during the season, and though perhaps I should not say so, they have been quite a success. Some good music—Nacora, the pianist, and Katherine Bird, the Australian contralto—in the big studio. Well, early in the afternoon, I was showing my guests my collection of medieval jewels. I keep them in the small wall safe over there. It is arranged like a cabinet inside, with a colored velvet background, to display the stones. Afterward we inspected the fans—in that case on the wall. Then we all went to the studio for music. It was not until after everyone had gone that I discovered the safe rifled! I must have failed to shut it properly, and someone had seized the opportunity to denude it of its contents. The rubies, M. Poirot, the emerald necklace—the collection of a lifetime! What would I not give to recover them! But there must be no publicity! You fully understand that, do you not, M. Poirot? My own guests, my personal friends—it would be a horrible scandal!"

"Who was the last person to leave this room when you went to the studio?"

"Mr. Johnston. You may know him? The South African millionaire. He has just rented the Abbotburys' house in Park Lane. He lingered behind a few moments, I remember. But surely, oh, surely it could not be he!"

"Did any of your guests return to this room during the afternoon on any pretext?"

"I was prepared for that question, M. Poirot. Countess Vera Rossakoff, Mr. Bernard Parker, and Lady Runcorn."

"Let us hear about them."

"The Countess Rossakoff is a very charming Russian lady, a member of the old régime. She has recently come to this country. She had bade me goodbye, and I was therefore somewhat surprised to find her in this room apparently gazing in rapture at my cabinet of fans. You know, M. Poirot, the more I think of it, the more suspicious it seems to me. Don't you agree?"

"Extremely suspicious; but let us hear about the others."

"Well, Parker simply came here to fetch a case of miniatures that I was anxious to show to Lady Runcorn."

"And Lady Runcorn herself?"

"As I dare say you know, Lady Runcorn is a middle-aged woman of considerable force of character who devotes most of her time to various charitable committees. She simply returned to fetch a handbag she had laid down somewhere."

"*Bien, monsieur.* So we have four possible suspects. The Russian countess, the English *grande dame,* the South African millionaire, and Mr. Bernard Parker. Who *is* Mr. Parker, by the way?"

The question appeared to embarrass Mr. Hardman.

"He is—er—he is a young fellow. Well, in fact, a young fellow I know."

"I had already deduced as much," replied Poirot gravely. "What does he do, this M. Parker?"

"He is a young man about town—not, perhaps, quite in the swim, if I may so express myself."

"How did he come to be a friend of yours, may I ask?"

"Well—er—on one or two occasions he has—performed certain little commissions for me."

"Continue, monsieur," said Poirot.

Hardman looked piteously at him. Evidently the last thing he wanted to do was to continue. But as Poirot maintained an inexorable silence, he capitulated.

"You see, M. Poirot—it is well known that I am interested in antique jewels. Sometimes there is a family heirloom to be disposed of—which, mind you, would never be sold in the open market or to a dealer. But a private sale to me is a very different matter. Parker arranges the details of such things—he is in touch with both sides, and thus any little embarrassment is avoided. He brings anything of that kind to my notice. For instance, the Countess Rossakoff has brought some family jewels with her from Russia. She is anxious to sell them. Bernard Parker was to have arranged the transaction."

"I see," said Poirot thoughtfully. "And you trust him implicitly?"

"I have had no reason to do otherwise."

"Mr. Hardman, of these four people, which do you yourself suspect?"

"Oh, M. Poirot, what a question! They are my friends, as I told you. I suspect none of them—or all of them, whichever way you like to put it."

"I do not agree. You suspect one of those four. It is not Countess Rossakoff. It is not Mr. Parker. Is it Lady Runcorn or Mr. Johnston?"

"You drive me into a corner, M. Poirot, you do indeed. I am most anxious to have no scandal. Lady Runcorn belongs to one of the oldest families in England; but it is true, it is most unfortunately true, that her aunt, Lady Caroline, suffered from a most melancholy affliction. It was understood, of course, by all her friends, and her maid returned the teaspoons, or whatever it was, as promptly as possible. You see my predicament!"

"So Lady Runcorn had an aunt who was a kleptomaniac? Very interesting. You permit that I examine the safe?"

Mr. Hardman assenting, Poirot pushed back the door of the safe and examined the interior. The empty velvet-lined shelves gaped at us.

"Even now the door does not shut properly," murmured Poirot, as he swung it to and fro. "I wonder why? Ah, what have we here? A glove, caught in the hinge. A man's glove."

He held it out to Mr. Hardman.

"That's not one of my gloves," the latter declared.

"Aha! Something more!" Poirot bent deftly and picked up a small object from the floor of the safe. It was a flat cigarette case made of black moiré.

"My cigarette case!" cried Mr. Hardman.

"Yours? Surely not, monsieur. Those are not your initials."

He pointed to an entwined monogram of two letters executed in platinum.

Hardman took it in his hand.

"You are right," he declared. "It is very like mine, but the initials are different. A B and a P. Good heavens—Bernard Parker!"

"It would seem so," said Poirot. "A somewhat careless young man—especially if the glove is his also. That would be a double clue, would it not?"

"Bernard Parker!" murmured Hardman. "What a relief! Well, M. Poirot, I leave it to you to recover the jewels. Place the matter in the hands of the police if you think fit—that is, if you are quite sure that it is he who is guilty."

"See you, my friend," said Poirot to me, as we left the house together, "he has one law for the titled, and another law for the plain, this Mr. Hardman. Me, I have not yet been ennobled, so I am on the side of the plain. I have sympathy for this young man. The whole thing was a little curious, was it not? There was Hardman suspecting Lady Runcorn; there was I, suspecting the Countess and Johnston; and all the time, the obscure Mr. Parker was our man."

"Why did you suspect the other two?"

"*Parbleu!* It is such a simple thing to be a Russian refugee or a South African millionaire! Any woman can call herself a Russian countess; anyone can buy a house in Park Lane and call himself a South African millionaire. Who is going to contradict them? But I observed that we are passing through Bury Street. Our careless young friend lives here. Let us, as you say, strike while the iron is in the fire."

Mr. Bernard Parker was at home. We found him reclining on some cushions, clad in an amazing dressing gown of purple and orange. I have seldom taken a greater dislike to anyone than I did to this particular young man with his white, effeminate face and affected lisping speech.

"Good morning, monsieur," said Poirot briskly. "I come from M. Hardman. Yesterday, at the party, somebody stole all his

35

jewels. Permit me to ask you, monsieur—is this your glove?"

Mr. Parker's mental processes did not seem very rapid. He stared at the glove, as though gathering his wits together.

"Where did you find it?" he asked at last.

"Is it your glove, monsieur?"

Mr. Parker appeared to make up his mind.

"No, it isn't," he declared.

"And this cigarette case, is that yours?"

"Certainly not. I always carry a silver one."

"Very well, monsieur. I go to put matters in the hands of the police."

"Oh, I say, I wouldn't do that, if I were you," cried Mr. Parker in some concern. "Beastly unsympathetic people, the police. Wait a bit. I'll go round and see old Hardman. Look here—oh, stop a minute."

But Poirot beat a determined retreat.

"We have given him something to think about, have we not?" he chuckled. "Tomorrow we will observe what has occurred."

But we were destined to have a reminder of the Hardman case that afternoon. Without the least warning the door flew open, and a whirlwind in human form invaded our privacy, bringing with her a swirl of sables (it was as cold as only an English June day can be) and a hat rampant with slaughtered ospreys. Countess Vera Rossakoff was a somewhat disturbing personality.

"You are M. Poirot? What is this that you have done? You accuse that poor boy! It is infamous. It is scandalous. I know him. He is a chicken, a lamb—never would he steal. He has done everything for me. Will I stand by and see him martyred and butchered?"

"Tell me, madame, is this his cigarette case?" Poirot held out the black moiré case.

The Countess paused for a moment while she inspected it.

"Yes, it is his. I know it well. What of it? Did you find it in the room? We were all there—he dropped it then, I suppose. Ah, you policemen, you are worse than—"

"And is this his glove?"

"How could I know? One glove is like another. Do not try to stop me—he must be set free. His character must be cleared. You shall do it. I will sell my jewels and give you much money."

"Madame—"

"It is agreed, then? No, no, do not argue. The poor boy! He

36

came to me, the tears in his eyes. 'I will save you,' I said. 'I will go to this man—this ogre, this monster! Leave it to Vera.' Now it is settled, I go."

With as little ceremony as she had come, she swept from the room, leaving an overpowering perfume of an exotic nature behind her.

"What a woman!" I exclaimed. "And what furs!"

"Ah, yes, *they* were genuine enough! Could a spurious countess have real furs? My little joke, Hastings. . . . No, she is truly Russian, I fancy. Well, well, so Master Bernard went bleating to her."

"The cigarette case is his. I wonder if the glove is also—"

With a smile Poirot drew from his pocket a second glove and placed it by the first. There was no doubt of their being a pair.

"Where did you get the second one, Poirot?"

"It was thrown down with a stick on the table in the hall in Bury Street. Truly, a very careless young man, Monsieur Parker. Well, well, *mon ami*—we must be thorough. Just for the form of the thing, I will make a little visit to Park Lane."

Needless to say, I accompanied my friend. Johnston was out, but we saw his private secretary. It transpired that Johnston had only recently arrived from South Africa. He had never been in England before.

"He is interested in precious stones, is he not?" hazarded Poirot.

"Gold mining is nearer the mark," said the secretary.

Poirot came away from the interview thoughtful. Late that evening, to my utter surprise, I found him earnestly studying a Russian grammar.

"Good heavens, Poirot!" I cried. "Are you learning Russian in order to converse with the Countess in her own language?"

"She certainly would not listen to my English, my friend!"

"But surely, Poirot, well-born Russians invariably speak French?"

"You are a mine of information, Hastings! I will cease puzzling over the intricacies of the Russian alphabet."

He threw the book from him with a dramatic gesture. I was not entirely satisfied. There was a twinkle in his eye which I knew of old. It was an invariable sign that Hercule Poirot was pleased with himself.

"Perhaps," I said patiently, "you doubt her being really a Russian. You are going to test her?"

"Ah, no, no, she is Russian."

"Well, then—"

"If you really want to distinguish yourself over this case, Hastings, I recommend *First Steps in Russian* as an invaluable aid."

Then he laughed and would say no more. I picked up the book from the floor and dipped into it curiously, but could make neither head nor tail of Poirot's remarks.

The following morning brought us no news of any kind, but that did not seem to worry my little friend. At breakfast, he announced his intention of calling upon Mr. Hardman early in the day. We found the elderly society butterfly at home, and seemingly a little calmer than on the previous day.

"Well, M. Poirot, any news?" he demanded eagerly.

Poirot handed him a slip of paper.

"That is the name of the person who took the jewels, monsieur. Shall I put matters in the hands of the police? Or would you prefer me to recover the jewels without bringing the police into the matter?"

Mr. Hardman was staring at the paper. At last he found his voice.

"Most astonishing. I should infinitely prefer to have no scandal in the matter. I give you *carte blanche*, M. Poirot. I am sure you will be discreet."

Our next procedure was to hail a taxi, which Poirot ordered to drive to the Carlton. There he inquired for Countess Rossakoff. In a few minutes we were ushered up into the lady's suite. She came to meet us with outstretched hands, arrayed in a marvelous négligée of barbaric design.

"M. Poirot!" she cried. "You have succeeded? You have cleared that poor infant?"

"Madame la Comtesse, your friend M. Parker is perfectly safe from arrest."

"Ah, but you are the clever little man! Superb! And so quickly, too."

"On the other hand, I have promised Mr. Hardman that the jewels shall be returned to him today."

"So?"

"Therefore, madame, I should be extremely obliged if you would place them in my hands without delay. I am sorry to hurry you, but I am keeping a taxi—in case it should be necessary for me to go on to Scotland Yard. And we Belgians, madame, we practice the thrift."

The Countess had lighted a cigarette. For some seconds she sat perfectly still, blowing smoke rings, and gazing steadily at Poirot. Then she burst into a laugh, and rose. She went across to the bureau, opened a drawer, and took out a silk handbag. She tossed it lighty to Poirot. Her tone, when she spoke, was perfectly light and unmoved.

"We Russians, on the contrary, practice prodigality," she said. "And to do that, unfortunately, one must have money. You need not look inside. They are all there."

Poirot rose.

"I congratulate you, madame, on your quick intelligence and your promptitude."

"Ah! But since you were keeping your taxi waiting, what else could I do?"

"You are too amiable, madame. You are remaining long in London?"

"I am afraid not—owing to you."

"Accept my apologies."

"We shall meet again elsewhere, perhaps."

"I hope so."

"And I—do not!" exclaimed the Countess with a laugh. "It is a great compliment that I pay you there—there are very few men in the world whom I fear. Goodbye, M. Poirot."

"Goodbye, Madame la Comtesse. Ah—pardon me, I forgot! Allow me to return you your cigarette case."

And with a bow he handed to her the little black moiré case we had found in the safe. She accepted it without any change of expression—just a lifted eyebrow and a murmured "I see!"

"What a woman! cried Poirot enthusiastically as we descended the stairs. *"Mon Dieu, quelle femme!* Not a word of argument—of protestation, of bluff! One quick glance, and she had sized up the position correctly. I tell you, Hastings, a woman who can accept defeat like that—with a careless smile—will go far! She is dangerous; she has the nerves of steel; she—" He tripped heavily.

"If you can manage to moderate your transports and look where you're going, it might be as well," I suggested. "When did you first suspect the Countess?"

"Mon ami, it was the glove and the cigarette case—the double

clue, shall we say?—that worried me. Bernard Parker might easily have dropped one or the other—but hardly both. Ah, no, that would have been *too* careless! In the same way, if someone else had placed them there to incriminate Parker, one would have been sufficient—the cigarette case *or* the glove—again not both. So I was forced to the conclusion that one of the two things did *not* belong to Parker. I imagined at first that the case was his, and that the glove was not. But when I discovered the fellow to the glove, I saw that it was the other way about. Whose, then, was the cigarette case? Clearly, it could not belong to Lady Runcorn. The initials were wrong. Mr. Johnston? Only if he were here under a false name. I interviewed his secretary, and it was apparent at once that everything was clear and above-board. There was no reticence about Mr. Johnston's past. The Countess, then? She was supposed to have brought jewels with her from Russia; she had only to take the stones from their settings, and it was extremely doubtful if they could ever be identified. What could be easier for her than to pick up one of Parker's gloves from the hall that day and thrust it into the safe? But, *bien sûr*, she did not intend to drop her own cigarette case."

"But if the case was hers, why did it have *B. P.* on it? The Countess' initials are *V. R.*"

Poirot smiled gently upon me.

"Exactly, *mon ami;* but in the Russian alphabet, *B* is *V* and *P* is *R.*"

"Well, you couldn't expect me to guess that. I don't know Russian."

"Neither do I, Hastings. That is why I bought my little book—and urged it on your attention."

He sighed.

"A remarkable woman. I have a feeling, my friend—a very decided feeling—I shall meet her again. Where, I wonder?"

THE DAUPHIN'S DOLL

BY ELLERY QUEEN

Ellery Queen is the pseudonym of cousins Manfred B. Lee and Frederick Dannay as well as the name of their fictional private detective. Their first novel, *The Roman Hat Mystery,* was published in 1929. They collaborated on dozens of novels and short stories and hundreds of radio plays. Several of their novels were written as by "Barnaby Ross." Frederic Dannay is editor of *Ellery Queen's Mystery Magazine,* founded in 1941, and many mystery anthologies. In 1978 Ellery Queen was awarded the Grand Prix de Littérature Policière for the 1964 novel *And On the Eighth Day.* Manfred Lee died in 1971.

THERE IS A LAW among story-tellers, originally passed by Editors at the cries (they say) of their constituents, which states that stories about Christmas shall have Children in them. This Christmas story is no exception; indeed, misopedists will complain that we have overdone it. And we confess in advance that this is also a story about Dolls, and that Santa Claus comes into it, and even a Thief; though as to this last, whoever he was—and that was one of the questions—he was certainly not Barabbas, even parabolically.

Another section of the statute governing Christmas stories provides that they shall incline toward Sweetness and Light. The first arises, of course, from the orphans and the never-souring savor of the annual Miracle; as for Light, it will be provided at the end, as usual, by that luminous prodigy, Ellery Queen. The reader of gloomier temper will also find a large measure of Darkness, in the person and works of one who, at least in Inspector Queen's harassed view, was surely the winged Prince of that region. His name, by the way, was not Satan, it was Comus; and this is paradox enow, since the original Comus, as everyone knows, was the god of festive joy and mirth, emotions not commonly associated with the Underworld. As Ellery struggled to embrace his phantom foe, he puzzled over this *non sequitur* in vain; in vain, that is, until Nikki Porter, no scorner of the obvious, suggested that he *might* seek the answer where any ordinary mortal would go at once. And there, to the great man's mortification, it was indeed to be found: On page 262b of Volume 6, *Coleb to Damasci,* of the 175th Anniversary edition of the Encyclopedia Britannica. A French conjuror of that name, performing in London in the year 1789, caused his wife to vanish from the top of a table—the very first time, it appeared, that this feat, uxorial or otherwise, had been accomplished without the aid of mirrors. To track his dark adversary's *nom de nuit* to its historic lair gave Ellery his only glint of satisfaction until that blessed moment when light burst all around him and exorcised the darkness, Prince and all.

But this is chaos.

Our story properly begins not with our invisible character but with our dead one.

Miss Ypson had not always been dead; *au contraire*. She had lived for seventy-eight years, for most of them breathing hard. As her father used to remark, "She was a very active little verb." Miss Ypson's father was a professor of Greek at a small Midwestern university. He had conjugated his daughter with the rather bewildered assistance of one of his brawnier students, an Iowa poultry heiress.

Professor Ypson was a man of distinction. Unlike most professors of Greek, he was a Greek professor of Greek, having been born Gerasymos Aghamos Ypsilonomon in Polykhnitos, on the island of Mytilini, "where," he was fond of recalling on certain occasions, "burning Sappho loved and sung"—a quotation he found unfailingly useful in his extracurricular activities; and, the Hellenic ideal notwithstanding, Professor Ypson believed wholeheartedly in immoderation in all things. This hereditary and cultural background explains the professor's interest in fatherhood—to his wife's chagrin, for Mrs. Ypson's own breeding prowess was confined almost exclusively to the barnyards on which her income was based; he held their daughter to be nothing less than a biological miracle.

The professor's mental processes also tended to confuse Mrs. Ypson. She never ceased to wonder why, instead of shortening his name to Ypson, her husband had not sensibly changed it to Jones. "My dear," the professor once replied, "you are an Iowa snob." "But nobody," Mrs. Ypson cried, "can spell it or pronounce it!" "This is a cross," murmured Professor Ypson, "which we must bear with Ypsilanti." "Oh," said Mrs. Ypson.

There was invariably something Sibylline about his conversation. His favorite adjective for his wife was "ypsiliform," a term, he explained, which referred to the germinal spot at one of the fecundation stages in a ripening egg and which was, therefore, exquisitely à propos. Mrs. Ypson continued to look bewildered; she died at an early age.

And the professor ran off with a Kansas City variety girl of considerable talent, leaving his baptized chick to be reared by an eggish relative of her mother's named Jukes.

The only time Miss Ypson heard from her father—except when he wrote charming and erudite little notes requesting, as he termed it, *lucrum*—was in the fourth decade of his Odyssey, when he sent her a handsome addition to her collection, a terra cotta play doll of Greek origin over three thousand years old which, unhappily, Miss Ypson felt duty-bound to return to the

Brooklyn museum from which it had unaccountably vanished. The note accompanying her father's gift had said, whimsically: *"Timeo Danaos et dona ferentes."*

There was poetry behind Miss Ypson's dolls. At her birth the professor, ever harmonious, signalized his devotion to fecundity by naming her Cytherea. This proved the Olympian irony. For, it turned out, her father's philoprogenitiveness throbbed frustrate in her mother's stony womb: even though Miss Ypson interred five husbands of quite adequate vigor, she remained infertile to the end of her days. Hence it is classically tragic to find her, when all passion was spent, a sweet little old lady with a vague if eager smile who, under the name of her father, pattered about a vast and echoing New York apartment playing enthusiastically with dolls.

In the beginning they were dolls of common clay: a Billiken, a kewpie, a Kathe Kruse, a Patsy, a Foxy Grandpa, and so forth. But then, as her need increased, Miss Ypson began her fierce sack of the past.

Down into the land of Pharaoh she went for two pieces of thin desiccated board, carved and painted and with hair of strung beads, and legless—so that they might not run away—which any connoisseur will tell you are the most superb specimens of ancient Egyptian paddle doll extant, far superior to those in the British Museum, although this fact will be denied in certain quarters.

Miss Ypson unearthed a foremother of "Letitia Penn," until her discovery held to be the oldest doll in America, having been brought to Philadelphia from England in 1699 by William Penn as a gift for a playmate of his small daughter's. Miss Ypson's find was a wooden-hearted "little lady" in brocade and velvet which had been sent by Sir Walter Raleigh to the first English child born in the New World. Since Virginia Dare had been born in 1587, not even the Smithsonian dared impugn Miss Ypson's triumph.

On the old lady's racks, in her plate-glass cases, might be seen the wealth of a thousand childhoods, and some riches—for such is the genetics of dolls—possessed by children grown. Here could be found "fashion babies" from fourteenth-century France, sacred dolls of the Orange Free State Fingo tribe, Satsuma paper dolls and court dolls from old Japan, beady-eyed "Kalifa" dolls of the Egyptian Sudan, Swedish birchbark dolls, "Katcina" dolls of the Hopis, mammoth-tooth dolls of the

Eskimos, feather dolls of the Chippewa, tumble dolls of the ancient Chinese, Coptic bone dolls, Roman dolls dedicated to Diana, *pantin* dolls which had been the street toys of Parisian exquisites before Madame Guillotine swept the boulevards, early Christian dolls in their *crèches* representing the Holy Family—to specify the merest handful of Miss Ypson's Briarean collection. She possessed dolls of pasteboard, dolls of animal skin, spool dolls, crab-claw dolls, eggshell dolls, cornhusk dolls, rag dolls, pine-cone dolls with moss hair, stocking dolls, dolls of *bisque,* dolls of palm leaf, dolls of *papier-mâché*, even dolls made of seed pods. There were dolls forty inches tall, and there were dolls so little Miss Ypson could hide them in her gold thimble.

Cytherea Ypson's collection bestrode the centuries and took tribute of history. There was no greater—not the fabled playthings of Montezuma, or Victoria's, or Eugene Field's; not the collection at the Metropolitan, or the South Kensington, or the royal palace in old Bucharest, or anywhere outside the enchantment of little girls' dreams.

It was made of Iowan eggs and the Attic shore, corn-fed and myrtle-clothed; and it brings us at last to Attorney John Somerset Bondling and his visit to the Queen residence one December twenty-third not so very long ago.

December the twenty-third is ordinarily not a good time to seek the Queens. Inspector Richard Queen likes his Christmas old-fashioned; his turkey stuffing, for instance, calls for twenty-two hours of over-all preparation and some of its ingredients are not readily found at the corner grocer's. And Ellery is a frustrated gift-wrapper. For a month before Christmas he turns his sleuthing genius to tracking down unusual wrapping papers, fine ribbons, and artistic stickers; and he spends the last two days creating beauty.

So it was that when Attorney John S. Bondling called, Inspector Queen was in his kitchen, swathed in a barbecue apron, up to his elbows in *fines herbes*, while Ellery, behind the locked door of his study, composed a secret symphony in glittering fuchsia metallic paper, forest-green moiré ribbon, and pine cones.

"It's almost useless," shrugged Nikki, studying Attorney Bondling's card, which was as crackly-looking as Attorney Bondling. "You say you know the Inspector personally, Mr. Bondling?"

"Just tell him Bondling the estate lawyer," said Bondling neurotically. "Park Row. He'll know."

"Don't blame me," said Nikki, "if you wind up in his stuffing. Goodness knows he's used everything else." And she went for Inspector Queen.

While she was gone, the study door opened noiselessly for one inch. A suspicious eye reconnoitered from the crack.

"Don't be alarmed," said the owner of the eye, slipping through the crack and locking the door hastily behind him. "Can't trust them, you know. Children, just children."

"Children!" Attorney Bondling snarled. "You're Ellery Queen, aren't you?"

"Yes."

"Interested in youth? Christmas? Orphans, dolls, that sort of thing?" Mr. Bondling went on in a remarkably nasty way.

"I suppose so."

"The more fool you. Ah, here's your father. Inspector Queen—!"

"Oh, that Bondling," said the old gentleman absently, shaking his visitor's hand. "My office called to say someone was coming up. Here, use my handkerchief; that's a bit of turkey liver. Know my son? His secretary, Miss Porter? What's on your mind, Mr. Bondling?"

"Inspector, I'm in charge of handling the Cytherea Ypson estate, and—"

"Cytherea Ypson," frowned the Inspector. "Oh, yes. She died only recently."

"Leaving me with the headache," said Mr. Bondling bitterly, "of disposing of her Dollection."

"Her what?" asked Ellery.

"Dolls—collection. Dollection. She coined the word."

Ellery strolled over to his armchair.

"Do I take this down?" sighed Nikki.

"Dollection," said Ellery.

"Spent about thirty years at it. Dolls!"

"Yes, Nikki, take it down."

"Well, well, Mr. Bondling," said Inspector Queen. "What's the problem? Christmas comes but once a year, you know."

"Will provides the Dollection be sold at auction," grated the attorney, "and the proceeds used to set up a fund for orphan children. I'm holding the public sale right after New Year's."

"Dolls and orphans, eh?" said the Inspector, thinking of

46

Javanese black pepper and Country Gentleman Seasoning Salt.

"That's *nice*," beamed Nikki.

"Oh, is it?" said Mr. Bondling softly. "Apparently, young woman, you've never tried to satisfy a Surrogate. I've administered estates for nineteen years without a whisper against me, but let an estate involve the interests of just one little fatherless child, and you'd think from the Surrogate's attitude I was Bill Sykes himself!"

"My stuffing," began the Inspector.

"I've had those dolls catalogued. The result is ominous! Did you know there's no set market for the damnable things? And aside from a few personal possessions, the Dollection constitutes the old lady's entire estate. Sank every nickel she had in it."

"But it should be worth a fortune," remarked Ellery.

"To whom, Mr. Queen? Museums always want such things as free and unencumbered gifts. I tell you, except for one item, those hypothetical orphans won't realize enough from that sale to keep them in—in bubble gum for two days!"

"Which item would that be, Mr. Bondling?"

"Number Six-seventy-four," the lawyer snapped. "This one."

"Number Six-seventy-four," read Inspector Queen from the fat catalogue Bondling had fished out of a large greatcoat pocket. "The Dauphin's Doll. Unique. Ivory figure of a boy Prince eight inches tall, clad in court dress, genuine ermine, brocade, velvet. Court sword in gold strapped to waist. Gold circlet crown surmounted by single blue brilliant diamond of finest water, weight approximately forty-nine carats—"

"How many carats?" exclaimed Nikki.

"Larger than the Hope and the Star of South Africa," said Ellery, with a certain excitement.

"—appraised," continued his father, "at one hundred and ten thousand dollars."

"Expensive dollie."

"Indecent!" said Nikki.

"This indecent—I mean exquisite royal doll," the Inspector read on, "was a birthday gift from King Louis XVI of France to Louis Charles, his second son, who became dauphin at the death of his elder brother in 1789. The little dauphin was proclaimed Louis XVII by the royalists during the French Revolution while in custody of the *sans-culottes*. His fate is shrouded in mystery. Romantic, historic item."

47

"Le prince perdu. I'll say," muttered Ellery. "Mr. Bondling, is this on the level?"

"I'm an attorney, not an antiquarian," snapped their visitor. "There are documents attached, one of them a sworn statement—holograph—by Lady Charlotte Atkyns, the English actress-friend of the Capet family—she was in France during the Revolution—or purporting to be in Lady Atkyns's hand. It doesn't matter, Mr. Queen. Even if the history is bad, the diamond's good!"

"I take it this hundred-and-ten-thousand-dollar dollie constitutes the bone, as it were, or that therein lies the rub?"

"You said it!" cried Mr. Bondling, cracking his knuckles in a sort of agony. "For my money the Dauphin's Doll is the only negotiable asset of that collection. And what's the old lady do? She provides by will that on the day preceding Christmas the Cytherea Ypson Dollection is to be publicly displayed . . . on the main floor of Nash's Department Store! *The day before Christmas, gentlemen!* Think of it!"

"But why?" asked Nikki, puzzled.

"Why? Who knows why? For the entertainment of New York's army of little beggars, I suppose! Have you any notion how many peasants pass through Nash's on the day before Christmas? My cook tells me—she's a very religious woman—it's like Armageddon."

"Day before Christmas," frowned Ellery. "That's tomorrow."

"It does sound chancy," said Nikki anxiously. Then she brightened. "Oh, well, maybe Nash's won't cooperate, Mr. Bondling."

"Oh, won't they!" howled Mr. Bondling. "Why, old lady Ypson had this stunt cooked up with that gang of peasant-purveyors for years! They've been snapping at my heels ever since the day she was put away!"

"It'll draw every crook in New York," said the Inspector, his gaze on the kitchen door.

"Orphans," said Nikki. "The orphans' interests *must* be protected." She looked at her employer accusingly.

"Special measures, dad," he said.

"Sure, sure," said the Inspector, rising. "Don't you worry about this, Mr. Bondling. Now if you'll be kind enough to excu—"

"Inspector Queen," hissed Mr. Bondling, leaning forward tensely, "that is not all."

48

"Ah," said Ellery briskly, lighting a cigarette. "There's a specific villain in this piece, Mr. Bondling, and you know who he is."

"I do," said the lawyer hollowly, "and then again I don't. I mean, it's Comus."

"*Comus!*" the Inspector screamed.

"Comus? said Ellery slowly.

"Comus?" said Nikki. "Who dat?"

"Comus," nodded Mr. Bondling. "First thing this morning. Marched right into my office, bold as day—must have followed me, I hadn't got my coat off, my secretary wasn't even in. Marched in and tossed this card on my desk."

Ellery seized it. "The usual, dad."

"His trademark," growled the Inspector, his lips working.

"But the card just says 'Comus,'" complained Nikki. "Who—?"

"Go on, Mr. Bondling!" thundered the Inspector.

"And he calmly announced to me," said Bondling, blotting his cheeks with an exhausted handkerchief, "that he's going to steal the Dauphin's Doll tomorrow, in Nash's."

"Oh, a maniac," said Nikki.

"Mr. Bondling," said the old gentleman in a terrible voice, "just what did this fellow look like?"

"Foreigner—black beard—spoke with a European accent of some sort. To tell you the truth, I was so thunderstruck I didn't notice details. Didn't even chase him till it was too late."

The Queens shrugged at each other, Gallically.

"The old story," said the Inspector; the corners of his nostrils were greenish. "The brass of the colonel's monkey and when he does show himself nobody remembers anything but beards and foreign accents. Well, Mr. Bondling, with Comus in the game it's serious business. Where's the collection right now?"

"In the vaults of the Life Bank and Trust, Forty-third Street branch."

"What time are you to move it over to Nash's?"

"They wanted it this evening. I said nothing doing. I've made special arrangements with the bank, and the collection's to be moved at seven thirty tomorrow morning."

"Won't be much time to set up," said Ellery thoughtfully, "before the store opens its doors." He glanced at his father.

"You leave Operation Dollie to us, Mr. Bondling," said the Inspector grimly. "Better give me a buzz this afternoon."

"I can't tell you, Inspector, how relieved I am—"

49

"Are you?" said the old gentleman sourly. "What makes you think he won't get it?"

When Attorney Bondling had left, the Queens put their heads together, Ellery doing most of the talking, as usual. Finally, the Inspector went into the bedroom for a session with his direct line to headquarters.

"Anybody would think," sniffed Nikki, "you two were planning the defense of the Bastille. Who on earth is this Comus, anyway?"

"We don't know, Nikki," said Ellery slowly. "Might be anybody. Began his criminal career about five years ago. He's in the grand tradition of Lupin—a saucy, highly intelligent rascal who's made stealing an art. He seems to take a special delight in stealing valuable things under virtually impossible conditions. Master of make-up—he's appeared in a dozen different disguises. And he's an uncanny mimic. Never been caught, photographed, or fingerprinted. Imaginative, daring—I'd say he's the most dangerous thief operating right now in the United States."

"If he's never been caught," said Nikki skeptically, "how do you know he commits these crimes?"

"You mean and not someone else?" Ellery smiled pallidly. "The techniques mark the thefts as his work. And then, like Arsène, he leaves a card—with the name 'Comus' on it—on the scene of each visit."

"Does he usually announce in advance that he's going to swipe the crown jewels?"

"No." Ellery frowned. "To my knowledge, this is the first such instance. Since he's never done anything without a reason, that visit to Bondling's office this morning must be part of his greater plan. I wonder if—"

The telephone in the living room rang clear and loud.

Nikki looked at Ellery. Ellery looked at the telephone.

"Do you suppose—?" began Nikki. But then she said, "Oh, it's too absurd."

"Where Comus is involved," said Ellery wildly, "nothing is too absurd!" and he leaped for the phone. "Hello!"

"A call from an old friend," announced a deep and hollowish male voice. "Comus."

"Well," said Ellery. "Hello again."

"Did Mr. Bondling," asked the voice jovially, "persuade you

50

to 'prevent' me from stealing the Dauphin's Doll in Nash's to-morrow?"

"So you know Bondling's been here."

"No miracle involved, Queen. I followed him. Are you taking the case?"

"See here, Comus," said Ellery. "Under ordinary circum-stances I'd welcome the sporting chance to put you where you belong. But these circumstances are not ordinary. That doll represents the major asset of a future fund for orphaned chil-dren. I'd rather we didn't play catch with it. Comus, what do you say we call this one off?"

"Shall we say," asked the voice gently, "Nash's Department Store—tomorrow?"

Thus the early morning of December twenty-fourth finds Messrs. Queen and Bondling, and Nikki Porter, huddled on the iron sidewalk of Forty-third Street before the holly-decked windows of the Life Bank & Trust Company, just outside a double line of armed guards. The guards form a channel be-tween the bank entrance and an armored truck, down which Cytherea Ypson's Dollection flows swiftly. And all about gapes New York, stamping callously on the aged, icy face of the street against the uncharitable Christmas wind.

Now is the winter of his discontent, and Mr. Queen curses.

"I don't know what you're beefing about," moans Miss Porter. "You and Mr. Bondling are bundled up like Yukon prospec-tors. Look at *me*."

"It's that rat-hearted public relations tripe from Nash's," says Mr. Queen murderously. "They all swore themselves to secrecy, Brother Rat included. Honor! Spirit of Christmas!"

"It was all over the radio last night," whimpers Mr. Bondling. "And in this morning's papers."

"I'll cut his creep's heart out. Here! Velie, keep those people away!"

Sergeant Velie says good-naturedly from the doorway of the bank, "You jerks stand back." Little does the Sergeant know the fate in store for him.

"Armored trucks," says Miss Porter bluishly. "Shotguns."

"Nikki, Comus made a point of informing us in advance that he meant to steal the Dauphin's Doll in Nash's Department Store. It would be just like him to have said that in order to make it easier to steal the doll en route."

"Why don't they hurry?" shivers Mr. Bondling. "Ah!" Inspector Queen appears suddenly in the doorway. His hands clasp treasure.

"Oh!" cries Nikki.

New York whistles.

It is magnificence, an affront to democracy. But street mobs, like children, are royalists at heart.

New York whistles, and Sergeant Thomas Velie steps menacingly before Inspector Queen, Police Positive drawn, and Inspector Queen dashes across the sidewalk between the bristling lines of guards.

Queen the Younger vanishes, to materialize an instant later at the door of the armored truck.

"It's just immorally, hideously beautiful, Mr. Bondling," breathes Miss Porter, sparkly-eyed.

Mr. Bondling cranes, thinly.

ENTER *Santa Claus, with bell.*

Santa. Oyez, oyez. Peace, good will. Is that the dollie the radio's been yappin' about, folks?

Mr. B. Scram.

Miss P. Why, Mr. Bondling.

Mr. B. Well, he's got no business here. Stand back, er, Santa. Back!

Santa. What eateth you, my lean and angry friend? Have you no compassion at this season of the year?

Mr. B. Oh . . . Here! (*Clink.*) Now will you kindly . . .?

Santa. Mighty pretty dollie. Where they takin' it, girlie?

Miss P. Over to Nash's, Santa.

Mr. B. You asked for it. Officer!!!

Santa. (*Hurriedly*) Little present for you, girlie. Compliments of old Santy. Merry, merry.

Miss P. For *me?* (EXIT *Santa, rapidly, with bell.*) Really, Mr. Bondling, was it necessary to . . . ?

Mr. B. Opium for the masses! What did that flatulent faker hand you, Miss Porter? What's in that unmentionable envelope?

Miss P. I'm sure I don't know, but isn't it the most touching idea? Why, it's addressed to *Ellery.* Oh! Elleryyyyyy!

Mr. B. (EXIT *excitedly*) Where is he? You—! Officer! Where did that baby-deceiver disappear to? A Santa Claus . . .

Mr. Q. (*Entering on the run*) Yes? Nikki, what is it? What's happened?

Miss P. A man dressed as Santa Claus just handed me this envelope. It's addressed to you.

Mr. Q. Note? (*He snatches it, withdraws a miserable slice of paper*

52

from it on which is block-lettered in pencil a message which he reads aloud with considerable expression.) "Dear Ellery, Don't you trust me? I said I'd steal the Dauphin in Nash's emporium today and that's exactly where I'm going to do it. Yours—" Signed . . .

Miss P. (*Craning*) "Comus." That Santa?
Mr. Q. (*Sets his manly lips. An icy wind blows*)

Even the master had to acknowledge that their defenses against Comus were ingenious.

From the Display Department of Nash's they had requisitioned four miter-jointed counters of uniform length. These they had fitted together, and in the center of the hollow square thus formed they had erected a platform six feet high. On the counters, in plastic tiers, stretched the long lines of Miss Ypson's babies. Atop the platform, dominant, stood a great chair of hand-carved oak, filched from the Swedish Modern section of the Fine Furniture Department; and on this Valhalla-like throne, a huge and rosy rotundity, sat Sergeant Thomas Velie of police headquarters, morosely grateful for the anonymity endowed by the scarlet suit and the jolly mask and whiskers of his appointed role.

Nor was this all. At a distance of six feet outside the counters shimmered a surrounding rampart of plate glass, borrowed in its various elements from *The Glass Home of the Future* display on the sixth floor rear, and assembled to shape an eight-foot wall quoined with chrome, its glistening surfaces flawless except at one point, where a thick glass door had been installed. But the edges fitted intimately and there was a formidable lock in the door, the key to which lay buried in Mr. Queen's right trouser pocket.

It was 8:51 A.M. The Queens, Nikki Porter, and Attorney Bondling stood among store officials and an army of plainclothesmen on Nash's main floor surveying the product of their labors.

"I think that about does it," muttered Inspector Queen at last. "Men! Positions around the glass partition."

Twenty-four assorted gendarmes in mufti jostled one another. They took marked places about the wall, facing it and grinning up at Sergeant Velie. Sergeant Velie, from his throne, glared back.

"Hagstrom and Piggott—the door."

Two detectives detached themselves from a group of reserves. As they marched to the glass door, Mr. Bondling

53

plucked at the Inspector's overcoat sleeve. "Can all these men be trusted, Inspector Queen?" he whispered. "I mean, this fellow Comus—"

"Mr. Bondling," replied the old gentleman coldly, "you do your job and let me do mine."

"But—"

"Picked men, Mr. Bondling! I picked 'em myself."

"Yes, yes, Inspector. I merely thought I'd—"

"Lieutenant Farber."

A little man with watery eyes stepped forward.

"Mr. Bondling, this is Lieutenant Geronimo Farber, headquarters jewelry expert. Ellery?"

Ellery took the Dauphin's Doll from his greatcoat pocket, but he said, "If you don't mind, dad, I'll keep holding on to it."

Somebody said, "Wow," and then there was silence.

"Lieutenant, this doll in my son's hand is the famous Dauphin's Doll with the diamond crown that—"

"Don't touch it, Lieutenant, please," said Ellery. "I'd rather nobody touched it."

"The doll," continued the Inspector, "has just been brought here from a bank vault which it ought never to have left, and Mr. Bondling, who's handling the Ypson estate, claims it's the genuine article. Lieutenant, examine the diamond and give us your opinion."

Lieutenant Farber produced a loupe. Ellery held the dauphin securely, and Farber did not touch it.

Finally, the expert said: "I can't pass an opinion about the doll itself, of course, but the diamond's a beauty. Easily worth a hundred thousand dollars at the present state of the market—maybe more. Looks like a very strong setting, by the way."

"Thanks, Lieutenant. Okay, son," said the Inspector. "Go into your waltz."

Clutching the dauphin, Ellery strode over to the glass gate and unlocked it.

"This fellow Farber," whispered Attorney Bondling in the Inspector's hairy ear. "Inspector, are you absolutely sure he's—?"

"He's really Lieutenant Farber?" The Inspector controlled himself. "Mr. Bondling, I've known Gerry Farber for eighteen years. Calm yourself."

Ellery was crawling perilously over the nearest counter.

54

Then, bearing the dauphin aloft, he hurried across the floor of the enclosure to the platform.

Sergeant Velie whined, "Maestro, how in hell am I going to sit here all day without washin' my hands?"

But Mr. Queen merely stooped and lifted from the floor a heavy little structure faced with black velvet consisting of a floor and a backdrop, with a two-armed chromium support. This object he placed on the platform directly between Sergeant Velie's massive legs.

Carefully, he stood the Dauphin's Doll in the velvet niche. Then he clambered back across the counter, went through the glass door, locked it with the key, and turned to examine his handiwork.

Proudly the prince's plaything stood, the jewel in his little golden crown darting "on pale electric streams" under the concentrated tide of a dozen of the most powerful floodlights in the possession of the great store.

"Velie," said Inspector Queen, "you're not to touch that doll. Don't lay a finger on it."

The sergeant said, "Gaaaaa."

"You men on duty. Don't worry about the crowds. Your job is to keep watching that doll. You're not to take your eyes off it all day. Mr. Bondling, are you satisfied?" Mr. Bondling seemed about to say something, but then he hastily nodded. "Ellery?"

The great man smiled. "The only way he can get that bawble," he said, "is by spells and incantations. Raise the portcullis!"

Then began the interminable day, *dies irae*, the last shopping day before Christmas. This is traditionally the day of the inert, the procrastinating, the undecided, and the forgetful, sucked at last into the mercantile machine by the perpetual pump of Time. If there is peace upon earth, it descends only afterward; and at no time, on the part of anyone embroiled, is there good will toward men. As Miss Porter expresses it, a cat fight in a bird cage would be more Christian.

But on this December twenty-fourth, in Nash's the normal bedlam was augmented by the vast shrilling of thousands of Children. It may be, as the Psalmist insists, that happy is the man that hath his quiver full of them; but no bowmen surrounded Miss Ypson's darlings this day, only detectives carrying revolvers, not a few of whom forbore to use same only by the most heroic self-discipline. In the black floods of humanity overflowing the main floor little folks darted about like electrically charged minnows, pursued by exasperated maternal shrieks and the imprecations of those whose shins and rumps and toes were at the mercy of hot, happy little limbs; indeed, nothing was sacred, and Attorney Bondling was seen to quail and wrap his greatcoat defensively about him against the savage innocence of childhood. But the guardians of the law, having been ordered to simulate store employees, possessed no such armor; and many a man earned his citation that day for unique cause. They stood in the very millrace of the tide; it churned about them, shouting, "Dollies! *Dollies!*" until the very word lost its familiar meaning and became the insensate scream of a thousand Loreleis beckoning strong men to destruction below the eye-level of their diamond Light.

But they stood fast.

And Comus was thwarted. Oh, he tried. At 11:18 A.M. a tottering old man holding fast to the hand of a small boy tried to wheedle Detective Hagstrom into unlocking the glass door "so my grandson here—he's terrible nearsighted—can get a closer look at the pretty dollies." Detective Hagstrom roared, "Rube!" and the old gentleman dropped the little boy's hand violently and with remarkable agility lost himself in the crowd. A spot investigation revealed that, coming upon the boy, who had been crying for his mommy, the old gentleman had promised to find her. The little boy, whose name—he said—was Lance Morganstern, was removed to the Lost and Found Department; and everyone was satisfied that the great thief had finally launched his attack. Everyone, that is, but Ellery Queen. He seemed puzzled. When Nikki asked him why, he merely said: "Stupidity, Nikki. It's not in character."

At 1:46 P.M., Sergeant Velie sent up a distress signal. Inspector Queen read the message aright and signaled back: "O.K. Fifteen minutes." Sergeant Santa C. Velie scrambled off his perch, clawed his way over the counter, and pounded urgently on the inner side of the glass door. Ellery let him out, relocking the door immediately, and the Sergeant's red-clad figure disappeared on the double in the general direction of the main-floor gentlemen's relief station, leaving the dauphin in solitary possession of the dais.

During the Sergeant's recess Inspector Queen circulated among his men repeating the order of the day.

56

The episode of Velie's response to the summons of Nature caused a temporary crisis. For at the end of the specified fifteen minutes he had not returned. Nor was there a sign of him at the end of a half-hour. An aide dispatched to the relief station reported back that the Sergeant was not there. Fears of foul play were voiced at an emergency staff conference held then and there and countermeasures were being planned even as, at 2:35 P.M. the familiar Santa-clad bulk of the Sergeant was observed battling through the lines, pawing at his mask.

"Velie," snarled Inspector Queen, "where have you been?"

"Eating my lunch," growled the Sergeant's voice, defensively. "I been taking my punishment like a good soldier all day, Inspector, but I draw the line at starvin' to death even in line of duty."

"Velie—!" choked the Inspector; but then he waved his hand feebly and said, "Ellery, let him back in there."

And that was very nearly all. The only other incident of note occurred at 4:22 P.M. A well-upholstered woman with a red face yelled, "Stop! Thief! He grabbed my pocketbook! Police!" about fifty feet from the Ypson exhibit. Ellery instantly shouted, *"It's a trick! Men, don't take your eyes off that doll!"*

"It's Comus disguised as a woman," exclaimed Attorney Bondling, as Inspector Queen and Detective Hesse wrestled the female figure through the mob. She was now a wonderful shade of magenta. "What are you *doing?*" she screamed. "Don't arrest *me!*—catch that crook who stole my pocketbook!" "No dice, Comus," said the Inspector. "Wipe off that makeup." "McComas?" said the woman loudly. "My name is Rafferty, and all these folks saw it. He was a fat man with a mustache." "Inspector," said Nikki Porter, making a surreptitious scientific test. "This is a female. Believe me." And so, indeed, it proved. All agreed that the mustachioed fat man had been Comus, creating a diversion in the desperate hope that the resulting confusion would give him an opportunity to steal the little dauphin.

"Stupid, stupid," muttered Ellery, gnawing his fingernails.

"Sure," grinned the Inspector. "We've got him nibbling his tail, Ellery. This was his do-or-die pitch. He's through."

"Frankly," sniffed Nikki, "I'm a little disappointed."

"Worried," said Ellery, "would be the word for me."

Inspector Queen was too case-hardened a sinner's nemesis to

57

lower his guard at his most vulnerable moment. When the 5:30 bells bonged and the crowds began struggling toward the exits, he barked: "Men, stay at your posts. Keep watching that doll!" So all hands were on the *qui vive* even as the store emptied. The reserves kept hustling people out. Ellery, standing on an Information booth, spotted bottlenecks and waved his arms.

At 5:50 P.M. the main floor was declared out of the battle zone. All stragglers had been herded out. The only persons visible were the refugees trapped by the closing bell on the upper floors, and these were pouring out of elevators and funneled by a solid line of detectives and accredited store personnel to the doors. By 6:05 they were a trickle; by 6:10 even the trickle had dried up. And the personnel itself began to disperse.

"No, men!" called Ellery sharply from his observation post. "Stay where you are till all the store employees are out!" The counter clerks had long since disappeared.

Sergeant Velie's plaintive voice called from the other side of the glass door. "I got to get home and decorate my tree. Maestro, make with the key."

Ellery jumped down and hurried over to release him. Detective Piggott jeered, "Going to play Santa to your kids tomorrow morning, Velie?" at which the Sergeant managed even through his mask to project a four-letter word distinctly, forgetful of Miss Porter's presence, and stamped off toward the gentlemen's relief station.

"Where you going, Velie?" asked the Inspector, smiling.

"I got to get out of these x-and-dash Santy clothes somewheres, don't I?" came back the Sergeant's mask-muffled tones, and he vanished in a thunderclap of his fellow-officers' laughter.

"Still worried, Mr. Queen?" chuckled the Inspector.

"I don't understand it." Ellery shook his head. "Well, Mr. Bondling, there's your dauphin, untouched by human hands."

"Yes. Well!" Attorney Bondling wiped his forehead happily. "I don't profess to understand it, either, Mr. Queen. Unless it's simply another case of an inflated reputation . . ." He clutched the Inspector suddenly. "Those men!" he whispered. *"Who are they?"*

"Relax, Mr. Bondling," said the Inspector good-naturedly. "It's just the men to move the dolls back to the bank. Wait a minute, you men! Perhaps, Mr. Bondling, we'd better see the dauphin back to the vaults ourselves."

"Keep those fellows back," said Ellery to the headquarters men, quietly, and he followed the Inspector and Mr. Bondling into the enclosure. They pulled two of the counters apart at one corner and strolled over to the platform. The dauphin was winking at them in a friendly way. They stood looking at him.

"Cute little devil," said the Inspector.

"Seems silly now," beamed Attorney Bondling. "Being so worried all day."

"Comus must have had *some* plan," mumbled Ellery.

"Sure," said the Inspector. "That old man disguise. And that purse-snatching act."

"No, no, dad. Something clever. He's always pulled something clever."

"Well, there's the diamond," said the lawyer comfortably. "He didn't."

"Disguise ..." muttered Ellery. "It's always been a disguise. Santa Claus costume—he used that once—this morning in front of the bank. . . . Did we see a Santa Claus around here today?"

"Just Velie," said the Inspector, grinning. "And I hardly think—"

"Wait a moment, please," said Attorney Bondling in a very odd voice.

He was staring at the Dauphin's Doll.

"Wait for what, Mr. Bondling?"

"What's the matter?" said Ellery, also in a very odd voice.

"But . . . not possible . . ." stammered Bondling. He snatched the doll from its black velvet repository. *"No!"* he howled. *"This isn't the dauphin! It's a fake—a copy!"*

Something happened in Mr. Queen's head—a little *click!* like the sound of a switch. And there was light.

"Some of you men!" he roared. *"After Santa Claus!"*

"After who, Ellery?" gasped Inspector Queen.

"Don't stand here! *Get him!"* screamed Ellery, dancing up and down. "The man I just let out of here! The Santa who made for the men's room!"

Detectives started running, wildly.

"But Ellery," said a small voice, and Nikki found that it was her own, "that was Sergeant Velie."

"It was *not* Velie, Nikki! When Velie ducked out just before two o'clock, *Comus waylaid him!* It was Comus who came back in Velie's Santa Claus rig, wearing Velie's whiskers and mask! *Comus has been on this platform all afternoon!"* He tore the dauphin

59

from Attorney Bondling's grasp. "Copy . . . He did it, he did it!"

"But Mr. Queen," whispered Attorney Bondling, "his voice. He spoke to us . . . in Sergeant Velie's voice."

"Yes, Ellery," Nikki heard herself saying.

"I told you yesterday Comus is a great mimic, Nikki. Lieutenant Farber! Is Farber still here?"

The jewelry expert, who had been gaping from a distance, shook his head and shuffled into the enclosure.

"Lieutenant," said Ellery in a strangled voice. "Examine this diamond. . . . I mean, *is* it a diamond?"

Inspector Queen removed his hands from his face and said froggily, "Well, Gerry?"

Lieutenant Farber squinted once through his loupe. "The hell you say. It's strass—"

"It's what?" said the Inspector piteously.

"Strass, Dick—lead glass—paste. Beautiful job of imitation —as nice as I've ever seen."

"Lead me to that Santa Claus," whispered Inspector Queen.

But Santa Claus was being led to him. Struggling in the grip of a dozen detectives, his red coat ripped off, his red pants around his ankles, but his whiskery mask still on his face, came a large shouting man.

"But I tell you," he was roaring, "I'm Sergeant Tom Velie! Just take the mask off—that's all!"

"It's a pleasure," growled Detective Hagstrom, trying to break their prisoner's arm, "we're reservin' for the Inspector."

"Hold him, boys," whispered the Inspector. He struck like a cobra. His hand came away with Santa's face.

And there, indeed, was Sergeant Velie.

"Why, it's Velie," said the Inspector wonderingly.

"I only told you that a thousand times," said the Sergeant, folding his great hairy arms across his great hairy chest. "Now who's the so-and-so who tried to bust my arm?" Then he said, "My pants!" and as Miss Porter turned delicately away, Detective Hagstrom humbly stooped and raised Sergeant Velie's pants.

"Never mind that," said a cold, remote voice.

It was the master, himself.

"Yeah?" said Sergeant Velie.

"Velie, weren't you attacked when you went to the men's room just before two?"

"Do I look like the attackable type?"

"You did go to lunch?—in person?"

"And a lousy lunch it was."

"It was *you* up here among the dolls all afternoon?"

"Nobody else, Maestro. Now, my friends, I want action. Fast patter. What's this all about? Before," said Sergeant Velie softly, "I lose my temper."

While divers headquarters orators delivered impromptu periods before the silent Sergeant, Inspector Richard Queen spoke.

"Ellery. Son. How in the name of the second sin did he do it?"

"Pa," replied the master, "you got me."

Deck the hall with boughs of holly, but not if your name is Queen on the evening of a certain December twenty-fourth. If your name is Queen on that lamentable evening you are seated in the living room of a New York apartment uttering no falalas but staring miserably into a somber fire. And you have company. The guest list is short, but select. It numbers two, a Miss Porter and a Sergeant Velie, and they are no comfort.

No, no ancient Yuletide carol is being trolled; only the silence sings.

Wail in your crypt, Cytherea Ypson; all was for nought; your little dauphin's treasure lies not in the empty coffers of the orphans but in the hot clutch of one who took his evil inspiration from a long-crumbled specialist in vanishments.

Fact: Lieutenant Geronimo Farber of police headquarters had examined the diamond in the genuine dauphin's crown a matter of seconds before it was conveyed to its sanctuary in the enclosure. Lieutenant Farber had pronounced the diamond a diamond, and not merely a diamond, but a diamond worth in his opinion over one hundred thousand dollars.

Fact: It was this genuine diamond and this genuine Dauphin's Doll which Ellery with his own hands had carried into the glass-enclosed fortress and deposited between the authenticated Sergeant Velie's verified feet.

Fact: All day—specifically, between the moment the dauphin had been deposited in his niche until the moment he was discovered to be a fraud; that is, during the total period in which a theft-and-substitution was even theoretically possible—no person whatsoever, male or female, adult or child, had set foot within the enclosure except Sergeant Thomas Velie, alias Santa Claus; and some dozens of persons with police training and specific instructions, not to mention the Queens themselves,

Miss Porter, and Attorney Bondling, testified unqualifiedly that Sergeant Velie had not touched the doll, at any time, all day.

Fact: All those deputized to watch the doll swore that they had done so without lapse or hindrance the everlasting day; moreover, that at no time had anything touched the doll— human or mechanical—either from inside or outside the enclosure.

Fact: Despite all the foregoing, at the end of the day they had found the real dauphin gone and a worthless copy in its place.

"It's brilliantly, unthinkably clever," said Ellery at last. "A master illusion. For, of course, it *was* an illusion. . . . ."

"Witchcraft," groaned the Inspector.

"Mass mesmerism," suggested Nikki Porter.

"Mass bird gravel," growled the Sergeant.

Two hours later Ellery spoke again.

"So Comus had a worthless copy of the dauphin all ready for the switch," he muttered. "It's a world-famous dollie, been illustrated countless times, minutely described, photographed. . . . All ready for the switch, but how did he make it? How? How?"

"You said that," said the Sergeant, "once or forty-two times."

"The bells are tolling," sighed Nikki, "but for whom? Not for us." And indeed, while they slumped there, Time, which Seneca named father of truth, had crossed the threshold of Christmas; and Nikki looked alarmed, for as that glorious song of old came upon the midnight clear, a great light spread from Ellery's eyes and beatified the whole contorted countenance, so that peace sat there, the peace that approximateth understanding; and he threw back that noble head and laughed with the merriment of an innocent child.

"Hey," said Sergeant Velie, staring.

"Son," began Inspector Queen, half-rising from his armchair; when the telephone rang.

"Beautiful!" roared Ellery. "Oh, exquisite! How did Comus make the switch, eh? Nikki—"

"From somewhere," said Nikki, handing him the telephone receiver, "a voice is calling, and if you ask me it's saying 'Comus.' Why not ask him?"

"Comus," whispered the Inspector, shrinking.

"Comus," echoed the Sergeant, baffled.

"Comus?" said Ellery heartily. "How nice. Hello there! Congratulations."

"Why, thank you," said the familiar deep and hollow voice. "I

62

called to express my appreciation for a wonderful day's sport and to wish you the merriest kind of Yuletide."

"You anticipate a rather merry Christmas yourself, I take it."

"*Laeti triumphantes*," said Comus jovially.

"And the orphans?"

"They have my best wishes. But I won't detain you, Ellery. If you'll look at the doormat outside your apartment door, you'll find on it—in the spirit of the season—a little gift, with the compliments of Comus. Will you remember me to Inspector Queen and to Attorney Bondling?"

Ellery hung up, smiling.

On the doormat he found the true Dauphin's Doll, intact except for a contemptible detail. The jewel in the little golden crown was missing.

"It was," said Ellery later, over pastrami sandwiches, "a fundamentally simple problem. All great illusions are. A valuable object is placed in full view in the heart of an impenetrable enclosure, it is watched hawkishly by dozens of thoroughly screened and reliable trained persons, it is never out of their view, it is not once touched by human hand or any other agency, and yet, at the expiration of the danger period, it is gone—exchanged for a worthless copy. Wonderful. Amazing. It defies the imagination. Actually, it's susceptible—like all magical hocus-pocus—to immediate solution if only one is able—as I was not—to ignore the wonder and stick to the fact. But then, the wonder is there for precisely that purpose: to stand in the way of the fact.

"What is the fact?" continued Ellery, helping himself to a dill pickle. "The fact is that between the time the doll was placed on the exhibit platform and the time the theft was discovered no one and no thing touched it. Therefore between the time the doll was placed on the platform and the time the theft was discovered *the dauphin could not have been stolen.* It follows, simply and inevitably, that the dauphin must have been stolen *outside that period.*

"Before the period began? No. I placed the authentic dauphin inside the enclosure with my own hands; at or about the beginning of the period, then, no hand but mine had touched the doll—not even, you'll recall, Lieutenant Farber's.

"Then the dauphin must have been stolen after the period closed."

Ellery brandished half the pickle. "And who," he demanded solemnly, "is the only one besides myself who handled that doll after the period closed and before Lieutenant Farber pronounced the diamond to be paste? *The only one?*"

The Inspector and the Sergeant exchanged puzzled glances, and Nikki looked blank.

"Why, Mr. Bondling," said Nikki, "and he doesn't count."

"He counts very much, Nikki," said Ellery, reaching for the mustard, "because the facts say Bondling stole the dauphin at that time."

"Bondling!" The Inspector paled.

"I don't get it," complained Sergeant Velie.

"Ellery, you must be wrong," said Nikki. "At the time Mr. Bondling grabbed the doll off the platform, the theft had already taken place. It was the worthless copy he picked up."

"That," said Ellery, reaching for another sandwich, "was the focal point of his illusion. How do we know it was the worthless copy he picked up? Why, he said so. Simple, eh? He said so and like the dumb bunnies we were, we took his unsupported word as gospel."

"That's right!" mumbled his father. "We didn't actually examine the doll till quite a few seconds later."

"Exactly," said Ellery in a munchy voice. "There was a short period of beautiful confusion, as Bondling knew there would be. I yelled to the boys to follow and grab Santa Claus—I mean, the Sergeant here. The detectives were momentarily demoralized. You, dad, were stunned. Nikki looked as if the roof had fallen in. I essayed an excited explanation. Some detectives ran; others milled around. And while all this was happening— during those few moments when nobody was watching the genuine doll in Bondling's hand because everyone thought it was a fake—Bondling calmly slipped it into one of his greatcoat pockets and from the other produced the worthless copy which he'd been carrying there all day. When I did turn back to him, it was the copy I grabbed from his hand. And his illusion was complete.

"I know," said Ellery dryly, "it's rather on the let-down side. That's why illusionists guard their professional secrets so closely; knowledge is disenchantment. No doubt the incredulous amazement aroused in his periwigged London audience by Comus the French conjuror's dematerialization of his wife from the top of a table would have suffered the same fate if he'd revealed the trap door through which she had dropped. A good trick, like a good woman, is best in the dark. Sergeant, have another pastrami."

"Seems like funny chow to be eating early Christmas morning," said the Sergeant, reaching. Then he stopped. Then he said, "Bondling," and shook his head.

"Now that we know it was Bondling," said the Inspector, who had recovered a little, "it's a cinch to get that diamond back. He hasn't had time to dispose of it yet. I'll just give downtown a buzz—"

"Wait, dad," said Ellery.

"Wait for what?"

"Whom are you going to sic the hounds on?"

"What?"

"You're going to call headquarters, get a warrant, and so on. Who's your man?"

The Inspector felt his head. "Why . . . Bondling, didn't you say?"

"It might be wise," said Ellery, thoughtfully searching with his tongue for a pickle seed, "to specify his alias."

"Alias?" said Nikki. "Does he have one?"

"What alias, son?"

"Comus."

"*Comus!*"

"*Comus?*"

"Oh, come off it," said Nikki, pouring herself a shot of coffee, straight, for she was in training for the Inspector's Christmas dinner. "How could Bondling be Comus when Bondling was with us all day?—and Comus kept making disguised appearances all over the place . . . that Santa who gave me the note in front of the bank—the old man who kidnapped Lance Morganstern—the fat man with the mustache who snatched Mrs. Rafferty's purse."

"Yeah," said the Sergeant. "How?"

"These illusions die hard," said Ellery. "Wasn't it Comus who phoned a few minutes ago to rag me about the theft? Wasn't it Comus who said he'd left the stolen dauphin—minus the diamond—on our doormat? Therefore Comus is Bondling.

"I told you Comus never does anything without a good reason," said Ellery. "Why did 'Comus' announce to 'Bondling' that he was *going* to steal the Dauphin's Doll? Bondling told us that—putting the finger on his *alter ego*—because he wanted us

65

to believe he and Comus were separate individuals. He wanted us to watch for *Comus* and take *Bondling* for granted. In tactical execution of this strategy Bondling provided us with three 'Comus' appearances during the day—obviously, confederates.

"Yes," said Ellery, "I think, dad, you'll find on backtracking that the great thief you've been trying to catch for five years has been a respectable estate attorney on Park Row all the time, shedding his quiddities and his quillets at night in favor of the soft shoe and the dark lantern. And now he'll have to exchange them all for a number and a grilled door. Well, well, it couldn't have happened at a more appropriate season; there's an old English proverb that says the Devil makes his Christmas pie of lawyers' tongues. Nikki, pass the pastrami."

THE COP KILLER

BY REX STOUT

Rex Todhunter Stout was born in Noblesville, Indiana, on December 1, 1886, and attended the University of Kansas. As a young man he developed the Educational Thrift System, a savings program for schoolchildren, the marketing of which enabled him to retire at forty-one. He began writing seriously, and his first four novels won critical acclaim but did not sell. In 1934, Stout's first Nero Wolfe book, *Fer-de-Lance,* was serialized in *The Saturday Evening Post* and was enormously successful. Over the next forty-one years Wolfe and Archie Goodwin appeared in nearly fifty books. Stout died on October 27, 1975.

THERE WERE SEVERAL REASONS why I had no complaints as I walked along West 35th Street that morning, approaching the stoop of Nero Wolfe's old brownstone house, where I both lived and worked. The day was sunny and sparkling, my new shoes felt fine after the brisk mile walk, a complicated infringement case had been polished off for a big client, and I had just deposited a check in five figures to Wolfe's account in the bank.

Five paces short of the stoop I became aware that two people, a man and a woman, were standing on the sidewalk across the street, staring either at the stoop or at me, or maybe both. That lifted me a notch higher, with the thought that while two rubbernecks might not put us in a class with the White House, still it was nothing to sneeze at, until a second glance made me realize that I had seen them before. But where? Instead of turning up the steps I faced them, just as they stepped off the curb and started toward me.

"Mr. Goodwin," the woman said, in a sort of gasping whisper.

She was fair-skinned and blue-eyed, young enough, kind of nice-looking, and neat in a dark-blue assembly-line coat. He was as dark as she was fair, not much bigger, with his nose slanting slightly to the left, and a full, wide mouth. My delay in recognizing him was because I had never seen him with a hat on before. He was the hat and coat and necktie custodian at the barbershop I went to.

"Oh, it's you, Carl—"

"Can we go in with you?" the woman asked in the same gasping whisper, and then I knew her, too. She was also from the barbershop, a manicurist. I had never hired her, since I do my own nails, but had seen her around and had heard her called Tina.

I looked down at her smooth, white little face with its pointed chin, and didn't care for the expression on it. I glanced at Carl, and he looked even worse.

"What's the matter?" I guess I was gruff. "Trouble?"

"Please, not out here," Tina pleaded. Her eyes darted left and right, and back up at me. "We just got enough brave to go to the door when you came. Please let us in?"

68

"You told me once," Carl practically whined, "that people in danger only have to mention your name."

"Nuts. A pleasantry. I talk too much." But I was stuck. "Okay, come in and tell me about it."

I led the way up the steps and let us in with my key. Inside, the first door on the left of the long, wide hall led to what we called the front room, and I opened it, thinking to get it over with in there, but Fritz was there dusting, so I took them along to the next door and on into the office. After moving a couple of chairs so they would be facing me, I sat at my desk and nodded at them impatiently. Tina had looked around, swiftly, before she sat.

"Such a nice, safe room," she said, "for you and Mr. Wolfe, two such great men."

"He's the great one," I corrected her. "I just caddie. What's this about danger?"

"We love this country," Carl said emphatically. All of a sudden he started trembling, first his hands, then his arms and shoulders, then all over. Tina darted to him and grabbed his elbows and shook him, not gently, and said things to him in some language I wasn't up on. He mumbled back at her, and after a little the trembling stopped.

"We do love this country," she declared.

I nodded. "Wait till you see Chillicothe, Ohio, where I was born. Then you *will* love it. How far west have you been— Tenth Avenue?"

"I don't think so." Tina was doubtful. "I think Eighth Avenue. But that's what we want to do, go west." She opened her blue leather handbag and, with no fingering or digging, took something from it. "But you see, we don't know where to go. This Ohio, maybe? I have fifty dollars here."

"That would get you there," I allowed.

She shook her head. "Oh, no. The fifty dollars is for you. You know our name—Vardas? You know we are married? So there is no question of morals; we are very high in morals; only, all we want is to do our work and live in private, Carl and me, and we think—"

Having heard the clatter of Wolfe's elevator descending from the plant rooms on the roof, I had known an interruption was coming, but had let her proceed. Now she stopped, as Wolfe's steps sounded and he appeared at the door. Carl and Tina both

69

bounced to their feet. Two paces in, after a quick glance at them, Wolfe stopped short and glowered at me.

"I didn't tell you we had callers," I said cheerfully, "because I knew you would be down soon. You know Carl, at the barber-shop? And Tina, you've seen her there, too. It's all right, they're married. They just dropped in to buy fifty bucks' worth of—"

Without a word or even a nod, Wolfe turned all of his seventh of a ton and beat it out toward the door to the kitchen at the rear. The Vardas family stared at the doorway a moment and then returned to me.

"Sit down," I invited them. "As you said, he's a great man. He's sore because I didn't notify him we had company, and he was expecting to sit there behind his desk"—I waved a hand—"and ring for beer and enjoy himself. He wouldn't wiggle a finger for fifty dollars. Maybe I won't, either, but let's see." I looked at Tina, who was back on the edge of her chair. "You were saying—"

"We don't want Mr. Wolfe mad at us," Tina said in distress.

"Forget it. He's only mad at me, which is chronic. What do you want to go to Ohio for?"

"Maybe not Ohio." She tried to smile again. "It's what I said—we love this country and we want to go more into it—far in. We want you to tell us where to go, to help us—"

"No, no." I was brusque. "Start from here. What's the danger Carl mentioned?"

"I don't think," she protested, "it makes any difference—"

"That's no good," Carl said harshly. His hands started trembling again, but he gripped the sides of his chair seat and they stopped. His dark eyes fastened on me. "I met Tina," he said in a low, level voice, trying to keep feeling out of it, "three years ago in a concentration camp in Russia. If you want me to I will tell you why it was that they would never have let us get out of there alive, not in one hundred years, but I would rather not talk so much about it. It makes me start to tremble, and I am trying to learn to act and talk of a manner so I can quit trembling."

I concurred. "Save it for some day after you stop trembling. But you did get out alive?"

"Plainly. We are here." There was an edge of triumph to the level voice. "I will not tell you about that, either. But they think we are dead. Of course, Vardas was not our name then, neither

70

of us. We took that name later, when we got married in Istanbul. Then we so managed—"

"You shouldn't tell any places," Tina scolded him. "No places at all and no people at all."

"You are most right," Carl admitted. He informed me: "It was not Istanbul. Anyway, we went many places, and at a certain time in a certain way we crossed the ocean. We had tried very hard to come to this country according to your rules, but it was in no way possible. When we did get into New York it was more by accident— No, I did not say that. Only I will say we got into New York. For a while it was so difficult, but it has been nearly a year now, since we got the jobs at the barbershop, that life has been so fine and sweet that we are almost healthy again. What we eat! We have even got us some money saved! We have got—"

"Fifty dollars," Tina said hastily.

"Most right," Carl agreed. "Fifty American dollars. I can say as a fact that we would be happy beyond our utmost dreams three years ago, except for the danger. The danger is that we did not follow your rules. I will not deny that they are good rules, but for us they were impossible. We cannot expect ourselves to be happy when we don't know what minute someone may come and ask us how we got here. We have found a way to learn what would happen, and we know where we would be sent back to. We know what would happen to us."

I glanced at Tina, but the expression on her face could have made me uncomfortable, so I looked back at Carl. "If I tried to figure a way out, I doubt if I would pick on spilling it to a guy named Archie Goodwin just because he came to the barbershop where I worked. He might be crazy about the rules you couldn't follow, and, anyhow, there are just as many minutes in Ohio as there are in New York."

"There is that fifty dollars." Carl extended his hands, not trembling, toward me.

Tina gestured impatiently. "That's nothing to you," she said, letting bitterness in it for the first time. "We know that; it's nothing. But the danger has come and we had to have someone tell us where to go. This morning a man came to the barbershop and asked us questions. An official! A policeman!"

"Oh." I glanced from one to the other. "That's different. A policeman in uniform?"

71

"No, in regular clothes, but he showed us a card in a case—New York Police Department. His name was on it, Jacob Wallen."

"What time this morning?"

"A little after nine o'clock, soon after the shop was open. He talked first with Mr. Fickler, the owner, and Mr. Fickler brought him around behind the partition to my booth, where I do customers when they're through in the chair or when they only want a manicure, and I was there getting things together, and he sat down and took out a notebook and asked me questions. Then he—"

"What kind of questions?"

"All about me. My name, where I live, where I came from, how long I've been working there, all that kind, and then about last night, where I was and what I was doing last night."

"What part of last night did he ask about? All of it?"

"Yes, from the time the shop closes, half-past six, from then on."

"Where did you tell him you came from?"

"I said Carl and I are DP's from Italy. That's what we had decided to say. We have to say something when people are just curious."

"I suppose you do. Did he ask to see your papers?"

"No. That will come next." She set her jaw. "We can't go back there. We have to leave New York today—right now."

"Did he question Carl, too?"

"Yes, but not right after me. He sent me away, and Mr. Fickler sent Philip to him in the next booth, and when Philip came out he sent Carl in, and when Carl came out he sent Jimmie in. Jimmie was still in the booth with him when I went to Carl, up front by the rack, and we knew we had to get out. We waited until Mr. Fickler had gone to the back of the shop for something, and then we just walked out. We went to our room down on the East Side and packed our bag and started for Grand Central with it, and then we realized we didn't know anything about where to go and might make some terrible mistake, so there in Grand Central we talked it over. We decided that the best thing would be to come to you and pay you to help us. You're a professional detective, and, anyway, Carl likes you about the best of all the customers. You only tip him a dime, so it's not that. I have noticed you myself, the way you look. You

72

look like a man who would break rules, too—if you had to."

I gave her a sharp look, suspicious, but if she was trying to butter me she was very good. All that showed in her blue eyes was the scare that had put them on the run and the hope of me they were hanging on to for dear life. I looked at Carl. The scare was there too, but I couldn't see the hope.

I was irritated. "You bring it here already broke," I protested. "What did you beat it for? That alone fixes you. And what about last night? What were you doing—breaking some more rules?"

They both started to answer, but she let him take it. He said no, they weren't. They had gone straight home from work and eaten in their room, as usual. Tina had washed some clothes and Carl had read a book. Around nine they had gone for a walk, and had been back in their room and in bed before ten thirty.

I was disgusted. "You sure did it up," I declared. "If you're clean for last night, why didn't you stay put? You must have something in your heads or you wouldn't have stayed alive and got this far. Why didn't you use it?"

Carl smiled at me. He really did smile, but it didn't make me want to smile back. "A policeman asking questions," he said in the level tone he had used before, "has a different effect on different people. If you have a country like this one, and you are innocent of crime, all the people of your country are saying it with you when you answer the questions. It takes a whole country to speak to a policeman, and Tina and I—we do not have one."

"You see," Tina said. "Here, take it." She got up and came to me, extending a hand with the money in it. "Take it, Mr. Goodwin! Just tell us where to go, all the little facts that will help us."

"Or we thought," Carl suggested, not hopefully, "that you might give us a letter to some friend, in this Ohio, perhaps. Not that we should expect too much for fifty dollars . . ."

I looked at them with my lips pressed together. The morning was shot now, anyway, with Wolfe sore and my chores not done. I swiveled to my desk and picked up the phone. Any one of three or four city employees would probably find out for me what kind of errand had taken a dick named Wallen to the Goldenrod Barbershop, unless it was something very special.

73

But with my finger in the dial hole I hesitated, and then replaced the phone. If it was something hot I would be starting PD cars for our address, and Wolfe and I both have a prejudice against cops yanking people out of his office, no matter who they are, unless we, ourselves, have got them ready for delivery. So I swiveled again.

"This is silly," I said. "If they're really after you, you'd be throwing your money away on carfare to Ohio or anywhere else. Save it for a lawyer. I'll have to go up there and see what it's all about." I got up, crossed to the soundproof door to the front room, and opened it. "You can wait here. In here, please?"

"We'll go," Tina said, back to her gasping whisper again. "We won't bother you any more. Come, Carl—"

"Skip it," I said curtly. "If this amounts to anything more than petty larceny you'd be nabbed sure as shooting. This is my day for breaking a rule, and I'll be back soon. Come on; I'll put you in here, and I advise you to stay put."

Tina moved. She came and passed through into the front room, and Carl was right behind her. I told them to sit down and relax and not get restless. Then I shut the door and went to the kitchen, where Wolfe was seated at the far end of the long table, drinking beer. I told him, "The check from Pendexter came and has been deposited. That pair of foreigners have got themselves in a mess. I put them in the front room and told them to stay there until I get back."

"Where are you going?" he demanded.

"A little detective work, not in your class. I won't be gone long. You can dock me."

The Goldenrod Barbershop was in the basement of an office building on Lexington Avenue, in the upper Thirties. I had been patronizing one of the staff, named Ed, for several years. Formerly, from away back, Wolfe had gone to an artist in a shop on 28th Street, named Fletcher. When Fletcher had retired a couple of years ago Wolfe had switched to Goldenrod, and after experimenting with the staff had settled on Jimmie. His position now, after two years, was that Jimmie was no Fletcher, especially with a shampoo, but that he was some better than tolerable.

Goldenrod, with only six chairs, and usually only four of them manned, and two manicurists, was not fancy, but it was

74

well equipped and clean. Anyhow, it had Ed, who had a razor so sharp and slick you never knew it was on you.

I hadn't shaved that morning, and as, at noon, I paid the taxi driver, entered the building, and descended the stairs to the basement, my plan of campaign was simple. I would get in Ed's chair, waiting if necessary, and ask him to give me a once-over, and the rest would be easy.

But it was neither simple nor easy. A medium-sized mob of white-collar workers, buzzing and chattering, was ranged three-deep along the wall of the corridor facing the door of the shop. Others, passing by in both directions, were stopping to try to look in, and a flatfoot, posted in the doorway, was telling them to keep moving.

I swerved aside and halted for a survey through the open door. Joel Fickler, the boss, was at the rack where Carl usually presided, taking a man's coat to put on a hanger. A man with his hat on was backed up to the cashier's counter, with his elbows on it, facing the whole shop. Two other men with their hats on were seated near the middle of the row of chairs for waiting customers, one of them next to the little table for magazines. They were discussing something without much enthusiasm. Two of the barbers' chairs, Ed's and Tom's, were occupied. The other two barbers, Jimmie and Philip, were on their stools against the wall. Janet, the other manicurist, was not in sight.

I stepped to the doorway and was going on in. The flatfoot blocked me. "Accident in here. Only customers with appointments allowed in. You got an appointment?"

"Certainly." I stuck my head through the doorway and yelled, "Ed! How soon?"

The man leaning on the counter straightened up and turned for a look. At sight of me he grunted. "Who whistled for you?"

The presence of my old friend and enemy, Sergeant Purley Stebbins, of Manhattan Homicide, gave the thing an entirely different flavor. Up to then I had just been mildly curious, floating along. Now I snapped to attention. Sergeant Stebbins is not interested in petty larceny. I didn't care for the possibility of having shown a pair of murderers to chairs in our front room.

Purley scowled at me. "Is this going to turn into one of them Nero Wolfe babies?"

"Not unless you turn it." I grinned at him. "Whatever it is. I

75

dropped in for a shave, that's all, and here you boys are, to my surprise." The flatfoot had given me leeway, and I had crossed the sill. "I'm a regular customer here." I turned to Fickler, who had trotted over to us: "How long have I been leaving my hair here, Joel?"

None of Fickler's bones was anywhere near the surface except on his bald head. He was six inches shorter than me, which may have been one reason why I never got a straight look into his narrow black eyes. He had never liked me much since the day he had forgotten to list an appointment with Ed I had made on the phone and I, under provocation, had made a few pointed remarks. Now he looked as if he had been annoyed by something much worse than remarks.

"Over six years, Mr. Goodwin," he said. "This," he told Purley, "is the famous detective, Mr. Archie Goodwin. Mr. Nero Wolfe comes here, too."

Purley snorted. "Famous!"

I shrugged. "Just a nuisance."

"Yeah. Don't let it get you down. You just dropped in for a shave?"

"Yes, sir. Write it down and I'll sign it."

"Who's your barber?"

"Ed."

"That's Graboff. He's busy."

"So I see. I'm not pressed. I'll chat with you or read a magazine or get a manicure."

"I don't feel like chatting." Purley had not relaxed the scowl. "You know a guy that works here named Carl Vardas? And his wife Tina, a manicurist?"

"I know Carl well enough to pay him a dime for my hat and coat and tie. I can't say I know Tina, but of course I've seen her here. Why?"

"I'm just asking. And to have it on the record in case it's needed, have you seen Vardas or his wife this morning?"

"Sure, I have." I stretched my neck to get closer to his ear and whispered, "I put them in our front room and told them to wait, and beat it up here to tell you, and if you'll step on it—"

"I don't care for gags," he growled. "Not right now. They killed a cop, or one of them did. You know how much we like that."

I did, indeed, and adjusted my face accordingly. "One of yours? Did I know him?"

76

"No. A dick from the Twentieth Precinct, Jake Wallen."

"Where and when?"

"This morning, right here. The other side of that partition, in Tina's manicure booth. Stuck a pair of scissors in his back and got his pump. Apparently, he never made a sound, but them massage things are going here off and on. By the time he was found, the Vardas pair had gone. It took us an hour to find out where they lived, and when we got there they had been and got their stuff and beat it."

I grunted sympathetically. "Is it tied up? Prints on the scissors or something?"

"We'll do all right without prints," Purley said grimly. "Didn't I say they lammed?"

"Yes, but," I objected, not aggressively, "some people can get awful scared at sight of a man with scissors sticking in his back. I wasn't intimate with Carl, but he didn't strike me as a man who would stab a cop just on principle. Was Wallen here to take him?"

Purley's reply was stopped before it got started. Tom had finished with his customer, and the two men with hats on in the row of chairs ranged along the partition were keeping their eyes on the customer as he went to the rack for his tie. Tom, having brushed himself off, had walked to the front and up to us. Usually Tom bounced around like a high-school kid, in spite of his white-haired sixty-some years, but today his feet dragged. Nor did he tell me hello, though he gave me a sort of glance before he spoke to Purley: "It's my lunchtime, Sergeant. I just go to the cafeteria at the end of the hall."

Purley called a name that sounded like Joffe, and one of the dicks on a chair by the partition got up and came.

"Yerkes is going to lunch," Purley told him. "Go along and stay with him."

They went, with Tom in front. Purley and I moved out of the way as the customer approached to pay his check and Fickler sidled around behind the cash register.

"I thought," I said politely, "you had settled for Carl and Tina. Why does Tom have to have company at lunch?"

"We haven't got Carl and Tina."

"But you soon will have, the way the personnel feels about cop killers. Why pester these innocent barbers? If one of them gets nervous and slices a customer, then what?"

Purley merely snarled.

I stiffened. "Excuse me. I'm not so partial to cop killers, either. It seemed only natural to show some interest. Luckily I can read, so I'll catch it in the evening paper."

"Don't bust a gut." Purley's eyes were following the customer as he walked to the door and on out past the flatfoot. "Sure, we'll get Carl and Tina, but if you don't mind we'll just watch these guys' appetites. You asked what Jake Wallen was here for."

"I asked if he came to take Carl."

"Yeah. I think he did, but I can't prove it yet. Last night around midnight a woman was hit by a car at Eighty-first and Broadway. She was killed. The car kept going. It was found later parked at Ninety-sixth and Broadway, just across from the subway entrance. We haven't found anyone who saw the driver, either at the scene of the accident or where the car was parked. The car was hot. It had been parked by its owner at eight o'clock on Forty-eighth Street between Ninth and Tenth, and was gone when he went for it at eleven thirty."

Purley paused to watch a customer enter. The customer got past the flatfoot with Joel Fickler's help, left things at the rack, and went and got on Jimmie's chair. Purley gave the customer another squint and returned to me:

"When the car was spotted by a squad car at Ninety-sixth and Broadway, with a dented fender and blood and other items that tagged it, the Twentieth Precinct sent Jake Wallen to it. He was the first one to give it a look. Later, there was a gang from all over, including the laboratory, going over it before they moved it. Wallen was supposed to go home at eight in the morning, when his trick ended, but he didn't. He phoned his wife that he had a hot lead on a hit-and-run killer and was going to handle it himself and grab a promotion. Not only that, he phoned the owner of the car, at his home in Yonkers, and asked him if he had any connection with the Goldenrod Barbershop or knew anyone who had, or if he had ever been there. The owner had never heard of it. Of course, we've collected all this since we were called here at ten fifteen and found Wallen DOA with scissors in his back."

I was frowning. "But what gave him the lead to this shop?"

"We'd like to know. It had to be something he found in the car—we don't know what. The poor fool kept it to himself and came here and got killed."

78

"Didn't he show it or mention it to anyone here?"

"They say not. All he had with him was a newspaper. We've got it—today's *Daily Press,* the early, out last night. We can't spot anything in it. There was nothing in his pockets, nothing on him, that helps any."

A phone rang. Fickler, by the cash register, looked at Purley, who stepped to the counter where the phone was and answered the call. It was for him. When, after a minute, it seemed to be going on, I moved away, and had gone a few paces when a voice came: "Hello, Mr. Goodwin."

It was Jimmie, Wolfe's man, using comb and scissors about his customer's right ear. He was the youngest of the staff, about my age, and by far the handsomest, with curly lips and white teeth and dancing dark eyes. I told him hello.

"Mr. Wolfe ought to be here," he said.

Under the circumstances I thought that a little tactless, and was even prepared to tell him so, when Ed called to me from two chairs down: "Fifteen minutes, Mr. Goodwin? All right?"

I told him okay, I would wait, and crossed to one of the chairs over by the partition, next to the table with magazines. I thought it would be fitting to pick up a magazine, but I had already read the one on top, the latest issue of *Ellery Queen's Mystery Magazine;* it was still in its full mailing wrapper, but I recognized it because the magazine had slid out of the wrapper a little, so that the upper part of the front cover showed outside the tan mailing-sheath. The other magazines didn't interest me, so I leaned back and let my eyes go, from left to right and back again.

Though I had been coming there for six years, I didn't really know those people, in spite of the reputation barbers have as conversationalists. I knew that Fickler, the boss, had once been attacked bodily there in the shop by his ex-wife; that Philip had had two sons killed in World War II; that Tom had once been accused by Fickler of swiping lotions and other supplies and had slapped Fickler's face; that Ed played the horses and was always in debt; that Jimmie had to be watched or he would take magazines from the shop while they were still current; and that Janet, who had been there only a year, was suspected of having a side line, maybe dope peddling. Aside from such items as those, they were strangers.

Suddenly Janet was there in front of me. She had come from

around the end of the partition, and not alone. The man with her was a broad-shouldered husky, gray-haired and gray-eyed, with an unlit cigar slanting up from a corner of his mouth. His eyes swept the whole shop, and since he started at the far right he ended up at me.

He stared. "For Pete's sake," he said. "You? Now what?"

I was surprised for a second to see Inspector Cramer himself, head of Manhattan Homicide, there on the job.

"Just waiting for a shave," I told him. "I'm an old customer here. You can ask Purley."

Purley came over and verified me, but Cramer checked with Ed, himself. Then he drew Purley aside and they mumbled back and forth a while, after which Cramer summoned Philip and escorted him around the end of the partition.

Janet seated herself in the chair next to mine. She looked even better in profile than head on, with her nice chin and straight little nose and long, homegrown lashes. I felt a little in debt to her, for the mild pleasure I had got occasionally as I sat in Ed's chair and glanced at her while she worked on the customer in the next chair.

"I was wondering where you were," I remarked.

She turned to me. "Did you say something?" she asked.

"Nothing vital. My name's Goodwin. Call me Archie."

"I know. You're a detective. How can I keep them from having my picture in the paper?"

"You can't, if they've already got it. Have they?"

"I think so. I wish I was dead."

"I don't." I made it not loud but emphatic.

"Why should you? I do. My folks in Michigan think I'm acting or modeling. I leave it vague. And here—oh, my heavens!" Her chin worked, but she controlled it.

"Work is work," I said. "My parents wanted me to be a college president, and I wanted to be a second baseman, and look at me. Anyhow, if your picture gets printed and it's a good likeness, who knows what will happen?"

"This is my Gethsemane," she said.

That made me suspicious, naturally. She had mentioned acting. "Come off it," I advised her. "Think of someone else. Think of the guy that got stabbed—no, he's out of it—think of his wife. How do you suppose she feels? Or Inspector Cramer, with the job he's got. What was he asking you just now?"

80

She didn't hear me. She said through clamped teeth, "I only wish I had some guts."

"Why? What would you do?"

"I'd tell all about it."

"You mean last night? Why not try it out on me and see how it goes? Just keep your voice down and let it flow."

She didn't hear a word. Her ears were disconnected. She kept her brown eyes, under the long lashes, straight at me:

"How it happened this morning. How I was going back to my booth after I finished Mr. Levinson in Philip's chair, and he called me into Tina's booth, and he seized me, with one hand on my throat so I couldn't scream, and there was no doubt at all what he intended, so I grabbed the scissors from the shelf and, without realizing what I was doing, plunged them into him with all my strength, and he collapsed onto the chair. That's what I would do if I really want a successful career. I would have to be arrested and have a trial, and then—"

"Hold it. Your pronouns. Mr. Levinson called you into Tina's booth?"

"Certainly not. That man that got killed." She tilted her head back. "See the marks on my throat?"

"Bravo," I said. "That would get you top billing anywhere."

"That's what I was saying."

"Then go ahead and tell it."

"I can't! I simply can't! It would be so darned vulgar."

At the moment I could have slapped her lovely young face with pleasure. "I understand your position," I said, "a girl as sweet and fine and strong as you, but it's bound to come out in the end, and I want to help. Incidentally, I am not married. I'll go to Inspector Cramer right now and tell him about it. He'll want to take photographs of your throat. Do you know any lawyers?"

She shook her head, answering, I thought, my question about lawyers, but no. She didn't believe in answering questions. "About your being married," she said, "I hadn't even thought. I think a girl must get her career established *first*. That's why when I see an attractive man I never wonder if he's married; by the time I'm ready for one these will be too old. I think a girl—"

If Ed hadn't signaled to me just then, his customer having left the chair, there's no telling how it would have ended. No words would have been any good, since she was deaf, but surely I

81

might have thought of something. As it was, I didn't want to keep Ed waiting, so I got up and crossed to his chair and climbed in.

"Just scrape the face," I told him.

He got a bib on me and tilted me back. "Did you phone?" he asked. "Did that fathead forget again?"

I told him no, that I had been caught midtown with a stubble and an unforeseen errand for which I should be presentable, and added, "You seem to have had some excitement."

He went to the cabinet for a tube of prefabricated lather, got some on me, started rubbing. "We sure did," he said with feeling. "Carl—you know Carl—he killed a man in Tina's booth. Then they both ran. I'm sorry for Tina—she was all right—but Carl—I don't know."

I couldn't articulate with him rubbing. He finished, went to wipe his fingers, and came with the razor. I remarked, "I'd sort of watch it, Ed. It's a little risky to go blabbing that Carl killed him unless you can prove it."

"Well, what did he run for?"

"I couldn't say. But the cops are still poking around here."

"Sure, they are; they're after evidence. You gotta have evidence." Ed pulled the skin tight over the jawbone. "For instance, they ask me did he show me anything or ask me anything about some article from the shop. I say he didn't. That would be evidence, see?"

"Yes, I get it." I could only mumble. "What did he ask you?"

"Oh, all about me—name, married or single, you know, insurance men, income tax, they all ask the same things. But when he asked about last night I told him where to get off, but then I thought, why not? And I told him.

"Of course," he said, "the police have to get it straight, but they can't expect us to remember everything. When he came in, first he talked with Fickler, maybe five minutes. Then Fickler took him to Tina's booth and he talked with Tina. After that Fickler sent Philip in, and then Carl and then Jimmie, and then Tom and then me, and then Janet. I think it's pretty good to remember that."

I mumbled agreement. He was at the corner of my mouth.

"But I can't remember everything and they can't make me. I don't know how long it was after Janet came back out before

Fickler went to Tina's booth and found him dead. They ask me was it nearer ten minutes or nearer fifteen, but I say I had a customer at the time, we all did but Philip, and I don't know. They ask me how many of us went behind the partition after Janet came out, to the steamer or the vat or to get the lamp or something, but I say again I had a customer at the time, and I don't know, except I know I didn't go because I was trimming Mr. Howell at the time. I was working the top when Fickler yelled and came running out. They can ask Mr. Howell."

"They probably have," I said, but to no one, because Ed had gone for a hot towel.

He returned, and used the towel, and got the lilac water. Patting it on, he resumed, "They ask me exactly when Carl and Tina went, they ask me that twenty times, but I can't say and I won't say. Carl did it, all right, but they can't prove it by me. They've gotta have evidence, but I don't. Cold towel today?"

"No, I'll keep the smell."

He brought a comb and brush. "Can I remember what I don't know?" he demanded.

"I know I can't."

"And I'm not great detective like you." Ed was a little rough with a brush. "And now I go for lunch but I've got to have a cop along. They searched all of us down to the skin, and they even brought a woman to search Janet. They took our fingerprints. I admit they've gotta have evidence." He flipped the bib off. "How was the razor, all right?"

I told him it was fine as usual, stepped down, fished for a quarter, and exchanged it for my check. Purley Stebbins, nearby, was watching both of us. There had been times when I had seen fit to kid Purley at the scene of a murder, but not now. A cop had been killed.

He spoke, not belligerently: "The inspector don't like your being here."

"Neither do I," I declared. "Fortunately, this didn't happen to be Mr. Wolfe's day for a haircut; you would never have believed it. I'm just a minor coincidence. Nice to see you."

I went and paid my check to Fickler, got my things on, and departed.

As I emerged into Lexington Avenue there were several things on my mind. The most immediate was this: If Cramer's suspicion had been aroused enough to spend a man on me, and if I were seen going directly home from the shop, there might be too much curiosity as to why I had chosen to spend six bits for a shave at that time of day. So, instead of taking a taxi, I walked, and when I got to a five-and-ten I used their aisles and exits to make sure I had no tail. That left my mind free for other things the rest of the way home.

One leading question was whether Carl and Tina would still be where I had left them, in the front room. That was what took me up the seven steps of the stoop two at a time, and on in quick. The answer to the question was no. The front room was empty. I strode down the hall to the office, but stopped there because I heard Wolfe's voice. It was coming from the dining room, and it was saying:

"No, Mr. Vardas, I cannot agree that mountain climbing is merely one manifestation of man's spiritual aspirations. I think, instead, it is an hyserical paroxysm of his infantile vanity. One of the prime ambitions of a jackass is to bray louder than any other jackass, and man is not . . ."

I crossed the hall and the dining-room sill. Wolfe was at his end of the table, and Fritz, standing at his elbow, had just removed the lid from a steaming platter. At his left was Tina, and Carl was at his right, my place when there was no company. Wolfe saw me but finished his lecture on mountain climbing before attending to me: "In time, Archie. You like veal and mushrooms."

Talk about infantile. His not being willing to sit down to his lunch with unfed people in the house was all well enough, but why not send trays in to them? That was easy. He was sore at me and I had called them foreigners.

I stepped to the end of the table and said, "I know you have a paroxysm if I try to bring up business during meals, but eighteen thousand cops would give a month's pay to get their hands on Carl and Tina, your guests."

"Indeed." Wolfe was serving the veal and accessories. "Why?"

"Have you talked with them?"

"No. I merely invited them to lunch."

"Then don't until I've reported. I ran into Cramer and Stebbins at the barbershop."

"Confound it." The serving spoon stopped en route.

"Yeah. It's quite interesting. But first lunch, of course. I'll go put the chain bolt on. Please dish me some veal."

84

Carl and Tina were speechless.

That lunch was one of Wolfe's best performances, I admit it. He didn't know a thing about Carl and Tina except that they were in a jam, he knew that Cramer and Stebbins dealt only with homicide, and he had a strong prejudice against entertaining murderers at his table. His only hope now was his knowledge that I was aware of his prejudice, and even shared it.

He must have been fairly tight inside, but he stayed the polite host clear to the end, with no sign of hurry even with the coffee. Then, however, the tension began to tell. Ordinarily his return to the office after a meal was leisurely and lazy, but this time he went right along, followed by his guests and me. He marched across to his chair behind the desk, got his bulk deposited, and snapped at me, "What have you got us into now?"

I was pulling chairs around so the Vardas family would be facing him, but stopped to give him an eye. "Us?" I inquired.

"Yes."

"Okay," I said courteously, "if that's how it is. I did not invite them to come here, let alone to lunch. They came on their own and I let them in, which is one of my functions. Having started it, I'll finish it. May I use the front room? I'll have them out of here in a minute."

"Pfui." He was supercilious. "I am now responsible for their presence, since they were my guests at lunch. . . . Sit down, sir. Sit down, Mrs. Vardas."

Carl and Tina didn't know what from which. I had to push the chairs up behind their knees. Then I went to my own chair and swiveled to face Wolfe.

"I have a question to ask them," I told him, "but first you need a couple of facts: They're in this country without papers. They were in a concentration camp in Russia, and they're not telling how they got here if they can help it. They could be spies, but I doubt it after hearing them talk. Naturally, they jump a mile if they hear someone say boo, and when a man came to the barbershop this morning and showed a police card and asked who they were and where they came from and what they were doing last night, they scooted the first chance they got. But they didn't know where to go, so they came here to buy fifty bucks' worth of advice. I got bighearted and went to the shop, myself."

"You went?" Tina gasped.

I turned to them. "Sure, I went. It's a complicated situation, but I think I can handle it if you two can be kept out of the way. It would be dangerous for you to stay here. I know a safe place up in the Bronx for you to lay low for a few days. You shouldn't take a chance on a taxi or the subway, so we'll go around the corner to the garage and get Mr. Wolfe's car, and you can drive it—"

"Excuse me," Carl said urgently. "You would drive us up there?"

"No, I'll be busy. Then I'll—"

"But I can't drive a car! I don't know how!"

"Then your wife will drive."

"She can't! She don't know, either!"

I sprang from my chair and stood over them. "Look," I said savagely; "save that for the cops. Can't drive a car? Certainly you can! Everybody can!"

They were looking up at me, Carl bewildered, Tina frowning. "In America, yes," she said. "But we are not Americans, not yet. We have never had a chance to learn."

"What's this?" Wolfe demanded.

I returned to my chair. "That," I said, "was the question I wanted to ask. It has a bearing, as you'll soon see." I regarded Carl and Tina. "If you're lying about this, not knowing how to drive a car, you won't be sent back home to die, you'll die right here. It will be a cinch to find out if you're lying."

"Why should we?" Carl asked. "What is so important in it?"

"Once more," I insisted, "can you drive a car?"

"No."

"Can you, Tina?"

"No!"

"Okay." I turned to Wolfe: "The caller at the barbershop this morning was a precinct dick named Wallen. Fickler took him to Tina's booth and he questioned Tina first. Then the others had a session with him in the booth, in this order: Philip, Carl, Jimmie, Tom, Ed, and Janet. You may not know that the manicure booths are around behind the long partition. After Janet came out there was a period of ten or fifteen minutes when Wallen was in the booth alone. Then Fickler went to see, and what he saw was Wallen's body with scissors buried in his back. Someone had stabbed him to death. Since Carl and Tina had lammed—"

Tina's cry was more of a gasp, a last gasp, an awful sound. With one leap she was out of her chair and at Carl, grasping him and begging wildly, "Carl, no! No, no! Oh, Carl—!"

"Make her stop," Wolfe snapped.

I had to try, because Wolfe would rather be in a room with a hungry tiger than with a woman out of hand. I went and got a grip on her shoulder, but released it at sight of the expression on Carl's face as he pushed to his feet against the pressure. It looked as if he could and would handle it. He did.

He eased her back to her chair and down onto it, and turned to me: "That man was killed there in Tina's booth?"

"Yes."

Carl smiled as he had once before, and I wished he would stop trying it. "Then of course," he said, as if he were conceding a point in a tight argument, "this is the end for us. But, please, I must ask you not to blame my wife. Because we have been through many things together she is ready to credit me with many deeds that are far beyond me. She has a big idea of me and I have a big idea of her. But I did not kill that man. I did not touch him." He frowned. "I don't understand why you suggested riding a car to the Bronx. Of course you will give us to the police."

"Forget the Bronx." I was frowning back. "Every cop in town has his eye peeled for you. Sit down."

He went to his chair and sat.

"About driving a car," Wolfe muttered. "Was that flummery?"

"No, sir, that comes next. Last night around midnight a hit-and-run driver in a stolen car killed a woman up on Broadway. The car was found parked at Broadway and Ninety-sixth Street. Wallen, from the Twentieth Precinct, was the first dick to look it over. In it he apparently found something that led him to the Goldenrod Barbershop—anyhow, he phoned his wife that he was on a hot one that would lead to glory and a raise, and then he showed up at the shop and called the roll, as described. With the result also as described. Cramer has bought it that the hit-and-run driver found himself cornered and used the scissors, and Cramer—don't quote me—is not a dope. To qualify as a hit-and-run driver you must meet certain specifications, and one of them is knowing how to drive a car. So the best plan would be for Carl and Tina to go back to the shop and report for duty and for the official quiz, if it wasn't for two things: First, the fact that they lammed will make it very tough, and, second, even though it is settled that they didn't kill a cop, their lack of documents will fix them anyhow."

I waved a hand. "So actually what's the difference? If they're sent back where they came from they're doomed, so they say. Between a doom here and a doom there, that's all they have to pick from. One interesting angle is that you are harboring fugitives from justice, and I am not. I told Purley they're here."

"You what?" Wolfe bellowed.

"What I said. That's the advantage of having a reputation for gags—you can say practically anything if you handle your face right. I told him they were here in our front room, and he sailed right over it. So I'm clean, but you're not. You can't even just show them out. If you don't want to call Cramer yourself I could get Purley at the shop and tell him they're still here, and why hasn't he sent for them?"

"It might be better," Tina said, not with hope, "just a little better, if you would let us go, ourselves? No?"

She got no answer. Wolfe was glaring at me. It wasn't that he needed my description of the situation to realize what a pickle he was in; I have never tried to deny that the interior decorator did a snappier job inside his skull than in mine. What had him boiling was my little stunt of getting it down that neither Carl nor Tina could drive a car. But for that it would still have been possible to let them meet the law and take what they got; now that was out of the question.

"There is," he said, glaring at me, "another alternative to consider."

"Yes, sir. What?"

"Let us just go," Tina said.

"Pfui." He moved the glare to her: "You would try to skedaddle, and be caught within an hour." Back to me: "You have told Mr. Stebbins they are here. We can simply keep them here and await developments. Since Mr. Cramer and Mr. Stebbins are still there at work, they may soon disclose the murderer."

"Sure, they may," I agreed, "but I doubt it. They're just being thorough, they've really settled for Carl and Tina, and what they're looking for is evidence, especially what it was that led Wallen to the barbershop—though I suppose they haven't much hope of that, since Carl and Tina could have taken it along."

Wolfe's eyes went to Carl: "Did you and your wife leave the shop together?"

Carl shook his head. "That might have been noticed, so she went first. When she was gone I waited until they were all busy and Mr. Fickler was walking behind the partition, then I ran upstairs to meet her there."

"When was that?" I asked. "Who was in Tina's booth with Wallen?"

"I don't think anybody was. Janet had come out a while before. She was at Jimmie's chair with a customer."

"Good heavens," I turned my palms up. "You left that place less than a minute, maybe only a few seconds, before Fickler found Wallen dead!"

"I don't know." Carl wasn't fazed. "I only know I didn't touch that man."

"This," I told Wolfe, "makes it even nicer. There was a slim chance we could get it that they left sooner."

"Yes." He regarded me. "It must be assumed that Wallen was alive when Ed left the booth, since that young woman—what's her name?"

"Janet."

"I call few men, and no women, by their first names. What's her name?"

"Stahl," Tina said. "Janet Stahl."

"Thank you. . . . Wallen was presumably alive when Ed left the booth, since Miss Stahl followed him. So Miss Stahl, who saw Wallen last, and Mr. Fickler, who reported him dead—manifestly they had opportunity. But they are not unique. What about the others?"

"You must remember," I told him, "that I had just dropped in for a shave. I had to show the right amount of intellectual curiosity, but I had to be careful not to carry it too far. From what Ed said, I gathered that opportunity is fairly wide open, except he excludes himself. As you know, they all keep darting behind that partition for one thing or another. Ed can't remember who did and who didn't, during that ten or fifteen minutes, and it's a safe bet that the others can't remember either. The fact that the cops were interested enough to ask shows that Carl and Tina haven't got a complete monopoly on it. As Ed remarked, they've gotta have evidence, and they're still looking."

Wolfe grunted in disgust.

"It also shows," I went on, "that they haven't got any real stopper to cork it, like prints from the car or localizing the scissors or anything they found on the corpse. They sure want Carl and Tina, and you know what happens when they get them, but they're still short on exhibits. If you like your suggestion to keep our guests here until Cramer and Stebbins get their paws on the right guy, it might work fine as a long-term policy, but you're against the idea of women living here, or even a woman, and after a few months it might get on your nerves."

"It is no good," Tina said, back to her gasping whisper again. "Just let us go! I beg you, do that!"

Wolfe ignored her. He leaned back, closed his eyes, and heaved a deep sigh, and from the way his nose began to twitch I knew he was coercing himself into facing the hard fact that he would have to go to work—either that or tell me to call Purley, and that was ruled out of bounds both by his self-respect and his professional vanity.

Wolfe sighed again, opened his eyes, and rasped at Tina, "Except for Mr. Fickler, that man questioned you first. Is that right?"

"Yes, sir."

"Tell me what he said. What he asked. I want every word."

I thought Tina did pretty well, under the circumstances. She wrinkled her brow and concentrated, and it looked as if Wolfe got it all out of her. But she couldn't give him what she didn't have.

He kept after it: "You are certain he showed you no object whatever?"

"Yes, I'm sure he didn't."

"He asked about no object, anything, in the shop?"

"No."

"He took nothing from his pocket?"

"No."

"The newspaper he had. Didn't he take that from his pocket?"

"No, like I said, he had it in his hand when he came in the booth."

"In his hand or under his arm?"

90

"In his hand. I think—yes, I'm sure."

"Was it folded up?"

"Well, of course newspapers are folded."

"Yes, Mrs. Vardas. Just remember the newspaper as you saw it in his hand. I'm making a point of it because there is nothing else to make a point of, and we must have a point if we can find one. Was the newspaper folded up as if he had had it in his pocket?"

"No, it wasn't." She was trying hard. "It wasn't folded that much. Like I said, it was a *Daily Press*. When he sat down he put it on the table, at the end by his right hand—yes, that's right, my left hand—I moved some of my things to make room—and it was the way it is on the newsstand, so that's all it was folded."

"But he didn't mention it?"

"No."

"And you noticed nothing unusual about it? I mean the newspaper?"

She shook her head. "It was just a newspaper."

Wolfe repeated the performance with Carl, and got more of the same. No object produced or mentioned, no hint of any. The only one on exhibit, the newspaper, had been there on the end of the table when Carl, sent by Fickler, had entered and sat, and Wallen had made no reference to it. Carl was more practical than Tina. He didn't work as hard as she had trying to remember Wallen's exact words, and I must say I couldn't blame him.

Wolfe gave up trying to get what they didn't have. He leaned back, compressed his lips, closed his eyes, and tapped with his forefingers on the ends of his chair arms. Finally he opened his eyes. "Confound it," he said peevishly, "it's impossible. Even if I had a move to make I couldn't make it. If I so much as stir a finger, Mr. Cramer will start yelping and I have no muzzle for him. Any effort to—"

The doorbell rang. During lunch Fritz had been told to leave it to me, so I arose, crossed to the hall, and went front. But not all the way. Four paces short of the door I saw, through the one-way glass panel, the red, rugged face and the heavy, broad shoulders. I wheeled and returned to the office, not dawdling, and told Wolfe, "The man to fix the chair."

"Indeed." His head jerked up. "The front room."

Carl and Tina, warned by our tone and tempo, were on their

feet. The bell rang again. I moved, fast, to the door to the front room and pulled it open, telling them, "In here, quick! Step on it!" They obeyed, without a word, as if they had known me and trusted me for years, but what choice did they have? When they had passed through I said, "Relax and keep quiet," shut the door, glanced at Wolfe and got a nod, went to the front door, opened it, and said morosely, "Hello. What now?"

"It took you long enough," Inspector Cramer growled, crossing the threshold.

Wolfe can move when he wants to. I have seen him prove it more than once, as he did then. By the time I was back in the office, following Cramer, he had scattered in front of him on his desk a dozen folders of plant germination records for which he had had to go to the filing cabinet. One of the folders was spread open and he was scowling at us above it. He grunted a greeting but not a welcome. Cramer grunted back, moved to the red leather chair, and sat down.

I got myself at my desk. I was wishing I wasn't involved so I could just enjoy it. If Wolfe succeeded in keeping Cramer's claws off the Vardas family, and at the same time kept himself out of jail, I would show my appreciation by not hitting him for a raise for a month.

Fritz entered with a tray, so Wolfe had found time to push a button, too. It was the fixed allotment, three bottles of beer. Wolfe told Fritz to bring another glass, but Cramer said no, thanks.

Suddenly Cramer looked at me and demanded, "Where did you go when you left the barbershop?"

My brows went up. "If you really cared you could have put a tail on me. If you didn't care enough to put a tail on me you're just being nosy, and I resent it. Next question."

"Why not answer that one?"

"Because some of the errands I get sent on are confidential, and I don't want to start a bad habit."

Cramer turned abruptly to Wolfe: "You know a police officer was killed this morning there in that shop?"

"Yes." Wolfe halted a foaming glass on its way to his mouth. "Archie told me about it."

"Maybe he did."

"Not maybe. He did."

"Okay." Cramer cocked his head and watched Wolfe empty

the glass and use his handkerchief on his lips. Then he said, "Look. This is what brought me here. I have learned over a stretch of years that when I find you within a mile of a murder, and Goodwin is a part of you, something fancy can be expected. I don't need to itemize that—your memory is as good as mine. . . . Wait a second; let me finish.

"I don't say there's no such thing as a coincidence. I know you've been going to that shop for two years, and Goodwin for six years. It wouldn't be so remarkable if he happened in there this particular day, two hours after a murder, if it wasn't for certain features. He told Graboff, his barber, that he needed an emergency shave to go to an appointment. Incidentally, it couldn't have been much of an emergency, since he waited nearly half an hour while Graboff finished with a customer, but I might concede that. The point is that Graboff and Fickler both say that in the six years Goodwin has been going there he has never gone just for a shave. Not once. He goes only for the works: haircut, scalp massage, shampoo, *and* shave. That makes it too remarkable. Just one day in six years an emergency sends him there for a shave. I don't believe it."

Wolfe shrugged. "Then you don't. I'm not responsible for your credulity quotient, Mr. Cramer. Neither is Mr. Goodwin. I don't see how we can help you."

"Nobody would believe it," Cramer said stubbornly, refusing to get riled. "That's why I'm here. I do believe that Goodwin went to that shop because he knew a man had been murdered there."

"Then you believe wrong," I told him. "Until I got there I hadn't the slightest idea or suspicion that a man had been murdered, there or anywhere else."

"You have been known to lie, Goodwin."

"Only within limits, and I know what they are. I will state that in an affidavit. Write it out, and there's a notary at the corner drugstore. That would be perjury, which I'm allergic to."

"Your going there had nothing whatever to do with the murder?"

"Put it that way if you prefer it. It did not."

Wolfe was pouring beer. "How," he inquired, not belligerently, "was Mr. Goodwin supposed to have learned of the murder? Had you fitted that in?"

"I don't know." Cramer gestured impatiently. "I didn't come

here with a diagram. I only know what it means when I'm on a homicide, and suddenly there you are, or Goodwin. And there Goodwin was, two hours after it happened. Frankly, I have no idea where you come in. You work only for big money. That hit-and-run driver could be a man with money, but if so it couldn't be someone who works in that shop. No one there has the kind of dough that hires Nero Wolfe. So I don't see how it could be money that pulled you in, and I frankly admit I have no idea what else could. I guess I'll have a little beer, after all, if you don't mind. I'm tired."

Wolfe leaned forward to push the button.

"What was on my mind," Cramer said, "was two things: First, I did not believe that Goodwin just happened to drop in at the scene of a murder. I admit he's not quite brazen enough to commit perjury." He looked at me. "I want that affidavit. Today."

"You'll get it," I assured him.

Fritz entered with another tray, put it down on the little table at Cramer's elbow, and uncapped the bottle. "Shall I pour, sir?"

"Thanks, I will." Cramer took the glass in his left hand, tilted it, and poured with his right. Unlike Wolfe, he didn't care for a lot of foam. "Second," he said, "I thought that what took Goodwin there might be something you would be ready to tell me about, but he wouldn't because you're the boss and he's a clam unless you say the word. I don't pretend to have anything to pry it out of you with. You know the law about withholding evidence as well as I do; you ought to, the stunts you've pulled—"

"You thought," Wolfe asked, "that I had sent Archie to the shop on business?"

"Yes. For the reason given."

"You're wrong. I didn't. Since you're to get an affidavit from Archie, you might as well have one from me too and get it settled. In it I will say that I did not send him to the barbershop, that I did not know he was going there, and that I heard and knew nothing of the murder until he returned and told me."

"You'll swear to that?"

"As a favor to you, yes. You've wasted your time coming here, and you might as well get a little something out of it." Wolfe reached for his second bottle. "By the way, I still don't know why you came. According to Archie, the murderer is known

94

and all you have to do is find him—that man at the clothes rack—uh, Carl. And his wife, you said, Archie?"

"Yes, sir. Tina, one of the manicurists. Purley told me straight they had done it and scooted."

Wolfe frowned at Cramer. "Then what could you expect to get from me? How could I help?"

"What I said, that's all," Cramer insisted doggedly, pouring the rest of his beer. "When I see Goodwin poking around I want to know why."

"I don't believe it," Wolfe said rudely. He turned to me: "Archie, I think you're responsible for this. I think it was something you did or said. What was it?"

"Sure; it's always me." I was hurt. "What I did, I got a shave, and Ed had a customer and I had to wait, so I talked with Purley and with Inspector Cramer and then with Janet—Miss Stahl to you—and with Ed while I was in the chair—that is, he talked—"

"What did you say to Mr. Cramer?"

"Practically nothing. Just answered a civil question."

"What did you say to Mr. Stebbins?"

I thought I knew now where he was headed, and hoped I was right. "Oh, just asked what was going on, and he told me. I've told you about it."

"Not verbatim. What did you say?"

"Nothing at all. Of course, Purley wanted to know what brought me there, and I told him I—Say, wait a minute! Maybe you're right, at that! He asked me if I had seen Carl or Tina this morning, and I said sure, I had put them here in the front room and told them to wait, and if he would step on—"

"Ha!" Wolfe snorted. "I knew it! Your confounded tongue. So that's it." He looked at Cramer. "Why have you waited to pounce?" he asked, trying not to sound too contemptuous, for, after all, Cramer was drinking his beer. "Since Archie has rashly disclosed our little secret, it would be useless for me to try to keep it. That's what we use the front room for mainly—to keep murderers in. You're armed, I suppose? Go in and get them. Archie, open the door for him."

I went to the door to the front room and pulled it open, not too wide.

"I'm scared of murderers, myself," I said courteously, "or I'd be glad to help."

Cramer had a glass half-full of beer in his hand, and it may well be that that took the trick. Bullheaded as he was, he might

95

have been capable of getting up and walking over for a look into the room, even though our build-up had convinced him it was empty. But the glass of beer complicated it. He would either have to take it with him or reach first to put it down on the little table—or throw it at Wolfe.

"Nuts," he said, and lifted the glass to drink.

I swung the door too carelessly, without bothering to see that it latched, and yawned on the way back to my chair.

"At least," Wolfe said, rubbing it in, "I can't be jailed for harboring a fugitive—one of your favorite threats. But I really don't know what you're after. If it was those two, you'll get them, of course. What else is there?"

"Nothing but a little more evidence." Cramer glanced at his wristwatch. "We'll get 'em, all right. It don't pay to kill a cop in this town." He stood up. "It wouldn't pay for anyone to hide a cop killer in their front room, either. Thanks for the beer. I'll be expecting those affidavits, and in case—"

The phone rang. I swiveled and got it. "Nero Wolfe's office, Archie Goodwin speaking."

"Inspector Cramer there?"

I said, yes, hold it. "For you," I told him, and moved aside. He spoke not more than twenty words altogether, between spells of listening. He dropped the phone onto the cradle and headed for the door.

"Have they found 'em?" I asked his back.

"No." He didn't turn. "Someone's hurt—the Stahl girl."

I marched after him, thinking the least I could do was co-operate by opening another door for him, but he was there and on out before I caught up, so I returned to the office.

Wolfe was standing up, and I wondered why all the exertion, but a glance at the wall clock showed me 3:55, nearly time for his afternoon visit to the plant rooms.

"He said Janet got hurt," I stated.

Wolfe, finishing his beer, grunted.

"I owe Janet something. Besides, it could mean that Carl and Tina are out of it. I can be there in ten minutes. Why not?"

"No." He looked at the clock, and moved. "Put those folders back, please." Halfway to the door, he turned. "Disturb me only if it is unavoidable. And admit no more displaced persons to the house. Two at a time is enough."

96

I put the folders away and then went to the front room. Tina, who was lying on the couch, sat up as I entered and saw to her skirt hem. She had nice legs, but my mind was occupied. Carl, on a chair near the foot of the couch, stood up and asked a string of questions with his eyes.

"As you were," I told them gruffly. I heartily agreed with Wolfe that two was enough. "I hope you didn't go near the windows."

"We have learned so long ago to stay away from windows," Carl said. "But we want to go. We will pay the fifty dollars gladly."

"You can't go." I was emphatic. "That was Inspector Cramer, a very important policeman. We told him you were in here, and so—"

"You told him—" Tina gasped.

"Yes. It's the Hitler-Stalin technique in reverse. They tell barefaced lies to have them taken for the truth, and we told the barefaced truth to have it taken for a lie. It worked. So now we're stuck, and you are, too. You stay here. We've told the cops you're in this room, and you're not going to leave it, at least not until bedtime. I'm locking you in." I pointed to a door. "That's a bathroom, and there's a glass if you want a drink. It has another door into the office, but I'll lock it. The windows have bars."

I crossed to the door to the hall and locked it with my master key. I went through to the office, entered the bathroom in the corner, turned the bolt flange on the door to the front room, opened the door an inch, returned to the office, locked that door with my key, and went back to the front room.

"All set," I told them. "Make yourselves comfortable. If you need anything don't yell, this room is soundproofed; push this button." I put my finger on it, under the edge of the table. "I'll give you the news as soon as there is any." I was going.

"But this is hanging in the air on a thread," Carl protested.

"You're right, it is," I agreed grimly. "Your only hope is that Mr. Wolfe has now put his foot in it and it's up to him to get both you and him loose, not to mention me. By the way, there is a small gleam. Inspector Cramer beat it back to the shop because he got a phone call that Janet had been hurt. If she got hurt with scissors with you not there, it may be a real break."

"Janet?" Tina was distressed. "Was she hurt much?"

"I don't know," I said, "and I'm not going to try to find out.

97

We'll have to sit it out, at least until six o'clock." I glanced at my wrist. "That's only an hour and twenty minutes. Then we'll see if Mr. Wolfe has cooked up a charade. If not, he may at least invite you to dinner. See you later."

I went to the door to the office, passed through, closed the door, and locked it. There in privacy I took a survey of the Vardas situation. Being smart enough to get in that neither Carl nor Tina could drive a car was all right as far as it went, but it proved nothing at all about the scissors in Jake Wallen's back; it merely showed that there are motives and motives. The cops thought Wallen had been killed by a cornered hit-and-run driver, but what did I think? And, even more important, what did Wolfe think? I was still trying to find the answers when the phone rang.

It was Sergeant Purley Stebbins: "Archie? . . . Purley. I'm at the barbershop. We want you here quick."

I responded courteously: "I'm busy, but I guess so. If you really want me. Do you care to specify?"

"When you get here. Grab a cab."

I buzzed Wolfe on the house phone and reported the development. Then I hopped. . . .

The crowd of spectators ganged up in the corridor outside the Goldenrod Barbershop was twice as big as it had been before, and inside the shop there was a fine assortment of cops and dicks to look at. The corridor sported not one flatfoot, but three, keeping people away from the entrance. I told one of them my name and errand and was ordered to wait, and in a minute Purley came and escorted me in.

I darted a glance around. The barber chairs were all empty. Fickler and three of the barbers, Jimmie, Ed, and Philip, were seated along the row of waiting chairs, each with a dick beside him. Tom was not in view.

Purley had guided me to the corner by the cash register. "How long have you known that Janet Stahl?" he demanded.

I shook my head reproachfully. "Not that way. You said I was needed and I came on the run. If you merely want my biography, call at the office any time during hours."

Purley's right shoulder twitched. It was only a reflex of his impulse to sock me, beyond his control and therefore nothing to resent. "Some day," he said, setting his jaw and then releasing it. "She was found on the floor of her booth, out from a blow on her head. We brought her to and she can talk, but she won't. She won't tell us anything. She says she won't talk to anybody except her friend Archie Goodwin. How long have you known her?"

"I'm touched," I said with emotion. "The only chat I've ever had with her was here today under your eye, but look what it did to her. Is it any wonder my opinion of myself is what it is?"

"Listen, Goodwin; we're after a murderer."

"I know you are. I'm all for it."

"You've never seen her outside this shop?"

"No."

"That can be checked, maybe. Right now we want you to get her to talk. She's stopped us dead. Come on." He moved.

I caught his elbow. "Hold it. If she sticks to it that she'll only talk with me I'll have to think up questions. I ought to know what happened."

"Yeah." Purley wanted no more delay, but obviously I had a point. "There were only three of us left—me here at the front, and Joffe and Sullivan there on chairs. The barbers were all working on customers. Fickler was moving around. I was on the phone half the time."

"Where was Janet?"

"I'm telling you. Toracco—that's Philip—finished with a customer, and a new one got in his chair—we were letting regular customers in. The new one wanted a manicure, and Toracco called Janet, but she didn't come. Fickler was helping the outgoing customer on with his coat. Toracco went behind the partition to get Janet, and there she was on the floor of her booth, cold. She had gone there fifteen minutes before, possibly twenty. I think all of them had gone behind the partition at least once during that time."

"How bad is she hurt?"

"Not enough for the hospital. Doc let us keep her here. She was hit above the right ear with a bottle taken from the supply shelf against the partition, six feet from the entrance to her booth. The bottle was big and heavy, full of oil. It was there by her on the floor."

"Prints?"

"For Pete's sake, start a school. He had a towel in his hand or something. Come on."

"One second. What did the doctor say when you asked him if

99

she could have been just hitting herself to test her skull?"

"He said it was possible, but he doubted it. Come and ask her."

I had never been behind the partition before. The space ran about half the length of the shop. Against the partition were steamers, vats, lamps, and other paraphernalia, and then a series of cupboards and shelves. Across a wide aisle were the manicure booths, four of them, though I had never seen more than two operators in the shop. As we passed the entrance to the first booth in the line, a glance showed me Inspector Cramer seated at a little table across from Tom, the barber with white hair. Cramer saw me and arose. I followed Purley to the third booth, and on in. Then steps behind me and Cramer was there.

It was a big booth, eight by eight, but was now crowded. In addition to us three and the furniture, a city employee was standing in a corner, and, on a row of chairs lined up against the right wall, Janet Stahl was lying on her back, her head resting on a stack of towels. She had moved her eyes, but not her head, to take in us visitors. She looked beautiful.

"Here's your friend Goodwin," Purley told her, trying to sound sympathetic.

"Hello, there," I said professionally. "What does this mean?"

The long, home-grown lashes fluttered at me. "You," she said.

"Yep. Your friend Archie Goodwin." There was a chair there, the only one she wasn't using, and I squeezed past Purley and sat, facing her. "How do you feel—terrible?"

"No, I don't feel at all. I am past feeling."

I reached for her wrist, got my fingers on the spot, and looked at my watch. In thirty seconds I said, "Your pump isn't bad. May I inspect your head?"

"If you're careful."

"Groan if it hurts." I used all fingers to part the fine brown hair, and gently but thoroughly investigated the scalp. She closed her eyes and flinched once, but there was no groan. "A lump to write home about," I announced. "Who did it?"

"Send them away and I'll tell you." I turned to the kibitzers. "Get out," I said sternly. "If I had been here this would never have happened."

They went without a word. I sat listening to the sound of

their retreating footsteps outside in the aisle, then thought I had better provide sound to cover in case they were careless tiptoeing back. They had their choice of posts, just outside the open entrance or in the adjoining booths. The partitions were only six feet high. "It was dastardly," I said. "He might have killed you. You're lucky you've got a good, strong, thick skull."

"I started to scream," she said, "but it was too late."

"What started you to scream? Seeing him, or hearing him?"

"It was both. I was in the customer's chair, with my back to the door—and there was a little noise behind me, like a stealthy step, and I looked up and saw him reflected in the partition glass, right behind me, with his arm raised, and I started to scream, but before I could get it out he struck—"

"Wait a minute." I got up and moved my chair to the outer side of the little table and sat in it. "These details are important. You were like this?"

"That's it. I was sitting thinking."

I felt that the opinion I had formed of her previously had not done her justice. The crinkly glass of the partition wall behind her could reflect no object whatever, no matter how the light was. Her contempt for mental processes was absolutely spectacular. I asked, "Did you recognize him?"

"Of course I did. That's why I wouldn't speak to them. That's why I had to see you. It was that big one with the big ears and gold tooth, the one they call Stebbins, or they call him sergeant."

I wasn't surprised. I knew the power of her imagination now. "You mean it was him that hit you with the bottle?"

"I can't say it was him that hit me. I think people should be careful what they accuse other people of. I only know it was him I saw standing behind me with his arm raised, and then something hit me. From that anyone can only draw conclusions, but there are other reasons, too. He was rude to me this morning, asking me questions, and all day he has been looking at me in a rude way, not the way a girl is willing for a man to look at her. And then you can just be logical. Would Ed want to kill me, or Philip or Jimmie or Tom or Mr. Fickler? Why would they? So it must have been him, even if I hadn't seen him."

"It does sound logical," I conceded. "But I've known Stebbins for years and have never known him to strike a woman without cause. What did he have against you?"

101

"I don't know." She frowned a little. "That's one of the first things you must tell me, how to answer things to the reporters. That's how you'll earn your ten per cent."

"My ten per cent of what?"

"Of everything I get. As my manager." She extended a hand. "Shake on it."

To avoid a contractual shake without offending, I grasped the back of her hand with my left, turning her palm up, and ran the fingers of my right from her wrist to her fingertips. "It's a darned good idea," I said appreciatively, "but we'll have to postpone it. I'm going through bankruptcy just now and it would be illegal for me to make a contract. Later on—"

"I don't need you later on. I need you right now."

"Here I am, you've got me, but not under contract yet." I got emphatic: "If you tell reporters I'm your manager, I'll give you a lump that will make that one seem as flat as a pool table. If they ask why he hit you, don't say you don't know; say it's a mystery. Now—"

"That's it!" She was delighted.

"Sure. Tell 'em that. Now we've got to consider the cops. Stebbins is a cop, and they won't want it hung on him. They've had one cop killed here today already. They'll try to tie this up with that. They'll try to make it that somebody here killed Wallen, and he found out that you knew something about it, so he tried to kill you. They may even think they have some kind of evidence—for instance, something you were heard to say. So we have to be prepared. We have to go back over it. Are you listening?"

"Certainly. What do I say when the reporters ask me if I'm going to go on working here? Couldn't I say I don't want to desert Mr. Fickler in a time of trouble?"

It took control to stay in that chair. But at home there were the guests locked in the front room, and some time, somehow, we had to get rid of them.

"That's the ticket," I said warmly. "Say you've got to be loyal to Mr. Fickler. Have you ever been interviewed before?"

"No, this will be the first, and I want to start right."

"Good for you. What they like best of all is to get the jump on the police. If you can tell them something the cops don't know they'll love you forever. For instance, the fact that Stebbins crowned you doesn't prove that he's the only one involved. He must have an accomplice here in the shop, or why did Wallen come here, in the first place? We'll call the accomplice X. Now listen:

"Some time today, some time or other after Wallen's body was found, you saw something or heard something, and X knew you did. He knew it, and he knew that if you told about it—if you told me, for example—it would put him and Stebbins on the spot. Naturally, both of them would want to kill you. It could have been X that tried to, but since you say you saw Stebbins reflected in the glass, we'll let it go at that for now. Here's the point:

"If you can remember what it was you saw or heard that scared X, and if you tell the reporters before the cops get wise to it, they'll be your friends for life. Concentrate. Remember everything you saw and heard here today, and everything you did and said, too."

She was frowning. "I don't remember anything that would scare anybody."

"Not right off the bat, who could?" Her hand was right there and I patted it. "I guess we'd better go over it together, right straight through. That's the way Nero Wolfe would do it. What time did you get to work this morning?"

"When I always do—a quarter to nine. I'm punctual."

"Were the others already here?"

"Some were and some weren't."

"Who was and who wasn't?"

"My heavens, I don't know. I didn't notice." She was resentful. "When I came to work I was thinking of something else, so how would I notice?"

I had to be patient. "Okay, we'll start at another point. You remember when Wallen came in and spoke with Fickler, and went to Tina's booth and talked with her, and when Tina came out Fickler sent Philip in to him. You remember that?"

She nodded. "I guess so."

"Guess won't get us anywhere. Just recall the situation. There's Philip, coming around the end of the partition after talking with Wallen. Did you hear him say anything? Did you say anything to him?"

"I don't think Philip was this X," she declared. "He is married, with children. I think it was Jimmie Kirk. He tried to make passes at me when I first came, and he drinks—you can ask Ed

103

about that—and he thinks he's superior. A barber being superior!" She looked pleased. "That's a good idea about Jimmie being X, because I don't have to say he really tried to kill me. I'll try to remember something he said. Would it matter exactly when he said it?"

I had had enough, but a man can't hit a woman when she's down, so I ended it without violence.

"Not at all," I told her, "but I've got an idea. I'll go and see if I can get something out of Jimmie. Meanwhile, I'll send a reporter in to break the ice with you, from the *Gazette* probably." I was on my feet. "Just use your common sense and stick to facts. See you later."

"But Mr. Goodwin! I want—"

I was gone. I strode down the aisle and around the end of the partition. There I halted, and it wasn't long before I was joined by Cramer and Purley. Their faces were expressive. I didn't have to ask if they had got it all.

"If you shoot her," I suggested, "send her brain to Johns Hopkins, if you can find it."

Cramer grunted. "Did she do it herself?"

"I doubt it. It was a pretty solid blow to raise that lump, and you didn't find her prints on the bottle. Bothering about prints is beneath her. I had to come up for air, but I left you an in. Better pick a strong character to play the role of reporter from the *Gazette*."

"Send for Biatti," Cramer snapped at Purley.

"Yeah," I agreed, "he can take it. Now I go home?"

"No. She might insist on seeing her manager again."

"I wouldn't pass that around," I warned them. "How would you like a broadcast of her line on Sergeant Stebbins? I'd like to be home for dinner. We're having fresh pork tenderloin."

"We would all like to be home for dinner." Cramer's look and tone were both sour. They didn't change when he shifted to Purley: "Is the Vardas pair still all you want?"

"They're what I want most," Purley said doggedly. "In spite of her getting it when they weren't here, but I guess we've got to spread out more. You can finish with them here and go home to dinner, and I suppose we've got to take 'em all downtown. I still want to be shown that the Stahl girl couldn't have used that bottle on herself, and I don't have to be shown that she could have used the scissors on Wallen if she felt like it. Or if she

104

performed with the bottle to have something to tell reporters about, the Vardases are still what I want most. But I admit the other 'if' is the biggest one. If someone here conked her, finding out who and why comes first until we get the Vardases."

Cramer stayed sour: "You haven't even started."

"Maybe that's a little too strong, Inspector. We were on the Vardases, but we didn't clear out of here; we kept close. Then, when we found the Stahl girl and brought her to, she shut the valve and had to see Goodwin. Even so, I wouldn't say we haven't made a start with the others. Ed Graboff plays the horses and owes a bookie nine hundred dollars, and he had to sell his car. Philip Toracco went off the rails in 1945 and spent a year in a booby hatch. Joel Fickler has been seen in public places with Horny Gallagher, and while that don't prove—"

Cramer cut in to shoot at me, "Is Fickler a racket boy?"

I shook my head. "Sorry. Blank. I've never been anything but a customer."

"If he is we'll get it." Purley was riled and didn't care who knew it. "Jimmie Kirk apparently only goes back three years, and he has expensive habits for a barber. Tom Yerkes did a turn in 1939 for assault—beat up a guy who took his young daughter for a fast weekend—and he is known for having a quick takeoff. So I don't think you can say we haven't even started."

"Are all alibis for last night being checked?" Cramer demanded.

"They have been."

"Do them over, and good. Get it going. Use as many men as you need. And not only alibis—records, too. I want the Vardas pair as much as you do, but if the Stahl girl didn't use that bottle on herself, I also want someone else. Get Biatti here. Let him have a try at her before you take her down."

"Yes, sir."

Purley moved. He went to the phone at the cashier's counter. I went to the one in the booth at the end of the clothes rack and dialed the number I knew best. Fritz answered, and I asked him to buzz the extension in the plantrooms, since it was still a few minutes short of six o'clock.

"Where are you?" Wolfe demanded. He was always testy when interrupted.

"At the barbershop." I was none too genial, myself. "Janet

was sitting in her booth and got hit on the head with a bottle of oil. They have gone through the routine and are still at the starting line. Her condition is no more critical than it was before she got hit. As I told you, she insisted on seeing me, and I have had a long, intimate talk with her. I can't say I made no progress, because she asked me to be her manager, and I am now giving you notice, quitting at the end of this week. Aside from that I got nowhere. I advise you to tell Fritz to increase the grocery orders until further notice."

Silence. Then. "Who is there?"

"Everybody. Cramer, Purley, squad men, the staff. The whole party will be moved downtown in an hour or so."

"Pfui." Silence. In a moment: "Stay there." The connection went.

I left the booth. Neither Purley nor Cramer was in sight. I moseyed toward the rear, with the line of empty barber chairs on my left and the row of waiting chairs against the partition on my right. Fickler was there, and three of the barbers—Ed being the missing one now—with dicks in between.

The chair on the left of the magazine table was empty, and I dropped into it. Apparently, no one had felt like reading today, since the same copy of *Ellery Queen's Mystery Magazine* was still on top. After sitting a few minutes I became aware that I was trying to analyze Janet. There must be some practical method of digging up from her memory the fact or facts that we had to have. Hypnotize her, maybe? That might work. I was considering suggesting it to Cramer when I became aware of movement over at the door and lifted my eyes.

A flatfoot was blocking the entrance to keep a man fully twice his weight from entering, and was explaining the situation. The man let him finish and then spoke:

"I know, I know." His eyes came at me over the flatfoot's shoulder, and he bellowed, "Archie! Where's Mr. Cramer?"

I got up and made for the door in no haste or jubilation.

"Okay, take it easy. I'll go see—"

But I didn't have to go. His bellow had carried within, and Cramer's voice came from right behind me:

"Well! Dynamite?"

The flatfoot had moved aside, leaving it to the brass, and Wolfe had crossed the sill. "I came to get a haircut," he stated, and marched past the sergeant and inspector to the rack, took off his hat, coat, vest, and tie, hung them up, crossed to Jimmie's chair, the second in the line, and got his bulk up onto the seat. In the mirrored wall fronting him he had a panorama of the row of barbers and dicks in his rear, and without turning his head he called, "Jimmie! If you please?"

Jimmie's dancing dark eyes came to Cramer and Purley, there by me. So did others. Cramer stood scowling at Wolfe. We all held our poses while Cramer slowly lifted his right hand and carefully and thoroughly scratched the side of his nose with his forefinger. That attended to, he decided to sit down. He went to the first chair in the line, turned it to face Wolfe.

"You want a haircut, huh?"

"Yes, sir. I need one."

"Yeah." Cramer turned his head. "All right, Kirk. Come and cut his hair."

Jimmie got up and went past the chair to the cabinet for an apron. Everybody stirred, as if a climax had been reached and passed. Purley strode to the third chair in the line, Philip's, and got on it. That way he and Cramer had Wolfe surrounded, and it seemed only fair for me to be handy, so I detoured around Cramer, pulled Jimmie's stool to one side, and perched on it.

Jimmie had Wolfe aproned and his scissors were singing above the right ear. Wolfe barred clippers.

"You just dropped in," Cramer rasped. "Like Goodwin this morning."

"Certainly not." Wolfe was curt but not pugnacious. "You summoned Mr. Goodwin. He told me on the phone of his fruitless talk with Miss Stahl, and I thought it well to come."

Cramer grunted. "Okay, you're here. And you're not going to leave until I know why, without any funny business about murderers in your front room."

"Not as short behind as last time," Wolfe commanded.

"Yes, sir." Jimmie had never had as big or attentive an audience, and he was giving a good show.

"Naturally," Wolfe said tolerantly, "I expected that. You can badger me, if that's what you're after, and get nowhere, but I offer a suggestion. Why not work first? Why don't we see if we can settle this business? Or would you rather harass me than catch a murderer?"

"I'm working now. I want the murderer. What about you?"

"Forget me for the moment. You can hound me any time. I

would like to propose certain assumptions about what happened here today. Do you care to hear them?"

"I'll listen, but don't drag it out."

"I won't. Please don't waste time challenging the assumptions; I don't intend to defend them, much less validate them. They are merely a basis of exploration, to be tested. The first is this—that Wallen found something in the car, the car that had killed the woman. . . . No, I don't like it this way. I want a direct view, not reflections. Jimmie, turn me around, please."

Jimmie whirled the chair a half-turn, so that Wolfe's back was to the mirrored wall, also to me, and he was facing those seated in the chairs against the partition.

I spoke up: "Ed isn't here."

"I left him in the booth," Purley rumbled.

"Get him," Wolfe instructed. "And Miss Stahl, where is she?"

"In her booth lying down."

"Archie. Bring Miss Stahl."

He had a nerve picking on me, with an inspector and a sergeant and three dicks there, but I postponed telling him so and went, as Purley went for Ed. In the booth Janet was still on her back on the chairs, her eyes wide open. At sight of me she fired immediately: "You said you were going to send a reporter—"

I raised my voice to stop her: "Listen to me, girlie. You're getting a break. Nero Wolfe is here with a suggestion and wants your opinion of it. Can you sit up?"

"Certainly I can, but—"

"Take it easy." I put an arm behind her shoulders. "Are you dizzy?"

"I'm never dizzy," she said scornfully, and shook me off and went on solo. She wasn't taking help from a man, and of course I wasn't her manager yet. She took the chair I had vacated when Wolfe appeared, next to the magazine table. Ed had been brought by Purley, who was back in Philip's chair, flanking Wolfe. I returned to the stool.

Jimmie had finished above the ears and was doing the back, so Wolfe's head was tilted forward.

"Your assumptions?" Cramer asked.

"Yes. I was saying, the first is that Wallen found something in the car that led him to this shop. It couldn't have been something he was told, for there was no one to tell him anything. It

108

was some object. I asked you not to challenge me, but I didn't mean to exclude contradictions. If there are facts that repudiate this assumption, or any other, I want them."

"We made that one without any help."

"And it still holds?"

"Yes."

"Good. That's fortunate, since all of my assumptions concern that object. The second is that Wallen had it with him when he came here. I can support that with sound—"

"You don't need to. We made it and we hold it."

"Very well. That saves time. . . . Not too short back there, Jimmie."

"No, sir."

"The third is that he had the object inside the newspaper he was carrying. This is slenderer, but it must be tested. He had not bought the paper shortly before coming here, for it was an early edition of the *Daily Press,* on sale last evening, not on sale this morning. It was not merely stuffed in his pocket, he had it in his hand; not rolled up, but folded over once. It is—"

"You know a lot about it," Cramer growled.

"Do me later," Wolfe snapped. "I know nothing you don't know. It is difficult to account for him carrying a stale newspaper in that manner except on the assumption that it was *a container for some object*—at least, the assumption is good enough to work on. The fourth is that whatever the object was, the murderer got it and disposed of it. More than an assumption, that is. No object that could have led him to this shop was found on Wallen's person or in the booth, so if he had it the murderer got it. The fifth assumption is that the murderer was neither Carl nor Tina. I shall—"

"Ah," Cramer said. "Tell us why."

"No. I shall not support that assumption; I merely make it and submit it to our test. Don't waste time clawing at me. Since Carl and Tina are not involved, and therefore didn't take the object away with them, it is still here in the shop. That is the sixth assumption, and it is good only if your surveillance of these people here, all these hours, has been constant and alert. What about it? Could any of them have removed such an object?"

"I want to know," Cramer demanded, "why you're excluding Carl and Tina."

109

"No. Not now." Wolfe and Cramer couldn't see each other because Jimmie was in between, starting on the top. "First we'll complete this test. We must know whether the object has been removed, *not* by Carl or Tina."

"No," Purley said.

"How good a no?"

"Good enough for me. No man has stepped outside this shop alone. Something could have been slipped to a customer, but that's stretching it, and we've had them under our eyes."

"Not, apparently, the one who assaulted Miss Stahl."

"That was in the shop. Is that a point?"

"I suppose not. Then we assume that the object is still here. The seventh and last assumption is this: that no proper search for such an object has been made. I hasten to add, Mr. Stebbins, that that is not a point, either. You and your men are unquestionably capable of making a proper search, but I assume that you haven't done so on account of Carl and Tina. Thinking them guilty, naturally you thought they wouldn't leave an incriminating object behind. Have you searched thoroughly?"

"We've looked."

"Yes. But granting all my assumptions, which of course you don't, has there been a proper search?"

"No."

"Then it's about time. Mr. Fickler!"

Fickler jerked his head up. "Me?"

"You run this place and can help us. However, I address all of you who work here. Put your minds on this. You too, Jimmie."

Jimmie backed off a step and stood.

"This," Wolfe said, "could take a few minutes or it could take all night. What we're after is an object with something on it that identifies it as coming from this shop. Ideally, it should be the name and address or phone number, but we'll take less if we have to. Since we're proceeding on my assumptions, we are supposing that it was inside the newspaper as Wallen was carrying it, so it is not a business card or match folder or bottle or comb or brush. It should be flat and of considerable dimensions. Another point: It should be easily recognizable. All of you went to the booth and were questioned by Wallen, but he showed you no such object and mentioned none. Is that correct?"

They nodded and mumbled affirmatives. Ed said, "Yes!"

"Then only the murder saw it or was told of it. Wallen must for some reason have shown it to him, or asked him about it, and not the rest of you; or its edge may have been protruding from the newspaper, unnoticed by the others; or the murderer may merely have suspected that Wallen had it. In any case, when opportunity offered later for him to dive into the booth and kill Wallen, he got the object. If Mr. Stebbins is right about the surveillance that has been maintained, it is still here in the shop. I put it to you, and especially to you, Mr. Fickler: What and where is it?"

They looked at one another and back at Wolfe. Philip said in his thin tenor, "Maybe it was the newspaper."

"Possibly. I doubt it. . . . Where is the newspaper, Mr. Cramer?"

"At the laboratory. There's nothing on it or in it that could have brought Wallen here."

"What else has been taken from here to the laboratory?"

"Nothing but the scissors and the bottle that was used on Miss Stahl."

"Then it's here. . . . All right, Jimmie, finish."

"It looks to me," Purley objected in his bass rumble, "like a turkey. Even with your assumptions. Say we find something like what you want, how do we know it's it? Even if we think it's it, where does that get us?"

Wolfe was curt: "For one thing, fingerprints."

"Nuts. If it belongs here, of course it will have their prints."

"Not *their* prints, Mr. Stebbins. *Wallen's prints!* If he picked it up in the car, he touched it. If he touched it, he left prints. As I understand it, he didn't go around touching things here. He entered, spoke to Mr. Fickler, was taken to the booth, and never left it alive. If we find anything with his prints on it, we've got it. Have you equipment here? If not, I advise you to send for it at once, and also for Wallen's prints."

Purley grunted. He didn't move.

"Go ahead," Cramer told him. "Phone. Give him what he wants."

"The search," Wolfe said, "must be thorough and will take time. First I ask all of you to search your minds. What object is here, belongs here, that meets the specifications as I have described them, Mr. Fickler?"

111

Fickler shook his head. "I don't know, unless it's a towel, and why would he carry a towel like that?"

"He wouldn't. Anyway, a towel wouldn't help us any. . . . Philip?"

"No, sir. I don't know what."

"Tom?"

Tom just shook his head, gloomily.

"Ed?"

"You've got me. Pass."

"Miss Stahl?"

"I think he might have been keeping the paper because there was something in it he wanted to read. I don't have time—"

"Yes. We'll consider that. . . . Jimmie?"

"I don't know a thing like that in the shop, Mr. Wolfe. Not a thing."

"Pfui." Wolfe was disgusted. "Either you have no brains at all, or you're all in a conspiracy. I'm looking straight at such an object right now."

From behind I couldn't see where his gaze was directed, but I didn't have to. The others could, and I saw them. Eleven pairs of eyes, including Purley's, who had finished at the phone and rejoined us, were aimed at the magazine table next to Janet's chair, from eleven different angles. Up to that moment my brain may have been as paralyzed as the others', but it could still react to a stimulus. I left the stool and stood right behind Wolfe, ready if and when needed.

"You mean the magazines?" Cramer demanded.

"Yes. You subscribe to them, Mr. Fickler? They come through the mail? Then the name and address is on them. For instance, that copy of *Ellery Queen's Mystery Magazine*—the name and address of Mr. Fickler, or of The Goldenrod Barbershop, is stenciled on the mailing-wrapper which is still around the magazine. Surely it deserves examination.

"What if he took it from here and had it in his pocket when he stole the car and drove up Broadway? And in the excitement of his misadventure he failed to notice that it had dropped from his pocket and was on the seat of the car? And Wallen found it there, took it, and saw the name and address on it? . . . You have sent for the equipment and Wallen's prints, Mr. Stebbins? Then we—"

"Oh! I remember!" Janet cried. She was pointing a finger.

112

"You remember, Jimmie? This morning, I was standing here, and you came by with a hot towel, and you had that magazine—the one sticking out of the mailing-wrapper—and you tossed it under there. That's why you must have been the one to hit me, because I asked if you had been steaming it, and you said—"

Jimmie leaped. I thought his prey was Janet, and in spite of everything I was willing to save her life, but Wolfe and the chair were in my way and cost me a fifth of a second. And it wasn't Janet he was after; it was the magazine—the copy of *Ellery Queen's Mystery Magazine.* He went for it in a hurtling dive, and got his hands on it, but then the three dicks, not to mention Cramer and Purley, were on his neck.

Janet didn't make a sound. I suppose she was considering what to say to the reporters.

"Confound it," Wolfe grumbled savagely behind me. "*My barber.*"

Anyhow, that haircut was done.

As stubborn as Cramer was, he never did learn why Wolfe went to get a haircut that day.

He learned plenty about Jimmie Kirk. Kirk was wanted as a bail jumper, under another name, in Wheeling, West Virginia, on an old charge as a car stealer, with various fancy complications such as slugging a respected citizen who had surprised him in the act. Apparently, he had gone straight in New York for a couple of years and then had hooked up with a car-stealing ring. Unquestionably, he had been fortified with liquids that Monday evening. Driving a stolen car while drunk is a risky operation, especially with a stolen magazine in your pocket. . . .

As for Carl and Tina, I took a strong position on them Tuesday evening in the office.

"You know very well what will happen," I told Wolfe. "Some day, maybe next week, maybe next year, they'll be confronted and they'll be in trouble. Being in trouble, they will come to me, because Carl likes me and because I rescued them—"

Wolfe snorted. "*You* did!"

"Yes, sir. I had already noticed that magazine there several times, and it just happened to catch your eye. Anyhow, I am secretly infatuated with Tina, so I'll try to help them and will get my finger caught, and you'll have to butt in again because you can't get along without me. It will go on like that year after year. Why not try to do something about it now? There are people in Washington you know—for instance, Carpenter. He might be able to help Tina and Carl. It will cost a measly buck for a phone call, and I can get that from the fifty they have earmarked for us. I have Carpenter's home number, and I might as well get him now."

No comment.

I put my hand on the phone. "Person to person, huh?"

Wolfe grunted. "I got my naturalization papers twenty-four years ago."

"I wasn't discussing you. You've caught it from Janet," I said coldly, and then lifted the phone and dialed.

114

THE CASE OF THE IRATE WITNESS

BY ERLE STANLEY GARDNER

Erle Stanley Gardner was born in Massachusetts. His
father was a mining engineer and Gardner traveled
often as a child—to the Klondike, Oregon, and California. He attended Valparaiso University in Indiana, was a
boxer, and typed for a law firm. He read law for fifty
hours a week for three years, and was admitted to the
California bar in 1911. His law practice still left him time
for writing and he sold his first mystery to a pulp
magazine in 1923. Besides hundreds of stories, including westerns as well as mysteries, he wrote more than
eighty novels about Perry Mason. He died in 1970.

THE EARLY-MORNING SHADOWS cast by the mountains still lay heavily on the town's main street as the big siren on the roof of the Jebson Commercial Company began to scream shrilly.

The danger of fire was always present, and at the sound, men at breakfast rose and pushed their chairs back from the table. Men who were shaving barely paused to wipe lather from their faces; men who had been sleeping grabbed the first available garments. All of them ran to places where they could look for the first telltale wisps of smoke.

There was no smoke.

The big siren was still screaming urgently as the men formed into streaming lines, like ants whose hill has been attacked. The lines all moved toward the Jebson Commercial Company.

There the men were told that the doors of the big vault had been found wide open. A jagged hole had been cut into one door with an acetylene torch.

The men looked at one another silently. This was the fifteenth of the month. The big, twice-a-month payroll, which had been brought up from the Ivanhoe National Bank the day before, had been the prize.

Frank Bernal, manager of the company's mine, the man who ruled Jebson City with an iron hand, arrived and took charge. The responsibility was his, and what he found was alarming.

Tom Munson, the night watchman, was lying on the floor in a back room, snoring in drunken slumber. The burglar alarm, which had been installed within the last six months, had been bypassed by means of an electrical device. This device was so ingenious that it was apparent that, if the work were that of a gang, at least one of the burglars was an expert electrician.

Ralph Nesbitt, the company accountant, was significantly silent. When Frank Bernal had been appointed manager a year earlier, Nesbitt had pointed out that the big vault was obsolete.

Bernal, determined to prove himself in his new job, had avoided the expense of tearing out the old vault and installing a new one by investing in an up-to-date burglar alarm and putting a special night watchman on duty.

Now the safe had been looted of $100,000 and Frank Bernal had to make a report to the main office in Chicago, with the disquieting knowledge that Ralph Nesbitt's memo stating that the antiquated vault was a pushover was at this moment reposing in the company files.

Some distance out of Jebson City, Perry Mason, the famous trial lawyer, was driving fast along a mountain road. He had planned a weekend fishing trip for a long time, but a jury which had waited until midnight before reaching its verdict had delayed Mason's departure and it was now 8:30 in the morning.

His fishing clothes, rod, wading boots, and creel were all in the trunk. He was wearing the suit in which he had stepped from the courtroom, and having driven all night he was eager for the cool, piny mountains.

A blazing red light, shining directly at him as he rounded a turn in the canyon road, dazzled his road-weary eyes. A sign, *STOP—POLICE*, had been placed in the middle of the road. Two men, a grim-faced man with a .30-30 rifle in his hands and a silver badge on his shirt, and a uniformed motorcycle officer, stood beside the sign.

Mason stopped his car.

The man with the badge, a deputy sheriff, said, "We'd better take a look at your driving license. There's been a big robbery at Jebson City."

"That so?" Mason said. "I went through Jebson City an hour ago and everything seemed quiet."

"Where you been since then?"

"I stopped at a little service station and restaurant for breakfast."

"Let's take a look at your driving license."

Mason handed it to him.

The man started to return it, then looked at it again. "Say," he said, "you're Perry Mason, the big criminal lawyer!"

"Not a criminal lawyer," Mason said patiently, "a trial lawyer. I sometimes defend men who are accused of crime."

"What are you doing up in this country?"

"Going fishing."

The deputy looked at him suspiciously. "Why aren't you wearing your fishing clothes?"

"Because," Mason said, and smiled, "I'm not fishing."

"You said you were going fishing."

"I also intend," Mason said, "to go to bed tonight. According to you, I should be wearing my pajamas."

The deputy frowned. The traffic officer laughed and waved Mason on.

The deputy nodded at the departing car. "Looks like a live clue to me," he said, "but I can't find it in that conversation."

"There isn't any," the traffic officer said.

The deputy remained dubious, and later on, when a news-hungry reporter from the local paper asked the deputy if he knew of anything that would make a good story, the deputy said that he did.

And that was why Della Street, Perry Mason's confidential secretary, was surprised to read stories in the metropolitan papers stating that Perry Mason, the noted trial lawyer, was rumored to have been retained to represent the person or persons who had looted the vault of the Jebson Commercial Company. All this had been arranged, it would seem, before Mason's "client" had even been apprehended.

When Perry Mason called his office by long-distance the next afternoon, Della said, "I thought you were going to the mountains for a vacation."

"That's right. Why?"

"The papers claim you're representing whoever robbed the Jebson Commercial Company."

"First I've heard of it," Mason said. "I went through Jebson City before they discovered the robbery, stopped for breakfast a little farther on, and then got caught in a roadblock. In the eyes of some officious deputy, that seems to have made me an accessory after the fact."

"Well," Della Street said, "they've caught a man by the name of Harvey L. Corbin, and apparently have quite a case against him. They're hinting at mysterious evidence which won't be disclosed until the time of trial."

"Was he the one who committed the crime?" Mason asked.

"The police think so. He has a criminal record. When his employers at Jebson City found out about it, they told him to leave town. That was the evening before the robbery."

"Just like that, eh?" Mason asked.

"Well, you see, Jebson City is a one-industry town, and the company owns all the houses. They're leased to the employees. I understand Corbin's wife and daughter were told they could stay until Corbin got located in a new place, but Corbin was told to leave town at once. You aren't interested, are you?"

118

"Not in the least," Mason said, "except that when I drive back I'll be going through Jebson City, and I'll probably stop to pick up the local gossip."

"Don't do it," she warned. "This man Corbin has all the ear-marks of being an underdog, and you know how you feel about underdogs."

A quality in her voice made Perry suspicious. "You haven't been approached, have you, Della?"

"Well," she said, "in a way. Mrs. Corbin read in the papers that you were going to represent her husband, and she was overjoyed. It seems that she thinks her husband's implication in this is a raw deal. She hadn't known anything about his criminal record, but she loves him and is going to stand by him."

"You've talked with her?" Mason asked.

"Several times. I tried to break it to her gently. I told her it was probably nothing but a newspaper story. You see, Chief, they have Corbin dead to rights. They took some money from his wife as evidence. It was part of the loot."

"And she has nothing?"

"Nothing. Corbin left her forty dollars, and they took it all as evidence."

"I'll drive all night," he said. "Tell her I'll be back tomorrow."

"I was afraid of that," Della Street said. "Why did you have to call up? Why couldn't you have stayed up there fishing? Why did you have to get your name in the papers?"

Mason laughed and hung up.

Paul Drake, of the Drake Detective Agency, came in and sat in the big chair in Mason's office and said, "You have a bear by the tail, Perry."

"What's the matter, Paul? Didn't your detective work in Jebson City pan out?"

"It panned out all right, but the stuff in the pan isn't what you want, Perry," Drake explained.

"How come?"

"Your client's guilty."

"Go on," Mason said.

"The money he gave his wife was some of what was stolen from the vault."

"How do they know it was the stolen money?" Mason asked.

Drake pulled a notebook from his pocket. "Here's the whole picture. The plant manager runs Jebson City. There isn't any

119

private property. The Jebson company controls everything."

"Not a single small business?"

Drake shook his head. "Not unless you want to consider garbage collecting as small business. An old coot by the name of George Addey lives five miles down the canyon; he has a hog ranch and collects the garbage. He's supposed to have the first nickel he ever earned. Buries his money in cans. There's no bank nearer than Ivanhoe City."

"What about the burglary? The men who did it must have moved in acetylene tanks and—"

"They took them right out of the company store," Drake said. And then he went on: "Munson, the watchman, likes to take a pull out of a flask of whiskey along about midnight. He says it keeps him awake. Of course, he's not supposed to do it, and no one was supposed to know about the whiskey, but someone did know about it. They doped the whiskey with a barbiturate. The watchman took his usual swig, went to sleep, and stayed asleep."

"What's the evidence against Corbin?" Mason asked.

"Corbin had a previous burglary record. It's a policy of the company not to hire anyone with a criminal record. Corbin lied about his past and got a job. Frank Bernal, the manager, found out about it, sent for Corbin about eight o'clock the night the burglary took place, and ordered him out of town. Bernal agreed to let Corbin's wife and child stay on in the house until Corbin could get located in another city. Corbin pulled out in the morning, and gave his wife this money. It was part of the money from the burglary."

"How do they know?" Mason asked.

"Now there's something I don't know," Drake said. "This fellow Bernal is pretty smart, and the story is that he can prove Corbin's money was from the vault."

Drake paused, then continued: "The nearest bank is at Ivanhoe City, and the mine pays off in cash twice a month. Ralph Nesbitt, the cashier, wanted to install a new vault. Bernal refused to okay the expense. So the company has ordered both Bernal and Nesbitt back to its main office at Chicago to report. The rumor is that they may fire Bernal as manager and give Nesbitt the job. A couple of the directors don't like Bernal, and this thing has given them their chance. They dug out a report Nesbitt had made showing the vault was a pushover. Bernal didn't act on that report." He sighed and then asked, "When's the trial, Perry?"

120

"The preliminary hearing is set for Friday morning. I'll see then what they've got against Corbin."

"They're laying for you up there," Paul Drake warned. "Better watch out, Perry. That district attorney has something up his sleeve, some sort of surprise that's going to knock you for a loop."

In spite of his long experience as a prosecutor, Vernon Flasher, the district attorney of Ivanhoe County, showed a certain nervousness at being called upon to oppose Perry Mason. There was, however, a secretive assurance underneath that nervousness.

Judge Haswell, realizing that the eyes of the community were upon him, adhered to legal technicalities to the point of being pompous both in rulings and mannerisms.

But what irritated Perry Mason was in the attitude of the spectators. He sensed that they did not regard him as an attorney trying to safeguard the interest of a client, but as a legal magician with a cloven hoof. The looting of the vault had shocked the community, and there was a tight-lipped determination that no legal tricks were going to do Mason any good *this* time.

Vernon Flasher didn't try to save his surprise evidence for a whirlwind finish. He used it right at the start of the case.

Frank Bernal, called as a witness, described the location of the vault, identified photographs, and then leaned back as the district attorney said abruptly, "You had reason to believe this vault was obsolete?"

"Yes, sir."

"It had been pointed out to you by one of your fellow employees, Mr. Ralph Nesbitt?"

"Yes, sir."

"And what did you do about it?"

"Are you," Mason asked in some surprise, "trying to cross-examine your own witness?"

"Just let him answer the question, and you'll see," Flasher replied grimly.

"Go right ahead and answer," Mason said to the witness.

Bernal assumed a more comfortable position. "I did three things," he said, "to safeguard the payrolls and to avoid the expense of tearing out the old vault and installing a new vault in its place."

121

"What were those three things?"

"I employed a special night watchman; I installed the best burglar alarm money could buy; and I made arrangements with the Ivanhoe National Bank, where we have our payrolls made up, to list the number of each twenty-dollar bill which was a part of each payroll."

Mason suddenly sat up straight.

Flasher gave him a glance of gloating triumph. "Do you wish the court to understand, Mr. Bernal," he said smugly, "that you have the numbers of the bills in the payroll which was made up for delivery on the fifteenth?"

"Yes, sir. Not *all* the bills, you understand. That would have taken too much time, but I have the numbers of all the twenty-dollar bills."

"And who recorded those numbers?" the prosecutor asked.

"The bank."

"And do you have that list of numbers with you?"

"I do. Yes, sir." Bernal produced a list. "I felt," he said, glancing coldly at Nesbitt, "that these precautions would be cheaper than a new vault."

"I move the list be introduced in evidence," Flasher said.

"Just a moment," Mason objected. "I have a couple of questions. You say this list is not in your handwriting, Mr. Bernal?"

"Yes, sir."

"Whose handwriting is it, do you know?" Mason asked.

"The assistant cashier of the Ivanhoe National Bank."

"Oh, all right," Flasher said. "We'll do it the hard way, if we have to. Stand down, Mr. Bernal, and I'll call the assistant cashier."

Harry Reedy, assistant cashier of the Ivanhoe Bank, had the mechanical assurance of an adding machine. He identified the list of numbers as being in his handwriting. He stated that he had listed the numbers of the twenty-dollar bills and put that list in an envelope which had been sealed and sent up with the money for the payroll.

"Cross-examine," Flasher said.

Mason studied the list. "These numbers are all in your handwriting?" he asked Reedy.

"Yes, sir."

"Did you yourself compare the numbers you wrote down with the numbers on the twenty-dollar bills?"

"No, sir. I didn't personally do that. Two assistants did that.

122

One checked the numbers as they were read off, one as I wrote them down."

"The payrolls are for approximately a hundred thousand dollars, twice each month?"

"That's right. And ever since Mr. Bernal took charge, we have taken this means to identify payrolls. No attempt is made to list the bills in numerical order. The serial numbers are simply read off and written down. Unless a robbery occurs, there is no need to do anything further. In the event of a robbery, we can reclassify the numbers and list the bills in numerical order."

"These numbers are in your handwriting—every number?"

"Yes, sir. More than that, you will notice that at the bottom of each page I have signed my initials."

"That's all," Mason said.

"I now offer once more to introduce this list in evidence," Flasher said.

"So ordered," Judge Haswell ruled.

"My next witness is Charles J. Oswald, the sheriff," the district attorney announced.

The sheriff, a long, lanky man with a quiet manner, took the stand. "You're acquainted with Harvey L. Corbin, the defendant in this case?" the district attorney asked.

"I am."

"Are you acquainted with his wife?"

"Yes, sir."

"Now, on the morning of the fifteenth of this month, the morning of the robbery at the Jebson Commercial Company, did you have any conversation with Mrs. Corbin?"

"I did. Yes, sir."

"Did you ask her about her husband's activities the night before?"

"Just a moment," Mason said. "I object to this on the ground that any conversation the sheriff had with Mrs. Corbin is not admissible against the defendant, Corbin; furthermore, that in this state a wife cannot testify against her husband. Therefore, any statement she might make would be an indirect violation of that rule. Furthermore, I object on the ground that the question calls for hearsay."

Judge Haswell looked ponderously thoughtful, then said, "It seems to me Mr. Mason is correct."

"I'll put it this way, Mr. Sheriff," the district attorney said.

"Did you, on the morning of the fifteenth, take any money from Mrs. Corbin?"

"Objected to as incompetent, irrelevant, and immaterial," Mason said.

"Your Honor," Flasher said irritably, "that's the very gist of our case. We propose to show that two of the stolen twenty-dollar bills were in the possession of Mrs. Corbin."

Mason said, "Unless the prosecution can prove the bills were given Mrs. Corbin by her husband, the evidence is inadmissible."

"That's just the point," Flasher said. "Those bills *were* given to her by the defendant."

"How do you know?" Mason asked.

"She told the sheriff so."

"That's hearsay," Mason snapped.

Judge Haswell fidgeted on the bench. "It seems to me we're getting into a peculiar situation here. You can't call the wife as witness, and I don't think her statement to the sheriff is admissible."

"Well," Flasher said desperately, "in this state, Your Honor, we have a community-property law. Mrs. Corbin had this money. Since she is the wife of the defendant, it was community property. Therefore, it's partially his property."

"Well now, there," Judge Haswell said, "I think I can agree with you. You introduce the twenty-dollar bills. I'll overrule the objection made by the defense."

"Produce the twenty-dollar bills, Sheriff," Flasher said triumphantly.

The bills were produced and received in evidence.

"Cross-examine," Flasher said curtly.

"No question of this witness," Mason said. "but I have a few questions to ask Mr. Bernal on cross-examination. You took him off the stand to lay the foundation for introducing the bank list, and I didn't have an opportunity to cross-examine him."

"I beg your pardon," Flasher said. "Resume the stand, Mr. Bernal."

His tone, now that he had the twenty-dollar bills safely introduced in evidence, had a gloating note to it.

Mason said, "This list which has been introduced in evidence is on the stationery of the Ivanhoe National Bank?"

"That's right. Yes, sir."

"It consists of several pages, and at the end there is the signature of the assistant cashier?"

"Yes, sir."

"And each page is initialed by the assistant cashier?"

"Yes, sir."

"This was the scheme which you thought of in order to safeguard the company against a payroll robbery?"

"Not to safeguard the company against a payroll robbery, Mr. Mason, but to assist us in recovering the money in the event there was a holdup."

"This was your plan to answer Mr. Nesbitt's objections that the vault was an outmoded model?"

"A part of my plan, yes. I may say that Mr. Nesbitt's objections had never been voiced until I took office. I felt he was trying to embarrass me by making my administration show less net returns than expected." Bernal tightened his lips and added, "Mr. Nesbitt had, I believe, been expecting to be appointed manager. He was disappointed. I believe he still expects to be manager."

In the spectator's section of the courtroom, Ralph Nesbitt glared at Bernal.

"You had a conversation with the defendant on the night of the fourteenth?" Mason asked Bernal.

"I did. Yes, sir."

"You told him that for reasons which you deemed sufficient you were discharging him immediately and wanted him to leave the premises at once?"

"Yes, sir. I did."

"And you paid him his wages in cash?"

"Mr. Nesbitt paid him in my presence, with money he took from the petty-cash drawer of the vault."

"Now, as part of the wages due him, wasn't Corbin given these two twenty-dollar bills which have been introduced in evidence?"

Bernal shook his head. "I had thought of that," he said, "but it would have been impossible. Those bills weren't available to us at that time. The payroll is received from the bank in a sealed package. Those two twenty-dollar bills were in that sealed package."

"And the list of the numbers of the twenty-dollar bills?"

"That's in a sealed envelope. The money is placed in the vault. I lock the list of numbers in my desk."

125

"Are you prepared to swear that neither you nor Mr. Nesbitt had access to these two twenty-dollar bills on the night of the fourteenth?"

"That is correct."

"That's all," Mason said. "No further cross-examination."

"I now call Ralph Nesbitt to the stand," District Attorney Flasher said. "I want to fix the time of these events definitely, Your Honor."

"Very well," Judge Haswell said. "Mr. Nesbitt, come forward."

Ralph Nesbitt, after answering the usual preliminary questions, sat down in the witness chair.

"Were you present at a conversation which took place between the defendant, Harvey L. Corbin, and Frank Bernal on the fourteenth of this month?" the district attorney asked.

"I was. Yes, sir."

"What time did that conversation take place?"

"About eight o'clock in the evening."

"And, without going into the details of that conversation, I will ask you if the general effect of it was that the defendant was discharged and ordered to leave the company's property?"

"Yes, sir."

"And he was paid the money that was due him?"

"In cash. Yes, sir. I took the cash from the safe myself."

"Where was the payroll then?"

"In the sealed package in a compartment in the safe. As cashier, I had the only key to that compartment. Earlier in the afternoon I had gone to Ivanhoe City and received the sealed package of money and the envelope containing the list of numbers. I personally locked the package of money in the vault."

"And the list of numbers?"

"Mr. Bernal locked that in his desk."

"Cross-examine," Flasher said.

"No questions," Mason said.

"That's our case, Your Honor," Flasher observed.

"May we have a few minutes' indulgence?" Mason asked Judge Haswell.

"Very well. Make it brief," the judge agreed.

Mason turned to Paul Drake and Della Street. "Well, there you are," Drake said. "You're confronted with the proof, Perry."

"Are you going to put the defendant on the stand?" Della Street asked.

Mason shook his head. "It would be suicidal. He has a record of a prior criminal conviction. Also, it's a rule of law that if one asks about any part of a conversation on direct examination, the other side can bring out all the conversation. That conversation, when Corbin was discharged, was to the effect that he had lied about his past record. And I guess there's no question that he did."

"And he's lying now," Drake said. "This is one case where you're licked. I think you'd better cop a plea, and see what kind of a deal you can make with Flasher."

"Probably not any," Mason said. "Flasher wants to have the reputation of having given me a licking—wait a minute, Paul. I have an idea."

Mason turned abruptly, walked away to where he could stand by himself, his back to the crowded courtroom.

"Are you ready?" the judge asked.

Mason turned. "I am quite ready, Your Honor. I have one witness whom I wish to put on the stand. I wish a subpoena *duces tecum* issued for that witness. I want him to bring certain documents which are in his possession."

The judge looked at him searchingly.

Mason walked quickly over to Paul Drake. "What's the name of that character who has the garbage-collecting business," he said softly, "the one you told me has the first nickel he'd ever made?"

"George Addey."

The lawyer turned to the judge. "The witness that I want is George Addey, and the documents that I want him to bring to court with him are all the twenty-dollar bills that he has received during the past sixty days."

"Your Honor," Flasher protested, "this is an outrage. This is making a travesty out of justice. It is exposing the court to ridicule."

Mason said, "I give Your Honor my assurance that I think this witness is material, and that the documents are material. I will make an affidavit to that effect if necessary. As attorney for the defendant, may I point out that if the court refuses to grant this subpoena, it will be denying the defendant due process of law."

"I'm going to issue the subpoena," Judge Haswell said, testily,

127

"and for your own good, Mr. Mason, the testimony had better be relevant."

George Addey, unshaven and bristling with indignation, held up his right hand to be sworn. He glared at Perry Mason.

"Mr. Addey," Mason said, "you have the contract to collect garbage from Jebson City?"

"I do."

"How long have you been collecting garbage there?"

"For over five years, and I want to tell you—"

Judge Haswell banged his gavel. "The witness will answer questions and not interpolate any comments."

"I'll interpolate anything I dang please," Addey said.

"That'll do," the judge said. "Do you wish to be jailed for contempt of court, Mr. Addey?"

"I don't want to go to jail, but I—"

"Then you'll remember the respect that is due the court," the judge said. "Now you sit there and answer questions. This is a court of law. You're in this court as a citizen, and I'm here as a judge, and I propose to see that the respect due to the court is enforced." There was a moment's silence while the judge glared angrily at the witness. "All right, go ahead, Mr. Mason," Judge Haswell said.

Mason said, "During the thirty days prior to the fifteenth of this month, did you deposit any money in any banking institution?"

"I did not."

"Do you have with you all the twenty-dollar bills that you received during the last sixty days?"

"I have, and I think making me bring them here is just like inviting some crook to come and rob me and—"

Judge Haswell banged with his gavel. "Any more comments of that sort from the witness and there will be a sentence imposed for contempt of court. Now you get out those twenty-dollar bills, Mr. Addey, and put them up here in the clerk's desk."

Addey, mumbling under his breath, slammed a roll of twenty-dollar bills down on the desk in front of the clerk.

"Now," Mason said, "I'm going to need a little clerical assistance. I would like to have my secretary, Miss Street, and the clerk help me check through the numbers on these bills. I will select a few at random."

Mason picked up three of the twenty-dollar bills and said, "I am going to ask my assistants to check the list of numbers introduced in evidence. In my hand is a twenty-dollar bill that has the number L 07083274 A. Is that bill on the list? The next bill that I pick up is number L 07579190 A. Are any of those bills on the list?"

The courtroon was silent. Suddenly, Della Street said, "Yes, here's one that's on the list—bill number L 07579190 A. It's on the list, on page eight."

"What?" the prosecutor shouted.

"Exactly," Mason said, smiling. "So, if a case is to be made against a person merely because he has possession of the money that was stolen on the fifteenth of this month, then your office should prefer charges against this witness, George Addey, Mr. District Attorney."

Addey jumped from the witness stand and shook his fist in Mason's face. "You're a cockeyed liar!" he screamed. "There ain't a one of those bills but what I didn't have it before the fifteenth. The company cashier changes my money into twenties, because I like big bills. I bury 'em in cans, and I put the date on the side of the can."

"Here's the list," Mason said. "Check it for yourself."

A tense silence gripped the courtroom as the judge and the spectators waited.

"I'm afraid I don't understand this, Mr. Mason," Judge Haswell said, after a moment.

"I think it's quite simple," Mason said. "And I now suggest the court take a recess for an hour and check these other bills against this list. I think the district attorney may be surprised."

And Mason sat down and proceeded to put papers in his brief case.

Della Street, Paul Drake, and Perry Mason were sitting in the lobby of the Ivanhoe Hotel.

"When are you going to tell us?" Della Street asked fiercely. "Or do we tear you limb from limb? How could the garbage man have—?"

"Wait a minute," Mason said. "I think we're about to get results. Here comes the esteemed district attorney, Vernon Flasher, and he's accompanied by Judge Haswell."

The two strode over to Mason's group and bowed with cold formality.

129

Mason got up.

Judge Haswell began in his best courtroom voice. "A most deplorable situation has occurred. It seems that Mr. Frank Bernal has—well—"

"Been detained somewhere," Vernon Flasher said.

"Disappeared," Judge Haswell said. "He's gone."

"I expected as much," Mason said.

"Now will you kindly tell me just what sort of pressure you brought to bear on Mr. Bernal to—?"

"Just a moment, Judge," Mason said. "The only pressure I brought to bear on him was to cross-examine him."

"Did you know that there had been a mistake in the dates on those lists?"

"There was no mistake. When you find Bernal, I'm sure you will discover there was a deliberate falsification. He was short in his accounts, and he knew he was about to be demoted. He had a desperate need for a hundred thousand dollars in ready cash. He had evidently been planning this burglary, or, rather, this embezzlement, for some time. He learned that Corbin had a criminal record. He arranged to have these lists furnished by the bank. He installed a burglar alarm, and, naturally, knew how to circumvent it. He employed a watchman he knew was addicted to drink. He only needed to stage his coup at the right time. He fired Corbin and paid him off with bills that had been recorded by the bank on page eight of the list of bills *in the payroll on the first of the month.*

"Then he removed page eight from the list of bills contained in the payroll *of the fifteenth,* before he showed it to the police, and substituted page eight of the list for the *first of the month* payroll. It was that simple.

"Then he drugged the watchman's whiskey, took an acetylene torch, burned through the vault doors, and took all the money."

"May I ask how you knew all this?" Judge Haswell demanded.

"Certainly," Mason said. "My client told me he received those bills from Nesbitt, who took them from the petty-cash drawer in the safe. He also told the sheriff that. I happened to be the only one who believed him. It sometimes pays, Your Honor, to have faith in a man, even if he has made a previous mistake. Assuming my client was innocent, I knew either Bernal or Nesbitt must be guilty. I then realized that only Bernal had custody of the *previous* lists of numbers.

130

"As an employee, Bernal had been paid on the first of the month. He looked at the numbers on the twenty-dollar bills in his pay envelope and found that they had been listed on page eight of the payroll for the first.

"Bernal only needed to abstract all twenty-dollar bills from the petty-cash drawer, substitute twenty-dollar bills from his own pay envelope, call in Corbin, and fire him. His trap was set.

"I let him know I knew what had been done by bringing Addey into court and proving my point. Then I asked for a recess. That was so Bernal would have a chance to skip out. You see, flight may be received as evidence of guilt. It was a professional courtesy to the district attorney. It will help him when Bernal is arrested."

THE MOST OBSTINATE MAN IN PARIS

BY GEORGES SIMENON

Georges Simenon was born in Belgium in 1903 and left
school at the age of sixteen to earn a living working in a
bakery, then in a bookstore, and finally on a newspaper.
He published his first novel at the age of seventeen, and
wrote his first Inspector Maigret novel in 1929 while
traveling by boat to the Netherlands. A vastly prolific
author, Simenon wrote hundreds of novels and short
stories before he retired from writing fiction in 1973.
Thomas Lask has called Simenon "a Gallic Ross Macdonald" and Howard Haycraft has praised Maigret as
"one of the few really distinctive and original detective
creations."

IN ALL THE ANNALS OF THE Paris police no one had ever posed so long or so assiduously for a *portrait parlé*. For hours on end—sixteen, to be exact—he seemed so stubbornly intent on attracting attention that Inspector Janvier himself came in to look him over at close range. Yet when it was necessary to detail his description, the outlines were blurred and inexact. And some of the dozen witnesses, none of them regularly given to flights of imagination, were sure that the stranger's ostentation was nothing less than a skillful trick.

It all happened on May 3—a warm, sunny day with the special feel of a Parisian spring in the air. The chestnut trees of the Boulevard Saint-Germain were in full bloom and their delicate, faintly sweet fragrance drifted into the cool interior of the café from morning till night.

As he did every day, Joseph opened the doors of the café at eight in the morning. He was in vest and shirtsleeves. The sawdust he had scattered on the floor the night before at closing time was still there and the chairs were piled high on the marble-topped tables. For the Café des Ministères, at the corner of the Boulevard Saint-Germain and the Rue des Saints-Pères, was one of the rare old-fashioned cafés still left in Paris. It had resisted the influx of the hurried drinkers who had only time for a quick one. And it had resisted the rage of gilt fixtures, indirect lighting, mirrored pillars, and flimsy plastic taborets.

It was a café of regulars, where every customer had his own table in his own corner and his own cards or chess set. Joseph the waiter knew them all by name—most of them bureau chiefs and government clerks from neighboring ministries.

Joseph himself was something of a personage in his own right. He had been a waiter for thirty years and it was difficult to imagine him wearing street clothes. Most of his regular customers would probably not recognize him if they met him on the street or in the suburbs where he had built himself a little house.

Eight o'clock was the hour of cleaning up and setting to rights. The double door was wide open on the Boulevard Saint-Germain. There was sunshine on the sidewalk, but inside the café there was only cool, bluish shadow, Joseph smoked as he went about the ritual of getting ready for the day's business. It was his only cigarette of the day. First he lit the gas under the coffee boiler, then polished the nickel until it shone like a mirror. Next he put the bottles on the shelves behind the bar, the apéritifs first, then the spirits. After that he swept up the sawdust and finally he set the chairs around the tables.

The man arrived at exactly ten minutes past eight. Joseph was busy at the coffee boiler and did not see him come in, a fact which he afterward regretted. Had the man rushed in furtively like someone being pursued? And why had he chosen the Café des Ministères, when the bar across the street was already bustling with customers drinking their morning coffee and eating croissants and rolls.

As Joseph later described it: "I turned around and saw somebody already inside—a man wearing a gray hat and carrying a small valise."

The café was really open without being open. It was open because the doors were not closed, but nobody ever came in at this hour. The water was barely warm in the coffee machine and some of the chairs were still piled on the tables.

"I won't be able to serve you for at least half an hour," Joseph said.

He thought that settled matters, but the man merely lifted a chair from a table and sat down, still holding tight to his traveling bag.

"It really doesn't matter," said the stranger calmly, with the air of a man who is not easily dissuaded.

His tone was enough to put the waiter in bad humor. Joseph was like a housewife who hates to have people around at cleaning time. He had a right to be alone while he was doing his housework. He grumbled:

"You'll have a long wait for your coffee."

He continued his daily routine until nine o'clock, favoring the stranger with an occasional glance. Ten times, twenty times, he passed very close to the man, brushed against him, even jostled him a few times while he was sweeping up the sawdust and taking down the remainder of the chairs.

At a few minutes past nine he reluctantly brought the man a cup of scalding coffee, a small pitcher of milk, and two lumps of sugar on a saucer.

134

"Don't you have any croissants?"

"The place across the street has croissants."

"It really doesn't matter," the stranger said.

It was a curious thing, but this man who must know he was in the way, who must know that he was in the wrong café at the wrong time, had a certain humility about him that made him rather likable. And there were other things which Joseph noted with appreciation. During a whole hour the man did not take a newspaper from his pocket, nor did he ask for a paper, nor did he consult the directory or the telephone book. Nor did he try to engage the waiter in conversation. And that was not all: he did not smoke, he did not cross and uncross his legs, he did not fidget. He merely sat.

Not many people could sit in a café for an hour without moving, without looking at the time every few minutes, without showing their impatience in one way or another. If this man was waiting for someone, he was certainly waiting with extraordinary equanimity.

At precisely ten o'clock Joseph finished his housework. The man was still there. Another curious detail struck Joseph: the stranger had not taken a chair by the window, but sat at the rear of the café near the mahogany stairway that led down to the washrooms. Joseph would be going downstairs soon himself to spruce up a little, but first he cranked down the orange-colored awning which gave a faint tint to the shadows inside.

Before going downstairs the waiter jingled a few coins in his vest pocket, hoping the man would take the hint, pay his bill, and leave. The man did nothing of the kind. Joseph left him sitting alone as he went down to change his starched collar and dickey, comb his hair, and put on his worn alpaca jacket. When he came back, the man was still there, still gazing into his empty coffee cup.

Mademoiselle Berthe, the cashier, had come in and was sitting at her desk, taking things out of her handbag. Joseph winked at her. The cashier winked back and started arranging the brass checks in regular piles. She was plump, soft, pink, and placid, and her hair was bleached. When she had finished with the checks, she looked down at the stranger from her throne-like perch.

"He gave me the impression of being a very gentle, very respectable person," she said later. "And I could have wagered

135

that he very probably dyed his mustache, like the Colonel."

It was true the blue-black tint of the man's little mustache suggested hair dye, just as the turned-up ends suggested the curling iron and wax.

Another part of the daily routine was the delivery of the ice. A giant with a piece of sacking on his shoulder carried in the opaline blocks, dripping a limpid trail as he put them away in the ice chest. He, too, noticed the solitary customer.

"He made me think of a sea lion," he said later.

Why a sea lion? The iceman couldn't say exactly.

As for Joseph, he kept strictly to his timetable. It was now time to remove yesterday's newspapers from their long-handled binders and to replace them with today's editions.

"Could I trouble you to pass me one of those?"

Well, well! The customer spoke at last—timidly, softly, but he spoke.

"Which paper do you want? *Le Temps? Le Figaro? Les Débats?*"

"It really doesn't matter."

That was another thing that made Joseph think the man was not a Parisian. He was not a foreigner either, for he had no accent. Probably just off the train from the provinces. And yet there was no railway station in the immediate vicinity. Why would a man come halfway across Paris to sit in a strange café? And it was a strange café, because Joseph, who had a memory for faces, was certain he had never seen the man before. Strangers who entered the Café des Ministères by chance knew at once they did not belong there and promptly went away.

Eleven o'clock—the hour of the boss's arrival. Monsieur Monnet came downstairs from his apartment, freshly shaven, his cheeks aglow, his gray hair neatly slicked down, his perennial patent leather shoes gleaming below his gray trousers. He could have retired from business long ago. He had bought a provincial café for each of his children, but he himself could live no other place in the world than this corner of the Boulevard Saint-Germain where all his customers were his friends.

"Everything all right, Joseph?"

The boss had spotted the stranger and his coffee cup immediately. His eyes asked questions. Behind the counter, Joseph whispered: "He's been here since eight this morning."

Monsieur Monnet walked back and forth in front of the stranger, rubbing his hands as if to invite conversation. Monsieur Monnet was used to talking to his customers. He played cards and dominoes with them. He knew their family troubles, their office gossip. But the stranger did not open his mouth.

"The man appeared very tired, like someone who had spent a sleepless night in a train," the boss said later.

And very much later Inspector Maigret asked the three of them, Joseph, Mademoiselle Berthe, and Monsieur Monnet: "Did he seem to be watching for somebody in the street?"

Their answers were different.

"No," said Monsieur Monnet.

"I got the impression he was waiting for a woman," said the cashier.

"Several times I caught him looking toward the bar across the street," said Joseph, "but each time he lowered his eyes almost immediately."

At twenty past eleven, the stranger ordered a small bottle of Vichy. Several of Joseph's customers drank mineral water, and for reasons which Joseph knew. Monsieur Blanc, for instance, of the War Ministry, was on a strict diet. Joseph noted that the stranger neither drank nor smoked, which was a most unusual circumstance.

For the next two hours he lost track of the man, for the regulars had begun to swarm in for their before-lunch apéritifs. Joseph knew in advance what each would drink and to which tables he should bring playing cards.

"*Garçon!*"

It was past one. The stranger was still there. His valise had been pushed under the red-plush banquette. Joseph pretended he thought the man was asking for the check, and he made his calculation half aloud.

"Eight francs fifty," he announced.

"Could you serve me a sandwich?"

"I'm sorry. We have none."

"Haven't you any rolls, either?"

"We don't serve any food here."

Which was both true and false. Sometimes in the evening a bridge player who had missed his dinner could get a ham sandwich, but it was not usual.

The man shook his head and murmured: "It really doesn't matter."

This time Joseph thought the man's lips trembled slightly. He was struck by the resigned, sorrowful expression on the stranger's face.

"Could I serve you something?"

"Another coffee, please, with plenty of milk."

The man was hungry and the milk would be a little nourishment. He did not ask for other newspapers. He had had time to read the first one from first line to last, including the classified ads.

The Colonel arrived and was distinctly unhappy because there was someone seated at his table. The Colonel was afraid of the slightest draught—spring draughts were the most treacherous of all—and always sat far back in the café.

Armand, the second waiter—he had been a waiter only three years and would never look like a real *garçon de café* if he remained a waiter all his life—came on duty at one thirty. Joseph immediately went behind the glass partition to eat the lunch brought down from the second floor.

Why did Armand think the stranger might have been a rug seller or a peanut vendor?

"He gave me the feeling of not being frank and open," said Armand later. "I didn't like the way he looked at you from under his eyelids. There was something oily, something too sweet in his face. If I had my way I'd have told him he was in the wrong pew and thown him out on his ear."

Others noticed the man, particularly those who came back in the evening and found him sitting in exactly the same place.

True, all these witnesses were amateurs, but the professional who was to come upon the scene later was just as vague and full of contradictions.

For the first ten years of his career Joseph had been a waiter at the Brasserie Dauphine, a few steps from the Quai des Orfèvres, which was frequented by most of the inspectors and detectives of the Police Judiciaire. He had become a close friend of Inspector Janvier, one of Maigret's best men, and in time married Janvier's sister-in-law.

At three o'clock in the afternoon, seeing the man still in the same place, Joseph began to get really irritated. He formulated a hypothesis, to wit, that if this fellow stubbornly clung to his banquette it was not for love of the atmosphere inside the Café des Ministeres but for fear of what lay outside. When he got off the train, Joseph reasoned, the man must have felt that he was

138

being followed, and had come to the café to avoid the police. So Joseph telephoned the Quai des Orfèvres and asked for Inspector Janvier.

"I've got a funny customer here who's been sitting in his corner since eight this morning and who seems determined not to budge," he said. "He hasn't eaten anything all day. Don't you think you ought to come over and take a look at him?"

The meticulous Janvier packed up a collection of the latest "Wanted" notices and headed for the Boulevard Saint-Germain. By a curious chance, at the very moment he stepped into the Café des Ministères, the place was empty.

"Flown the coop?" he asked Joseph.

The waiter pointed to the basement stairs. "Gone to telephone."

What a pity! A few minutes sooner and Janvier could have had the call monitored. As it was, the Inspector sat down and ordered Calvados.

The stranger came back to his table, still calm, perhaps a trifle worried, but certainly not nervous. Joseph, who was getting to know the man, thought him rather relaxed.

For the next twenty minutes Janvier scrutinized the stranger from head to foot. He had plenty of time to compare the plump, rather vague features with the photos of the most-wanted criminals. Then he shrugged.

"He's not on our lists," Janvier told Joseph. "He looks to me like some poor guy who's been stood up by a woman. He's probably an insurance agent or something of the sort." He chuckled. "I wouldn't be surprised if he turned out to be a coffin salesman. Anyhow, I don't see that I have any right to pick him up. There's no law against a man going without lunch, if he wants to, or sitting all day in a café as long as he pays his tab."

After chatting with Joseph a while longer, Janvier returned to the Quai des Orfèvres for an appointment with Maigret. The two Inspectors were so engrossed in a gambling case that Janvier forgot even to mention the man of the Boulevard Saint-Germain to Maigret.

The dying rays of the sun slanted so low that they slid under the awnings of the Café des Ministères. At five o'clock three tables were taken by *belote* players. Monsieur Monnet himself took a hand at a table just opposite the stranger. From time to time he glanced at the man who still sat motionless.

By six o'clock the café was jammed. Joseph and Armand hurried from table to table, their trays loaded with bottles and glasses. The aroma of Pernod soon overpowered the delicate scent of the blossoming chestnut trees on the boulevard.

Each of the two waiters, during the rush hour, had his own tables. The man was sitting at a table in Armand's section. Not only was Armand less observant than his colleague, but he occasionally slipped behind the counter to toss off a glass of white wine. It was understandable, therefore, that the events of the evening may have seemed somewhat blurred to him.

All he could say for sure was that a woman finally came in.

"She was a brunette, well dressed, respectable looking, not at all one of these women who sometimes drop into a café and try to strike up a conversation with strangers."

She was, according to Armand, a woman who would wait in a public place only because she had a date with her husband. There were several vacant tables, but she sat down at the table next to the man.

"I'm sure they didn't speak to one another," Armand said later. "She ordered a glass of port. I think I remember that besides her handbag—a brown or black leather bag—she was carrying a small package in her hand. I noticed it on the table when she ordered the port. It was tied up in paper. But when I brought her order, the package was no longer on the table. She had probably put it on the banquette beside her."

Too bad that Joseph did not see the woman more clearly.

Mademoiselle Berthe saw her all right, from her high-perched desk.

"Rather nicely turned out," the cashier said later. "She wore a blue tailored suit, a white blouse, and almost no makeup. I don't know why I say this, but I don't think she was a married woman."

There was a constant flow of customers in and out of the café until eight o'clock, the dinner hour. Then the vacant tables began to be more numerous. At nine o'clock only six other tables were occupied, two by bridge players who never missed a daily session, and four by the chess players.

"One thing is certain," Joseph said later, "the man knew bridge. And chess, too. I'd say he was a demon at both. I could tell by the way he was watching the games around him."

So he was not at all preoccupied? Or was Joseph mistaken?

At ten o'clock only three other tables were occupied. The men from the ministries went to bed early. At half-past ten, Armand went home. His wife was expecting a baby and he had arranged with the boss to leave early.

The man was still there, still sitting quietly.

Since ten minutes past eight that morning he had drunk three cups of coffee, a split of Vichy, and a bottle of lemon pop—nothing stronger. He had not smoked. He had read *Le Temps* during the morning and late in the afternoon he had bought an evening paper from a news vendor who passed through the café.

At eleven o'clock Joseph started piling the chairs on the tables, as he did every evening, although two tables were still occupied. He also scattered the sawdust on the floor, as usual.

A little later one game broke up. Monsieur Monnet shook hands with his partners, one of whom was the Colonel, went to the cashier's desk for the little canvas bag into which Mademoiselle Berthe had stuffed the sheafs of banknotes and the small change, and climbed the stairs to his apartment.

Before leaving he glanced once more at the obstinate customer who had been a topic of general conversation that evening and said to Joseph:

"If he makes any trouble, ring me."

There was a push-button behind the bar which set off an alarm in Monsieur Monnet's private apartment.

And what was the whole story. When Maigret started his investigation next day, there was little more to be learned.

Mademoiselle Berthe had left at ten minutes to eleven to catch the last bus for Epinay. She, too, had looked at the stranger one final time before leaving.

"I can't say that he was nervous, exactly, but he wasn't exactly calm either. If I'd met him in the street, for instance, he would have scared me, if you know what I mean. And if he'd got off the bus at my stop in Epinay, I wouldn't have dared walk home all alone."

"Why?"

"Well, he had one of those inward looks."

"What do you mean by that?"

"He didn't pay attention to anything that was going on around him."

141

"Were the shutters of the café closed?"

"No. Joseph doesn't lower them until the last minute."

"From your desk you can see the street corner and the bar across the street. Did you notice any suspicious movements in either place? Did you see anyone who might have been watching for him, waiting for him?"

"I wouldn't have noticed. As quiet as it is on the Boulevard Saint-Germain side, there's quite a bit of traffic in the Rue des Saints-Pères. And there's always people coming in and going out of the bar across the street."

"You didn't notice anyone outside this café when you left to go home?"

"Nobody. No, wait. There was a police officer at the corner."

The statement was confirmed by the district police station. Unfortunately the policeman was to leave his post a few minutes later.

Only two other tables were now taken, one by a couple who had dropped in for a drink after the movies, a doctor and his wife who lived a few doors down and often had a nightcap on their way home. They were considered regulars of the Café des Ministères. They had paid their check and were leaving.

The doctor said, "We were sitting just opposite him, and I observed that he was not a well man."

"In your opinion, Doctor, what was wrong with him?"

"His liver, no doubt about it."

"How old would you say he was?"

"It's hard to say. I'm sorry now that I didn't pay more careful attention. In my opinion he was one of those men who look older than their age. Some people would say he was forty-five or even more because of the dyed mustache."

"He did dye his mustache, then? You're sure of that?"

"I think he did. However, I've known patients of thirty-five with the same flabby, colorless flesh, the same lifeless air . . ."

"Don't you think the fact that he had nothing to eat all day may have given him his lifeless air?"

"Possibly. Nevertheless, that would not change my diagnosis. The man had a bad stomach, a bad liver, and, I may add, a defective intestinal tract."

The bridge game at the last occupied table—the last except the stranger's—went on and on. Every time game and rubber seemed on the point of ending the contest, the declarer failed to make his bid. At last a contract of five clubs, doubled and redoubled, was miraculously made, thanks to the nervous error of a tired player who unintentionally established the dummy's long side suit.

It was ten minutes before midnight when Joseph piled the last chairs on a table and announced: "We're closing, *messieurs*."

The stranger did not move while the bridge players were settling their bill, and Joseph would have admitted that at that moment he was frightened. He was on the point of asking the four regulars to wait while he put the man out, but somehow he didn't dare. The regulars filed out, still talking about the last hand. They continued arguing for a moment on the street corner and then separated.

"Eighteen francs seventy-five," Joseph said, a shade too loudly. He was now alone with the stranger. He had already extinguished half the lights.

"I had my eye on an empty siphon of seltzer left over on the corner of the bar," he confessed to Maigret afterward. "One move and I would have bashed his head in."

"Did you put the siphon bottle there for that express purpose?"

Obviously he had. Sixteen hours spent with the enigmatic stranger had put Joseph's nerves on edge. The man had become a personal enemy, almost. Little by little Joseph had practically convinced himself that the man was there on the waiter's account exclusively, that he was waiting only for a propitious moment, a moment when they would be alone, to attack and rob him.

And yet Joseph made one mistake. While the man was fumbling in his pockets for change, still seated at his table, the waiter had gone out to crank down the iron shutters. He was afraid of missing his bus. True, the door was still wide open and there were still pedestrians on the boulevard, taking advantage of the midnight coolness.

"Here you are, *garçon*."

Twenty-one francs! Two francs twenty-five tip for whole day! Joseph was furious. Only his professional composure of thirty years kept him from throwing the change back on the table.

"And maybe you were a little afraid of him, too?" Inspector Maigret suggested.

"I really don't know. Anyhow, I was in a hurry to be rid of

143

him. In all my life I've never been infuriated by a customer like that. If I'd only foreseen that morning that he was going to stay all day!"

"Where were you at the exact moment he left the café?"

"Let me see . . . First I had to remind him that he had a valise under the banquette. He was going off without it."

"Did he seem annoyed that you reminded him of it?"

"No."

"Did he seem relieved?"

"He didn't act pleased or displeased. Indifferent, I would say. If I was looking for a cool customer, this was a cool customer. I've seen all kinds and shapes in the thirty years I've been a waiter, but I've never seen one who could sit behind a marble-topped table for sixteen hours straight without getting ants in his legs."

"And where were you standing?"

"Near the cashier's desk. I was ringing up the eighteen francs seventy-five. You've noticed there are two entrances here—the big double door that opens on the boulevard and the little one on the Rue des Saints-Pères. When he headed for the side door, I was going to call him back and show him the main entrance, but then I thought, *What's the difference? It's all the same to me.* I was through for the night, except to change my clothes and lock up."

"In what hand was he carrying his valise?"

"I didn't notice."

"And I suppose you didn't notice either if he had one hand in his pocket?"

"I don't know. He wasn't wearing a topcoat. I didn't actually see him go out on account of the chairs piled on the tables. They cut off my view."

"You kept standing in the same place?"

"Yes, right here. I was taking the ticket out of the cash register with one hand, and with the other I was fishing in my pocket for the last of the day's brass checks. Then I heard an explosion—like a motor backfiring. Only I knew right away it wasn't a car. I said to myself, 'Well, well! So he got it after all!'

"You think very fast at a time like that. You have to in my line of business. I've seen some pretty tough brawls in my life. I'm always amazed at how fast a man thinks.

"I was mad at myself. After all, he was just a poor guy who

144

had hid out here because he knew he'd get knocked off the minute he stuck his nose outside. So I was sorry for him. He didn't eat anything all day, so maybe he didn't have the money to call a taxi and make a getaway before he got ambushed."

"Did you rush right out to help him?"

"Well, as a matter of fact . . ." Joseph was embarrassed. "I think I probably hesitated a moment. I've got a wife and three children, you know. So first I pushed the button that rings in the boss's bedroom. Then I heard voices outside, and the sound of people running in the street. I heard a woman say, 'You stay out of this, Gaston.' Then I heard a police whistle.

"I went out. I saw three people standing in the Rue des Saints-Pères, several meters from the door."

"Eight meters," said Inspector Maigret, consulting the police report.

"Possibly. I didn't measure. A man was lying in the street and another man was stooping over him. I found out afterwards it was a doctor who was on his way home from the theater and who just happens to be a customer of ours. We have quite a few doctors among our regulars.

"The doctor stood up and said, 'He's had it. The bullet entered the back of his neck and came out through the left eye.'

"Then the police officer arrived and I knew I'd be questioned. Believe it or not, I just couldn't look at the ground. That business about the left eye made me sick to my stomach. I didn't want to look at my customer in that shape, with his eye shot out. I told myself that it was partly my fault, that perhaps I should have— But after all, what could I have done?

"I can still hear the voice of the police officer, standing there with his notebook in his hand, asking: 'Doesn't anybody know this man?' And I answered automatically, 'I do. At least I think I—'

"Finally I forced myself to bend down and look. I swear to you, Monsieur Maigret—and you know me well enough, what with all the thousands of glasses of beer and Calvados I used to serve you over at the Brasserie Dauphine, Inspector, to understand I'm not given to exaggerating—I swear to you I never had such a shock in my life.

"*It was not the man!* It was not the stranger who had sat all day in the café.

"It was somebody I didn't know, somebody I never saw

before—a tall, skinny man in a raincoat. On a fine spring day, a night warm enough to sleep under the stars, and he was wearing a tan raincoat.

"I felt better. Maybe it's silly, but I was glad it wasn't our customer. If my customer had been the victim instead of the murderer, I would have felt guilty about it all my life. You see, since early morning I felt there was something not quite right about my man. I would have put my hand in the fire, that he was a wrong one. It wasn't for nothing that I phoned Janvier. Only Janvier, even if he is practically my brother-in-law, always does everything according to the rules. When I called him, why didn't he ask to see the man's identity papers? They would have told him something, certainly. A decent law-abiding citizen doesn't sit all day in a café and then go out and shoot somebody on the sidewalk at midnight.

"Because you'll note that he didn't loiter after the shot was fired. Nobody saw him. If he wasn't the one that pulled the trigger, he would have stayed right there. He couldn't have walked more than a dozen steps by the time I heard the gun go off.

"The only thing I don't understand is about this woman—the one that ordered a glass of port from Armand. How does she fit into this? Because there's no doubt she had something to do with this man. We don't get many unescorted women in our café—it's not that kind of a place."

"I thought," Inspector Maigret objected, "that the man and the woman did not speak to each other."

"Did they have to speak? Didn't she have a little package in her hand when she came in? Armand saw it, and Armand is not a liar. He saw it on the table and then he saw it wasn't on the table any more and he supposed she'd put it on the banquette. And when this lady left, Mademoiselle Berthe watched her go out because she was admiring her handbag and wishing she had one like it. Now Mademoiselle Berthe didn't notice that she was carrying a package then, and you must admit that women do notice such things.

"You can say what you like, but I still think I spent the whole day with a murderer. And I think I got off very lucky."

Dawn brought one of those perfect spring days such as Paris manages to produce about every third year, a day meant for nothing more strenuous than nibbling at a sherbet or remembering the carefree days of childhood. Everything was good, light, heady, and of rare quality: the limpid blue of the sky, the fleecy whiteness of the few clouds, the softness of the breeze that kissed your cheek as you turned a corner and that rustled the chestnut just enough to make you raise your eyes to admire the clusters of sweet flowers. A cat on a window sill, a dog stretched out on the sidewalk, a shoemaker in his leather apron leaning in his doorway for a breath of air, ordinary green-and-yellow bus rumbling by—they were all precious that day, all designed to instill gaiety into the soul.

That is probably why Inspector Maigret has always kept such a delightful memory of the corner of the Boulevard Saint-Germain and the Rue des Saints-Pères. It is also the reason he was later to stop frequently at a certain café for a spot of shade and a glass of beer. Unfortunately, the beer never tasted quite the same after that day.

The case he was investigating was destined to become famous, not because of the inexplicable obstinacy of the stranger in the Café des Ministères, or of the midnight shooting, but because of the strange motive for the crime.

At eight the next morning Inspector Maigret was at his desk in the Quai des Orfèvres, all of his windows open to the blue-and-gold panorama of the Seine. He smoked his pipe with small, gluttonous puffs as he skimmed through the reports—and thus made his first contact with the man of the Café des Ministères and with the death in the Rue des Saints-Pères.

The police of the district Commissariat had put in a good night's work. Dr. Paul, the medical examiner, had finished his autopsy by six in the morning. The bullet and the empty shell case, which had both been found on the sidewalk, had already been submitted to Gastinne-Renette, the ballistic expert, and a report was expected shortly.

The dead man's clothes, together with the contents of his pockets and several photographs of the scene made by Identification, were on Maigret's desk. Maigret picked up his phone.

"Would you step into my office, Janvier? According to the report, you seem to be somewhat involved in this case."

And so on that beautiful spring day Maigret and Janvier were once again teammates.

Maigret studied the clothing while he waited. The suit was of

147

good quality and less worn than it seemed. It was the suit of a man who lived alone, without a woman to brush it off occasionally or to make him send it to the cleaners before it looked as though he had slept in it—which perhaps he had. The shirt was new and had not yet been to the laundry, but it had been worn for at least a week. The socks looked no better.

There were no papers in the pockets, no letters, no clues to the man's identity. The usual miscellany had some unusual additions: a corkscrew; a pocketknife with numerous blades; a dirty handkerchief; a button off his jacket; a single key; a well-caked pipe and a tobacco pouch; a wallet containing two thousand three hundred and fifty francs and a snapshot of half a dozen bare-bosomed native girls standing in front of an African straw hut; a piece of string; and a third-class railway ticket from Juvisy to Paris, bearing yesterday's date. And finally there was a toy printing set, the kind with which children could fit rubber letters into a small wooden frame and make their own rubber stamps.

The rubber letters in the frame formed the words:

I'LL GET YOU YET.

The medical examiner's report contained several interesting details. The shot had been fired from behind at a distance of not more than ten feet. Death had been instantaneous. The dead man had numerous scars. The ones on his feet were obviously caused by chigoes, African chiggers which burrow under the skin and have to be dug out with the point of a knife. His liver was in pitiful condition, a real drunkard's liver. And finally the man killed in the Rue des Saints-Pères had been suffering from a bad case of malaria.

"Here you are!" Maigret reached for his hat. "Let's go, Janvier, old man."

They walked to the Café des Ministères. Through the window they could see Joseph busy with his morning housework. But curiously enough, Maigret was more interested in the café across the street.

The two cafés were opposite in more ways than geographically. Joseph's domain was old-fashioned and quiet. The bar on the opposite corner—the sign read Chez Léon—was aggressively and vulgarly modern. At the long bar two waiters in shirtsleeves worked busily behind pyramids of croissants, sandwiches, and hard-boiled eggs. Now they were serving little but coffee and white wine. Later it would be red wine and anise-flavored apéritifs.

At the far end of the bar the proprietor and his wife alternated at the tobacco counter. Beyond was the back room, garish with its red-and-gold pillars, its one-legged tables in rainbow plastic, and its chairs covered with goffered plush of an incredible red hue.

All the bay windows opened on the street and crowds swarmed in and out of Chez Léon from morning to night—masons in powdery smocks, clerks and typists, delivery boys rushing in for quick ones before reclaiming their parked tricycle carriers; people in a hurry, people looking for a phone, and most of all, people who were thirsty.

"One up! . . . Two Beaujolais! . . . Three bocks!"

The cash register played a continuous tune. The waiters and barmen sweated as they worked, sometimes mopping their brows with bar towels. Dirty glasses, dipped in murky water, did not even have time to dry before they were filled with red or white wine.

"Two dry whites," Maigret ordered. He loved the din and tumult of the morning rush. And he liked the rascally aftertaste of the white wine which he never found anywhere but in bistros of this sort.

"Tell me, *garçon*, do you remember this man?"

Identification had done a good job. Photographing a dead man may be an ignoble way of earning a living, but it is an essential and delicate art. The inexpert result is often hard to recognize, especially if the face has been damaged. So the gentlemen from Identification first touch up the corpse, then retouch the negative so that the subject looks almost alive.

"That's him, all right. Isn't it, Louis?"

The other waiter looked over his partner's shoulder.

"Sure, that's the guy who bothered hell out of us all day yesterday. How could we forget him?"

"Do you remember what time he first came in?"

"Well, that's hard to say. He's not a regular. But I remember around ten o'clock this guy was all steamed up about something. He couldn't sit still. He came to the bar and asked for a slug of white. He gulped it down, paid, and went out. Ten

149

minutes later he was back, sitting at a table, yelling for another slug of white."

"So he was in here all day?"

"I think so. Anyhow I saw him at least ten or fifteen times. He kept getting more and more jittery. He had a funny way of looking at you, and his hands trembled when he handed you the money. Like an old woman's. Didn't he break a glass on you, Louis?"

"He did. And he insisted on picking all the pieces out of the sawdust himself. He'd say, 'It's white glass. That's good luck. And do I need good luck, 'specially today. You ever been in the Gabon, lad?' he'd keep asking."

"He talked to me about the Gabon, too," said the other waiter. "He was eating hard-boiled eggs. He'd eaten twelve or thirteen in a row, and I thought he was going to bust, particularly as he'd had quite a lot to drink. So he said to me, 'Don't be afraid, lad. One time in the Gabon I made a bet I could swallow three dozen, with thirty-six beers along with the eggs, and I won.'"

"Did he seem preoccupied?" Maigret asked.

"Depends on what you mean by that. He kept going out and coming back. I thought he was waiting for somebody. Sometimes I caught him laughing all by himself, like he'd been telling himself jokes. And once he cornered an old man who comes in every afternoon for two-three slugs of red, a nice old man. He grabbed the old man's lapels and talked his ear off for an hour."

"Did you know he was armed?"

"How could I know that?"

"Because a man of his type is apt to show off his revolver in a bar."

It was indeed a revolver. The police had found it on the sidewalk beside the body. It was a large-caliber gun, loaded, but unfired.

"Let's have more of that white wine."

Maigret was in such high spirits that he could not resist the solicitations of a barefooted flower girl who came in at that moment. She was a skinny, dirty little elf with the most beautiful eyes in the world. Impulsively he bought a bouquet of violets which he then did not know what to do with, so he stuffed it into his coat pocket.

It must be said that this was a day for white wine. A little later

150

Maigret and Janvier crossed the street and entered the savory gloom of the Café des Ministères. Joseph rushed to meet them.

Here they tried to straighten out the blurred portrait of the man with the little valise and the blue-black mustache. Or perhaps "blurred" is not the word. The picture was rather one in which either the subject or the camera had moved, or had been developed from a film with double or triple exposure.

No two descriptions matched. Everyone saw the stranger in a different light. And now there was even one witness—the Colonel—who swore that the minute he saw the man he was sure he was up to no good.

Some remembered the man as terribly nervous, others as amazingly calm. Maigret listened to them all, nodding, stuffing his pipe with a meticulous forefinger, lighting it with great care, smoking with little puffs, narrowing his eyes like a man enjoying a wonderful day—a day on which heaven, in a fit of good humor, had decided to be generous to all mankind.

"About this woman—"

"You mean the girl?"

Joseph, who had only caught a glimpse of her, was convinced it was a girl—a pretty girl, distinguished and obviously of good family. He was sure she did not work for a living. He imagined her in comfortable bourgeois surroundings, baking pastry or making genteel desserts for her family.

Mademoiselle Berthe, on the other hand, had doubts.

"I for one," the cashier said, "would hesitate to give her absolution without confession. However, I do admit that she seemed a lot more decent than the man."

There were moments when Maigret wanted to yawn and stretch himself, as though he were in the country, lying in the sun. That morning he found life enchanting at the corner of the Boulevard Saint-Germain and the Rue des Saints-Pères. He was fascinated by the bus stopping and starting, by the passengers climbing aboard, by the ritual gesture of the conductor reaching for the bell. And what could be more lovely than the moving shadow patterns on the sidewalk, the leafy tapestry of the chestnut trees?

"I'll wager he hasn't gone very far," Maigret grumbled to Janvier who was still vexed at not being able to give a more exact description of the man, after having looked him right in the face.

151

The two detectives left the café and paused a moment at the curb, staring at the bar across the street. Two men, two bars, one for each. It would appear that Fate has planted each man in his proper atmosphere: in one the calm man with the little mustache, the man who could sit all day without moving, who could live on coffee and soda, who did not even protest when Joseph told him there was nothing to eat. And across the street, in the noise and confusion of little people, of the press of secretaries and workmen and delivery boys, in the mad rush of white wine and hard-boiled eggs, the man who was too excited to wait, who popped in and out, buttonholing people to talk to them of the Gabon.

"I'll wager that there's a third café," said Maigret, staring across the boulevard.

In that he was wrong. True, there was across the street a window that commanded a view of both corners and a window that obviously belonged to a public place of some kind. But it was neither bar nor café. It was a restaurant called A l'Escargot.

The restaurant consisted of one long, low-ceilinged room which was reached by two steps down from the street level. It was obviously a restaurant with a regular clientèle, for along the wall there was a row of pigeonholes in which the diners could leave their napkins. The pleasant garlicky aroma of good cooking permeated the place. It was the proprietress herself who emerged from the kitchen to greet them.

"What is it, *messieurs?*"

Maigret identified himself. He then said, "I'd like to know if you had a customer here last night who lingered over his dinner much longer than is usual in your restaurant."

The woman hesitated. There was no one in the dining room. The tables were already set for lunch. At each plate there were tiny decanters of red and white wine.

"I spend most of my time in the kitchen," she said. "My husband would know. He's usually at the cash desk, but he's out right now buying fruit. Our waiter, François, doesn't come on until eleven, but he won't be long now. May I serve you something while you're waiting? We have a little Corsican wine which you might like. My husband has it shipped direct."

Everybody was charming this fine spring day. The little Corsican wine was charming, too. And the low-ceilinged dining

152

room where the two detectives waited for François was delightful. They watched the parade of pedestrians and the two cafés across the boulevard.

"You have an idea, Chief?"

"I've got several. But which is the right one, that's the question."

François arrived. He was a white-thatched old man who would never be taken for anything but a restaurant waiter. He backed halfway into a closet to change his clothes.

"Tell me, waiter. Do you remember a diner last night who acted rather strangely? A girl with dark hair?"

"A lady," François corrected. "Anyhow, I noticed she wore a wedding ring, a red-gold band. I noticed it because my wife and I wear red-gold wedding rings, too. Look."

"Was she young?"

"I'd say about thirty. Quite a proper person, well spoken, with almost no makeup."

"What time did she come in?"

"At quarter past six, just as I finished setting the tables for dinner. Our regular clientèle hardly ever gets here before seven. She seemed surprised by the empty room and started to turn around. 'Do you want dinner?' I asked, because sometimes people come in by mistake, thinking this is a café. 'Come in,' I said. 'I can serve you dinner in about fifteen minutes. Would you like something to drink while you're waiting?' And she ordered a glass of port."

Maigret and Janvier exchanged satisfied glances.

"She sat down near the window. I had to ask her to move because she was sitting at the table of the gentlemen from the Registry Office. They've been coming here regularly for ten years and they don't like to sit at any other table. . . . Actually, she had to wait nearly half an hour because the snails were not ready. She wasn't impatient, though. I brought her a newspaper, but she didn't read it. She just sat quietly and looked out the window."

Just like the man with the blue-black mustache. A calm man and a calm woman. And at the other corner a madcap with nerves as taut as violin strings. Only at this point in the drama it was the madcap who had the gun. It was the madcap who had a rubber stamp in his pocket with the threat: *I'LL GET YOU YET.*

And it was the madcap who had died without firing his gun.

"A very gentle woman," François was saying. "I thought she must be somebody from the neighborhood who had forgotten her key and was waiting for her husband to come home. That happens oftener than people think, you know."

"Did she eat with good appetite?"

"Let me see . . . A dozen snails . . . Then some sweetbreads, some cheese, and some strawberries and cream. I remember because those dishes all cost extra on the menu. She drank a small carafe of white wine and then a cup of coffee.

"She stayed quite late. That's what made me think she was waiting for somebody. She wasn't quite the last to leave, but there were only two other people here when she asked for her check. It must have been after ten o'clock. We usually close at ten thirty."

"Do you know which direction she took when she left?"

"I hope you gentlemen don't mean any harm to this lady?" The old waiter seemed to have an affection for his one-night customer. "Good. So then I can tell you that when I left here myself at quarter to eleven, I was surprised to see her across the street, standing near a tree. Look, it was the second tree to the left of the lamp post."

"Was she still waiting for someone?"

"She must have been. She's not the sort you're thinking of. When she saw me, she turned her head away, as if she was embarrassed."

"Tell me, waiter, did she have a handbag?"

"Of course."

"Was it big? Small? Did you see her open it?"

"Just a moment. . . . No, she didn't open it. She put it on the window sill next to her table. It was of dark leather, rectangular, fairly large. It had a big letter on it—an M, I think, in silver or some other metal."

"Well, Janvier, old man?"

"Well, Chief?"

If they drank many more of these little glasses here and there, they would end up this fine spring day by acting like a couple of schoolboys on vacation.

"Do you think she killed him?"

"We know he was killed from behind, at not more than ten feet."

"But the man in the Café des Ministères could have—"

"Just a moment, Janvier. Which of these two men was going to attack the other?"

"The dead man."

"Who was not yet dead, but who was certainly armed. So he was the menace, the ambusher. He was a threat to the other. Under these conditions, unless he was dead drunk by midnight, it is unlikely that the other could have surprised *him* and shot *him* from behind on emerging from the Café des Ministères, especially at such short range. On the other hand, the woman—"

"What do we know now?"

If Maigret followed his inclination, they would have loitered a while longer in the neighborhood. He liked the atmosphere. He would go back for another white wine with Joseph. Then back to the bar across the street. Sniff around. Drink a little more wine. Play different variations on the same theme: a man with a waxed mustache here; a man across the street, rotten with fever and alcohol; and finally a woman so respectable-looking that she had conquered the heart of old François, eating snails, sweetbreads, and strawberries and cream.

"I'll wager she's used to simple family cooking and eats out very rarely," said Maigret.

"Why do you say that, Chief?"

"The menu. She ordered three dishes that cost more than the regular dinner. People who eat out regularly don't do that, particularly two of the dishes which you rarely get at home—snails and sweetbreads. The two don't go together. The fact that she ordered them indicates she is something of a gourmand."

"You think a woman about to commit murder gives much thought to what she's eating?"

"First of all, my dear Janvier, we know nothing that *proves* she was going to kill anyone last night."

"If she did kill him, she must have been armed. Right? I got the drift of your questions about the handbag. I was waiting for you to ask the waiter if he thought it might be heavy."

"Second," Maigret went on, ignoring the interruption, "even the most poignant tragedy will not make most human beings unaware of what they are eating. You must have seen it as clearly as I have. Somebody is dead. The house is upside down. The place is filled with tears and wailing. Life will never resume

155

its normal rhythm. Then somebody comes in to fix dinner—an old aunt, a neighbor, a neighbor's maid. 'I couldn't swallow a mouthful,' the widow swears. Everybody coaxes her. They make her sit down to the table. The whole family abandons the corpse and sits down with her. After a minute everybody is eating with gusto. And the widow is asking for the salt and pepper because the ragoût needs seasoning. . . . Let's go, my dear Janvier."

"Where to, Chief?"

"To Juvisy."

They really should have caught a suburban train at the Gare de Lyon, but Maigret was horrified at the thought of ending a perfect spring day by fighting crowds of commuters at the ticket windows and on the platforms, ending up either in a No Smoking compartment or standing in the corridor. So, refusing to envisage what the auditor at Police Judiciaire might say about his expense account, Maigret hailed a taxi—an open car, almost brand-new—and spread himself luxuriously on the cushions.

"Juvisy," he told the driver. "Drop us across from the railway station."

He half closed his eyes and spent the journey in a delicious trance, only the trail of smoke from his pipe indicating that he was not asleep.

For a long time, whenever he was asked to tell the story of one of his most famous cases, Inspector Maigret used to describe some investigation in which his stubborn persistence, his intuition and his sense of human values, literally forced the truth to the surface.

Nowadays, however, the story he likes to tell is the case of the two cafés in the Boulevard Saint-Germain, even though his own part in it was a rather slim one. And when he finishes with a satisfied smile that is almost a smacking of the lips, someone inevitably asks, "But what is the true story?"

Maigret smiles even more and says, "It's up to you. Pick the one you like best."

For on at least one point the whole truth was never discovered by Maigret or by anyone else.

It was half-past twelve when the taxi dropped the two Inspectors opposite the suburban railway station of Juvisy. The detectives first entered the Restaurant du Triage, an undistinguished oasis with a terrace surrounded by bay trees in green tubs. They exchanged questioning glances. Could they enter a café—especially today—without taking a drink? Maigret shrugged. Inasmuch as they had devoted themselves so far to white wine, like the dead man of the Rue des Saints-Pères, they might as well continue.

Maigret produced his retouched photograph of the cadaver and showed it to the prizefighter-looking man who was operating behind the zinc bar.

"Tell me, *patron*," he said, "do you recognize this face?"

The man behind the bar held the picture at arm's length and squinted at it, as if he were far-sighted.

"Julie, come here a minute," he called. "Isn't this the bird from next door?"

His wife came in, wiping her hands on her blue-denim apron. She took the photograph gingerly in her fingers.

"Why, sure it is!" she exclaimed. "But he has a funny expression in this picture, hasn't he?" Turning to Maigret she added, "Probably stiff again. He's a great drinker. Just last night he kept us up past eleven o'clock, tossing them off."

"Last night?" Maigret was startled.

"No, wait a minute. It must have been the night before last. Yesterday I did my washing and last night I went to the movies."

"Can we have lunch here?"

"Sure you can have lunch. What do you want to eat? Veal fricandeau? Roast pork with lentils? And you can start with a good homemade pâté."

They ate outside on the terrace, next to the taxi driver they had asked to wait. From time to time the tavern-keeper came out to talk to them.

"My neighbor next door can tell you a lot more than I can," he said. "He rents rooms. We don't. Your man has been staying there for the last month or two. When it comes to drinking, though, he drinks all over town. Why, just yesterday morning—"

"Are you sure it was yesterday?"

"Positive. I was just opening up at six thirty when he came in. He tossed off two or three glasses of white wine. 'To kill the worms,' he said. Then all of a sudden he grabbed his raincoat and ran for the station. The Paris train was just leaving."

The tavern-keeper knew nothing about the man except that

he drank a lot of wine, that he talked about the Gabon with or without the slightest provocation, that he was contemptuous of anyone who had not lived in Africa, and that he bore a bitter grudge against somebody. Who? The tavern-keeper didn't know, but he repeated a speech the man with the raincoat had once made:

"Some people think they are very clever, but they're not clever enough. I'll get them in the end. Sure, anybody can be a skunk at times, but there's a limit on how much of a skunk a man can be."

Half an hour later Janvier and Maigret were talking to the proprietor of the Hôtel du Chemin de Fer. It looked exactly like the place next door except that there were no bay trees around the terrace and the chairs were painted red, not green.

The proprietor had been behind the bar when they came in, reading a newspaper aloud to his wife and his waiter. When Maigret saw the likeness of the dead man on page one, he knew that the first editions of the evening papers had reached Juvisy. He himself had sent the photographs to the press.

"That your tenant?" Maigret asked.

The proprietor darted a suspicious glance. He put down the paper.

"Yes. So?"

"Nothing. I just wanted to know if he was your tenant."

"Good riddance, in any case."

Maigret hesitated. They were going to have to drink something again and it was too soon after lunch to drink any more white wine.

"Calvados," he ordered. "Two."

"You from the police?"

"Yes."

"I thought so. Your face is familiar. So?"

"I'm asking what you think of the murder."

"I would have thought that he was the one to shoot somebody else, not get shot himself. Although it wouldn't have surprised me if he'd got his face kicked in. He was impossible when he was drunk, and he was drunk every night."

"Do you have his registration blank?"

With great dignity, to show that he had nothing to hide, the proprietor went for his register which he offered to Inspector Maigret with just a touch of contempt. The entry read:

158

Ernest Combarieu. Age 47. Born at Marsily, La Rochelle arrondissement (Charente-Maritime). Occupation: woodcutter. Coming from: Libreville, French Equatorial Africa.

"I hear he stayed with you for six weeks."

"Six weeks too long."

"Didn't he pay his bill?"

"He paid regularly every week. But he was a lunatic—stark crazy. He used to stay in bed with the fever two or three days at a time, and he'd order rum sent up to cure him. He drank the rum right out of the bottle. Then he'd get up and make the rounds of every bistro in town. Sometimes he'd forget to come home, sometimes he'd wake us up at three o'clock in the morning to let him in. Sometimes I had to undress him and put him to bed. He used to vomit on the stairway carpet or on the rug in his room."

"Did he have any family here in town?"

Husband and wife looked at each other.

"He knew somebody here, that's certain. If it was a relative, our friend didn't like him, I can guarantee you that. He used to say to me, 'One of these days you're going to hear news about me and a scoundrel who everybody thinks is an honest man, but who is really a dirty hypocrite and the worst thief in the world.' "

"You never knew which man he was talking about?"

"All I know is that our tenant was unbearable and that when he was drunk he had the crazy habit of pulling out a big revolver, aiming across the room, and shouting, 'Bang! Bang!' Then he would burst out laughing and order another drink."

"You'll have a little drink with us, won't you?" said Maigret. "One more question. Do you know a gentleman in Juvisy who is medium height, plump but not fat, with a fine turned-up black mustache and who sometimes carries a small valise?"

The proprietor turned to his wife. "That mean anything to you, *bobonne?*"

The woman shook her head slowly. "No . . . Unless—No, he's shorter than medium and I never thought of him as plump."

"Who is this?"

"Monsieur Auger. He lives in one of those villas in the new subdivision."

"Is he married?"

"Oh, yes, to a very nice wife. Madame Auger is very pretty,

very sweet—a homebody who almost never leaves Juvisy. *Tiens!* That reminds me—"

The three men looked at her expectantly.

"Yesterday while I was doing my laundry in the yard, I saw her walking toward the railway station. She must have been taking the four thirty-seven for Paris."

"She has dark hair, hasn't she? And she carried a black leather handbag?"

"I can't tell you the color of her handbag but she was wearing a blue tailleur and a white blouse."

"What does Monsieur Auger do for a living?"

"He sells postage stamps," the landlord said. "You've seen his name in the classified ads—*Stamps for Collectors.* An envelope of a thousand foreign stamps for so many francs. Five hundred assorted for so much. A mail-order business, C.O.D."

"Does he travel much?"

"He goes to Paris from time to time. On stamp business, I suppose. He always carries his little valise. Two or three times when his train was late he stopped in here for a cup of coffee or a split of Vichy."

It was too easy. This wasn't even an investigation any more. It was a day in the country, an outing enlivened by a laughing spring sun and an ever-increasing number of the cups that cheer. And yet Maigret's eyes sparkled as though he had already guessed that behind this apparently banal affair lay one of the most extraordinary human mysteries he had ever encountered in his long career.

They gave him the address of the Augers. The new subdivision was quite a distance away, near the Seine. Hundreds, perhaps thousands, of little villas had arisen there, each in its own little garden, some of stone, some of pink brick, others of blue or yellow stucco. The worst part of it was that the villas had names instead of numbers, and it took the two Inspectors a long time to find the villa *Mon Repos.*

The taxi rolled along new streets lined with half-finished sidewalks and newly planted trees as skinny as skeletons. Vacant lots separated many of the houses. They had to ask their way several times. After a number of wrong addresses, they finally reached their goal: a pink villa with a blood-red roof. A curtain in the corner window stirred slightly as Maigret and Janvier got out of the taxi.

160

"Should I wait outside, Chief?"

"Maybe you'd better. I don't expect any trouble, though. As long as there is somebody home."

He found the tiny bell-push in the too-new door. He heard the ring inside. Then he heard other sounds—whispering, footsteps, a door closing.

At last the street door opened. Standing before Maigret was the young woman of the Café des Ministères and the Escargot. She was wearing the same blue tailleur and white blouse she had worn the night before.

"I'm Inspector Maigret of the Police Judiciaire."

"I thought it might be the police. Come in."

He climbed a few steps. The stairway seemed to have just come from the carpenter's shop. So did all the woodwork. The plaster on the walls was scarcely dry.

"Come this way, please."

She signaled through a half-open door to someone Maigret could not see. Then she ushered the Inspector into the living room—the corner room with the curtains that had stirred a moment ago. There was a sofa with brightly colored silk cushions, books, bric-a-brac. On a coffee table there was the noon edition of a Paris newspaper with the dead man's photograph staring from the front page.

"Please sit down. Am I allowed to offer you something to drink?"

"Thank you, no."

"I should have suspected that it wasn't done. My husband will be here in a moment. You needn't worry. He won't try to run away. His conscience is clear. However, he has not been well all morning. We took the first train home today. He has a heart condition. He had a slight attack when we got home. He's up and dressed now, though. He's shaving."

Maigret nodded. He had heard the water running in the bathroom. The walls were not very thick in the new subdivision. He smiled at Madame Auger. She was quite pretty, in a wholesome, middle-class way. And she was quite calm.

"You must have guessed that I was the one who killed my brother-in-law," she said. "It was high time. If I had not killed him, my husband would be dead today. And after all, Raymond is worth a hundred Ernests."

"Raymond is your husband?"

161

"For the last eight years. We have nothing to hide, Monsieur l'Inspecteur. I know that we should have gone to the police with the whole story last night. Raymond wanted to do it, but I wouldn't let him. Because of his heart condition, I wanted him to get over the first shock before facing added complications. And I knew you would come here sooner or later."

"You mentioned your brother-in-law a moment ago. His name is different from your husband's."

"Combarieu was the husband of my sister Marthe. He used to be quite a nice fellow. Perhaps a little mad. . . ."

"One moment. May I smoke?"

"Please do. My husband doesn't smoke because of his heart, but tobacco doesn't bother me a bit."

"Where were you born?"

"In Melun. We were sisters, Marthe and I, twin sisters. My name is Isabelle. We looked so much alike when we were tots that my parents—they're both dead now—used to put different colored ribbons in our hair so they could tell us apart. Sometimes we would play a joke on them and change the ribbons."

"Which one of you married first?"

"We were married the same day. Combarieu used to work at the Prefecture in Melun. Auger was an insurance broker. They knew each other because, as two bachelors, they used to eat in the same restaurant. My sister and I met them together, so we were married together. We even lived on the same street in Melun early in our marriage."

"During this time, Combarieu was still working at the Prefecture and your husband was still in the insurance business?"

"Yes. But Auger was already interested in philately. He started his own stamp collection for pleasure, but he realized that stamps could be a lucrative business."

"What about Combarieu?"

"He was ambitious. He was impatient, and he was always short of money. He met a man just back from the colonies who gave him the idea of going to Africa and making his fortune there. He wanted my sister to go with him, but she refused. She had heard that the climate was very unhealthy, particularly for women."

"So he went alone?"

"Yes. He was gone for two years. He came back with his pockets bulging with money. But he spent it faster than he had made it. He had already begun to drink. When he was in his cups he would proclaim to the world that my husband was a mouse instead of a man. A real man, he used to say, would not spend his life selling insurance or postage stamps."

"He went back to Africa?"

"Yes, but the second trip was less successful. His letters were as boastful as ever, but reading between the lines we could feel that things were not going too well for him. Then two winters ago my sister Marthe died of pneumonia. We wrote the bad news to her husband who began drinking more than ever to drown his grief.

"A little later my husband and I moved here to Juvisy. For a long time we had been wanting to build our own home, and live closer to Paris. My husband had discovered he could make a comfortable living with his stamp business and had given up his insurance connections completely."

She spoke slowly, quietly, weighing every word. She seemed to be listening to the sounds from the bathroom.

"Five months ago my brother-in-law returned here without a word of warning," she continued. "Our doorbell rang one night and when I opened the door, there he was, weaving drunk. He gave me a funny look, and without even saying hello, how are you, he sneered and said, 'Just as I suspected.'

"At that time I hadn't the slightest idea what he was talking about. He didn't look well, and from the way he was dressed, he didn't seem too prosperous. In other words, it was not the brilliant homecoming he had enjoyed before, even if he had not been so drunk.

"He came in and for a few minutes talked a lot of incoherent nonsense. Neither of us could make out what he meant. Suddenly he got up and said to my husband, 'You're not only a scoundrel but you're the king of scoundrels. Admit it, now.' Without another word he left. We had no idea where he went.

"A few weeks later he returned, still drunk. He said to me, 'Well, well, my little Marthe.' 'You know very well I'm not Marthe,' I told him; 'I'm Isabelle.' He put on his best sneer. 'We'll see about that some day, won't we?' he said. 'As for your blackguard of a husband who sells postage stamps—'

"I don't know if you understand what was happening, Monsieur l'Inspecteur, but we didn't at first. He wasn't crazy, exactly, although he certainly drank too much. But he had this

163

fixed idea which we were slow to grasp. For weeks we didn't understand his threatening gestures, his sardonic smiles, his insinuations. Then my husband began to get threats by mail. Just one phrase: *I'LL GET YOU YET.*"

"In a word," Maigret interrupted quietly, "your brother-in-law Combarieu for one reason or another got it into his head that his wife was still alive and that it was Auger's wife who had died of pneumonia."

It was a startling idea: twin sisters so alike that their parents had to dress them differently to tell them apart . . . Combarieu far away in darkest Africa, learning that his wife was dead . . . imagining on his return—correctly or not—that there had been a switch, that it was Isabelle who had died and that his own wife Marthe had taken her place in Auger's bed.

Maigret's eyes were half closed as he considered the situation. He puffed more slowly on his pipe.

"Life has been a nightmare for us these past months," Madame Auger continued. "The menacing letters became more frequent. Combarieu would stagger in here at all hours of the day and night, draw his revolver, point it at my husband, then put it away again and laugh. 'No, not yet,' he would sneer; 'It would be too good for you.'

"Then he took a room here in town so that he could torment us more often. He's as sly as a monkey, even when he's drunk. He knows very well what he is doing."

"He knew," Maigret corrected her.

"I'm sorry." She colored slightly. "You're right. He knew. And I don't think he was too anxious to get into trouble. That's why we felt fairly safe here. If he had killed Auger here in Juvisy, everybody would know that he was the murderer.

"My husband hardly dared leave the house. Yesterday, however, he simply had to go to Paris on business. I wanted to go along but he wouldn't hear of it. He took the first train out, the early express, hoping that Combarieu would still be sleeping off his wine and wouldn't see him leave, even though Combarieu had a room just opposite the railway station.

"He was wrong. In the afternoon he telephoned me to come to Paris and bring his pistol to a café in the Boulevard Saint-Germain.

"I could see that my husband had come to the end of his rope, that he wanted to settle things once and for all. He told

164

me on the phone that he would not leave the café before closing time. I brought him his Browning. I also bought a revolver for myself. You must understand, Monsieur l'Inspecteur."

"I understand that you had made up your mind to shoot before your husband was shot. Right?"

"I swear to you that when I pressed the trigger, Combarieu was raising his gun to aim at my husband. . . . That's all I have to say. I'll be glad to answer any questions you want to ask me."

"How is it that your handbag is still marked with the initial *M*?"

"Because the handbag used to belong to my sister. If Combarieu was right, if there really had been this switch he was talking about so much, don't you suppose I'd have made sure to change the initial?"

"In a word, you are enough in love with a man to—"

"I love my husband."

"I was going to say you are enough in love with a man, whether he is your husband or not, to—"

"But he *is* my husband!"

"You are enough in love with this man, meaning Auger, that you would commit murder to save his life or to prevent him from committing murder?"

"Yes," she said.

There was a faint noise at the door.

"Come in," she said.

At last Maigret cast eyes on the man who had been described so differently by so many witnesses—the man with the blue-black mustache, the patience of an angel, and the obstinacy of a mule. In his domestic setting, he was a great disappointment. After the young woman's declaration of love, the man impressed Maigret as despairingly commonplace, the very quintessence of mediocrity.

Auger looked about him uneasily.

The woman smiled and said, "Sit down, I've told the Inspector everything . . . *Your heart?*"

Auger poked vaguely at his chest and said, "Seems all right."

A jury in the Court of Assizes for the Department of the Seine found Madame Auger not guilty on grounds of legitimate self-defense.

Every time Maigret has told about the case, he has always

165

concluded with an ironic: "And that's the whole story."

"Does that mean," someone would always ask, "that you have reservations?"

"It means nothing at all—except that it is not impossible for a very commonplace little man to inspire a very great love, a passion of heroic proportions, even if he has a weak heart and sells postage stamps for a living."

"What about Combarieu?"

"Well, what about him?"

"Was he crazy when he imagined that his wife was not dead at all but was passing herself off as Isabelle?"

Maigret would shrug and mockingly declaim:

"A very great love? A grand passion!"

And sometimes when he was in particularly good humor, perhaps sipping some fine old Calvados that he had warmed gently by holding the inhaler between the palms of his hands, he would continue:

"Is it always the husband who inspires these great loves and mad passions? And don't sisters often have the grievous habit of swooning over the same man? Remember that Combarieu was far away. . . ."

Then, puffing great clouds of smoke from his pipe, he would conclude:

"Too bad the parents were dead, so we couldn't question them about the twins who couldn't be told apart. Anyhow, it was a fine day—The most beautiful spring day I ever saw. And I doubt if I ever drank so much on any one case. If you catch Janvier in an unguarded moment, he might even tell you we were surprised to find ourselves singing duets in the taxi coming back to Paris. And Madame Maigret has always wondered why I had a bouquet of violets in my pocket when I got home. . . . What a Jezebel, that Marthe! Excuse me, I mean, that Isabelle!"

166

THE MURDERS IN THE RUE MORGUE

BY EDGAR ALLAN POE

Edgar Allan Poe was born in Boston, Massachusetts, in 1809, the son of an actress and actor. Orphaned at the age of two, he was taken into the family of John Allan, a wealthy merchant in Richmond, Virginia. He went to school in England, attended the University of Virginia for a time, and entered West Point in 1830 but was expelled. While editing a literary magazine in Richmond, he married his cousin Virginia Clemm in 1836. *The Murders in the Rue Morgue*, first published in 1841, is considered the first modern detective story. Poe died in 1849.

What song the Syrens sang, or what name Achilles assumed
when he hid himself among women, although puzzling questions, are not beyond *all* conjecture.

Sir Thomas Browne

THE MENTAL FEATURES DISCOURSED OF as the analytical, are,
in themselves, but little susceptible of analysis. We appreciate
them only in their effects. We know of them, among other
things, that they are always to their possessor, when in-
ordinately possessed, a source of the liveliest enjoyment. As the
strong man exults in his physical ability, delighting in such
exercises as call his muscles into action, so glories the analyst in
that moral activity which *disentangles*. He derives pleasure from
even the most trivial occupations bringing his talent into play.
He is fond of enigmas, of conundrums, hieroglyphics; exhibiting in his solutions of each a degree of *acumen* which appears to
the ordinary apprehension praeternatural. His results, brought
about by the very soul and essence of method, have, in truth,
the whole air of intuition.

The faculty of resolution is possibly much invigorated by
mathematical study, and especially by that highest branch of it
which, unjustly, and merely on account of its retrograde oper-
ations, has been called, as if *par exellence,* analysis. Yet to calcu-
late is not in itself to analyze. A chess-player, for example, does
the one, without effort at the other. It follows that the game of
chess, in its effects upon mental character, is greatly misunderstood. I am not now writing a treatise, but simply prefacing a
somewhat peculiar narrative by observations very much at
random; I will, therefore, take occasion to assert that the higher
powers of the reflective intellect are more decidedly and more
usefully tasked by the unostentatious game of draughts than by
all the elaborate frivolity of chess. In this latter, where the
pieces have different and *bizarre* motions, with various and
variable values, what is only complex, is mistaken (a not unusual
error) for what is profound. The *attention* is here called power-
fully into play. If it flag for an instant, an oversight is com-

168

mitted, resulting in injury or defeat. The possible moves being not only manifold, but involute, the chances of such oversights are multiplied; and in nine cases out of ten, it is the more concentrative rather than the more acute player who conquers. In draughts, on the contrary, where the moves are *unique* and have but little variation, the probabilities of inadvertence are diminished, and the mere attention being left comparatively unemployed, what advantages are obtained by either party are obtained by superior *acumen*. To be less abstract, let us suppose a game of draughts where the pieces are reduced to four kings, and where, of course, no oversight is to be expected. It is obvious that here the victory can be decided (the players being at all equal) only by some *recherché* movement, the result of some strong exertion of the intellect. Deprived of ordinary resources, the analyst throws himself into the spirit of his opponent, identifies himself therewith, and not unfrequently sees thus, at a glance, the sole methods (sometimes indeed absurdly simple ones) by which he may seduce into error or hurry into miscalculation.

Whist has long been known for its influence upon what is termed the calculating power; and men of the highest order of intellect have been known to take an apparently unaccountable delight in it, while eschewing chess as frivolous. Beyond doubt there is nothing of a similar nature so greatly tasking the faculty of analysis. The best chess-player in Christendom *may* be little more than the best player of chess; but proficiency in whist implies capacity for success in all these more important undertakings where mind struggles with mind. When I say proficiency, I mean that perfection is the game which includes a comprehension of *all* the sources whence legitimate advantage may be derived. These are not only manifold, but multiform, and lie frequently among recesses of thought altogether inaccessible to the ordinary understanding. To observe attentively is to remember distinctly; and, so far, the concentrative chess-player will do very well at whist; while the rules of Hoyle (themselves based upon the mere mechanism of the game) are sufficiently and generally comprehensible. Thus to have a retentive memory, and proceed by "the book" are points commonly regarded as the sum total of good playing. But it is in matters beyond the limits of mere rule that the skill of the analyst is evinced. He makes, in silence, a host of observations and inferences. So, perhaps, do his companions; and the difference in the extent of the information obtained, lies not so much in the validity of the inference as in the quality of the observation. The necessary knowledge is that of *what* to observe. Our player confines himself not at all; nor, because the game is the object, does he reject deductions from things external to the game. He examines the countenance of his partner, comparing it carefully with that of each of his opponents. He considers the mode of assorting the cards in each hand; often counting trump by trump, and honor by honor, through the glances bestowed by their holders upon each. He notes every variation of face as the play progresses, gathering a fund of thought from the differences in the expression of certainty, of surprise, of triumph, or chagrin. From the manner of gathering up a trick he judges whether the person taking it, can make another in the suit. He recognizes what is played through feint, by the manner with which it is thrown upon the table. A casual or inadvertent word; the accidental dropping or turning of a card, with the accompanying anxiety or carelessness in regard to its concealment; the counting of the tricks, with the order of their arrangement; embarrassment, hesitation, eagerness, or trepidation—all afford, to his apparently intuitive perception, indications of the true state of affairs. The first two or three rounds having been played, he is in full possession of the contents of each hand, and thenceforward puts down his cards with as absolute a precision of purpose as if the rest of the party had turned outward the faces of their own.

The analytical power should not be confounded with simple ingenuity; for while the analyst is necessarily ingenious, the ingenious man is often remarkably incapable of analysis. The constructive or combining power, by which ingenuity is usually manifested, and to which the phrenologists (I believe erroneously) have assigned a separate organ, supposing it a primitive faculty, has been so frequently seen in those whose intellect bordered otherwise upon idiocy, as to have attracted general observation among writers on morals. Between ingenuity and the analytic ability there exists a difference far greater, indeed, than that between the fancy and the imagination, but of a character very strictly analogous. It will be found, in fact, that the ingenious are always fanciful, and the *truly* imaginative never otherwise than analytic.

170

The narrative which follows will appear to the reader somewhat in the light of a commentary upon the propositions just advanced.

Residing in Paris during the spring and part of the summer of 18—, I there became acquainted with a Monsieur C. Auguste Dupin. This young gentleman was of an excellent, indeed of an illustrious family, but, by a variety of untoward events, had been reduced to such poverty that the energy of his character succumbed beneath it, and he ceased to bestir himself in the world, or to care for the retrieval of his fortunes. By courtesy of his creditors, there still remained in his possession a small remnant of his patrimony; and, upon the income arising from this, he managed, by means of a rigorous economy, to procure the necessities of life, without troubling himself about its superfluities. Books, indeed, were his sole luxuries, and in Paris these are easily obtained.

Our first meeting was at an obscure library in the Rue Montmartre, where the accident of our both being in search of the same very rare and very remarkable volume, brought us into closer communion. We saw each other again and again. I was deeply interested in the little family history which he detailed to me with all that candor which a Frenchman indulges whenever mere self is the theme. I was astonished, too, at the vast extent of his reading; and, above all, I felt my soul enkindled within me by the wild fervor, and the vivid freshness of his imagination. Seeking in Paris the objects I then sought, I felt that the society of such a man would be to me a treasure beyond price; and this feeling I frankly confided to him. It was at length arranged that we should live together during my stay in the city; and as my wordly circumstances were somewhat less embarrassed than his own, I was permitted to be at the expense of renting, and furnishing in a style which suited the rather fantastic gloom of our common temper, a time-eaten and grotesque mansion, long deserted through superstitions into which we did not inquire, and tottering to its fall in a retired and desolate portion of the Faubourg St. Germain.

Had the routine of our life at this place been known to the world, we should have been regarded as madmen—although, perhaps, as madmen of a harmless nature. Our seclusion was perfect. We admitted no visitors. Indeed the locality of our retirement had been carefully kept a secret from my own former associates; and it had been many years since Dupin had ceased to know or be known in Paris. We existed within ourselves alone.

It was a freak of fancy in my friend (for what else shall I call it?) to be enamored of the night for her own sake; and into this *bizarrerie,* as into all his others, I quietly fell; giving myself up to his wild whims with a perfect *abandon.* The sable divinity would not herself dwell with us always; but we could counterfeit her presence. At the first dawn of the morning we closed all the massy shutters of our old building; lighted a couple of tapers which, strongly perfumed, threw out only the ghastliest and feeblest of rays. By the aid of these we then busied our souls in dreams—reading, writing, or conversing, until warned by the clock of the advent of the true Darkness. Then we sallied forth into the streets, arm in arm, continuing the topics of the day, or roaming far and wide until a late hour, seeking, amid the wild lights and shadows of the populous city, that infinity of mental excitement which quiet observation can afford.

At such times I could not help remarking and admiring (although from his rich ideality I had been prepared to expect it) a peculiar analytic ability in Dupin. He seemed, too, to take an eager delight in its exercise—if not exactly in its display—and did not hesitate to confess the pleasure thus derived. He boasted to me, with a low chuckling laugh, that most men, in respect to himself, wore windows in their bosoms, and was wont to follow up such assertions by direct and very startling proofs of his intimate knowledge of my own. His manner at these moments was frigid and abstract; his eyes were vacant in expression; while his voice, usually a rich tenor, rose into a treble which would have sounded petulant but for the deliberateness and entire distinctness of the enunciation. Observing him in these moods, I often dwelt meditatively upon the old philosophy of the Bi-Part Soul, and amused myself with the fancy of a double Dupin—the creative and the resolvent.

Let it not be supposed, from what I have just said, that I am detailing any mystery, or penning any romance. What I have described in the Frenchman was merely the result of an excited, or perhaps of a diseased, intelligence. But of the character of his remarks at the periods in question an example will best convey the idea.

We were strolling one night down a long dirty street, in the vicinity of the Palais Royal. Being both, apparently, occupied with thought, neither of us had spoken a syllable for fifteen minutes at least. All at once Dupin broke forth with these words:

"He is a very little fellow, that's true, and would do better for the *Théâtre des Variétés*."

"There can be no doubt of that," I replied, unwittingly, and not at first observing (so much had I been absorbed in reflection) the extraordinary manner in which the speaker had chimed in with my meditations. In an instant afterward I recollected myself, and my astonishment was profound.

"Dupin," said I, gravely, "this is beyond my comprehension. I do not hesitate to say that I am amazed, and can scarcely credit my senses. How was it possible you should know I was thinking of ——?" Here I paused, to ascertain beyond a doubt whether he really knew of whom I thought.

"—— of Chantilly," said he, "why do you pause? You were remarking to yourself that his diminutive figure unfitted him for tragedy."

This was precisely what had formed the subject of my reflections. Chantilly was a *quondam* cobbler of the Rue St. Denis, who, becoming stage-mad, had attempted the *rôle* of Xerxes, in Crébillon's tragedy so called, and been notoriously Pasquinaded for his pains.

"Tell me, for Heaven's sake," I exclaimed, "the method—if method there is—by which you have been enabled to fathom my soul in this matter." In fact, I was even more startled that I would have been willing to express.

"It was the fruiterer," replied my friend, "who brought you to the conclusion that the mender of soles was not of sufficient height for Xerxes *et id genus omne*."

"The fruiterer!—you astonish me—I know no fruiterer whomsoever."

"The man who ran up against you as we entered the street—it may have been fifteen minutes ago."

I now remembered that, in fact, a fruiterer, carrying upon his head a large basket of apples, had nearly thown me down, by accident, as we passed from the Rue C—— into the thoroughfare where we stood; but what this had to do with Chantilly I could not possibly understand.

There was not a particle of *charlatânerie* about Dupin. "I will

173

explain," he said, "and that you may comprehend all clearly, we will first retrace the course of your meditations, from the moment in which I spoke to you until that of the *rencontre* with the fruiterer in question. The larger links of the chain run thus—Chantilly, Orion, Dr. Nichols, Epicurus, Stereotomy, the street stones, the fruiterer."

There are few persons who have not, at some period of their lives, amused themselves in retracing the steps by which particular conclusions of their own minds have been attained. The occupation is often full of interest; and he who attempts it for the first time is astonished by the apparently illimitable distance and incoherence between the starting-point and the goal. What, then, must have been my amazement, when I heard the Frenchman speak what he had just spoken, and when I could not help acknowledging that he had spoken the truth. He continued:

"We had been talking of horses, if I remember aright, just before leaving the Rue C——. This was the last subject we discussed. As we crossed into this street, a fruiterer, with a large basket upon his head, brushing quickly past us, thrust you upon a pile of paving-stones collected at a spot where the causeway is undergoing repair. You stepped upon one of the loose fragments, slipped, slightly strained your ankle, appeared vexed or sulky, muttered a few words, turned to look at the pile, and then proceeded in silence. I was not particularly attentive to what you did; but observation has become with me, of late, a species of necessity.

"You kept your eyes upon the ground—glancing, with a petulant expression, at the holes and ruts in the pavement (so that I saw you were still thinking of the stones), until we reached the little alley called Lamartine, which has been paved, by way of experiment, with the overlapping and riveted blocks. Here your countenance brightened up, and, perceiving your lips move, I could not doubt that you murmured the word 'stereotomy,' a term very affectedly applied to this species of pavement. I knew that you could not say to yourself 'stereotomy' without being brought to think of atomies, and thus of the theories of Epicurus; and since, when we discussed this subject not very long ago, I mentioned to you how singularly, yet with how little notice, the vague guesses of that noble Greek had met with confirmation in the late nebular cosmogony, I felt that you

174

could not avoid casting your eyes upward to the great *nebula* in Orion, and I certainly expected that you would do so. You did look up; and I was now assured that I had correctly followed your steps. But in that bitter *tirade* upon Chantilly, which appeared in yesterday's '*Musée*,' the satirist, making some disgraceful allusions to the cobbler's change of name upon assuming the buskin, quoted a Latin line about which we have often conversed. I mean the line

> Perdidit antiquum litera prima sonum.

I had told you that this was in reference to Orion, formerly written Urion; and, from certain pugencies connected with this explanation, I was aware that you could not have forgotten it. It was clear, therefore, that you would not fail to combine the two ideas of Orion and Chantilly. That you did combine them I saw by the character of the smile which passed over your lips. You thought of the poor cobbler's immolation. So far, you had been stooping in your gait; but now I saw you draw yourself up to your full height. I was then sure that you reflected upon the diminutive figure of Chantilly. At this point I interrupted your meditations to remark that as, in fact, he *was* a very little fellow—that Chantilly—he would do better at the *Théâtre des Variétés*."

Not long after this, we were looking over an evening edition of the *Gazette des Tribunaux*, when the following paragraphs arrested our attention.

"EXTRAORDINARY MURDERS.—This morning, about three o'clock, the inhabitants of the Quartier St. Roch were roused from sleep by a succession of terrific shrieks, issuing, apparently, from the fourth story of a house in the Rue Morgue, known to be in the sole occupancy of one Madame L'Espanaye, and her daughter, Mademoiselle Camille L'Espanaye. After some delay, occasioned by a fruitless attempt to procure admission in the usual manner, the gateway was broken in with a crowbar, and eight or ten of the neighbors entered, accompanied by two *gendarmes*. By this time the cries had ceased; but, as the party rushed up the first flight of stairs, two or more rough voices, in angry contention, were distinguished, and seemed to proceed from the upper part of the house. As the second landing was reached, these sounds, also, had ceased, and everything remained perfectly quiet. The party spread

175

themselves, and hurried from room to room. Upon arriving at a large back chamber in the fourth story (the door of which, being found locked, with the key inside, was forced open), a spectacle presented itself which struck every one present not less with horror than with astonishment.

"The apartment was in the wildest disorder—the furniture broken and thrown about in all directions. There was only one bedstead; and from this the bed had been removed, and thown into the middle of the floor. On a chair lay a razor, besmeared with blood. On the hearth were two or three long and thick tresses of gray human hair, also dabbled with blood, and seeming to have been pulled out by the roots. Upon the floor were found four Napoleons, an earring of topaz, three large silver spoons, three smaller of *métal d' Alger*, and two bags, containing nearly four thousand francs in gold. The drawers of a *bureau*, which stood in one corner, were open, and had been, apparently, rifled, although many articles still remained in them. A small iron safe was discovered under the *bed* (not under the bedstead). It was open, with the key still in the door. It had no contents beyond a few old letters, and other papers of little consequence.

"Of Madame L'Espanaye no traces were here seen; but an unusual quantity of soot being observed in the fire-place, a search was made in the chimney, and (horrible to relate!) the corpse of the daughter, head downward, was dragged therefrom; it having been thus forced up the narrow aperture for a considerable distance. The body was quite warm. Upon examining it, many excoriations were perceived, no doubt occasioned by the violence with which it had been thrust up and disengaged. Upon the face were many severe scratches, and, upon the throat, dark bruises, and deep indentations of finger nails, as if the deceased had been throttled to death.

"After a thorough investigation of every portion of the house without further discovery, the party made its way into a small paved yard in the rear of the building, where lay the corpse of the old lady, with her throat so entirely cut that, upon an attempt to raise her, the head fell off. The body, as well as the head, was fearfully mutilated—the former so much so as scarcely to retain any semblance of humanity.

"To this horrible mystery there is not as yet, we believe, the slightest clue."

The next day's paper had these additional particulars:

"*The Tragedy in the Rue Morgue.*—Many individuals have been examined in relation to this most extraordinary and frightful affair' " [the world '*affaire*' has not yet, in France, that levity of import which it conveys with us], "but nothing whatever has transpired to throw light upon it. We give below all the material testimony elicited.

"*Pauline Dubourg,* laundress, deposes that she has known both the deceased for three years, having washed for them during that period. The old lady and her daughter seemed on good terms—very affectionate toward each other. They were excellent pay. Could not speak in regard to their mode or means of living. Believes that Madame L. told fortunes for a living. Was reputed to have money put by. Never met any person in the house when she called for the clothes or took them home. Was sure that they had no servant in employ. There appeared to be no furniture in the building except in the fourth story.

"*Pierre Moreau,* tobacconist, deposes that he has been in the habit of selling small quantities of tobacco and snuff to Madame L'Espanaye for nearly four years. Was born in the neighborhood, and has always resided there. The deceased and her daughter had occupied the house in which the corpses were found, for more than six years. It was formerly occupied by a jeweler, who under-let the upper rooms to various persons. The house was the property of Madame L. She became dissatisfied with the abuse of the premises by her tenant, and moved into them herself, refusing to let any portion. The old lady was childish. Witness had seen the daughter some five or six times during the six years. The two lived an exceedingly retired life—were reputed to have money. Had heard it said among the neighbors that Madame L. told fortunes—did not believe it. Had never seen any person enter the door except the old lady and her daughter, a porter once or twice, and a physician some eight or ten times.

"Many other persons, neighbors, gave evidence to the same effect. No one was spoken of as frequenting the house. It was not known whether there were any living connections of Madame L. and her daughter. The shutters of the front windows were seldom opened. Those in the rear were always closed, with the exception of the large back room, fourth story. The house was a good house—not very old.

177

"*Isidore Musèt, gendarme,* deposes that he was called to the house about three o'clock in the morning, and found some twenty or thirty persons at the gateway, endeavoring to gain admittance. Forced it open, at length, with a bayonet—not with a crowbar. Had but little difficulty in getting open, on account of its being a double or folding gate, and bolted neither at bottom nor top. The shrieks were continued until the gate was forced—and then suddenly ceased. They seemed to be screams of some person (or persons) in great agony—were loud and drawn out, not short and quick. Witness led the way upstairs. Upon reaching the first landing, heard two voices in loud and angry contention—the one of a gruff voice, the other much shriller—a very strange voice. Could distinguish some words of the former, which was that of a Frenchman. Was positive that it was not a woman's voice. Could distinguish the words '*sacré*' and '*diable.*' The shrill voice was that of a foreigner. Could not be sure whether it was the voice of a man or of a woman. Could not make out what was said, but believed the language to be Spanish. The state of the room and of the bodies was described by this witness as we described them yesterday.

"*Henri Duval,* a neighbor, and by trade a silversmith, deposes that he was one of the party who first entered the house. Corroborates the testimony of Muset in general. As soon as they forced an entrance, they reclosed the door, to keep out the crowd, which collected very fast, notwithstanding the lateness of the hour. The shrill voice, this witness thinks, was that of an Italian. Was certain it was not French. Could not be sure that it was a man's voice. It might have been a woman's. Was not acquainted with the Italian language. Could not distinguish the words, but was convinced by the intonation that the speaker was an Italian. Knew Madame L. and her daughter. Had conversed with both frequently. Was sure that the shrill voice was not that of either of the deceased.

"—— *Odenheimer, restaurateur.*—This witness volunteered his testimony. Not speaking French, was examined through an interpreter. Is a native of Amsterdam. Was passing the house at the time of the shrieks. They lasted for several minutes—probably ten. They were long and loud—very awful and distressing. Was one of those who entered the building. Corroborated the previous evidence in every respect but one. Was sure that the shrill voice was that of a man—of a Frenchman. Could

178

not distinguish the words uttered. They were loud and quick—unequal—spoken apparently in fear as well as in anger. The voice was harsh—not so much shrill as harsh. Could not call it a shrill voice. The gruff voice said repeatedly, '*sacré,*' '*diable,*' and once '*mon Dieu.*'

"*Jules Mignaud,* banker, of the firm of Mignaud et Fils, Rue Deloraine. Is the elder Mignaud. Madame L'Espanaye had some property. Had opened an account with his banking house in the spring of the year —— (eight years previously). Made frequent deposits in small sums. Had checked for nothing until the third day before her death, when she took out in person the sum of 4,000 francs. This sum was paid in gold, and a clerk sent home with the money.

"*Adolphe Le Bon,* clerk to Mignaud et Fils, deposes that on the day in question, about noon, he accompanied Madame L'Espanaye to her residence with the 4,000 francs, put up in two bags. Upon the door being opened, Mademoiselle L. appeared and took from his hands one of the bags, while the old lady relieved him of the other. He then bowed and departed. Did not see any person in the street at the time. It is a by-street—very lonely.

"*William Bird,* tailor, deposes that he was one of the party who entered the house. Is an Englishman. Has lived in Paris two years. Was one of the first to ascend the stairs. Heard the voices in contention. The gruff voice was that of a Frenchman. Could make out several words, but cannot now remember all. Heard distinctly '*sacré*' and '*mon Dieu.*' There was a sound at the moment as if of several persons struggling—a scraping and scuffling sound. The shrill voice was very loud—louder than the gruff one. Is sure that it was not the voice of an Englishman. Appeared to be that of a German. Might have been a woman's voice. Does not understand German.

"Four of the above-named witnesses, being recalled, deposed that the door of the chamber in which was found the body of Mademoiselle L. was locked on the inside when the party reached it. Everything was perfectly silent—no groans or noises of any kind. Upon forcing the door no person was seen. The windows, both of the back and front room, were down and firmly fastened from within. A door between the two rooms was closed but not locked. The door leading from the front room into the passage was locked, with the key on the inside. A small room in the front of the house, on the fourth story, at the head of the passage, was open, the door being ajar. This room was crowded with old beds, boxes, and so forth. These were carefully removed and searched. There was not an inch of any portion of the house which was not carefully searched. Sweeps were sent up and down the chimneys. The house was a four-story one, with garrets *(mansardes)*. A trap-door on the roof was nailed down very securely—did not appear to have been opened for years. The time elapsing between the hearing of the voices in contention and the breaking open of the room door was variously stated by the witnesses. Some made it as short as three minutes—some as long as five. The door was opened with difficulty.

"*Alfonzo Garcio,* undertaker, deposes that he resides in the Rue Morgue. Is a native of Spain. Was one of the party who entered the house. Did not proceed upstairs. Is nervous, and was apprehensive of the consequences of agitation. Heard the voices in contention. The gruff voice was that of a Frencman. Could not distinguish what was said. The shrill voice was that of an Englishman—is sure of this. Does not understand the English language, but judges by the intonation.

"*Alberto Montani,* confectioner, deposes that he was among the first to ascend the stairs. Heard the voices in question. The gruff voice was that of a Frenchman. Distinguished several words. The speaker appeared to be expostulating. Could not make out the words of the shrill voice. Spoke quick and unevenly. Thinks it the voice of a Russian. Corroborates the general testimony. Is an Italian. Never conversed with a native of Russia.

"Several witnesses, recalled, here testified that the chimneys of all the rooms on the fourth story were too narrow to admit the passage of a human being. By 'sweeps' were meant cylindrical sweeping-brushes, such as are employed by those who clean chimneys. These brushes were passed up and down every flue in the house. There is no back passage by which any one could have descended while the party proceeded upstairs. The body of Mademoiselle L'Espanaye was so firmly wedged in the chimney that it could not be got down until four or five of the party united their strength.

"*Paul Dumas,* physician, deposes that he was called to view the bodies about daybreak. They were both then lying on the sacking of the bedstead in the chamber where Mademoiselle L. was found. The corpse of the young lady was much bruised and excoriated. The fact that it had been thrust up the chimney would sufficiently account for these appearances. The throat was greatly chafed. There were several deep scratches just below the chin, together with a series of livid spots which were evidently the impression of fingers. The face was fearfully discolored, and the eyeballs protruded. The tongue had been partially bitten through. A large bruise was discovered upon the pit of the stomach, produced, apparently, by the pressure of a knee. In the opinion of M. Dumas, Mademoiselle L'Espanaye had been throttled to death by some person or persons unknown. The corpse of the mother was horribly mutilated. All the bones of the right leg and arm were more or less shattered. The left *tibia* much splintered, as well as all the ribs of the left side. Whole body dreadfully bruised and discolored. It was not possible to say how the injuries had been inflicted. A heavy club of wood, or a broad bar of iron—a chair—any large, heavy, and obtuse weapon would have produced such results, if wielded by the hands of a very powerful man. No woman could have inflicted the blows with any weapon. The head of the deceased, when seen by witness, was entirely separated from the body, and was also greatly shattered. The throat had evidently been cut with some very sharp instrument—probably with a razor.

"*Alexandre Etienne,* surgeon, was called with M. Dumas to view the bodies. Corroborated the testimony, and the opinion of M. Dumas.

"Nothing further of importance was elicited, although several other persons were examined. A murder so mysterious, and so perplexing in all its particulars, was never before committed in Paris—if indeed a murder has been committed at all. The police are entirely at fault—an unusual occurrence in affairs of this nature. There is not, however, the shadow of a clue apparent."

The evening edition of the paper stated that the greatest excitement still continued in the Quartier St. Roch—that the premises in question had been carefully re-searched, and fresh examinations of witnesses instituted, but all to no purpose. A postscript, however, mentioned that Adolphe Le Bon had been arrested and imprisoned—although nothing appeared to incriminate him beyond the facts already detailed.

Dupin seemed singularly interested in the progress of this affair—at least so I judged from his manner, for he made no comments. It was only after the announcement that Le Bon had been imprisoned, that he asked me my opinion respecting the murders. I could merely agree with all Paris in considering them an insoluble mystery. I saw no means by which it would be possible to trace the murderer.

"We must not judge of the means," said Dupin, "by this shell of an examination. The Parisian police, so much extolled for *acumen*, are cunning, but no more. There is no method in their proceeding, beyond the method of the moment. They make a vast parade of measures; but, not unfrequently, these are so ill-adapted to the objects proposed, as to put us in mind of Monsieur Jourdain's calling for his *robe-de-chambre—pour mieux entendre la musique.* The results attained by them are not infrequently surprising, but, for the most part, are brought about by simple diligence and activity. When these qualities are unavailing, their schemes fail. Vidocq, for example, was a good guesser, and a persevering man. But, without educated thought, he erred continually by the very intensity of his investigations. He impaired his vision by holding the object too close. He might see, perhaps, one or two points with unusual clearness, but in so doing he, necessarily, lost sight of the matter as a whole. Thus there is such a thing as being too profound. Truth is not always in a well. In fact, as regards the more important knowledge, I do believe that she is invariably superficial. The depth lies in the valleys where we seek her, and not upon the mountain-tops where she is found. The modes and sources of this kind of error are well typified in the contemplation of the heavenly bodies. To look at a star by glances—to view it in a side-long way, by turning toward it the exterior portions of the *retina* (more susceptible of feeble impressions of light than the interior), is to behold the star distinctly—is to have the best appreciation of its luster—a luster which grows dim just in proportions as we turn our vision *fully* upon it. A greater number of rays actually fall upon the eye in the latter case, but in the former, there is the more refined capacity for comprehension. By undue profundity we perplex and enfeeble thought; and it is possible to make even Venus herself vanish from the firmament by a scrutiny too sustained, too concentrated, or too direct.

"As for these murders, let us enter into some examinations for ourselves, before we make up an opinion respecting them. An inquiry will afford us amusement," [I thought this an odd term, so applied, but said nothing] "and besides, Le Bon once rendered me a service for which I am not ungrateful. We will go and see the premises with our own eyes. I know G——, the Prefect of Police, and shall have no difficulty in obtaining the necessary permission."

The permission was obtained, and we proceeded at once to the Rue Morgue. This is one of those miserable thoroughfares which intervene between the Rue Richelieu and the Rue St. Roch. It was late in the afternoon when we reached it, as this quarter is at a great distance from that in which we resided. The house was readily found; for there were still many persons gazing up at the closed shutters, with an objectless curiosity, from the opposite side of the way. It was an ordinary Parisian house, with a gateway, on one side of which was a glazed watch-box, with a sliding panel in the window, indicating a *loge de concierge.*

Before going in we walked up the street, turned down an alley, and then, again turning, passed in the rear of the building—Dupin, meanwhile, examining the whole neighborhood, as well as the house, with a minuteness of attention for which I could see no possible object.

Retracing our steps, we came again to the front of the dwelling, rang, and, having shown our credentials, were admitted by the agents in charge. We went upstairs—into the chamber where the body of Mademoiselle L'Espanaye had been found, and where both the deceased still lay. The disorders of the room had, as usual, been suffered to exist. I saw nothing beyond what had been stated in the *Gazette des Tribunaux.* Dupin scrutinized every thing—not excepting the bodies of the victims. We then went into the other rooms, and into the yard; a *gendarme* accompanying us throughout. The examination occupied us until dark, when we took our departure. On our way home my companion stepped in for a moment at the office of one of the daily papers.

I have said that the whims of my friend were manifold, and that *Je les ménagais:*—for this phrase there is no English equivalent. It was his humor, now, to decline all conversation on the subject of the murder, until about noon the next day. He then

183

asked me, suddenly, if I had observed anything *peculiar* at the scene of the atrocity.

There was something in his manner of emphasizing the word "*peculiar,*" which caused me to shudder, without knowing why.

"No, nothing *peculiar,*" I said; "nothing more, at least, than we both saw stated in the paper."

"The *Gazette,*" he replied, "has not entered, I fear, into the unusual horror of the thing. But dismiss the idle opinions of this print. It appears to me that this mystery is considered insoluble, for the very reason which should cause it to be regarded as easy of solution—I mean for the *outré* character of its features. The police are confounded by the seeming absence of motive—not for the murder itself—but for the atrocity of the murder. They are puzzled, too, by the seeming impossibility of reconciling the voices heard in contention, with the facts that no one was discovered upstairs but the assassinated Mademoiselle L'Espanaye, and that there were no means of egress without the notice of the party ascending. The wild disorder of the room; the corpse thrust, with the head downward, up the chimney; the frightful mutilation of the body of the old lady; these considerations, with those just mentioned, and others which I need not mention, have sufficed to paralyze the powers, by putting completely at fault the boasted *acumen,* of the government agents. They have fallen into the gross but common error of confounding the unusual with the abstruse. But it is by these deviations from the plane of t̃ e ordinary, that reason feels its way, if at all, in its search for ̣ıe true. In investigations such as we are now pursuing, it shc ̣ld not be so much asked 'what has occurred,' as 'what has occurred that has never occurred before.' In fact, the facility with which I shall arrive, or have arrived, at the solution of this mystery, is in the direct ratio of its apparent insolubility in the eyes of the police."

I stared at the speaker in mute astonishment.

"I am now awaiting," continued he, looking toward the door of our apartment—"I am now awaiting a person who, although perhaps not the perpetrator of these butcheries, must have been in some measure implicated in their perpetration. Of the worst portion of the crimes committed, it is probable that he is innocent. I hope that I am right in this supposition; for upon it I build my expectation of reading the entire riddle. I look for the man here—in this room—every moment. It is true that he may not arrive; but the probability is that he will. Should he come, it will be necessary to detain him. Here are pistols; and we both know how to use them when occasion demands their use."

I took the pistols, scarcely knowing what I did, or believing what I heard, while Dupin went on, very much as if in a soliloquy. I have already spoken of his abstract manner at such times. His discourse was addressed to myself; but his voice, although by no means loud, had that intonation which is commonly employed in speaking to some one at a great distance. His eyes, vacant in expression, regarded only the wall.

"That the voices heard in contention," he said, "by the party upon the stairs, were not the voices of the women themselves, was fully proved by the evidence. This relieves us of all doubt upon the question whether the old lady could have first destroyed the daughter, and afterward have committed suicide. I speak of this point chiefly for the sake of method; for the strength of Madame L'Espanaye would have been utterly unequal to the task of thrusting her daughter's corpse up the chimney as it was found; and the nature of the wounds upon her own person entirely precludes the idea of self-destruction. Murder, then, has been committed by some third party; and the voices of this third party were those heard in contention. Let me now advert—not to the whole testimony respecting these voices—but to what was *peculiar* in that testimony. Did you observe any thing peculiar about it?"

I remarked that, while all the witnesses agreed in supposing the gruff voice to be that of a Frenchman, there was much disagreement in regard to the shrill, or, as one individual termed it, the harsh voice.

"That's the evidence itself," said Dupin, "but it was not the peculiarity of the evidence. You have observed nothing distinctive. Yet there *was* something to be observed. The witnesses, as you remark, agreed about the gruff voice; they were here unanimous. But in regard to the shrill voice, the peculiarity is—not that they disagreed—but that, while an Italian, an Englishman, a Spaniard, a Hollander, and a Frenchman attempted to describe it, each one spoke of it as that *of a foreigner.* Each sure that it was not the voice of one of his own countrymen. Each likens it—not to the voice of an individual of any nation with whose language he is conversant—but the converse. The Frenchman supposes it the voice of a Spaniard, and 'might have distinguished some words *had he been acquainted with the Spanish.*' The Dutchman maintains it to have been that of a Frenchman; but we find it stated that *'not understanding French this witness was examined through an interpreter.'* The Englishman thinks it the voice of a German, and *'does not understand German.'* The Spaniard 'is sure' that it was that of an Englishman, but 'judges by the intonation' altogether, *'as he has no knowledge of the English.'* The Italian believes it the voice of a Russian, but *'has never conversed with a native of Russia.'* A second Frenchman differs, moreover, with the first, and is positive that the voice was that of an Italian; but, *not being cognizant of that tongue,* is, like the Spaniard, 'convinced by the intonation.' Now, how strangely unusual must that voice have really been, about which such testimony as this *could* have been elicited!—in whose *tones,* even, denizens of the five great divisions of Europe could recognize nothing familiar! You will say that it might have been the voice of an Asiatic—of an African. Neither Asiatics nor Africans abound in Paris; but, without denying the inference, I will now merely call your attention to three points. The voice is termed by one witness 'harsh rather than shrill.' It is represented by two others to have been 'quick and *unequal.*' No words—no sounds resembling words—were by any witness mentioned as distinguishable.

"I know not," continued Dupin, "what impression I may have made, so far, upon your own understanding; but I do not hesitate to say that legitimate deductions even from this portion of the testimony—the portion respecting the gruff and shrill voices—are in themselves sufficient to engender a suspicion which should give direction to all farther progress in the investigation of the mystery. I said 'legitimate deductions'; but my meaning is not thus fully expressed. I designed to imply that the deductions are the *sole* proper ones, and that the suspicion arises *inevitably* from them as the single result. What the suspicion is, however, I will not say just yet. I merely wish you to bear in mind that, with myself, it was sufficiently forcible to give a definite form—a certain tendency—to my inquiries in the chamber.

"Let us now transport ourselves, in fancy, to this chamber. What shall we first seek here? The means of egress employed by the murderers. It is not too much to say that neither of us believe in praeternatural events. Madame and Mademoiselle L'Espanaye were not destroyed by spirits. The doers of the deed were material and escaped materially. Then how? Fortunately there is but one mode of reasoning upon the point, and that mode *must* lead us to a definite decision. Let us examine, each by each, the possible means of egress. It is clear that the assassins were in the room where Mademoiselle L'Espanaye was found, or at least in the room adjoining, when the party ascended the stairs. It is, then, only from these two apartments that we have to seek issues. The police have laid bare the floors, the ceiling, and the masonry of the walls, in every direction. No *secret* issues could have escaped their vigilance. But, not trusting to *their* eyes, I examined with my own. There were, then, no secret issues. Both doors leading from the rooms into the passage were securely locked, with the keys inside. Let us turn to the chimneys. These, although of ordinary width for some eight or ten feet above the hearths, will not admit, throughout their extent, the body of a large cat. The impossibility of egress, by means already stated, being thus absolute, we are reduced to the windows. Through those of the front room no one could have escaped without notice from the crowd in the street. The murderers *must* have passed, then, through those of the back room. Now, brought to this conclusion in so unequivocal a manner as we are, it is not our part, as reasoners, to reject it on account of apparent impossibilities. It is only left for us to prove that these apparent 'impossibilities' are, in reality, not such.

"There are two windows in the chamber. One of them is unobstructed by furniture, and is wholly visible. The lower portion of the other is hidden from view by the head of the unwieldy bedstead which is thrust close up against it. The former was found securely fastened from within. It resisted the utmost force of those who endeavored to raise it. A large gimlet-hole had been pierced in its frame to the left, and a very stout nail was found fitted therein, nearly to the head. Upon examining the other window, a similar nail was seen similarly fitted in it; and a vigorous attempt to raise this sash failed also. The police were now entirely satisfied that egress had not been in these directions. And, *therefore,* it was thought a matter of supererogation to withdraw the nails and open the windows.

"My own examination was somewhat more particular, and was so for the reason I have just given—because here it was, I knew, that all apparent impossibilities *must* be proved to be not such in reality.

"I proceed to think thus—*a posteriori.* The murderers *did* escape from one of these windows. This being so, they could not have refastened the sashes from the inside, as they were found fastened;—the consideration which put a stop, through its obviousness, to the scrutiny of the police in this quarter. Yet the sashes *were* fastened. They *must,* then, have the power of fastening themselves. There was no escape from this conclusion. I stepped to the unobstructed casement, withdrew the nail with some difficulty, and attempted to raise the sash. It resisted all my efforts, as I had anticipated. A concealed spring must, I now knew, exist; and this corroboration of my idea convinced me that my premises, at least, were correct, however mysterious still appeared the circumstances attending the nails. A careful search soon brought to light the hidden spring. I pressed it, and, satisfied with the discovery, forbore to upraise the sash.

"I now replaced the nail and regarded it attentively. A person passing out through this window might have reclosed it, and the spring would have caught—but the nail could not have been replaced. The conclusion was plain, and again narrowed in the field of my investigations. The assassins *must* have escaped through the other window. Supposing, then, the springs upon each sash to be the same, as was probable, there *must* be found a difference between the nails, or at least between the modes of their fixture. Getting upon the sacking of the bedspread, I looked over the headboard minutely at the second casement. Passing my hand down behind the board, I readily discovered and pressed the spring, which was, as I had supposed, identical in character with its neighbor. I now looked at the nail. It was as stout as the other, and apparently fitted in the same manner—driven in nearly up to the head.

"You will say that I was puzzled; but, if you think so, you must have misunderstood the nature of the inductions. To use a sporting phrase, I had not been once 'at fault.' The scent had never for an instant been lost. There was no flaw in any link of the chain. I had traced the secret to its ultimate result,—and that result was *the nail.* It had, I say, in every respect, the appearance of its fellow in the other window; but this fact was an absolute nullity (conclusive as it might seem to be) when compared with the consideration that here, at this point, terminated the clue. 'There *must* be something wrong,' I said, 'about the nail.' I touched it; and the head, with about a quarter of an inch of the shank, came off in my fingers. The rest of the shank was in the gimlet-hole, where it had been broken off. The fracture was an old one (for its edges were incrusted with rust), and had apparently been accomplished by the blow of a hammer, which had partially imbedded, in the top of the bottom sash, the head portion of the nail. I now carefully replaced this head portion in the indentation whence I had taken it, and the resemblance to a perfect nail was complete—the fissure was invisible. Pressing the spring, I gently raised the sash for a few inches; the head went up with it, remaining firm in its bed. I closed the window, and the semblance of the whole nail was again perfect.

"This riddle, so far, was now unriddled. The assassin had escaped through the window which looked upon the bed. Dropping of its own accord upon his exit (or perhaps purposely closed), it had become fastened by the spring; and it was the retention of this spring which had been mistaken by the police for that of the nail,—farther inquiry being thus considered unnecessary.

"The next question is that of the mode of descent. Upon this point I had been satisfied in my walk with you around the building. About five feet and a half from the casement in question there runs a lightning-rod. From this rod it would have been impossible for anyone to reach the window itself, to say nothing of entering it. I observed, however, that the shutters of the fourth story were of the peculiar kind called by Parisian carpenters *ferrades*—a kind rarely employed at the present day, but frequently seen upon very old mansions at Lyons and Bordeaux. They are in the form of an ordinary door (a single, not a folding door), except that the lower half is latticed or worked in open trellis—thus affording an excellent hold for the hands. In the present instance these shutters are fully three feet and a half broad. When we saw them from the rear of the house, they were both about half open—that is to say, they stood off at right angles from the wall. It is probable that the police, as well as myself, examined the back of the tenement; but, if so, in looking at these *ferrades* in the line of their breadth (as they must have done), they did not perceive this great breadth itself, or, at all events, failed to take it into due consideration. In fact, having once satisfied themselves that no egress could have been made in this quarter, they would naturally bestow here a very cursory examination. It was clear to me, however, that the shutter belonging to the window at the head of the bed, would if swung fully back to the wall, reach to within two feet of the lightning-rod. It was also evident that, by exertion of a very unusual degree of activity and courage, an entrance into the window, from the rod, might have been thus effected. By reaching to the distance of two feet and a half (we now suppose the shutter open to its whole extent) a robber might have taken a firm grasp upon the trellis-work. Letting go, then, his hold upon the rod, placing his feet securely against the wall, and springing boldly from it, he might have swung the shutter so as to close it, and, if we imagine the window open at the time, might even have swung himself into the room.

"I wish you to bear especially in mind that I have spoken of a *very* unusual degree of activity as requisite to success in so hazardous and so difficult a feat. It is my design to show you first, that the thing might possibly have been accomplished:— but, secondly and *chiefly*, I wish to impress upon your understanding the *very extraordinary*—the almost praeternatural character of that agility which could have accomplished it.

"You will say, no doubt, using the language of the law, that 'to make out my case,' I should rather undervalue than insist upon a full estimation of the activity required in this matter. This may be the practice in law, but it is not the usage of reason. My ultimate object is only the truth. My immediate purpose is to lead you to place in juxtaposition, that *very unusual* activity of which I have just spoken, with that *very peculiar* shrill (or harsh) and *unequal* voice, about whose nationality no two persons could be found to agree, and in whose utterance no syllabification could be detected."

At these words a vague and half-formed conception of the meaning of Dupin flitted over my mind. I seemed to be upon the verge of comprehension, without power to comprehend—as men, at times, find themselves upon the brink of remembrance, without being able, in the end, to remember. My friend went on with his discourse.

"You will see," he said, "that I have shifted the question from the mode of egress to that of ingress. It was my design to convey the idea that both were effected in the same manner, at the same point. Let us now revert to the interior of the room. Let us survey the appearances here. The drawers of the bureau, it is said, had been rifled, although many articles of apparel still remained within them. The conclusion here is absurd. It is a mere guess—a very silly one—and no more. How are we to know that the articles found in the drawers were not all these drawers had originally contained? Madame L'Espanaye and her daughter lived an exceedingly retired life—saw no company—seldom went out—had little use for numerous changes of habiliment. Those found were at least of as good quality as any likely to be possessed by these ladies. If a thief had taken any, why did he not take the best—why did he not take all? In a word, why did he abandon four thousand francs in gold to encumber himself with a bundle of linen? The gold *was* abandoned. Nearly the whole sum mentioned by Monsieur Mignaud, the banker, was discovered, in bags, upon the floor. I wish you therefore, to discard from your thoughts the blundering idea of *motive*, engendered in the brains of the police by that portion of the evidence which speaks of money delivered at the door of the house. Coincidences ten times as remarkable as this (the delivery of the money, and murder committed within three days upon the party receiving it), happen to all of us every hour of our lives, without attracting even momentary notice. Coincidences, in general, are great stumbling-blocks in the way of that class of thinkers who have been educated to know nothing of the theory of probabilities—that theory to which the most glorious objects of human research are indebted for the most glorious of illustrations. In the present instance, had the gold been gone, the fact of its delivery three days before would have formed something more than a coincidence. It would have been corroborative of this idea of motive. But, under the real circumstances of the case, if we are to suppose gold the motive of this outrage, we must also imagine the perpetrator so vacillating an idiot as to have abandoned his gold and his motive together.

"Keeping now steadily in mind the point to which I have drawn your attention—that peculiar voice, that unusual agility, and that startling absence of motive in a murder so singularly atrocious as this—let us glance at the butchery itself. Here is a woman strangled to death by manual strength, and thrust up a chimney head downward. Ordinary assassins employ no such mode of murder as this. Least of all, do they thus dispose of the murdered. In the manner of thrusting the corpse up the chimney, you will admit that there was something *excessively outré*—something altogether irreconcilable with our common notions of human action, even when we suppose the actors the most depraved of men. Think, too, how great must have been that strength which could have thrust the body *up* such an aperture so forcibly that the united vigor of several persons was found barely sufficient to drag it *down!*

"Turn, now, to other indications of the employment of a vigor most marvelous. On the hearth were thick tresses—very thick tresses—of gray human hair. These had been torn out by the roots. You are aware of the great force necessary in tearing thus from the head even twenty or thirty hairs together. You saw the locks in question as well as myself. Their roots (a hideous sight!) were clotted with fragments of the flesh of the scalp—sure token of the prodigious power which had been exerted in uprooting perhaps half a million of hairs at a time. The throat of the old lady was not merely cut, but the head absolutely severed from the body: the instrument was a mere razor. I wish you also to look at the *brutal* ferocity of these deeds. Of the bruises upon the body of Madame L'Espanaye I do not speak. Monsieur Dumas, and his worthy coadjutor Monsieur Etienne, have pronounced that they were inflicted by some obtuse instrument; and so far these gentlemen are very correct. The obtuse instrument was clearly the stone pavement in the yard, upon which the victim had fallen from the window which looked in upon the bed. This idea, however simple it may now seem, escaped the police for the same reason that the breadth of the shutters escaped them—because, by the affair of the nails, their perceptions had been hermetically sealed against the possibility of the windows having ever been opened at all.

"If now, in addition to all these things, you have properly reflected upon the odd disorder of the chamber, we have gone so far as to combine the ideas of an agility astounding, a strength superhuman, a ferocity brutal, a butchery without motive, a *grotesquerie* in horror absolutely alien from humanity, and a voice foreign in tone to the ears of men of many nations, and devoid of all distinct or intelligible syllabification. What result, then, has ensued? What impression have I made upon your fancy?"

I felt a creeping of the flesh as Dupin asked me the question. "A madman," I said, "has done this deed—some raving maniac, escaped from a neighboring *Maison de Santé.*"

"In some respects," he replied, "your idea is not irrelevant. But the voices of madmen, even in their wildest paroxysms, are never found to tally with that peculiar voice heard upon the stairs. Madmen are of some nation, and their language, however incoherent in its words, has always the coherence of syllabification. Besides, the hair of a madman is not such as I now hold in my hand. I disentangled this little tuft from the rigidly clutched fingers of Madame L'Espanaye. Tell me what you can make of it."

"Dupin!" I said, completely unnerved; "this hair is most unusual—this is no *human* hair."

"I have not asserted that it is," said he; "but, before we decide this point, I wish you to to glance at the little sketch I have here traced upon this paper. It is a *facsimile* drawing of what has been described in one portion of the testimony as 'dark bruises and deep indentations of finger nails' upon the throat of Mademoiselle L'Espanaye, and in another (by Messrs. Dumas and Etienne) as a 'series of livid spots, evidently the impression of fingers.'

"You will perceive," continued my friend, spreading out the paper upon the table before us, "that this drawing gives the idea of a firm and fixed hold. There is no *slipping* apparent. Each finger has retained—possibly until the death of the victim—the fearful grasp by which it originally imbedded itself. Attempt, now, to place all your fingers, at the same time, in the respective impressions as you see them."

I made the attempt in vain.

"We are possibly not giving this matter a fair trial," he said. "The paper is spread out upon a plane surface; but the human throat is cylindrical. Here is a billet of wood, the circumference of which is about that of the throat. Wrap the drawing around it, and try the experiment again."

I did so; but the difficulty was even more obvious than before. "This," I said, "is the mark of no human hand."

"Read now," replied Dupin, "this passage from Cuvier."

It was a minute anatomical and generally descriptive account of the large fulvous Ourang-Outang of the East Indian Islands. The gigantic stature, the prodigious strength and activity, the wild ferocity, and the imitative propensities of these mammalia are sufficiently well-known to all. I understood the full horrors of the murder at once.

"The description of the digits," said I, as I made an end of the reading, "is in exact accordance with this drawing. I see that no animal but an Ourang-Outang, of the species here mentioned, could have impressed the indentations as you have traced them. This tuft of tawny hair, too, is identical in character with that of the beast of Cuvier. But I cannot possibly comprehend the particulars of this frightful mystery. Besides, there were *two* voices heard in contention, and one of them was unquestionably the voice of a Frenchman."

"True; and you will remember an expression attributed almost unanimously, by the evidence, to this voice,—the expression, *'mon Dieu!'* This, under the circumstances, has been justly characterized by one of the witnesses (Montani, the confectioner) as an expression of remonstrance or expostulation. Upon these two words, therefore, I have mainly built my hopes of a full solution of the riddle. A Frenchman was cognizant of the murder. It is possible—indeed it is far more than probable—that he was innocent of all participation in the bloody transactions which took place. The Ourang-Outang may have escaped from him. He may have traced it to the chamber; but, under the agitating circumstances which ensued, he could never have recaptured it. It is still at large. I will not pursue these guesses—for I have no right to call them more—since the shades of reflection upon which they are based are scarcely of sufficient depth to be appreciable by my own intellect, and since I could not pretend to make them intelligible to the understanding of another. We will call them guesses, then, and speak of them as such. If the Frenchman in question is indeed, as I suppose, innocent of this atrocity, this advertisement, which I left last night, upon our return home, at the office of *Le Monde* (a paper devoted to the shipping interest, and much sought by sailors), will bring him to our residence."

He handed me a paper, and I read thus:

"CAUGHT—*In the Bois de Boulogne, early in the morning of the —— inst.* (the morning of the murder), *a very large, tawny Ourang-Outang of the Bornese species. The owner (who is ascertained to be a sailor, belonging to a Maltese vessel) may have the animal again, upon identifying it satisfactorily, and paying a few charges arising from its capture and keeping. Call at No —— Rue ——, Faubourg St. Germain—au troisième.*"

"How was it possible," I asked, "that you should know the

man to be a sailor, and belonging to a Maltese vessel?"

"I do *not* know it," said Dupin. "I am not *sure* of it. Here, however, is a small piece of ribbon, which from its form, and from its greasy appearance, has evidently been used in tying the hair in one of those long *queues* of which sailors are so fond. Moreover, this knot is one which few besides sailors can tie, and is peculiar to the Maltese. I picked the ribbon up at the foot of the lightning-rod. It could not have belonged to either of the deceased. Now if, after all, I am wrong in my induction from this ribbon, that the Frenchman was a sailor belonging to a Maltese vessel, still I can have done no harm in saying what I did in the advertisement. If I am in error, he will merely suppose that I have been misled by some circumstance into which he will not take the trouble to inquire. But if I am right, a great point is gained. Cognizant although innocent of the murder, the Frenchman will naturally hesitate about replying to the advertisement—about demanding the Ourang-Outang. He will reason thus:—'I am innocent; I am poor; my Ourang-Outang is of great value—to one in my circumstances a fortune in itself—why should I lose it through idle apprehensions of danger? Here it is, within my grasp. It was found in the Bois de Boulogne—at a vast distance from the scene of that butchery. How can it ever be suspected that a brute beast should have done that deed? The police are at fault—they have failed to procure the slightest clue. Should they even trace the animal, it would be impossible to prove me cognizant of the murder, or to implicate me in guilt on account of that cognizance. Above all, *I am known*. The advertiser designates me as the possessor of the beast. I am not sure to what limit his knowledge may extend. Should I avoid claiming a property of so great value, which it is known that I possess, I will render the animal at least, liable to suspicion. It is not my policy to attract attention either to myself or to the beast. I will answer the advertisement, get the Ourang-Outang, and keep it close until this matter has blown over.'"

At this moment we heard a step upon the stairs.

"Be ready," said Dupin, "with your pistols, but neither use them nor show them until at a signal from myself."

The front door of the house had been left open, and the visitor had entered, without ringing, and advanced several steps upon the staircase. Now, however, he seemed to hesitate.

195

Presently we heard him descending. Dupin was moving quickly to the door, when we again heard him coming up. He did not turn back a second time, but stepped up with decision, and rapped at the door of our chamber.

"Come in," said Dupin, in a cheerful and hearty tone.

A man entered. He was a sailor, evidently,—a tall, stout, and muscular-looking person, with a certain daredevil expression of countenance, not altogether unprepossessing. His face, greatly sunburnt, was more than half hidden by whiskers and *mustachio*. He had with him a huge oaken cudgel, but appeared to be otherwise unarmed. He bowed awkwardly, and bade us "good evening," in French accents, which, although somewhat Neufchatelish, were still sufficiently indicative of a Parisian origin.

"Sit down, my friend," said Dupin. "I suppose you have called about the Ourang-Outang. Upon my word, I almost envy you the possession of him; a remarkably fine, and no doubt a very valuable animal. How old do you suppose him to be?"

The sailor drew a long breath, with the air of a man relieved of some intolerable burden, and then replied, in an assured tone:

"I have no way of telling—but he can't be more than four or five years old. Have you got him here?"

"Oh, no; we had no conveniences for keeping him here. He is at a livery stable in the Rue Dubourg, just by. You can get him in the morning. Of course you are prepared to identify the property?"

"To be sure I am, sir."

"I shall be sorry to part with him," said Dupin.

"I don't mean that you should be at all this trouble for nothing, sir," said the man. "Couldn't expect it. Am very willing to pay a reward for the finding of the animal—that is to say, anything in reason."

"Well," replied my friend, "that is all very fair, to be sure. Let me think!—what should I have? Oh! I will tell you. My reward shall be this. You shall give me all the information in your power about these murders in the Rue Morgue."

Dupin said the last words in a very low tone, and very quietly. Just as quietly, too, he walked toward the door, locked it, and put the key in his pocket. He then drew a pistol from his bosom and placed it, without the least flurry, upon the table.

196

The sailor's face flushed up as if he were struggling with suffocation. He started to his feet and grasped his cudgel; but the next moment he fell back into this seat, trembling violently, and with the countenance of death itself. He spoke not a word. I pitied him from the bottom of my heart.

"My friend," said Dupin, in a kind tone, "you are alarming yourself unnecessarily—you are indeed. We mean you no harm whatever. I pledge you the honor of a gentleman, and of a Frenchman, that we intend you no injury. I perfectly well know that you are innocent of the atrocities in the Rue Morgue. It will not do, however, to deny that you are in some measure implicated in them. From what I have already said, you must know that I have had means of information about this matter—means of which you could never have dreamed. Now the thing stands thus. You have done nothing which you could have avoided—nothing, certainly, which renders you culpable. You were not even guilty of robbery, when you might have robbed with impunity. You have nothing to conceal. You have no reason for concealment. On the other hand, you are bound by every principle of honor to confess all you know. An innocent man is now imprisoned, charged with that crime of which you can point out the perpetrator."

The sailor had recovered his presence of mind, in a great measure, while Dupin uttered these words; but his original boldness of bearing was all gone.

"So help me God!" said he, after a brief pause, "I *will* tell you all I know about this affair;—but I do not expect you to believe one half I say—I would be a fool indeed if I did. Still, I *am* innocent, and I am determined to make a clean breast if I die for it.".

What he stated was, in substance, this. He had lately made a voyage to the Indian Archipelago. A party, of which he formed one, landed at Borneo, and passed into the interior on an excursion of pleasure. Himself and a companion had captured the Ourang-Outang. This companion dying, the animal fell into his own exclusive possession. After great trouble, occasioned by the intractable ferocity of his captive during the home voyage, he at length succeeded in lodging it safely at his own residence in Paris, where, not to attract toward himself the unpleasant curiosity of his neighbors, he kept it carefully secluded, until such time as it should recover from a wound in the foot, received from a splinter on board ship. His ultimate design was to sell it.

Returning home from some sailors' frolic on the night, or rather in the morning, of the murder, he found the beast occupying his own bedroom, into which it had broken from a closet adjoining, where it had been, as was thought, securely confined. Razor in hand, and fully lathered, it was sitting before a looking-glass, attempting the operation of shaving, in which it had no doubt previously watched its master through the key-hole of the closet. Terrified at the sight of so dangerous a weapon in the possession of an animal so ferocious, and so well able to use it, the man, for some moments, was at a loss what to do. He had been accustomed, however, to quiet the creature, even in its fiercest moods, by the use of a whip, and to this he now resorted. Upon sight of it, the Ourang-Outang sprang at once through the door of the chamber, down the stairs, and thence, through a window, unfortunately open, into the street.

The Frenchman followed in despair; the ape, razor still in hand, occasionally stopping to look back and gesticulate at his pursuer, until the latter had nearly come up with it. It then again made off. In this manner the chase continued for a long time. The streets were profoundly quiet, as it was nearly three o'clock in the morning. In passing down an alley in the rear of the Rue Morgue, the fugitive's attention was arrested by a light gleaming from the open window of Madame L'Espanaye's chamber, in the fourth story of her house. Rushing to the build-ing, it perceived the lightning-rod, clambered up with incon-ceivable agility, grasped the shutter, which was thrown fully back against the wall, and, by its means, swung itself directly upon the headboard of the bed. The whole feat did not occupy a minute. The shutter was kicked open again by the Ourang-Outang as it entered the room.

The sailor, in the meantime, was both rejoiced and per-plexed. He had strong hopes of now recapturing the brute, as it could scarcely escape from the trap into which it had ventured, except by the rod, where it might be intercepted as it came down. On the other hand, there was much cause for anxiety as to what it might do in the house. This latter reflection urged the man still to follow the fugitive. A lightning-rod is ascended without difficulty, especially by a sailor; but, when he had ar-rived as high as the window, which lay far to his left, his career

198

was stopped; the most that he could accomplish was to reach over so as to obtain a glimpse of the interior of the room. At this glimpse he nearly fell from his hold through excess of horror. Now it was that those hideous shrieks arose upon the night, which had startled from slumber the inmates of the Rue Morgue. Madame L'Espanaye and her daughter, habited in their night clothes, had apparently been occupied in arranging some papers in the iron chest already mentioned, which had been wheeled into the middle of the room. It was open, and its contents lay beside it on the floor. The victims must have been sitting with their backs toward the window; and, from the time elapsing between the ingress of the beast and the screams, it seems probable that it was not immediately perceived. The flapping-to of the shutter would naturally have been attributed to the wind.

As the sailor looked in, the gigantic animal had seized Madame L'Espanaye by the hair (which was loose, as she had been combing it), and was flourishing the razor about her face, in imitation of the motions of a barber. The daughter lay prostrate and motionless; she had swooned. The screams and struggles of the old lady (during which the hair was torn from her head) had the effect of changing the probably pacific purposes of the Ourang-Outang into those of wrath. With one determined sweep of its muscular arm it nearly severed her head from her body. The sight of blood inflamed its anger into frenzy. Gnashing its teeth, and flashing fire from its eyes, it flew upon the body of the girl, and imbedded its fearful talons in her throat, retaining its grasp until she expired. Its wandering and wild glances fell at this moment upon the head of the bed, over which the face of its master, rigid with horror, was just discernible. The fury of the beast, who no doubt bore still in mind the dreaded whip, was instantly converted into fear. Conscious of having deserved punishment, it seemed desirous of concealing its bloody deeds, and skipped about the chamber in an agony of nervous agitation; throwing down and breaking the furniture as it moved, and dragging the bed from the bedstead. In conclusion, it seized first the corpse of the daughter, and thrust it up the chimney, as it was found; then that of the old lady, which it immediately hurled through the window headlong.

As the ape approached the casement with its mutilated

burden the sailor shrank aghast to the rod, and, rather gliding than clambering down it, hurried at once home—dreading the consequences of the butchery, and gladly abandoning, in his terror, all solicitude about the fate of the Ourang-Outang. The words heard by the party upon the staircase were the Frenchman's exclamations of horror and affright, commingled with the fiendish jabberings of the brute.

I have scarcely anything to add. The Ourang-Outang must have escaped from the chamber, by the rod, just before the breaking of the door. It must have closed the window as it passed through it. It was subsequently caught by the owner himself, who obtained for it a very large sum at the *Jardin des Plantes*. Le Bon was instantly released, upon our narration of the circumstances (with some comments from Dupin) at the *bureau* of the Prefect of Police. This functionary, however well disposed to my friend, could not altogether conceal his chagrin at the turn which affairs had taken, and was fain to indulge in a sarcasm or two about the propriety of every person minding his our business.

"Let him talk," said Dupin, who had not thought it necessary to reply. "Let him discourse; it will ease his conscience. I am satisfied with having defeated him in his own castle. Nevertheless, that he failed in the solution of this mystery, is by no means that matter for wonder which he supposes it; for, in truth, our friend the Prefect is somewhat too cunning to be profound. In his wisdom is no *stamen*. It is all head and no body, like the pictures of the Goddess Laverna—or, at best, all head and shoulders, like a codfish. But he is a good creature after all. I like him especially for one master stroke of cant, by which he has attained his reputation for ingenuity. I mean the way he has '*de nier ce qui est, et d'expliquer ce qui n'est pas.*' "[1]

---

[1] Rousseau—Nouvelle Héloise.

A MAN CALLED SPADE

BY DASHIELL HAMMETT

Dashiell Hammett was born in Maryland, in 1894, and worked as a newsboy, railroad laborer, messenger, stevedore, advertising manager, and Pinkerton detective, then served in the Army during World War I. His first detective stories appeared in the pulps in the 1920s, and his first novel, *Red Harvest,* was published in 1929. The creator of Sam Spade, Nick and Nora Charles, and the Continental Op, Hammett also collaborated with artist Alexander Raymond on the comic strip, *Secret Agent X-9*. Hammett was devoted to left-wing causes and served time in prison during the McCarthy era. He died in New York on January 10, 1961.

SAMUEL SPADE PUT HIS telephone aside and looked at his watch. It was not quite four o'clock.

He called, "Yoo-hoo!"

Effie Perine came in from the outer office. She was eating a piece of chocolate cake.

"Tell Sid Wise I won't be able to keep that date this afternoon," he said.

She put the last of the cake into her mouth and licked the tips of forefinger and thumb. "That's the third time this week."

When he smiled, the v's of his chin, mouth, and brows grew longer. "I know, but I've got to go out and save a life." He nodded at the telephone. "Somebody's scaring Max Bliss."

She laughed. "Probably somebody named John D. Conscience."

He looked up at her from the cigarette he had begun to make. "Know anything I ought to know about him?"

"Nothing you don't know. I was just thinking about the time he let his brother go to San Quentin."

Spade shrugged. "That's not the worst thing he's done." He lit his cigarette, stood up, and reached for his hat. "But he's all right now. All Samuel Spade clients are honest, God-fearing folk. If I'm not back at closing time just run along."

He went to a tall apartment building on Nob Hill, pressed a button set in the frame of a door marked 10K. The door was opened immediately by a burly dark man in wrinkled dark clothes. He was nearly bald and carried a gray hat in one hand.

The burly man said, "Hello, Sam." He smiled, but his small eyes lost none of their shrewdness. "What are you doing here?"

Spade said, "Hello, Tom." His voice was expressionless. "Bliss in?"

"Is he!" Tom pulled down the corners of his thick-lipped mouth. "You don't have to worry about that."

Spade's brows came together. "Well?"

A man appeared in the vestibule behind Tom. He was smaller than either Spade or Tom, but compactly built. He had a ruddy, square face and a close-trimmed, grizzled mustache. His clothes were neat. He wore a black bowler perched on the back of his head.

Spade addressed this man over Tom's shoulder: "Hello, Dundy."

Dundy nodded briefly and came to the door. His blue eyes were hard and prying.

"What is it?" he asked Tom.

"B-l-i-s-s, M-a-x," Spade spelled patiently. "I want to see him. He wants to see me. Catch on?"

Tom laughed. Dundy did not. Tom said, "Only one of you gets your wish." Then he glanced sidewise at Dundy and abruptly stopped laughing. He seemed uncomfortable.

Spade scowled. "All right," he demanded irritably; "is he dead or has he killed somebody?"

Dundy thrust his square face up at Spade and seemed to push his words out with his lower lip. "What makes you think either?"

Spade said, "Oh, sure! I come calling on Mr. Bliss and I'm stopped at the door by a couple of men from the police Homicide Detail, and I'm supposed to think I'm just interrupting a game of rummy."

"Aw, stop it, Sam," Tom grumbled, looking at neither Spade nor Dundy. "He's dead."

"Killed?"

Tom wagged his head slowly up and down. He looked at Spade now. "What've you got on it?"

Spade replied in a deliberate monotone, "He called me up this afternoon—say at five minutes to four—I looked at my watch after he hung up and there was still a minute or so to go—and said somebody was after his scalp. He wanted me to come over. It seemed real enough to him—it was up in his neck all right." He made a small gesture with one hand. "Well, here I am."

"Didn't say who or how?" Dundy asked.

Spade shook his head. "No. Just somebody had offered to kill him and he believed them, and would I come over quick as I could."

"Didn't he—?" Dundy began quickly.

"He didn't say anything else," Spade said. "Don't you people tell me anything?"

Dundy said curtly, "Come in and take a look at him."

Tom said, "It's a sight."

They went across the vestibule and through a door into a green and rose living room.

A man near the door stopped sprinkling white powder on the end of a glass-covered small table to say, "Hello, Sam."

Spade nodded, said, "How are you, Phels?" and then nodded at the two men who stood talking by a window.

The dead man lay with his mouth open. Some of his clothes had been taken off. His throat was puffy and dark. The end of his tongue showing in a corner of his mouth was bluish, swollen. On his bare chest, over the heart, a five-pointed star had been outlined in black ink and in the center of it a T.

Spade looked down at the dead man and stood for a moment silently studying him. Then he asked, "He was found like that?"

"About," Tom said. "We moved him around a little." He jerked a thumb at the shirt, undershirt, vest, and coat lying on a table. "They were spread over the floor."

Spade rubbed his chin. His yellow-gray eyes were dreamy. "When?"

Tom said, "We got it at four twenty. His daughter gave it to us." He moved his head to indicate a closed door. "You'll see her."

"Know anything?"

"Heaven knows," Tom said wearily. "She's been kind of hard to get along with so far." He turned to Dundy. "Want to try her again now?"

Dundy nodded, then spoke to one of the men at the window. "Start sifting his papers, Mack. He's supposed to've been threatened."

Mack said, "Right." He pulled his hat down over his eyes and walked towards a green secretaire in the far end of the room.

A man came in from the corridor, a heavy man of fifty with a deeply lined, grayish face under a broad-brimmed black hat. He said, "Hello, Sam," and then told Dundy, "He had company around half past two, stayed just about an hour. A big blond man in brown, maybe forty or forty-five. Didn't send his name up. I got it from the Filipino in the elevator that rode him both ways."

"Sure it was only an hour?" Dundy asked.

The gray-faced man shook his head. "But he's sure it wasn't more than half past three when he left. He says the afternoon papers came in then, and this man had ridden down with him before they came." He pushed his hat back to scratch his head, then pointed a thick finger at the design inked on the dead man's breast and asked somewhat plaintively, "What the deuce do you suppose that thing is?"

Nobody replied. Dundy asked, "Can the elevator boy identify him?"

"He says he could, but that ain't always the same thing. Says he never saw him before." He stopped looking at the dead man. "The girl's getting me a list of his phone calls. How you been, Sam?"

Spade said he had been all right. Then he said slowly, "His brother's big and blond and maybe forty or forty-five."

Dundy's blue eyes were hard and bright. "So what?" he asked.

"You remember the Graystone Loan swindle. They were both in it, but Max eased the load over on Theodore and it turned out to be one to fourteen years in San Quentin."

Dundy was slowly wagging his head up and down. "I remember now. Where is he?"

Spade shrugged and began to make a cigarette.

Dundy nudged Tom with an elbow. "Find out."

Tom said, "Sure, but if he was out of here at half past three and this fellow was still alive at five to four—"

"And he broke his leg so he couldn't duck back in," the gray-faced man said jovially.

"Find out," Dundy repeated.

Tom said, "Sure, sure," and went to the telephone.

Dundy addressed the gray-faced man: "Check up on the newspapers; see what time they were actually delivered this afternoon."

The gray-faced man nodded and left the room.

The man who had been searching the secretaire said, "Uh-huh," and turned around holding an envelope in one hand, a sheet of paper in the other.

Dundy held out his hand. "Something?"

The man said, "Uh-huh," again and gave Dundy the paper.

Spade was looking over Dundy's shoulder.

It was a small sheet of common white paper bearing a penciled message in neat, undistinguished handwriting:

When this reaches you I will be too close for you to escape—this time. We will balance our accounts—for good.

The signature was a five-pointed star enclosing a T, the design on the dead man's left breast.

Dundy held out his hand again and was given the envelope. Its stamp was French. The address was typewritten:

MAX BLISS, ESQ.
AMSTERDAM APARTMENTS
SAN FRANCISCO, CALIF.   U.S.A.

"Postmarked Paris," he said, "the second of the month." He counted swiftly on his fingers. "That would get it here today, all right." He folded the message slowly, put it in the envelope, put the envelope in his coat pocket. "Keep digging," he told the man who found the message.

The man returned to the desk.

Dundy looked at Spade. "What do you think of it?"

Spade's brown cigarette wagged up and down with his words. "I don't like any of it."

Tom put down the telephone. "He got out the fifteenth of last month," he said. "I got them trying to locate him. Shouldn't take long."

Spade went to the telephone, called a number, and asked for Mr. Darrell. Then: "Hello, Harry, this is Sam Spade. . . . Fine. How's Lil? . . . Yes. . . . Listen, Harry, what does a five-pointed star with a capital T in the middle mean? . . . What? How do you spell it? . . . Yes, I see. . . . And if you found it on a body? . . . Neither do I. . . . Yes, and thanks. I'll tell you about it when I see you. . . . Yes, give me a ring. . . . Thanks. . . . 'Bye."

Dundy and Tom were watching him closely when he turned from the telephone. He said, "That's a fellow who knows things sometimes. He says it's a pentagram with a Greek tau—t-a-u— in the middle; a sign magicians used to use. Maybe Rosicrucians still do."

"What's a Rosicrucian?" Tom asked.

"It could be Theodore's first initial, too," Dundy said.

Spade moved his shoulders, said carelessly, "Yes, but if he wanted to autograph the job it'd been just as easy for him to sign his name."

He then went on more thoughtfully, "There are Rosicrucians at both San Jose and Point Loma. I don't go much for this, but maybe we ought to look them up."

Dundy nodded.

Spade looked at the dead man's clothes on the table. "Anything in his pockets?"

"Only what you'd expect to find," Dundy replied. "It's on the table there."

Spade went to the table and looked down at the little pile of watch and chain, keys, wallet, address book, money, gold pencil, handkerchief, and spectacle case beside the clothing. He did not touch them, but slowly picked up, one at a time, the dead man's shirt, undershirt, vest, and coat. A blue necktie lay on the table beneath them. He scowled irritably at it. "It hasn't been worn," he complained.

Dundy, Tom, and the coroner's deputy, who had stood silent all this while by the window—he was a small man with a slim, dark, intelligent face—came together to stare down at the unwrinkled blue silk.

Tom groaned miserably. Dundy cursed under his breath. Spade lifted the necktie to look at its back. The label was a London haberdasher's.

Spade said cheerfully, "Swell. San Francisco, Point Loma, San Jose, Paris, London."

The gray-faced man came in. "The papers got here at three thirty, all right," he said. His eyes widened a little. "What's up?" As he crossed the room towards them he said, "I can't find anybody that saw Blondy sneak back in here again." He looked uncomprehendingly at the necktie until Tom growled, "It's brand-new"; then he whistled softly.

Dundy turned to Spade. "The deuce with all this," he said bitterly. "He's got a brother with reasons for not liking him. The brother just got out of stir. Somebody who looks like his brother left here at half past three. Twenty-five minutes later he phoned you he'd been threatened. Less than half an hour after that his daughter came in and found him dead— strangled." He poked a finger at the small, dark-faced man's chest. "Right?"

"Strangled," the dark-faced man said precisely, "by a man. The hands were large."

"O. K." Dundy turned to Spade again. "We find a threatening letter. Maybe that's what he was telling you about, maybe it was something his brother said to him. Don't let's guess. Let's stick to what we know. We know he—"

The man at the secretaire turned around and said, "Got another one." His mien was somewhat smug.

The eyes with which the five men at the table looked at him were identically cold, unsympathetic.

He, nowise disturbed by their hostility, read aloud:

"Dear Bliss:

"I am writing this to tell you for the last time that I want my money back, and I want it back by the first of the month, all of it. If I don't get it I am going to do something about it, and you ought to be able to guess what I mean. And don't think I am kidding.

"Yours truly,

"Daniel Talbot."

He grinned. "That's another T for you." He picked up an envelope. "Postmarked San Diego, the twenty-fifth of last month. And that's another city for you."

Spade shook his head. "Point Loma's down that way," he said.

He went over with Dundy to look at the letter. It was written in blue ink on white stationery of good quality, as was the address on the envelope, in a cramped, angular handwriting that seemed to have nothing in common with that of the penciled letter.

Spade said ironically, "Now we're getting somewhere."

Dundy made an impatient gesture. "Let's stick to what we know," he growled.

"Sure," Spade agreed. "What is it?"

There was no reply.

Spade took tobacco and cigarette papers from his pocket. "Didn't somebody say something about talking to a daughter?" he asked.

"We'll talk to her." Dundy turned on his heel, then suddenly frowned at the dead man on the floor. He jerked a thumb at the small, dark-faced man. "Through with it?"

"I'm through."

Dundy addressed Tom curtly: "Get rid of it." He addressed the gray-faced man: "I want to see both elevator boys when I'm finished with the girl."

He went to the closed door Tom had pointed out to Spade and knocked on it.

A slightly harsh female voice within asked, "What is it?"

"Lieutenant Dundy. I want to talk to Miss Bliss."

There was a pause; then the voice said, "Come in."

Dundy opened the door and Spade followed him into a black, gray, and silver room, where a big-boned and ugly middle-aged woman in black dress and white apron sat beside a bed on which a girl lay.

The girl lay, elbow on pillow, cheek on hand, facing the big-boned, ugly woman. She was apparently about eighteen years old. She wore a gray suit. Her hair was blonde and short, her face firm-featured and remarkably symmetrical. She did not look at the two men coming into the room.

Dundy spoke to the big-boned woman, while Spade was lighting his cigarette: "We want to ask you a couple of questions, too, Mrs. Hooper. You're Bliss's housekeeper, aren't you?"

The woman said, "I am." Her slightly harsh voice, level gaze of her deep-set gray eyes, the stillness and size of her hands lying in her lap, all contributed to the impression she gave of resting strength.

"What do you know about this?"

"I don't know anything about it. I was let off this morning to go over to Oakland to my nephew's funeral, and when I got back you and the other gentlemen were here and—and this had happened."

Dundy nodded, asked, "What do you think about it?"

"I don't know what to think," she replied simply.

"Didn't you know he expected it to happen?"

Now the girl suddenly stopped watching Mrs. Hooper. She sat up in bed, turning wide, excited eyes on Dundy, and asked, "What do you mean?"

"I mean what I said. He'd been threatened. He called up Mr. Spade"—he indicated Spade with a nod—"and told him so just a few minutes before he was killed."

"But who—?" she began.

"That's what we're asking you." Dundy said. "Who had that much against him?"

She stared at him in astonishment. "Nobody would—"

This time Spade interrupted her, speaking with a softness that made his words seem less brutal than they were. "Somebody did." When she turned her stare on him he asked, "You don't know of any threat?"

She shook her head from side to side with emphasis.

He looked at Mrs. Hooper. "You?"

"No, sir," she said.

He returned his attention to the girl. "Do you know Daniel Talbot?"

"Why, yes," she said. "He was here for dinner last night."

"Who is he?"

"I don't know, except that he lives in San Diego, and he and Father had some sort of business together. I'd never met him before."

"What sort of terms were they on?"

She frowned a little, said slowly, "Friendly."

Dundy spoke: "What business was your father in?"

"He was a financier."

"You mean a promoter?"

"Yes, I suppose you could call it that."

"Where is Talbot staying, or has he gone back to San Diego?"

"I don't know."

"What does he look like?"

She frowned again, thoughtfully. "He's kind of large, with a red face and white hair and a white mustache."

"Old?" Dundy asked.

"I guess he must be sixty; fifty-five at least."

Dundy looked at Spade, who put the stub of his cigarette in a tray on the dressing table and took up the questioning. "How long since you've seen your uncle?"

Her face flushed. "You mean Uncle Ted?"

He nodded.

"Not since," she began, and bit her lip. Then she said, "Of course, you know. Not since he first got out of prison."

"He came here?"

"Yes."

"To see your father?"

"Of course."

"What sort of terms were they on?"

She opened her eyes wide. "Neither of them is very demonstrative," she said, "but they are brothers, and Father was giving him money to set him up in business again."

"Then they were on good terms?"

"Yes," she replied in the tone of one answering an unnecessary question.

"Where does he live?"

"On Post Street," she said, and gave a number.

"And you haven't seen him since?"

"No. He was shy, you know, about having been in prison—" She finished the sentence with a gesture of one hand.

Spade addressed Mrs. Hooper: "You've seen him since?"

"No, sir."

210

He pursed his lips, asked slowly, "Either of you know he was here this afternoon?"

They said, "No," together.

"Where did—?"

Someone knocked on the door.

Dundy said, "Come in."

Tom opened the door far enough to stick his head in. "His brother's here," he said.

The girl leaning forward, called, "Oh, Uncle Ted!"

A big blond man in brown appeared behind Tom. He was sunburned to an extent that made his teeth seem whiter, his clear eyes bluer, than they were.

He asked, "What's the matter, Miriam?"

"Father's dead," she said, and began to cry.

Dundy nodded at Tom, who stepped out of Theodore Bliss's way and let him come into the room.

A woman came in behind him, slowly, hesitantly. She was a tall woman in her late twenties, blonde, not quite plump. Her features were generous, her face pleasant and intelligent. She wore a small brown hat and a mink coat.

Bliss put an arm around his niece, kissed her forehead, sat on the bed beside her. "There, there," he said awkwardly.

She saw the blonde woman, stared through her tears at her for a moment, then said, "Oh, how do you do, Miss Barrow."

The blonde woman said, "I'm awfully sorry to—"

Bliss cleared his throat, and said, "She's Mrs. Bliss now. We were married this afternoon."

Dundy looked angrily at Spade. Spade, making a cigarette, seemed about to laugh.

Miriam Bliss, after a moment's surprised silence, said, "Oh, I do wish you all the happiness in the world." She turned to her uncle while his wife was murmuring, "Thank you" and said, "And you too, Uncle Ted."

He patted her shoulder and squeezed her to him. He looked questioningly at Spade and Dundy.

"Your brother died this afternoon," Dundy said. "He was murdered."

Mrs. Bliss caught her breath. Bliss's arm tightened around his niece with a little jerk, but there was not yet any change in his face. "Murdered?" he repeated uncomprehendingly.

"Yes." Dundy put his hands in his coat pockets. "You were here this afternoon."

Theodore Bliss paled a little under his sunburn, but said, "I was," steadily enough.

"How long?"

"About an hour. I got here about half past two and—" He turned to his wife. "It was almost half past three when I phoned you, wasn't it?"

She said, "Yes."

"Well, I left right after that."

"Did you have a date with him?" Dundy asked.

"No. I phoned his office"—he nodded at his wife—"and was told he'd left for home, so I came on up. I wanted to see him before Elise and I left, of course, and I wanted him to come to the wedding, but he couldn't. He said he was expecting somebody. We sat here and talked longer than I had intended, so I had to phone Elise to meet me at the Municipal Building."

After a thoughtful pause, Dundy asked, "What time?"

"That we met there?" Bliss looked inquiringly at his wife, who said, "It was just quarter to four." She laughed a little. "I got there first and I kept looking at my watch."

Bliss said very deliberately, "It was a few minutes after four that we were married. We had to wait for Judge Whitefield—about ten minutes, and it was a few more before we got started—to get through with the case he was hearing. You can check it up—Superior Court, Part Two, I think."

Spade whirled around and pointed at Tom. "Maybe you'd better check it up."

Tom said, "Oke," and went away from the door.

"If that's so, you're all right, Mr. Bliss," Dundy said, "but I have to ask these things. Now, did your brother say who he was expecting?"

"No."

"Did he say anything about having been threatened?"

"No. He never talked much about his affairs to anybody, not even to me. Had he been threatened?"

Dundy's lips tightened a little. "Were you and he on intimate terms?"

"Friendly, if that's what you mean."

"Are you sure?" Dundy asked. "Are you sure neither of you held any grudge against the other?"

Theodore Bliss took his arm free from around his niece. Increasing pallor made his sunburned face yellowish. He said, "Everybody here knows about my having been in San Quentin.

You can speak out, if that's what you're getting at."

"It is," Dundy said, and then, after a pause, "Well?"

Bliss stood up. "Well, what?" he asked impatiently. "Did I hold a grudge against him for that? No. Why should I? We were both in it. He could get out; I couldn't. I was sure of being convicted whether he was or not. Having him sent over with me wasn't going to make it any better for me. We talked it over and decided I'd go it alone, leaving him outside to pull things together. And he did. If you look up his bank account you'll see he gave me a check for twenty-five thousand dollars two days after I was discharged from San Quentin, and the registrar of the National Steel Corporation can tell you a thousand shares of stock have been transferred from his name to mine since then."

He smiled apologetically and sat down on the bed again. "I'm sorry. I know you have to ask things."

Dundy ignored the apology. "Do you know Daniel Talbot?" he asked.

Bliss said, "No."

His wife said, "I do; that is I've seen him. He was in the office yesterday."

Dundy looked her up and down carefully before asking, "What office?"

"I am—I was Mr. Bliss's secretary, and—"

"Max Bliss's?"

"Yes, and a Daniel Talbot came in to see him yesterday afternoon, if it's the same one."

"What happened?"

She looked at her husband, who said, "If you know anything, for heaven's sake tell them."

She said, "But nothing really happened. I thought they were angry with each other at first, but when they left together they were laughing and talking, and before they went Mr. Bliss rang for me and told me to have Trapper—he's the bookkeeper—make out a check to Mr. Talbot's order."

"Did he?"

"Oh, yes. I took it in to him. It was for seventy-five hundred and some dollars."

"What was it for?"

She shook her head. "I don't know."

"If you were Bliss's secretary," Dundy insisted, "you must have some idea of what his business with Talbot was."

"But I haven't," she said, "I'd never even heard of him before."

Dundy looked at Spade. Spade's face was wooden. Dundy glowered at him, then put a question to the man on the bed: "What kind of necktie was your brother wearing when you saw him last?"

Bliss blinked, then stared distantly past Dundy, and finally shut his eyes. When he opened them he said, "It was green with—I'd know it if I saw it. Why?"

Mrs. Bliss said, "Narrow diagonal stripes of different shades of green. That's the one he had on at the office this morning."

"Where does he keep his neckties?" Dundy asked the housekeeper.

She rose, saying, "In a closet in his bedroom. I'll show you."

Dundy and the newly married Blisses followed her out.

Spade put his hat on the dressing table and asked Miriam Bliss, "What time did you go out?" He sat on the foot of her bed.

"Today? About one o'clock. I had a luncheon engagement for one and I was a little late, and then I went shopping, and then—" She broke off with a shudder.

"And then you came home at what time?" His voice was friendly, matter-of-fact.

"Some time after four, I guess."

"And what happened?"

"I f-found Father lying there and I phoned—I don't know whether I phoned downstairs or the police, and then I don't know what I did. I fainted or had hysterics or something, and the first thing I remember is coming to and finding those men here and Mrs. Hooper." She looked him full in the face now.

"You didn't phone a doctor?"

She lowered her eyes again. "No, I don't think so."

"Of course you wouldn't, if you knew he was dead," he said casually.

She was silent.

"You knew he was dead?"

She raised her eyes and looked blankly at him. "But he was dead," she said.

He smiled. "Of course; but what I'm getting at is, did you make sure before you phoned?"

She put a hand to her throat. "I don't remember what I did," she said earnestly. "I think I just knew he was dead."

He nodded understandingly. "And if you phoned the police it was because you knew he had been murdered."

She worked her hands together and looked at them and said, "I suppose so. It was awful. I don't know what I thought or did."

Spade leaned forward and made his voice low and persuasive. "I'm not a police detective, Miss Bliss. I was engaged by your father—a few minutes too late to save him. I am, in a way, working for you now, so if there is anything I can do—maybe something the police wouldn't—" He broke off as Dundy, followed by the Blisses and the housekeeper, returned to the room. "What luck?"

Dundy said, "The green tie's not there." His suspicious gaze darted from Spade to the girl. "Mrs. Hooper says the blue tie we found is one of half a dozen new ones he just got from England."

Bliss asked, "What's the importance of the tie?"

Dundy scowled at him. "He was partly undressed when we found him. The tie with his clothes had never been worn."

"Couldn't he have been changing clothes when whoever killed him came, and was killed before he had finished dressing?"

Dundy's scowl deepened. "Yes, but what did he do with the green tie? Eat it?"

Spade said, "He wasn't changing clothes. If you'll look at the shirt collar you'll see Bliss must have had it on when he was choked."

Tom came to the door. "Checks all right," he told Dundy. "The judge and a bailiff named Kittredge say they were there from about a quarter to four till five or ten minutes after. I told Kittredge to come over and take a look at them to make sure they're the same ones."

Dundy said, "Right," without turning his head and took the penciled threat signed with the T in a star from his pocket. He folded it so only the signature was visible. Then he asked, "Anybody know what this is?"

Miriam Bliss left the bed to join the others in looking at it. From it they looked at one another blankly.

"Anybody know anything about it?" Dundy asked.

Mrs. Hooper said, "It is like what was on poor Mr. Bliss's chest, but—" The others said, "No."

"Anybody ever seen anything like it before?"

They said they had not.

Dundy said, "All right. Wait here. Maybe I'll have something else to ask you after a while."

Spade said, "Just a minute. Mr. Bliss, how long have you known Mrs. Bliss?"

Bliss looked curiously at Spade. "Since I got out of prison," he replied somewhat cautiously. "Why?"

"Just since last month," Spade said as if to himself. "Meet her through your brother?"

"Of course—in his office. Why?"

"And at the Municipal Building this afternoon, were you together all the time?"

"Yes, certainly." Bliss spoke sharply. "What are you getting at?"

Spade smiled at him, a friendly smile. "I have to ask things," he said.

Bliss smiled too. "It's all right." His smile broadened. "As a matter of fact, I'm a liar. We weren't actually together all the time. I went out into the corridor to smoke a cigarette, but I assure you every time I looked through the glass of the door I could see her still sitting in the courtroom where I had left her."

Spade's smile was as light as Bliss's. Nevertheless, he asked, "And when you weren't looking through the glass you were in sight of the door? She couldn't've left the courtroom without your seeing her?"

Bliss's smile went away. "Of course she couldn't," he said, "and I wasn't out there more than five minutes."

Spade said, "Thanks," and followed Dundy into the living-room, shutting the door behind him.

Dundy looked sidewise at Spade. "Anything to it?"

Spade shrugged.

Max Bliss's body had been removed. Besides the man at the secretaire and the gray-faced man, two Filipino boys in plum-colored uniforms were in the room. They sat close together on the sofa.

Dundy said, "Mack, I want to find a green necktie. I want this house taken apart, this block taken apart, and the whole neighborhood taken apart till you find it."

The man at the secretaire rose, said "Right," pulled his hat down over his eyes and went out.

Dundy scowled at the Filipinos. "Which of you saw the man in brown?"

216

The smaller stood up. "Me, sir."

Dundy opened the bedroom door and said, "Bliss."

Bliss came to the door.

The Filipino's face lighted up. "Yes, sir, him."

Dundy shut the door in Bliss's face. "Sit down."

The boy sat down hastily.

Dundy stared gloomily at the boys until they began to fidget. Then, "Who else did you bring up to this apartment this afternoon?"

They shook their heads in unison from side to side. "Nobody else, sir," the smaller one said. A desperately ingratiating smile stretched his mouth wide across his face.

Dundy took a threatening step towards them. "Nuts!" he snarled. "You brought up Miss Bliss."

The larger boy's head bobbed up and down. "Yes, sir. Yes, sir. I bring them up. I think you mean other people." He too tried a smile.

Dundy was glaring at him. "Never mind what you think I mean. Tell me what I ask. Now, what do you mean by 'them'?"

The boy's smile died under the glare. He looked at the floor between his feet and said, "Miss Bliss and the gentleman."

"What gentleman? The gentleman in there?" He jerked his head toward the door he had shut on Bliss.

"No, sir. Another gentleman, not an American gentleman." He had raised his head again and now brightness came back into his face. "I think he is Armenian."

"Why?"

"Because he not like us Americans, not talk like us."

Spade laughed, asked, "Ever seen an Armenian?"

"No sir. That is why I think he—" He shut his mouth with a click as Dundy made a growling noise in his throat.

"What'd he look like?" Dundy asked.

The boy lifted his shoulders, spread his hands. "He tall, like this gentleman." He indicated Spade. "Got dark hair, dark mustache. Very"—he frowned earnestly—"very nice clothes. Very nice looking man. Cane, gloves, spats, even, and—"

"Young?" Dundy asked.

The head went up and down again. "Young. Yes, sir."

"When did he leave?"

"Five minutes," the boy replied.

Dundy made a chewing motion with his jaws, then asked, "What time did they come in?"

217

The boy spread his hands, lifted his shoulders again. "Four o'clock—maybe ten minutes after."

"Did you bring anybody else up before we got here?"

The Filipinos shook their heads in unison once more.

Dundy spoke out the side of his mouth to Spade: "Get her."

Spade opened the bedroom door, bowed slightly, said, "Will you come out a moment, Miss Bliss?"

"What is it?" she asked warily.

"Just for a moment," he said, holding the door open. Then he suddenly added, "And you'd better come along, too, Mr. Bliss."

Miriam Bliss came slowly into the living-room followed by her uncle, and Spade shut the door behind them. Miss Bliss's lower lip twitched a little when she saw the elevator boys. She looked apprehensively at Dundy.

He asked, "What's this fiddlededee about the man that came in with you?"

Her lower lip twitched again. "Wh-what?" She tried to put bewilderment on her face. Theodore Bliss hastily crossed the room, stood for a moment before her as if he intended to say something, and then, apparently changing his mind, took up a position a foot or so behind her, his arms crossed over the back of a chair.

"The man who came in with you," Dundy said harshly, rapidly. "Who is he? Where is he? Why'd he leave? Why didn't you say something about him?"

The girl put her hands over her face and began to cry. "He didn't have anything to do with it," she blubbered through her hands. "He didn't, and it would just make trouble for him."

"Nice boy," Dundy said. "So, to keep his name out of the newspapers, he runs off and leaves you alone with your murdered father."

She took her hands away from her face. "Oh, but he had to," she cried. "His wife is so jealous, and if she knew he had been with me again she'd certainly divorce him, and he hasn't a cent in the world of his own."

Dundy looked at Spade. Spade looked at the goggling Filipinos and jerked a thumb at the outer door. "Scram," he said. They went out quickly.

"And who is this gem?" Dundy asked the girl.

"But he didn't have any—"

"Who is he?"

Her shoulders drooped a little and she lowered her eyes. "His name is Boris Smekalov," she said wearily.

"Spell it."

She spelled it.

"Where does he live?"

"At the St. Mark Hotel."

"Does he do anything for a living except marry money?"

Anger came into her face as she raised it, but went away as quickly. "He doesn't do anything."

Dundy wheeled to address the gray-faced man. "Get him."

The gray-faced man grunted and went out.

Dundy faced the girl again. "You and this Smekalov in love with each other?"

Her face became scornful. She looked at him with scornful eyes and said nothing.

He said, "Now your father's dead, will you have enough money for him to marry if his wife divorces him?"

She covered her face with her hands.

He said, "Now your father's dead, will—?"

Spade, leaning far over, caught her as she fell. He lifted her easily and carried her into the bedroom. When he came back he shut the door behind him and leaned against it. "Whatever the rest of it was," he said, "the faint's a phony."

"Everything's a phony," Dundy said. "There ought to be a law making criminals give themselves up."

Mr. Bliss smiled and sat down at his brother's desk by the window.

Dundy's voice was disagreeable. "You got nothing to worry about," he said to Spade. "Even your client's dead and can't complain. But if I don't come across I've got to stand for riding from the captain, the chief, the newspapers, and heaven knows who all."

"Stay with it," Spade said soothingly; "you'll catch a murderer sooner or later yet." His face became serious except for the lights in his yellow-gray eyes. "I don't want to run this job up any more alleys than we have to, but don't you think we ought to check up on the funeral the housekeeper said she went to? There's something funny about that woman."

After looking suspiciously at Spade for a moment, Dundy nodded.

"Tom'll do it."

Spade turned about and, shaking his finger at Tom, said, "It's

219

a ten-to-one bet there wasn't any funeral. Check on it . . . don't miss a trick."

Then he opened the bedroom door and called Mrs. Hooper. "Sergeant Polhaus wants some information from you," he told her.

While Tom was writing down names and addresses that the woman gave him, Spade sat on the sofa and made and smoked a cigarette, and Dundy walked the floor slowly, scowling at the rug. With Spade's approval, Theodore Bliss rose and rejoined his wife in the bedroom.

Presently Tom put his notebook in his pocket, said, "Thank you," to the housekeeper, "Be seeing you," to Spade and Dundy, and left the apartment.

The housekeeper stood where he had left her, ugly, strong, serene, patient.

Spade twisted himself around on the sofa until he was looking into her deep-set, steady eyes. "Don't worry about that," he said, flirting a hand toward the door Tom had gone through. "Just routine." He pursed his lips, asked, "What do you honestly think of this thing, Mrs. Hooper?"

She replied calmly, in her strong, somewhat harsh voice, "I think it's the judgment of God."

Dundy stopped pacing the floor.

Spade said, "What?"

There was certainty and no excitement in her voice: "The wages of sin is death."

Dundy began to advance towards Mrs. Hooper in the manner of one stalking game. Spade waved him back with a hand which the sofa hid from the woman. His face and voice showed interest, but were now as composed as the woman's. "Sin?" he asked.

She said, " 'Whosoever shall offend one of these little ones that believe in me, it were better for him that a millstone were hanged around his neck, and he were cast into the sea.' " She spoke, not as if quoting, but as if saying something she believed deeply.

Dundy barked a question at her. "What little one?"

She turned her grave gray eyes on him, then looked past him at the bedroom door.

"Her," she said; "Miriam."

Dundy frowned at her. "His daughter?"

The woman said, "Yes, his own adopted daughter."

Angry blood mottled Dundy's square face. "What the heck is this?" he demanded. He shook his head as if to free it from some clinging thing. "She's not really his daughter?"

The woman's serenity was in no way disturbed by his anger. "No. His wife was an invalid most of her life. They didn't have any children."

Dundy moved his jaws as if chewing for a moment and when he spoke again his voice was cooler. "What did he do to her?"

"I don't know," she said, "but I truly believe that when the truth's found out you'll see that the money her father—I mean her real father—left her has been—"

Spade interrupted her, taking pains to speak very clearly, moving one hand in small circles with his words. "You mean you don't actually know he's been gypping her? You just suspect it?"

She put her hand over her heart. "I know it here."

Dundy looked at Spade, Spade at Dundy, and Spade's eyes were shiny with not altogether pleasant merriment. Dundy cleared his throat and addressed the woman again. "And you think this"—he waved a hand at the floor where the dead man had lain—"was the judgment of God, huh?"

"I do."

He kept all but the barest trace of craftiness out of his eyes. "Then whoever did it was just acting as the hand of God?"

"It's not for me to say," she replied.

Red began to mottle his face again.

"That'll be all right now," he said in a choking voice, but by the time she had reached the bedroom door his eyes became alert again and he called, "Wait a minute." And when they were facing each other: "Listen, do you happen to be a Rosicrucian?"

"I wish to be nothing but a Christian."

He growled, "All right, all right," and turned his back on her. She went into the bedroom and shut the door. He wiped his right hand and complained wearily, "Great Scott, what a family!"

Spade shrugged. "Try investigating your own some time."

Dundy's face whitened. His lips, almost colorless, came back tight over his teeth. He balled his fists and lunged towards Spade. "What do you—? The pleasantly surprised look on Spade's face stopped him. He averted his eyes, wet his lips with the tip of his tongue, looked at Spade again and away, essayed an embarrassed smile, and mumbled, "You mean any family.

221

Uh-huh, I guess so." He turned hastily towards the corridor door as the doorbell rang.

The amusement twitching Spade's face accentuated his likeness to a blond satan.

An amiable, drawling voice came in through the corridor door: "I'm Jim Kittredge, Superior Court. I was told to come over here."

Dundy's voice: "Yes, come in."

Kittredge was a roly-poly ruddy man in too-tight clothes with the shine of age on them. He nodded at Spade and said, "I remember you, Mr. Spade, from the Burke-Harris suit."

Spade said, "Sure," and stood up to shake hands with him.

Dundy had gone to the bedroom door to call Theodore Bliss and his wife. Kittredge looked at them, smiled at them amiably, said, "How do you do?" and turned to Dundy. "That's them, all right." He looked around as if for a place to spit, found none, and said, "It was just about ten minutes to four that the gentleman there came in the courtroom and asked me how long His Honor would be, and I told him about ten minutes, and they waited there; and right after court adjourned at four o'clock we married them."

Dundy said, "Thanks." He sent Kittredge away, the Blisses back to the bedroom, scowled with dissatisfaction at Spade, and said, "So "what?"

Spade, sitting down again, replied, "So you couldn't get from here to the Municipal Building in less than fifteen minutes on a bet, so he couldn't've ducked back here while he was waiting for the judge, and he couldn't have hustled over here to do it after the wedding and before Miriam arrived."

The dissatisfaction in Dundy's face increased. He opened his mouth, but shut it in silence when the gray-faced man came in with a tall, slender, pale young man who fitted the description the Filipino had given of Miriam Bliss's companion.

The gray-faced man said, "Lieutenant Dundy, Mr. Spade, Mr. Boris—uh—Smekalov."

Dundy nodded curtly.

Smekalov began to speak immediately. His accent was not heavy enough to trouble his hearers much, though his r's sounded more like w's. "Lieutenant, I must beg of you that you keep this confidential. If it should get out it will ruin me, Lieutenant, ruin me completely and most unjustly. I am most innocent, sir, I assure you, in heart, spirit, and deed, not only

222

innocent, but in no way whatever connected with any part of the whole horrible matter. There is no—"

"Wait a minute." Dundy prodded Smekalov's chest with a blunt finger. "Nobody's said anything about you being mixed up in anything—but it'd look better if you'd stuck around."

The young man spread his arms, his palms forward, in an expansive gesture. "But what can I do? I have a wife who—" He shook his head violently. "It is impossible. I cannot do it."

The gray-faced man said to Spade in an inadequately subdued voice, "Goofy, these Russians."

Dundy screwed up his eyes at Smekalov and made his voice judicial. "You've probably put yourself in a pretty tough spot."

Smekalov seemed about to cry. "But only put yourself in my place," he begged, "and you—"

"Wouldn't want to." Dundy seemed, in his callous way, sorry for the man. "Murder's nothing to play with in this country."

"Murder! But I tell you, Lieutenant, I happen' to enter into this situation by the merest mischance only. I am not—"

"You mean you came in here with Miss Bliss by accident?"

The young man looked as if he would like to say "Yes." He said, "No," slowly, then went on with increasing rapidity: "But that was nothing sir, nothing at all. We had been to lunch. I escorted her home and she said, 'Will you come in for a cocktail?' and I would. That is all, I give you my word." He held out his hands, palms up. "Could it not have happened so to you?" He moved his hands in Spade's direction. "To you?"

Spade said, "A lot of things happen to me. Did Bliss know you were running around with his daughter?"

"He knew we were friends, yes."

"Did he know you had a wife?"

Smekalov said cautiously, "I do not think so."

Dundy said, "You know he didn't."

Smekalov moistened his lips and did not contradict the lieutenant.

Dundy asked, "What do you think he'd have done if he found out?"

"I do not know, sir."

Dundy stepped close to the young man and spoke through his teeth in a harsh, deliberate voice: "What *did* he do when he found out?"

The young man retreated a step, his face white and frightened.

223

The bedroom door opened and Miriam Bliss came into the room. "Why don't you leave him alone?" she asked indignantly. "I told you he had nothing to do with it. I told you he didn't know anything about it." She was beside Smekalov now and had one of his hands in hers. "You're simply making trouble for him without doing a bit of good. I'm awfully sorry, Boris, I tried to keep them from bothering you."

The young man mumbled unintelligibly.

"You tried, all right," Dundy agreed. He addressed Spade: "Could it've been like this, Sam? Bliss found out about the wife, knew they had the lunch date, came home early to meet them when they came in, threatened to tell the wife, and was choked to stop him." He looked sidewise at the girl. "Now, if you want to fake another faint, hop to it."

The young man screamed and flung himself at Dundy, clawing with both hands. Dundy gruntled—"Uh!"—and struck him in the face with a heavy fist. The young man went backwards across the room until he collided with a chair. He and the chair went down on the floor together. Dundy said to the gray-faced man, "Take him down to the Hall—material witness."

The gray-faced man said, "Oke," picked up Smekalov's hat and went over to help pick him up.

Theodore Bliss, his wife, and the housekeeper had come to the door Miriam Bliss had left open. Miriam Bliss was crying, stamping her foot, threatening Dundy: "I'll report you, you coward. You had no right to . . ." and so on. Nobody paid much attention to her; they watched the gray-faced man help Smekalov to his feet, take him away. Smekalov's nose and mouth were red smears.

Then Dundy said, "Hush," negligently to Miriam Bliss and took a slip of paper from his pocket. "I got a list of the calls from here today. Sing out when you recognize them."

He read a telephone number.

Mrs. Hooper said, "That is the butcher. I phoned him before I left this morning." She said the next number Dundy read was the grocer's. He read another.

"That's the St. Mark," Miriam Bliss said. "I called up Boris." She identified two more numbers as those of friends she had called.

The sixth number, Bliss said, was his brother's office. "Probably my call to Elise to ask her to meet me."

Spade said, "Mine," to the seventh number, and Dundy said, "That one's police emergency." He put the slip back in his pocket.

Spade said cheerfully, "And that gets us a lot of places."

The doorbell rang.

Dundy went to the door. He and another man could be heard talking in voices too low for their words to be recognized in the living room.

The telephone rang. Spade answered it. "Hello. . . . No, this is Spade. Wait a min— All right." He listened. "Right, I'll tell him. . . . I don't know. I'll have him call you soon as he can. . . . Right."

When he turned from the telephone Dundy was standing, hands behind him, in the vestibule doorway. Spade said, "O'Gar says your Russian friend went completely nuts on the way to the Hall. They had to shove him into a straitjacket."

"He ought to been there long ago," Dundy growled. "Come here."

Spade followed Dundy into the vestibule. A uniformed policeman stood in the outer doorway.

Dundy brought his hands from behind him. In one was a necktie with a narrow diagonal stripes in varying shades of green, in the other was a platinum scarfpin in the shape of a crescent set with small diamonds.

Spade bent over to look at three small, irregular spots on the tie. "Blood?"

"Or dirt," Dundy said. "He found them crumpled up in a newspaper in the rubbish can on the corner."

"Yes, sir," the uniformed man said proudly: "there I found them, all wadded up in—" He stopped because nobody was paying any attention to him.

"Blood's better," Spade was saying. "It gives a reason for taking the tie away. Let's go in and talk to people."

Dundy stuffed the tie in one pocket, thrust his hand holding the pin into another. "Right—and we'll call it blood."

They went into the living-room. Dundy looked from Bliss to Bliss's wife, to Bliss's niece, to the housekeeper, as if he did not like any of them. He took his fist from his pocket, thrust it straight out in front of him, and opened it to show the crescent pin lying in his hand. "What's that?" he demanded.

Miriam Bliss was the first to speak. "Why, it's Father's pin," she said.

"So it is?" he said disagreeably. "And did he have it on today?"

"He always wore it." She turned to the others for confirmation.

Mrs. Bliss said, "Yes," while the others nodded.

"Where did you find it?" the girl asked.

Dundy was surveying them one by one again, as if he liked them less than ever. His face was red. "He always wore it," he said angrily, "but there wasn't one of you could say, 'Father always wore a pin. Where is it?' No, we got to wait till it turns up before we can get a word out of you about it."

Bliss said, "Be fair. How were we to know—?"

"Never mind what you were to know," Dundy said. "It's coming around to the point where I'm going to do some talking about what I know." He took the green necktie from his pocket. "This is his tie?"

Mrs. Hooper said, "Yes, sir."

Dundy said, "Well, it's got blood on it, and it's not his blood, because he didn't have a scratch on him that we could see." He looked narrow-eyed from one to another of them. "Now, suppose you were trying to choke a man that wore a scarfpin and he was wrestling with you, and—"

He broke off to look at Spade.

Spade had crossed to where Mrs. Hooper was standing. Her big hands were clasped in front of her. He took her right hand, turned it over, took the wadded handkerchief from her palm, and there was a two-inch-long fresh scratch in the flesh.

She had passively allowed him to examine her hand. Her mien lost none of its tranquility. She said nothing.

"Well?" he asked.

"I scratched it on Miss Miriam's pin fixing her on the bed when she fainted," the housekeeper said calmly.

Dundy's laugh was brief, bitter. "It'll hang you just the same," he said.

There was no change in the woman's face. "The Lord's will be done," she replied.

Spade made a peculiar noise in his throat as he dropped her hand. "Well, let's see how we stand." He grinned at Dundy. "You don't like that star-T, do you?"

Dundy said, "Not by a long shot."

"Neither do I," Spade said. "The Talbot threat was probably on the level, but that debt seems to have been squared.

226

Now— Wait a minute." He went to the telephone and called his office. "The tie thing looked pretty funny, too, for a while," he said while he waited, "but I guess the blood takes care of that."

He spoke into the telephone again: "Hello, Effie. Listen: Within half an hour or so of the time Bliss called me, did you get any call that maybe wasn't on the level? Anything that could have been a stall? . . . Yes, before . . . Think now."

He put his hand over the mouthpiece and said to Dundy, "There's a lot of deviltry going on in this world."

He spoke into the telephone again: "Yes? . . . Yes . . . Kruger? . . . Yes. Man or woman? . . . Thanks. . . . No, I'll be through in half an hour. Wait for me and I'll buy your dinner. 'Bye."

He turned away from the telephone. "About half an hour before Bliss phoned, a man called my office and asked for Mr. Kruger."

Dundy frowned. "So what?"

"Kruger wasn't there."

Dundy's frown deepened. "Who's Kruger?"

"I don't know," Spade said blandly. "I never heard of him." He took tobacco and cigarette papers from his pockets. "All right, Bliss, where's your scratch?"

Theodore Bliss said, "What?" while the others stared blankly at Spade.

"Your scratch," Spade repeated in a consciously patient tone. His attention was on the cigarette he was making. "The place where your brother's pin gouged you when you were choking him."

"Are you crazy?" Bliss demanded. "I was—"

"Uh-huh, you were being married when he was killed. You were not." Spade moistened the edge of his cigarette paper and smoothed it with his forefingers.

Mrs. Bliss spoke now, stammering a little: "But he—but Max Bliss called—"

"Who says Max Bliss called me?" Spade asked. "I don't know that. I wouldn't know his voice. All I know is a man called me and said he was Max Bliss. Anybody could say that."

"But the telephone records here show the call came from here," she protested.

He shook his head and smiled. "They show I had a call from here, and I did, but not that one. I told you somebody called up half an hour or so before the supposed Max Bliss call and asked for Mr. Kruger." He nodded at Theodore Bliss. "He was smart

227

enough to get a call from this apartment to my office on the record before he left to meet you."

She stared from Spade to her husband with dumbfounded blue eyes.

Her husband said lightly, "It's nonsense, my dear. You know—"

Spade did not let him finish that sentence. "You know he went out to smoke a cigarette in the corridor while waiting for the judge, and he knew there were telephone booths in the corridor. A minute would be all he needed." He lit his cigarette and returned his lighter to his pocket.

Bliss said, "Nonsense!" more sharply. "Why should I want to kill Max?" He smiled reassuringly into his wife's horrified eyes. "Don't let this disturb you, dear. Police methods are sometimes—"

"All right," Spade said, "let's look you over for scratches."

Bliss wheeled to face him more directly. "Damned if you will!" He put a hand behind him.

Spade, wooden-faced and dreamy-eyed, came forward.

Spade and Effie Perine sat at a small table in Julia's Castle on Telegraph Hill. Through the window beside them ferryboats could be seen carrying lights to and from the cities' lights across the bay.

". . . hadn't gone there to kill him, chances are," Spade was saying; "just to shake him down for some more money; but when the fight started, once he got his hands on his throat, I guess, his grudge was too hot in him for him to let go till Max was dead. Understand, I'm just putting together what the evidence says, and what we got out of his wife, and the not much that we got out of him."

Effie nodded. "She's a nice, loyal wife."

Spade drank coffee, shrugged. "What for? She knows now that he made his play for her only because she was Max's secretary. She knows that when he took out the marriage license a couple of weeks ago it was only to string her along so she'd get him the photostatic copies of the records that tied Max up with the Graystone Loan swindle. She knows—well, she knows she wasn't just helping an injured innocent to clear his good name."

He took another sip of coffee. "So he calls on his brother this afternoon to hold San Quentin over his head for a price again, and there's a fight, and he kills him, and gets his wrist scratched

228

by the pin while he's choking him. Blood on the tie, a scratch on his wrist—that won't do. He takes the tie off the corpse and hunts up another, because the absence of a tie will set the police to thinking. He gets a bad break there: Max's new ties are on the front of the rack, and he grabs the first one he comes to. All right. Now he's got to put it around the dead man's neck—or wait—he gets a better idea. Pull off some more clothes and puzzle the police. The tie'll be just as inconspicuous off as on, if the shirt's off too. Undressing him, he gets another idea. He'll give the police something else to worry about so he draws a mystic sign he has seen somewhere on the dead man's chest."

Spade emptied his cup, set it down, and went on: "By now he's getting to be a regular mastermind at bewildering the police. A threatening letter signed with the thing on Max's chest. The afternoon mail is on the desk. One envelope's as good as another so long as it's typewritten and has no return address, but the one from France adds a touch of the foreign, so out comes the original letter and in goes the threat. He's overdoing it now; see? He's giving us so much that's wrong that we can't help suspecting things—the phone call, for instance.

"Well, he's ready for the phone calls now—his alibi. He picks my name out of the private detectives in the phone book and does the Mr. Kruger trick; but that's after he calls the blonde Elise and tells her that not only have the obstacles to their marriage been removed, but he's had an offer to go in business in New York and has to leave right away, and will she meet him in fifteen minutes and get married? There's more than just an alibi to that. He wants to make sure *she* is dead sure he didn't kill Max, because she knows he doesn't like Max, and he doesn't want her to think he was just stringing her along to get the dope on Max, because she might be able to put two and two together and get something like the right answer.

"With that taken care of, he's ready to leave. He goes out quite openly, with only one thing to worry about now—the tie and pin in his pocket. He takes the pin along because he's not sure the police mightn't find traces of blood around the setting of the stones, no matter how carefully he wipes it. On his way out he picks up a newspaper—buys one from the newsboy he meets at the street door—wads tie and pin up in a piece of it, and drops it in the rubbish can at the corner. That seems all right. No reason for the police to look for the tie. No reason for the street cleaner who empties the can to investigate a crumpled piece of newspaper, and if something does go wrong—what the deuce!—the murderer dropped it there, but he, Theodore, can't be the murderer, because he's going to have an alibi.

"Then he jumps in his car and drives to the Municipal Building. He knows there are plenty of phones there and he can always say he's got to wash his hands, but it turns out he doesn't have to. While they are waiting for the judge to get through with a case he goes out to smoke a cigarette, and there you are—'Mr. Spade, this is Max Bliss and I've been threatened.' "

Effie Perine nodded, then asked, "Why do you suppose he picked on a private detective instead of the police?"

"Playing safe. If the body had been found, meanwhile, the police might've heard of it and trace the call. A private detective wouldn't be likely to hear about it till he read it in the papers."

She laughed, then said, "And that was your luck."

"Luck? I don't know." He looked gloomily at the back of his left hand. "I hurt a knuckle stopping him and the job only lasted an afternoon. Chances are whoever's handling the estate'll raise hobs if I send them a bill for any decent amount of money." He raised a hand to attract the waiter's attention. "Oh, well, better luck next time. Want to catch a movie or have you got something else to do?"

THE BLAST OF THE BOOK

BY G. K. CHESTERTON

Gilbert Keith Chesterton was born in London on May 29, 1874. He attended St. Paul's School, where he won a prize for poetry, and Slade, the art school of University College, London. His first novel, *The Napoleon of Notting Hill,* was a futuristic tale, and his first mystery fiction, *The Club of Queer Trades,* was a collection of short stories. His famous fictional detective, Father Brown, is partially modeled after Father John O'Connor, who converted Chesterton to Catholicism in 1922. Chesterton wrote poetry, reviews, stories, and essays on literature, politics, religion, and philosophy. He died on June 14, 1936.

PROFESSOR OPENSHAW ALWAYS lost his temper, with a loud bang, if anybody called him a Spiritualist; or believer in Spiritualism. This, however, did not exhaust his explosive elements: for he also lost his temper if anybody called him a disbeliever in Spiritualism. It was his pride to have given his whole life to investigating Psychic Phenomena; it was also his pride never to have given a hint of whether he thought they were really psychic or merely phenomenal. He enjoyed nothing so much as to sit in a circle of devout Spiritualists and give devastating descriptions of how he had exposed medium after medium and detected fraud after fraud: for indeed he was a man of much detective talent and insight, when once he had fixed his eye on an object, and he always fixed his eye on a medium, as a highly suspicious object. There was a story of his having spotted the same Spiritualistic mountebank under three different disguises: dressed as a woman, a white-bearded old man and a Brahmin of a rich chocolate brown. These recitals made the true believers rather restless, as indeed they were intended to do; but they could hardly complain, for no Spiritualist denies the existence of fraudulent mediums; only the Professor's flowing narrative might well seem to indicate that all mediums were fraudulent.

But woe to the simple-minded and innocent Materialist (and Materialists as a race are rather innocent and simple-minded) who, presuming on this narrative tendency, should advance the thesis that ghosts were against the laws of nature, or that such things were only old superstitions; or that it was all tosh, or, alternatively, bunk. Him would the Professor, suddenly reversing all his scientific batteries, sweep from the field with a cannonade of unquestionable cases and unexplained phenomena, of which the wretched rationalist had never heard in his life, giving all the dates and details, stating all the attempted and abandoned natural explanations; stating everything, indeed, except whether he, John Oliver Openshaw, did or did not believe in Spirits; and that neither Spiritualist nor Materialist could ever boast of finding out.

Professor Openshaw, a lean figure with pale leonine hair and hypnotic blue eyes, stood exchanging a few words with Father Brown, who was a friend of his, on the steps outside the hotel where both had been breakfasting that morning and sleeping the night before. The Professor had come back rather late from one of his grand experiments in general exasperation, and was still tingling with the fight that he always waged alone and against both sides.

"Oh, I don't mind you," he said laughing. "You don't believe in it even if it's true. But all these people are perpetually asking me what I'm trying to prove. They don't seem to understand that I'm a man of science. A man of science isn't trying to prove anything. He's trying to find out what will prove itself."

"But he hasn't found out yet," said Father Brown.

"Well, I have some little notions of my own, that are not quite so negative as most people think," answered the Professor, after an instant of frowning silence; "anyhow, I've begun to fancy that if there is something to be found, they're looking for it along the wrong line. It's all too theatrical; it's showing off, all their shiny ectoplasm and trumpets and voices and the rest; all on the model of old melodramas and mouldy historical novels about the Family Ghost. If they'd go to history instead of historical novels, I'm beginning to think they'd really find something. But not Apparitions."

"After all," said Father Brown, "Apparitions are only Appearances. I suppose you'd say the Family Ghost is only keeping up appearances."

The Professor's gaze, which had commonly a fine abstracted character, suddenly fixed and focused itself as it did on a dubious medium. It had rather the air of a man screwing a strong magnifying-glass into his eye. Not that he thought the priest was in the least like a dubious medium; but he was startled into attention by his friend's thought following so closely on his own.

"Appearances!" he muttered. "Crikey, but it's odd you should say that just now. The more I learn, the more I fancy they lose by merely looking for Appearances. Now if they'd look a little into Disappearances—"

"Yes," said Father Brown, "after all, the real fairy legends weren't so very much about the appearance of famous fairies; calling up Titania or exhibiting Oberon by moonlight. But there were no end of legends about people *disappearing*, because they were stolen by the fairies. Are you on the track of Kilmeny or Thomas the Rhymer?"

"I'm on the track of ordinary modern people you've read of in the newspapers," answered Openshaw. "You may well stare; but that's my game just now; and I've been on it for a long time. Frankly, I think a lot of psychic appearances could be explained away. It's the disappearances I can't explain, unless they're psychic. These people in the newspapers who vanish and are never found—if you knew the details as I do . . . and now only this morning I got confirmation; an extraordinary letter from an old missionary, quite a respectable old boy. He's coming to see me at my office this morning. Perhaps you'd lunch with me or something; and I'd tell the results—in confidence."

"Thanks; I will—unless," said Father Brown modestly, "the fairies have stolen me by then."

With that they parted and Openshaw walked round the corner to a small office he rented in the neighborhood; chiefly for the publication of a small periodical, of psychical and psychological notes of the driest and most agnostic sort. He had only one clerk, who sat at a desk in the outer office, totting up figures and facts for the purposes of the printed report; and the Professor paused to ask if Mr. Pringle had called. The clerk answered mechanically in the negative and went on mechanically adding up figures; and the Professor turned towards the inner room that was his study. "Oh, by the way, Berridge," he added, without turning round, "if Mr. Pringle comes, send him straight in to me. You needn't interrupt your work; I rather want those notes finished tonight if possible. You might leave them on my desk tomorrow, if I am late."

And he went into his private office, still brooding on the problem which the name of Pringle had raised; or rather, perhaps, had ratified and confirmed in his mind. Even the most perfectly balanced of agnostics is partially human; and it is possible that the missionary's letter seemed to have greater weight as promising to support his private and still tentative hypothesis. He sat down in his large and comfortable chair, opposite the engraving of Montaigne; and read once more the short letter from the Rev. Luke Pringle, making the appointment for that morning. No man knew better than Professor Openshaw the marks of the letter of the crank; the crowded details; the spidery handwriting; the unnecessary length and repetition. There were none of these things in this case; but a brief and businesslike typewritten statement that the writer had encountered some curious cases of Disappearance, which seemed to fall within the province of the Professor as a student of psychic problems. The professor was favorably impressed; nor had he any unfavorable impression, in spite of a slight movement of surprise, when he looked up and saw that the Rev. Luke Pringle was already in the room.

"Your clerk told me I was to come straight in," said Mr. Pringle apologetically, but with a broad and rather agreeable grin. The grin was partly masked by masses of reddish-gray beard and whiskers; a perfect jungle of a beard, such as is sometimes grown by white men living in the jungles; but the eyes above the snub nose had nothing about them in the least wild or outlandish. Openshaw had instantly turned on them that concentrated spotlight or burning-glass of skeptical scrutiny which he turned on many men to see if they were mountebanks or maniacs; and, in this case, he had a rather unusual sense of reassurance. The wild beard might have belonged to a crank, but the eyes completely contradicted the beard; they were full of that quite frank and friendly laughter which is never found in the faces of those who are serious frauds or serious lunatics. He would have expected a man with those eyes to be a Philistine, a jolly skeptic, a man who shouted out shallow but hearty contempt for ghosts and spirits; but anyhow, no professional humbug could afford to look as frivolous as that. The man was buttoned up to the throat in a shabby old cape, and only his broad limp hat suggested the cleric; but missionaries from wild places do not always bother to dress like clerics.

"You probably think all this is another hoax, Professor," said Mr. Pringle, with a sort of abstract enjoyment, "and I hope you will forgive my laughing at your very natural air of disapproval. All the same, I've got to tell my story to somebody who knows, because it's true. And, all joking apart, it's tragic as well as true. Well, to cut it short, I was a missionary in Nya-Nya, a station in West Africa, in the thick of the forests, where almost the only other white man was the officer in command of the district, Captain Wales; and he and I grew rather thick. Not that he liked missions; he was, if I may say so, thick in many ways; one of those square-headed, square-shouldered men of action who hardly need to think, let alone believe. That's what makes it all the queerer. One day he came back to his tent in the forest, after a short leave, and said he had gone through a jolly rum experience, and didn't know what to do about it. He was holding a rusty old book in a leather binding, and he put it down on a table beside his revolver and an old Arab sword he kept, probably as a curiosity. He said this book had belonged to a man on the boat he had just come off; and the man swore that nobody must open the book, or look inside it; or else they would be carried off by the devil, or disappear, or something. Wales said this was all nonsense, of course; and they had a quarrel; and the upshot seems to have been that this man, taunted with cowardice or superstition, actually did look into the book; and instantly dropped it; walked to the side of the boat—"

"One moment," said the Professor, who had made one or two notes. "Before you tell me anything else, did this man tell Wales where he had got the book, or who it originally belonged to?"

"Yes," replied Pringle, now entirely grave. "It seems he said he was bringing it back to Dr. Hankey, the Oriental traveler now in England, to whom it originally belonged, and who had warned him of its strange properties. Well, Hankey is an able man and a rather crabbed and sneering sort of man; which makes it queerer still. But the point of Wales's story is much simpler. It is that the man who had looked into the book walked straight over the side of the ship, and was never seen again."

"Do you believe it yourself?" asked Openshaw after a pause.

"Well, I do," replied Pringle. "I believe it for two reasons. First, that Wales was an entirely unimaginative man; and he added one touch that only an imaginative man could have added. He said that the man walked straight over the side on a still and calm day; but there was no splash."

The Professor looked at his notes for some seconds in silence; and then said: "And your other reason for believing it?"

"My other reason," answered the Rev. Luke Pringle, "is what I saw myself."

There was another silence, until he continued in the same matter-of-fact way. Whatever he had, he had nothing of the eagerness with which the crank, or even the believer, tries to convince others.

"I told you that Wales put down the book on the table beside the sword. There was only one entrance to the tent; and it happened that I was standing in it, looking out into the forest, with my back to my companion. He was standing by the table grumbling and growling about the whole business; saying it was tomfoolery in the twentieth century to be frightened of opening a book; asking why the devil he shouldn't open it himself. Then some instinct stirred in me and I said that he had better not do that, it had better be returned to Dr. Hankey. 'What harm could it do?' he said restlessly. 'What harm did it do?' I answered obstinately. 'What happened to your friend on the boat?' He didn't answer; indeed I didn't know what he could answer; but I pressed my logical advantage in mere vanity. 'If it comes to that,' I said, 'what is your version of what really happened on the boat?' Still he didn't answer; and I looked round and saw that he wasn't there.

"The tent was empty. The book was lying on the table; open, but on its face, as if he had turned it downwards. But the sword was lying on the ground near the other side of the tent; and the canvas of the tent showed a great slash, as if somebody had hacked his way out with the sword. The gash in the tent gaped at me; but showed only the dark glimmer of the forest outside. And when I went across and looked through the rent I could not be certain whether the tangle of the tall plants and the undergrowth had been bent or broken; at least no farther than a few feet. I have never seen or heard of Captain Wales from that day.

"I wrapped the book up in brown paper, taking good care not to look at it; and I brought it back to England, intending at first to return it to Dr. Hankey. Then I saw some notes in your paper suggesting a hypothesis about such things; and I decided to stop on the way and put the matter before you, as you have a name for being balanced and having an open mind."

Professor Openshaw laid down his pen and looked steadily at the man on the other side of the table; concentrating in that single stare all his long experience of many entirely different types of humbug, and even some eccentric and extraordinary types of honest men. In the ordinary way, he would have begun with the healthy hypothesis that the story was a pack of lies. On the whole he did incline to assume that it was a pack of lies. And yet he could not fit the man into his story; if it were only that he could not see that sort of liar telling that sort of lie. The man was not trying to look honest on the surface, as most quacks and impostors do; somehow, it seemed all the other way; as if the man *was* honest, in spite of something else that was merely on the surface. He thought of a good man with one innocent delusion; but again the symptoms were not the same; there was even a sort of virile indifference; as if the man did not care much about his delusion, if it was a delusion.

"Mr. Pringle," he said sharply, like a barrister making a witness jump, "where is this book of yours now?"

The grin reappeared on the bearded face which had grown grave during the recital.

"I left it outside," said Mr. Pringle. "I mean in the outer office. It was a risk, perhaps; but the less risk of the two."

"What do you mean?" demanded the Professor. "Why didn't you bring it straight in here?"

"Because," answered the missionary, "I knew that as soon as you saw it, you'd open it—before you had heard the story. I thought it possible you might think twice about opening it—after you'd heard the story."

Then after a silence he added: "There was nobody out there but your clerk; and he looked a stolid steady-going specimen, immersed in business calculations."

Openshaw laughed unaffectedly. "Oh, Babbage," he cried, "your magic tomes are safe enough with him, I assure you. His name's Berridge—but I often call him Babbage; because he's so exactly like a Calculating Machine. No human being, if you can call him a human being, would be less likely to open other people's brown paper parcels. Well, we may as well go and bring it in now; though I assure you I will consider seriously the course to be taken with it. Indeed, I tell you frankly," and he stared at the man again, "that I'm not quite sure whether we ought to open it here and now, or send it to this Dr. Hankey."

The two had passed together out of the inner into the outer office; and even as they did so, Mr. Pringle gave a cry and ran forward towards the clerk's desk. For the clerk's desk was there; but not the clerk. On the clerk's desk lay a faded old leather book, torn out of its brown-paper wrappings, and lying closed, but as if it had just been opened. The clerk's desk stood against the wide window that looked out into the street; and the window was shattered with a huge ragged hole in the glass; as if a human body had been shot through it into the world without. There was no other trace of Mr. Berridge.

Both the two men left in the office stood as still as statues; and then it was the Professor who slowly came to life. He looked even more judicial than he had ever looked in his life, as he slowly turned and held out his hand to the missionary.

"Mr. Pringle," he said, "I beg your pardon. I beg your pardon only for thoughts that I have had; and half-thoughts at that. But nobody could call himself a scientific man and not face a fact like this."

"I suppose," said Pringle doubtfully, "that we ought to make some inquiries. Can you ring up his house and find out if he has gone home?"

"I don't know that he's on the telephone," answered Openshaw, rather absently; "he lives somewhere up Hampstead way, I think. But I suppose somebody will inquire here, if his friends or family miss him."

"Could we furnish a description," asked the other, "if the police want it?"

"The police!" said the Professor, starting from his reverie. "A description. . . . Well, he looked awfully like everybody else, I'm afraid, except for goggles. One of those clean-shaven chaps. But the police . . . look here, what *are* we to do about this mad business?"

"I know what I ought to do," said the Rev. Mr. Pringle firmly. "I am going to take this book straight to the only original Dr. Hankey, and ask him what the devil it's all about. He lives not very far from here, and I'll come straight back and tell you what he says."

"Oh, very well," said the Professor at last, as he sat down rather wearily; perhaps relieved for the moment to be rid of the responsibility. But long after the brisk and ringing footsteps of the little missionary had died away down the street, the Professor sat in the same posture, staring into vacancy like a man in a trance.

He was still in the same seat and almost in the same attitude, when the same brisk footsteps were heard on the pavement without and the missionary entered, this time, as a glance assured him, with empty hands.

"Dr. Hankey," said Pringle gravely, "wants to keep the book for an hour and consider the point. Then he asks us both to call, and he will give us his decision. He specially desired, Professor, that you should accompany me on the second visit."

Openshaw continued to stare in silence; then he said, suddenly:

"Who the devil is Dr. Hankey?"

"You sound rather as if you meant he was the devil," said Pringle, smiling, "and I fancy some people have thought so. He had quite a reputation in your own line; but he gained it mostly in India, studying local magic and so on, so perhaps he's not so well known here. He is a yellow skinny little devil with a lame leg, and a doubtful temper; but he seems to have set up in an ordinary respectable practice in these parts, and I don't know anything definitely wrong about him—unless it's wrong to be the only person who can possibly know anything about all this crazy affair."

Professor Openshaw rose heavily and went to the telephone; he rang up Father Brown, changing the luncheon engagement to a dinner, that he might hold himself free for the expedition to the house of the Anglo-Indian doctor; after that he sat down again, lit a cigar and sank once more into his own unfathomable thoughts..

Father Brown went round to the restaurant appointed for dinner, and kicked his heels for some time in a vestibule full of mirrors and palms in pots; he had been informed of Openshaw's afternoon engagement, and, as the evening closed in dark and stormy round the glass and the green plants, guessed that it had produced something unexpected and unduly prolonged. He even wondered for a moment whether the Professor would turn up at all; but when the Professor eventually did, it was clear that his own more general guesses had been justified. For it was a very wild-eyed and even wild-haired Professor who eventually drove back with Mr. Pringle from the expedition to the north of London, where suburbs are still fringed with heathy wastes and scraps of common, looking more somber under the rather thunderous sunset. Nevertheless, they had apparently found the house, standing a little apart though within hail of other houses; they had verified the brass plate duly engraved: "J. D. Hankey, M.D., M.R.C.S." Only they did not find J. D. Hankey, M.D., M.R.C.S. They found only what a nightmare whisper had already subconsciously prepared them to find: a commonplace parlor with the accursed volume lying on the table, as if it had just been

240

read; and beyond, a back door burst open and a faint trail of footsteps that ran a little way up so steep a garden path that it seemed that no lame man could have run up so lightly. But it was a lame man who had run; for in those few steps there was the misshapen unequal mark of some sort of surgical boot; then two marks of that boot alone (as if the creature had hopped) and then nothing. There was nothing further to be learned from Dr. J. D. Hankey, except that he had made his decision. He had read the oracle and received the doom.

When the two came into the entrance under the palms, Pringle put the book down suddenly on a small table, as if it burned his fingers. The priest glanced at it curiously; there was only some rude lettering on the front with a couplet:

They that looked into this book
Them the Flying Terror took;

and underneath, as he afterward discovered, similar warnings in Greek, Latin and French. The other two had turned away with a natural impulsion towards drinks, after their exhaustion and bewilderment; and Openshaw had called to the waiter, who brought cocktails on a tray.

"You will dine with us, I hope," said the Professor to the missionary; but Mr. Pringle amiably shook his head.

"If you'll forgive me," he said, "I'm going off to wrestle with this book and this business by myself somewhere. I suppose I couldn't use your office for an hour or so?"

"I suppose—I'm afraid it's locked," said Openshaw in some surprise.

"You forget there's a hole in the window." The Rev. Luke Pringle gave the very broadest of all his broad grins and vanished into the darkness without.

"A rather odd fellow, that, after all," said the Professor, frowning.

He was rather surprised to find Father Brown talking to the waiter who had brought the cocktails, apparently about the waiter's most private affairs; for there was some mention of a baby who was now out of danger. He commented on the fact with some surprise, wondering how the priest came to know the man; but the former only said, "Oh, I dine here every two or three months, and I've talked to him now and then."

The Professor, who himself dined there about five times a

week, was conscious that he had never thought of talking to the man; but his thoughts were interrupted by a strident ringing and a summons to the telephone. The voice on the telephone said it was Pringle; it was rather a muffled voice, but it might well be muffled in all those bushes of beard and whisker. Its message was enough to establish identity.

"Professor," said the voice, "I can't stand it any longer. I'm going to look for myself. I'm speaking from your office and the book is in front of me. If anything happens to me, this to say good-bye. No—it's no good trying to stop me. You wouldn't be in time, anyhow. I'm opening the book now. I . . ."

Openshaw thought he heard something like a sort of thrilling or shivering yet almost soundless crash; then he shouted the name of Pringle again and again; but he heard no more. He hung up the receiver, and, restored to a superb academic calm, rather like the calm of despair, went back and quietly took his seat at the dinner-table. Then, as coolly as if he were describing the failure of some small silly trick at a *séance,* he told the priest every detail of this monstrous mystery.

"Five men have now vanished in this impossible way," he said. "Every one is extraordinary; and yet the one case I simply can't get over is my clerk, Berridge. It's just because he was the quietest creature that he's the queerest case."

"Yes," replied Father Brown, "it was a queer thing for Berridge to do, anyway. He was awfully conscientious. He was always so jolly careful to keep all the office business separate from any fun of his own. Why, hardly anybody knew he was quite a humorist at home and—"

"Berridge!" cried the Professor. "What on earth are you talking about? Did you know him?"

"Oh, no," said Father Brown carelessly, "only as you say I know the waiter. I've often had to wait in your office, till you turned up; and of course I passed the time of day with poor Berridge. He was rather a card. I remember he once said he would like to collect valueless things, as collectors did the silly things they thought valuable. You know the old story about the woman who collected valueless things."

"I'm not sure I know what you're talking about," said Openshaw. "But even if my clerk was eccentric (and I never knew a man I should have thought less so), it wouldn't explain what happened to him; and it certainly wouldn't explain the others."

242

"What others?" asked the priest.

The Professor stared at him and spoke distinctly, as if to a child.

"My dear Father Brown, five men have disappeared."

"My dear Professor Openshaw, no men have disappeared."

Father Brown gazed back at his host with equal steadiness and spoke with equal distinctness. Nevertheless, the Professor required the words repeated, and they were repeated as distinctly.

"I say that no men have disappeared."

After a moment's silence, he added, "I suppose the hardest thing is to convince anybody that 0 plus 0 = 0. Men believe the oddest things if they are in a series; that is why Macbeth believed the three words of the three witches; though the first was something he knew himself; and the last something he could only bring about himself. But in your case the middle term is the weakest of all."

"What do you mean?"

"You saw nobody vanish. You did not see the man vanish from the boat. You did not see the man vanish from the tent. All that rests on the word of Mr. Pringle, which I will not discuss just now. But you'll admit this; you would never have taken his word yourself, *unless* you had seen it confirmed by your clerk's disappearance; just as Macbeth would never have believed he would be king, if he had not been confirmed in believing he would be Cawdor."

"That may be true," said the Professor, nodding slowly. "But *when* it was confirmed, I knew it was the truth. You say I saw nothing myself. But I did; I saw my own clerk disappear. Berridge did disappear."

"Berridge did not disappear," said Father Brown. "On the contrary."

"What the devil do you mean by 'on the contrary'?"

"I mean, said Father Brown, "that he never disappeared. He appeared."

Openshaw stared across at his friend, but the eyes had already altered in his head, as they did when they concentrated on a new presentation of a problem. The priest went on:

"He appeared in your study, disguised in a bushy red beard and buttoned up in a clumsy cape, and announced himself as the Rev. Luke Pringle. And you had never noticed your own clerk enough to know him again, when he was in so rough-and-ready a disguise."

"But surely," began the Professor.

"Could you describe him for the police?" asked Father Brown. "Not you. You probably knew he was clean-shaven and wore tinted glasses; and merely taking off those glasses was a better disguise than putting on anything else. You had never seen his eyes any more than his soul; jolly laughing eyes. He had planted his absurd book and all the properties; then he calmly smashed the window, put on the beard and cape and walked into your study; knowing that you had never looked at him in your life."

"But why should he play me such an insane trick?" demanded Openshaw.

"Why, *because* you had never looked at him in your life," said Father Brown; and his hand slightly curled and clinched, as if he might have struck the table, if he had been given to gesture. "You called him the Calculating-Machine, because that was all you ever used him for. You never found out even what a stranger strolling into your office could find out, in five minutes' chat: that he was a character; that he was full of antics; that he had all sorts of views on you and your theories and your reputation for 'spotting' people. Can't you understand his itching to prove that you couldn't spot your own clerk? He has nonsense notions of all sorts. About collecting useless things, for instance. Don't you know the story of the woman who bought the two most useless things; an old doctor's brass-plate and a wooden leg? With those your ingenious clerk created the character of the remarkable Dr. Hankey; as easily as the visionary Captain Wales. Planting them in his own house—"

"Do you mean that place we visited beyond Hampstead was Berridge's own house?" asked Openshaw.

"Did *you* know his house—or even his address?" retorted the priest. "Look here, don't think I'm speaking disrespectfully of you or your work. You are a great servant of truth and you know I could never be disrespectful to that. You've seen through a lot of liars, when you put your mind to it. But don't *only* look at liars. Do, just occasionally, look at honest men—like the waiter."

"Where is Berridge now?" asked the Professor, after a long silence.

"I haven't the least doubt," said Father Brown, "that he is back in your office. In fact, he came back into your office at the exact moment when the Rev. Luke Pringle read the volume and faded into the void."

There was another long silence and then Professor Openshaw laughed; with the laugh of a great man who is great enough to look small. Then he said abruptly:

"I suppose I do deserve it; for not noticing the nearest helpers I have. But you must admit the accumulation of incidents was rather formidable. Did you *never* feel just a momentary awe of the awful volume?"

"Oh that," said Father Brown. "I opened it as soon as I saw it lying there. It's all blank pages. You see, I am not superstitious."

A MATTER OF TASTE

BY DOROTHY L. SAYERS

Dorothy Leigh Sayers was born in Oxford, England, and grew up in the East Anglia fen country familiar to readers of her *The Nine Tailors.* She received a degree in medieval literature from Somerville College, Oxford, which later served as a background for her novel *Gaudy Night,* disguised as "Shrewsbury College." After graduation she edited several volumes of poetry and was a copywriter for a London advertising agency, which she later satirized in *Murder Must Advertise.* Her first novel about Lord Peter Wimsey, published in 1923, was *Whose Body?* Miss Sayers was an anthologist, playwright, lecturer, and translator of Dante.

"HALTE-LA! . . . ATTENTION . . . F—e!"

The young man in the gray suit pushed his way through the protesting porters and leaped nimbly for the footboard of the guard's van as the Paris-Evreux express steamed out of the Invalides. The guard, with an eye to a tip, fielded him adroitly from among the detaining hands.

"It is happy for monsieur that he is so agile," he remarked. "Monsieur is in a hurry?"

"Somewhat. Thank you. Do you know if I can get through by the corridor?"

"But certainly. The *premières* are two coaches away, beyond the luggage van."

The young man rewarded his rescuer, and made his way forward, mopping his face. As he passed the piled-up luggage, something caught his eye, and he stopped to investigate. It was a suitcase, nearly new, of expensive-looking leather, labeled conspicuously:

LORD PETER WIMSEY,
Hôtel Saumon d'Or,
Verneuil-sur-Eure.

and bore witness to its itinerary thus:

LONDON—PARIS
(Waterloo) (Gare St. Lazare)
via Southampton-Havre.
PARIS—VERNEUIL
(Ch. de Fer de l'Ouest)

The young man whistled, and sat down on a trunk to think it out.

Somewhere there had been a leakage, and they were on his trail. Nor did they care who knew it. There were hundreds of people in London and Paris who would know the name of Wimsey, not counting the police of both countries. In addition to belonging to one of the oldest ducal families in England, Lord Peter had made himself conspicuous by his meddling with crime detection. A label like this was a gratuitous advertisement.

247

But the amazing thing was that the pursuers were not troubling to hide themselves from the pursued. That argued very great confidence. That he should have got into the guard's van was, of course, an accident, but, even so, he might have seen it on the platform, or anywhere.

An accident? It occurred to him—not for the first time, but definitely now, and without doubt—that it was indeed an accident for them that he was here. The series of maddening delays that had held him up between London and the Invalides presented itself to him with an air of prearrangement. The preposterous accusation, for instance, of the woman who had accosted him in Piccadilly, and the slow process of extricating himself at Marlborough Street. It was easy to hold a man up on some trumped-up charge till an important plan had matured.

Then there was the lavatory door at Waterloo, which had so ludicrously locked itself upon him. Being athletic, he had climbed over the partition, to find the attendant mysteriously absent. And, in Paris, was it by chance that he had a deaf taxi driver, who mistook the direction "Quai d'Orléans" for "Gare de Lyon," and drove a mile and a half in the wrong direction before the shouts of his fare attracted his attention?

They were clever, the pursuers, and circumspect. They had accurate information; they would delay him, but without taking any overt step; they knew that, if only they could keep time on their side, they needed no other ally.

Did they know he was on the train? If not, he still kept the advantage, for they would travel in a false security, thinking him to be left, raging and helpless, in the Invalides. He decided to make a cautious reconnaissance.

The first step was to change his gray suit for another of inconspicuous navy-blue cloth, which he had in his small black bag. This he did in the privacy of the men's room, substituting for his gray soft hat a large traveling cap, which pulled well down over his eyes.

There was little difficulty in locating the man he was in search of. He found him seated in the inner corner of a first-class compartment, facing the engine, so that the watcher could approach unseen from behind. On the rack was a handsome dressing case, with the initials P.D.B.W. The young man was familiar with Wimsey's narrow, beaky face, flat yellow hair, and insolent dropped eyelids. He smiled a little grimly.

"He is confident," he thought, "and has regrettably made the mistake of underrating the enemy. Good! This is where I retire into a *seconde* and keep my eyes open. The next act of this melodrama will take place, I fancy, at Dreux."

It is a rule on the Chemin de Fer l'Ouest that all Paris-Evreux trains, whether of Grande Vitesse or what Lord Peter Wimsey preferred to call Grande Paresse, shall halt for an interminable period at Dreux. The young man (now in navy-blue) watched his quarry safely into the refreshment room, and slipped unobtrusively out of the station.

In a quarter of an hour he was back—this time in a heavy motoring coat, helmet, and goggles, at the wheel of a powerful hired Peugeot. Coming quietly onto the platform, he took up his station behind the wall of the *lampisterie,* where he could keep an eye on the train and the buffet door. After fifteen minutes his patience was rewarded by the sight of his man again boarding the express, dressing case in hand.

The porters slammed the doors, crying, "Next stop Verneuil!" The engine panted and groaned; the long train of gray-green carriages clanked slowly away. The motorist drew a breath of satisfaction, and, hurrying past the barrier, started up the car. He knew that he had a good eighty miles an hour under his hood, and there is no speed limit in France.

Mon Souci, the seat of that eccentric and eremitical genius the Comte de Rueil, is situated three kilometers from Verneuil. It is a sorrowful and decayed château, desolate at the termination of its neglected avenue of pines. The mournful state of a nobility without an allegiance surrounds it. The stone nymphs droop greenly over their dry and moldering fountains. An occasional peasant creaks with a single wagonload of wood along the ill-forested glades. It has the atmosphere of sunset at all hours of the day. The woodwork is dry and gaping for lack of paint. Through the jalousies one sees the prim *salon,* with its beautiful and faded furniture. Even the last of its ill-dressed, ill-favored women has withered away from Mon Souci, with her inbred, exaggerated features and her long white gloves.

But at the rear of the château a chimney smokes incessantly. It is the furnace of the laboratory, the only living and modern thing among the old and dying; the only place tended and loved, petted and spoiled, heir to the long solicitude which Counts of a more light-hearted day had given to stable and kennel, portrait gallery and ballroom. And below, in the cool cellar, lie row upon row the dusty bottles, each an enchanted glass coffin in which the Sleeping Beauty of the vine grows ever more ravishing.

As the Peugeot came to a standstill in the courtyard, the driver observed with considerable surprise that he was not the Count's only visitor. An immense super-Renault, like a *merveilleuse* of the Directoire, all hood and no body, had been drawn so ostentatiously across the entrance as to embarrass the approach of any newcomer. Its glittering panels were embellished with a coat of arms, and the Count's elderly servant was at that moment staggering beneath the weight of two large and elaborate suitcases, bearing in silver letters that could be read a mile away the legend: LORD PETER WIMSEY.

The Peugeot driver gazed with astonishment at this display, and grinned sardonically. "Lord Peter seems rather ubiquitous in this country," he observed to himself. Then, taking pen and paper from his bag, he busied himself with a little letter writing.

By the time that the suitcases had been carried in, and the Renault had purred its smooth way to the outbuildings, the document was complete and enclosed in an envelope addressed to the Comte de Rueil. "The hoist with his own petard touch," said the young man, and, stepping up to the door, presented the envelope to the manservant.

"I am the bearer of a letter of introduction to Monsieur le Comte," he said. "Will you have the obligingness to present it to him? My name is Bredon—Death Bredon."

The man bowed, and begged him to enter.

"If monsieur will have the goodness to seat himself in the hall for a few moments. Monsieur le Comte is engaged with another gentleman, but I will lose no time in making monsieur's arrival known."

The young man sat down and waited. The windows of the hall looked out upon the entrance, and it was not long before the château's sleep was disturbed by the hooting of yet another motor horn. A station taxicab came noisily up the avenue. The man from the first-class carriage and the luggage labeled P.D.B.W. were deposited on the doorstep. Lord Peter Wimsey dismissed the driver and rang the bell.

"Now," said Mr. Bredon, "the fun is going to begin." He effaced himself as far as possible in the shadow of a tall *armoire normande*.

"Good evening," said the newcomer to the manservant, in admirable French, "I am Lord Peter Wimsey. I arrive upon the invitation of Monsieur le Comte de Rueil. Monsieur le Comte is at liberty?"

"Milord Peter Wimsey? Pardon, monsieur, but I do not understand. Milord de Wimsey is already arrived and is with Monsieur le Comte at this moment."

"You surprise me," said the other, with complete imperturbability, "for certainly no one but myself has any right to that name. It seems as though some person more ingenious than honest has had the bright idea of impersonating me."

The servant was clearly at a loss.

"Perhaps," he suggested, "monsieur can show his *papiers d'identité.*"

"Although it is somewhat unusual to produce one's credentials on the doorstep when paying a private visit," replied his lordship, with unaltered good humor, "I have not the slightest objection. Here is my passport, here is a *permis de séjour* granted to me in Paris, here my visiting card, and here a quantity of correspondence addressed to me at the Hôtel Meurice, Paris, at my flat in Piccadilly, London, at the Marlborough Club, London, and at my brother's house at King's Denver. Is that sufficiently in order?"

The servant perused the documents carefully, particularly impressed by the *permis de séjour.*

"It appears there is some mistake," he murmured dubiously. "If monsieur will follow me, I will acquaint Monsieur le Comte."

They disappeared through the folding doors at the back of the hall, and Bredon was left alone.

"Quite a little boom in Richmonds today," he observed, "each of us more unscrupulous than the last. The occasion obviously calls for a refined subtlety of method."

After what he judged to be a hectic ten minutes in the Count's library, the servant reappeared, searching for him.

"Monsieur le Comte's compliments, and would monsieur step this way?"

Bredon entered the room with a jaunty step. He had created for himself the mastery of this situation. The Count, a thin, elderly man, his fingers deeply stained with chemicals, sat, with a perturbed expression, at his desk. In two armchairs sat the two Wimseys.

Bredon noted that, while the Wimsey he had seen in the train (whom he mentally named Peter I) retained his unruffled smile, Peter II (he of the Renault) had the flushed and indignant air of an Englishman affronted. The two men were superficially alike—both fair, lean, and long-nosed, with the nondescript, inelastic face which predominates in any assembly of well-bred Anglo-Saxons.

"Mr. Bredon," said the Count, "I am charmed to have the pleasure of making your acquaintance, and regret that I must at once call upon you for a service as singular as it is important. You have presented to me a letter of introduction from your cousin, Lord Peter Wimsey. Will you now be good enough to inform me which of these gentlemen he is?"

Bredon let his glance pass slowly from the one claimant to the other, meditating what answer would best serve his own ends. One, at any rate, of the men in this room was a formidable intellect, trained in the detection of imposture.

"Well?" said Peter II. "Are you going to acknowledge me, Bredon?"

Peter I extracted a cigarette from a silver case. "Your confederate does not seem very well up in his part," he remarked, with a quiet smile at Peter II.

"Monsieur le Comte," said Bredon, "I regret extremely that I cannot assist you in the matter. My acquaintance with my cousin, like your own, has been made and maintained entirely through correspondence on a subject of common interest. My profession," he added, "has made me unpopular with my family."

There was a very slight sigh of relief somewhere. The false Wimsey—whichever he was—had gained a respite. Bredon smiled.

"An excellent move, Mr. Bredon," said Peter I, "but it will hardly explain—allow me." He took the letter from the Count's hesitating hand. "It will hardly explain the fact that the ink of this letter of recommendation, dated three weeks ago, is even now scarcely dry—though I congratulate you on the very plausible imitation of my handwriting."

"If *you* can forge my handwriting," said Peter II, "so can this Mr. Bredon." He read the letter aloud over his double's shoulder.

" 'Monsieur le Comte—I have the honor to present to you my friend and cousin, Mr. Death Bredon, who, I understand, is to

252

be traveling in your part of France next month. He is very anxious to view your interesting library. Although a journalist by profession, he really knows something about books.' I am delighted to learn for the first time that I have such a cousin. An interviewer's trick, I fancy, Monsieur le Comte. Fleet Street appears well informed about our family names. Possibly it is equally well informed about the object of my visit to Mon Souci?"

"If," said Bredon boldly, "you refer to the acquisition of the Rueil formula for poison gas for the British Government, I can answer for my own knowledge, though possibly the rest of Fleet Street is less completely enlightened." He weighed his words carefully now, warned by his slip. The sharp eyes and detective ability of Peter II alarmed him far more than the caustic tongue of Peter I.

The Count uttered an exclamation of dismay.

"Gentlemen," he said, "one thing is obvious—that there has been somewhere a disastrous leakage of information. Which of you is the Lord Peter Wimsey to whom I should entrust the formula, I do not know. Both of you are supplied with papers of identity; both appear completely instructed in this matter; both of your handwritings correspond with the letters I have previously received from Lord Peter, and both of you have offered me the sum agreed upon in Bank of England notes.

"In addition, this third gentleman arrives endowed with an equal facility in handwritings, an introductory letter surrounded by most suspicious circumstances, and a degree of acquaintance with this whole matter which alarms me. I can see but one solution. All of you must remain here at the château while I send to England for some elucidation of this mystery. To the genuine Lord Peter I offer my apologies, and assure him that I will endeavor to make his stay as agreeable as possible. Will this satisfy you? It will? I am delighted to hear it. My servants will show you to your bedrooms, and dinner will be at half-past seven."

"It is delightful to think," said Mr. Bredon, as he fingered his glass and passed it before his nostrils with the air of a connoisseur, "that whichever of these gentlemen has the right to the name he assumes is assured tonight of a truly Olympian satisfaction." His impudence had returned to him, and he challenged the company with an air. "Your cellars, Monsieur le

Comte, are as well known among men endowed with a palate as your talents among men of science. No eloquence could say more."

The two Lord Peters murmured assent.

"I am the more pleased by your commendation," said the Count, "that it suggests to me a little test which, with your kind cooperation, will, I think, assist us very much in determining which of you gentlemen is Lord Peter Wimsey and which his talented impersonator. Is it not matter of common notoriety that Lord Peter has a palate for wine almost unequaled in Europe?"

"You flatter me, Monsieur le Comte," said Peter II modestly.

"I wouldn't like to say unequaled," said Peter I, chiming in like a well-trained duet; "let's call it fair to middling. Less liable to misconstruction and all that."

"Your lordship does yourself an injustice," said Bredon, addressing both men with impartial deference. "The bet which you won from Mr. Frederick Arbuthnot at the Egotists Club, when he challenged you to name the vintage years of seventeen wines blindfolded, received its due prominence in the *Evening Wire.*"

"I was in extra form that night," said Peter I.

"A fluke," laughed Peter II.

"The test I propose, gentlemen, is on similar lines," pursued the Count, "though somewhat less strenuous. There are six courses ordered for dinner tonight. With each we will drink a different wine, which my butler shall bring in with the label concealed. You shall each in turn give me your opinion upon the vintage. By this means we shall perhaps arrive at something, since the most brilliant forger—of whom I gather I have at least two at my table tonight—can scarcely forge a palate for wine. If too hazardous a mixture of wines should produce a temporary incommodity in the morning, you will, I feel sure, suffer it gladly this once in the cause of truth."

The two Wimseys bowed.

"*In vino veritas,*" said Mr. Bredon, with a laugh. He at least was well seasoned, and foresaw opportunities for himself.

"Accident, and my butler, having placed you at my right hand, monsieur," went on the Count, addressing Peter I, "I will ask you to begin by pronouncing, as accurately as may be, upon the wine which you have just drunk."

"That is scarcely a searching ordeal," said the other, with a

254

smile. "I can say definitely that it is a very pleasant and well-matured Chablis Moutonne; and, since ten years is an excellent age for a Chablis—a real Chablis—I should vote for 1916, which was perhaps the best of the war vintages in that district."

"Have you anything to add to that opinion, monsieur?" inquired the Count deferentially of Peter II.

"I wouldn't like to be dogmatic to a year or so," said that gentleman critically, "but if I must commit myself, don't you know, I should say 1915—decidedly 1915."

The Count bowed, and turned to Bredon.

"Perhaps you, too, monsieur, would be interested to give an opinion," he suggested, with the exquisite courtesy always shown to the plain man in the society of experts.

"I'd rather not set a standard which I might not be able to live up to," replied Bredon a little maliciously. "I know that it is 1915, for I happened to see the label."

Peter II looked a little disconcerted.

"We will arrange matters better in future," said the Count. "Pardon me." He stepped apart for a few moments' conference with the butler, who presently advanced to remove the oysters and bring in the soup.

The next candidate for attention arrived swathed to the lip in damask.

"It is your turn to speak first, monsieur," said the Count to Peter II. "Permit me to offer you an olive to cleanse the palate. No haste, I beg. Even for the most excellent political ends, good wine must not be used with disrespect."

The rebuke was not unnecessary, for, after a preliminary sip, Peter II had taken a deep draft of the heady white richness. Under Peter I's quizzical eye he wilted quite visibly.

"It is—it is Sauterne," he began, and stopped. Then, gathering encouragement from Bredon's smile, he said, with more aplomb, "Château Yquem, 1911—ah! the queen of white wines, sir, as what's-his-name says." He drained his glass defiantly.

The Count's face was a study as he slowly detached his fascinated gaze from Peter II to fix it on Peter I.

"If I had to be impersonated by somebody," murmured the latter gently, "it would have been more flattering to have had it undertaken by a person to whom all white wines were *not* alike. Well, now, sir, this admirable vintage is, of course, a Montrachet of—let me see"—he rolled the wine delicately on his tongue—"of 1911. And a very attractive wine it is, though, with all due deference to yourself, Monsieur le Comte, I feel that it is perhaps slightly too sweet to occupy its present place in the menu. True, with this excellent *consommé marmite,* a sweetish wine is not altogether out of place, but, in my own humble opinion, it would have shown to better advantage with the *confitures.*"

"There, now," said Bredon innocently, "it just shows how one may be misled. Had not I had the advantage of Lord Peter's expert opinion—for certainly nobody who could mistake Montrachet for Sauterne has any claim to the name of Wimsey—I should have pronounced this to be, not the Montrachet-Aîné, but the Chevalier-Montrachet of the same year, which is a trifle sweeter. But no doubt, as your lordship says, drinking it with the soup has cauused it to appear sweeter to me than it actually is."

The Count looked sharply at him, but made no comment.

"Have another olive," said Peter I kindly. "You can't judge wine if your mind is on other flavors."

"Thanks frightfully," said Bredon. "And that reminds me—" He launched into a rather pointless story about olives, which lasted out the soup and bridged the interval to the entrance of an exquisitely cooked sole.

The Count's eye followed the pale amber wine rather thoughtfully as it trilled into the glasses. Bredon raised his in the approved manner to his nostrils, and his face flushed a little. With the first sip he turned excitedly to his host.

"Good God, sir—" he began.

The lifted hand cautioned him to silence.

Peter I sipped, inhaled, sipped again, and his brows clouded. Peter II had by this time apparently abandoned his pretensions. He drank thirstily, with a beaming smile and a lessening hold upon reality.

"Eh bien, monsieur?" inquired the Count gently.

"This," said Peter I, "is certainly hock, and the noblest hock I have ever tasted, but I must admit that for the moment I cannot precisely place it."

"No?" said Bredon. His voice was like bean-honey now; sweet and harsh together. "Nor the other gentleman? And yet I fancy I could place it within a couple of miles, though it is a wine I had hardly looked to find in a French cellar at this time. It is hock, as your lordship says, and at that is Johannisberger. Not the plebeian cousin, but the *echter* Schloss Johannisberger from

256

the castle vineyard itself. Your lordship must have missed it—to your great loss—during the war years. My father laid some down the year before he died, but it appears that the ducal cellars at Denver were less well furnished."

"I must set about remedying the omission," said the remaining Peter, with determination.

The *poulet* was served to the accompaniment of an argument over the Lafitte, his lordship placing it at 1878, Bredon maintaining it to be a relic of the glorious 'seventy-fives, slightly overmatured, but both agreeing as to its great age and noble pedigree.

As to the Clos-Vougeôt, on the other hand, there was complete agreement; after a tentative suggestion of 1915, it was pronounced finally by Peter I to belong to the equally admirable though slightly lighter 1911 crop. The *pré-salé* was removed amid general applause, and the dessert was brought in.

"Is it necessary," asked Peter I, with a slight smile in the direction of Peter II—now happily murmuring, "Damn good wine, damn good dinner, damn good show"—"is it necessary to prolong this farce any further?"

"Your lordship will not, surely, refuse to proceed with the discussion?" cried the Count.

"The point is sufficiently made, I fancy."

"But no one will surely ever refuse to discuss wine," said Bredon, "least of all your lordship, who is so great an authority."

"Not on this," said the other. "Frankly, it is a wine I do not care about. It is sweet and coarse, qualities that would damn any wine in the eyes—the mouth, rather—of a connoisseur. Did your excellent father have this laid down also, Mr. Bredon?"

Bredon shook his head.

"No," he said, "no. Genuine Imperial Tokay is beyond the opportunities of Grub Street, I fear. Though I agree with you that it is horribly overrated—with all due deference to yourself, Monsieur le Comte."

"In that case," said the Count, "we will pass at once to the liqueur. I admit that I had thought of puzzling these gentlemen with the local product, but, since one competitor seems to have scratched, it shall be brandy—the only fitting close to a good wine list."

In a slightly embarrassing silence the huge, round-bellied balloon glasses were set upon the table, and the few precious drops poured gently into each and set lightly swinging to release the bouquet.

"This," said Peter I, charmed again into amiability, "is, indeed, a wonderful old French brandy. Half a century old, I suppose."

"Your lordship's praise lacks warmth," replied Bredon. "This is *the* brandy—the brandy of brandies—the superb—the incomparable—the true Napoleon. It should be honored like the emperor it truly is."

He rose to his feet, his napkin in his hand.

"Sir," said the Count, turning to him, "I have on my right a most admirable judge of wine, but you are unique." He motioned to the butler, who solemnly brought forward the empty bottles, unswathed now, from the humble Chablis to the stately Napoleon, with the imperial seal blown in the glass. "Every time you have been correct as to growth and year. There cannot be six men in the world with such a palate as yours, and I thought that but one of them was an Englishman. Will you not favor us, this time, with your real name?"

"It doesn't matter what his name is," said Peter I. He rose. "Put up your hands, all of you. Count, the formula!"

Bredon's hands came up with a jerk, still clutching the napkin. The white folds spurted flame as his shot struck the other's revolver cleanly between trigger and barrel, exploding the charge, to the extreme detriment of the glass chandelier. Peter I stood shaking his paralyzed hand and cursing.

Bredon kept him covered while he cocked a wary eye at Peter II, who, his rosy visions scattered by the report, seemed struggling back to aggressiveness.

"Since the entertainment appears to be taking a lively turn," observed Bredon, "perhaps you would be so good, Count, as to search these gentlemen for further firearms. Thank you. Now, why should we not all sit down again and pass the bottle round?"

"You—*you* are—" growled Peter I.

"Oh, my name is Bredon all right," said the young man cheerfully. "I loathe aliases. Like another fellow's clothes, you know—never seem quite to fit. Peter Death Bredon Wimsey—a bit lengthy and all that, but handy when taken in installments. I've got a passport and all those things, too, but I didn't offer them, as their reputation here seems a little blown upon, so to speak.

"As regards the formula, I think I'd better give my personal check for it—all sorts of people seem able to go about flourishing Bank of England notes. Personally, I think all this secret diplomacy work is a mistake, but that's the War Office's pigeon. I suppose we all brought similar credentials. Yes, I thought so. Some bright person seems to have sold himself very successfully in two places at once. But you two must have been having a lively time, each of you thinking the other was me."

"My lord," said the Count heavily, "these two men are, or were, Englishmen, I suppose. I do not care to know what Governments have purchased their treachery. But where they stand, I, alas! stand too. To our venal and corrupt Republic I, as a Royalist, acknowledge no allegiance. But it is in my heart that I have agreed to sell my country to England because of my poverty. Go back to your War Office and say I will not give you the formula. If war should come between our countries—which may God avert!—I will be found on the side of France. That, my lord, is my last word."

Wimsey bowed.

"Sir," said he, "it appears that my mission has, after all, failed. I am glad of it. This trafficking in destruction is a dirty kind of business after all. Let us shut the door on these two, who are neither flesh nor fowl, and finish the brandy in the library."

THE ADOPTED DAUGHTER

BY MELVILLE DAVISSON POST

Melville Davisson Post was born at Romines Mills, West
Virginia, on April 19, 1871. He attended rural schools
and received his B.A. and LL.B. degrees from West Virginia University. He practiced criminal and corporate
law for eleven years and was active in local politics. His
numerous short stories involved many series characters,
including the (at first) unscrupulous lawyer Randolph
Mason, and Uncle Abner, a Virginia squire turned detective. Among his other characters are Sir Henry
Marquis of Scotland Yard, Walker of the Secret Service,
and Monsieur Jonquelle, Prefect of the Paris Police. Post
traveled extensively in his later years. He died in 1930.

"ISN'T SHE A BEAUTY—eh, Randolph?"

Vespatian Flornoy had a tumbler of French brandy. He sucked in a mouthful. Then he put it on the table.

The house was the strangest in Virginia. It was of some foreign model. The whole second floor on the side lying toward the east was in two spacious chambers lighted with great casement windows to the ceiling. Outside, on this brilliant morning, the world was yellow and dried-up, sere and baked. But the sun was thin and the autumn air hard and vital.

My uncle, Squire Randolph, the old country doctor, Storm, and the host, Vespatian Flornoy, were in one of these enormous rooms. They sat about a table, a long mahogany piece made in England and brought over in a sailing ship.

There were a squat bottle of French brandy and some tumblers. Flornoy drank and recovered his spirit of abandon. He leered at Randolph, and at the girl he had just called in.

He was a man one would have traveled far to see—yesterday or the day ahead of that. He had a figure out of Athens, a face cast in some forgotten foundry by the Arno, thick-curled mahogany-colored hair, and eyes like the velvet hull on an Italian chestnut. These excellencies the heavenly workman had turned out, and now by some sorcery of the pit they were changed into abominations.

Hell charms, one thought of, when one looked the creature in the face. Drops of some potent liquor, and devil words had done it, on yesterday or the day ahead of yesterday. Surely not the things that really had done it—time and the iniquities of Gomorrah. His stock and his fine ruffled shirt were soiled. His satin waistcoat was stained with liquor.

"A daughter of a French marquis, eh!" he went on. "Sold into slavery by a jest of the gods—stolen out of the garden of a convent! It's the fabled history of every octoroon in New Orleans!"

Fabled or not, the girl might have been the thing he said. The contour of the face came to a point at the chin and the skin was a soft Oriental olive. She was the perfect expression of a type. One never could wish to change a line of her figure or a feature of her face.

She stood now in the room before the door in the morning sun, in the quaint, alluring costume of a young girl of the time—a young girl of degree, stolen out of the garden of a convent! She had entered at Flornoy's drunken call, with the aspect of terror on her.

The man went on in his thick, abominable voice. "My brother Sheppard, coming north to an inspection of our joint estate, presents her as his adopted daughter. But when he dropped dead in this room last night and I went about the preparation of his body for your inquisition—eh, what, my gentlemen! I find a bill of sale running back ten years for the dainty baggage!

"French, and noble, stolen from the garden of a convent, perhaps! Perhaps!—but not by my brother Sheppard. His adopted daughter—sentimentally, perhaps. But legally a piece of property, I think descending to his heirs. Eh, Randolph!"

And he thrust a folded yellow paper across the table.

The justice put down his glass with the almost untasted liquor in it and examined the bill of sale.

"It is in form," he said. "And you interpret it correctly, Flornoy, by the law's letter. But you will not wish to enforce it, I imagine!"

"And why not, Randolph?" cried the man.

The Justice looked him firmly in the face.

"You take enough by chance, sir. You and your brother Sheppard held the estate jointly at your father's death, and now at your brother's death you hold it as sole heir. You will not wish, also, to hold his adopted daughter?"

Then he added, "This bill of sale would hold in the courts against any unindentured purpose, not accompanied by an intention expressed in some overt act. It would also fix the status of the girl against any pretended or legendary exemption of birth. The judges might believe that your brother Sheppard was convinced of this pretension when he rescued the child by purchase, and made his informal adoption at a tender age. But they would hold the paper, like a deed, irrevocable, and not to be disturbed by his conjecture."

"It will hold," cried the man, "and I will hold! You make an easy disclaimer of the rights of other men."

Then his face took on the aspect of a satyr's.

"Give her up, eh! To be a lady! Why, Randolph, I would have given Sheppard five hundred golden eagles for this little beauty—five hundred golden eagles in his hand! Look at her,

262

Randolph. You are not too old to forget the points—the trim ankle, the slender body, the snap of a thoroughbred. There's the blood of the French marquis, on my honor!"

And he laughed, snapping his fingers at his wit.

"It only makes the noble lady merchandise! And perhaps, as you say, perhaps it isn't there, in fact. Egad, old man, I would have bid a thousand eagles if Sheppard had put her up. A thousand eagles!—and now I get her for nothing! He falls dead in my house and I take her by inheritance."

It was the living truth. The two men, Vespatian Flornoy and his brother Sheppard, took their father's estate jointly at his death. They were unmarried, and now at the death of Sheppard, the surviving brother Vespatian was sole heir, under the law, to the dead man's properties: houses and lands and slaves. The bill of sale made the girl an item in the inventory of the dead man's estate, to descend with the manor-house and lands.

The thing had happened—as fortune is predisposed to change, in a moment, as by the turning of dice.

At daybreak on this morning Vespatian Flornoy had sent a Negro at a gallop to summon the old country doctor, Storm, Squire Randolph, and my Uncle Abner. At midnight, in this chamber where they now sat, Sheppard as he got on his feet, with his candle, fell and died, Vespatian said, before he could reach his body. He lay now shaven and clothed for burial in the great chamber that adjoined.

Old Storm had stripped the body and found no mark. The man was dead with no scratch or bruise.

He could not say what vital organ had suddenly played out—perhaps a string of the heart had snapped. At any rate, the dead man had not gone out by any sort of violence, nor by any poison. Every drug or herb that killed left its stamp and superscription, old Storm said, and one could see it, if one had the eye, as one could see the slash of a knife or the bruise of an assassin's fingers.

It was plain death "by the Providence of God"—that was Randolph's verdict. So the Justice and old Storm summed up the thing and they represented the inquiry and the requirements of the law.

My Uncle Abner made no comment on this conclusion. He came and looked and was silent. He demurred to the "Providence of God" in Randolph's verdict, with a great gesture of rejection. He disliked this term in any human horror. "By the abandonment of God," he said, these verdicts ought rather to be written. But he gave no sign that his objection was of any special tenor. He seemed profoundly puzzled.

When the girl came in, at Vespatian's command, he continued silent. At the man's speech, and evident intent, his features and his great jaw hardened, as though under the sunburned skin the bony structure of the face were metal.

He sat in his chair, a little way out beyond the table, as he sat on a Sunday before the pulpit, on a bench, motionless, in some deep concern.

Randolph and Vespatian Flornoy were in this dialogue. Old Storm sat with his arms folded across his chest, his head down. His interest in the matter had departed with his inspection of the dead man, or remained in the adjoining chamber where the body lay, the eyelids closed forever on the land of living men, shut up tight like the shutters of a window in a house of mystery. He only glanced at the girl with no interest, as at a bauble.

And now while the dialogue went on and Dr. Storm looked down his nose, the girl, silent and in terror, appealed to my uncle in a furtive glance, swift, charged with horror and like a flash of shadow. The great table had a broad board connecting the carved legs beneath, a sort of shelf raised a little from the floor. In her glance, swift and fearful, she directed my uncle's attention to this board.

It was a long piece of veneered mahogany, making a shelf down the whole length of the table. On it my uncle saw a big folded cloth of squares white and black, and a set of huge ivory chessmen. The cloth was made to spread across the top of the table, and the chessmen were of unusual size in proportion to the squares; the round knobs on the heads of the pawns were as big as marbles. Beside these things was a rosewood box for dueling pistols, after the fashion of the time.

My uncle stooped over, took up these articles, and set them on the table.

"And so, Flornoy," he said, "you played at chess with your brother Sheppard."

The man turned swiftly; then he paused and drank his glass of liquor.

"I entertained my brother," he said, "as I could. There is no coffeehouse to enter, nor any dancing women to please the eye, in the mountains of Virginia."

"For what stake?" said my uncle.

"I have forgotten, Abner," replied the man, "—some trifle."

"And who won?" said my uncle.

"I won," replied the man. He spoke promptly.

"You won," said my uncle, "and you remember that; but what you won, you have forgotten! Reflect a little on it, Flornoy."

The man cursed, his face in anger.

"Does it matter, Abner, a thing great or small? It is all mine today!"

"But it was not all yours last night," said my uncle.

"What I won was mine," replied the man.

"Now, there," replied my uncle, "lies a point that I would amplify. One might win, but might not receive the thing one played for. One might claim it for one's own, and the loser might deny it. If the stake were great, the loser might undertake to repudiate the bargain. And how would one enforce it?"

The man put down his glass, leaned over, and looked steadily at my uncle.

Abner slipped the silver hooks on the rosewood box, slowly, with his thumb and finger.

"I think," he said, "that if the gentleman you have in mind won and were met with a refusal, he would undertake to enforce his claim, not in the courts or by any legal writ, but the methods which gentlemen such as you have in mind are accustomed to invoke."

He opened the box and took out two pistols of the time. Then his face clouded with perplexity. Both weapons were clean and loaded.

The man, propping his wonderful face in the hollow of his hand, laughed. He had the face and the laughter of the angels cast out with Satan, when in a moment of some gain over the hosts of Michael they forgot the pit.

"Abner," he cried, "you are hag-ridden by a habit, and it leads you into the wildest fancies!"

His laughter chuckled and gurgled in his throat.

"Let me put your theory together. It is a very pretty theory, lacking in some trifles, but spirited and packed with dramatic tension. Let me sketch it out as it stands before your eye. . . . Have no fear, I shall not mar it by any delicate concern for the cunning villain, or any suppression of his evil nature. I shall uncover the base creature amid his deeds of darkness!"

He paused, and mocked the tragedy of actors.

"It is the hour of yawning graveyards—midnight in this

house. Vespatian Flornoy sits at this table with his good brother Sheppard. He has the covetousness of David, the son of Jesse, in his evil heart. He would possess the noble daughter of the Latin marquis, by a sardonic fate sold at childhood into slavery, but by the ever watchful Providence of God, for such cases made and provided, purchased by the good brother Sheppard and adopted for his daughter!

"Mark, Abner, how beautifully it falls into the formula of the tragic poets!

"The wicked Vespatian Flornoy, foiled in every scheme of purchase, moved by the instigation of the Devil, and with no fear of God before his eyes, plays at chess with his good brother Sheppard, wins his interest in the manor-house and lands, and his last gold piece—taunts and seduces him into a final game with everything staked against this Iphigenia. The evil one rises invisible but sulphurous to Vespatian's aid. He wins. In terror, appalled, aghast at the realization of his folly, the good brother Sheppard repudiates the bargain. They duel across the table, and Vespatian, being the better shot, killed his good brother Sheppard!

"Why, Abner, it is the plan of the 'Poetics.' It lacks no element of completeness. It is joined and fitted for the diction of Euripides!"

The man declaimed, his wonderful fouled face, his Adonis head with its thick curled hair, virile and spirited with the liquor and the momentum of his words. Old Storm gave no attention. Randolph listened as to the periods of an oration. And my uncle sat, puzzled, before the articles on the table. The girl now and then, when the speaker's eyes were on my uncle, by slight indicatory signs affirmed the speech, and continued strongly to indicate the chessmen.

My uncle began to turn the pieces over under the protection of his hand, idly, like one who fingers about a table in abstraction. Presently he stopped and covered one of the pieces with his hand. It was a pawn, large, like the other chessmen, but the round ivory knob at the top of it was gone. Sawed off!

The man Flornoy, consumed with his idea, failed to mark the incident, and moved by the tenor of his speech, went on. "This is the Greek plan for a tragedy. It is the plan of Athens in the fifth century. It is the plan of Sophocles and Aeschylus. Mark how it turns upon the Hellenic idea of a dominating Fate—a Fate in control over the affairs of men, pagan and not good.

266

The innocent and virtuous have no gain above the shrewd and wicked. The good Sheppard dies and the evil Vespatian takes his daughter, his goods and lands to enjoy in a gilded life, long and happy!"

He thought the deep reflection in my uncle's face was confusion at his wit.

"That ending would not please you, Abner. Luther and Calvin and John Wesley have lived after Aristotle assembled this formula in his 'Poetics.' And they will have the evil punished—a dagger in the wicked Vespatian's heart, and the virgin slave, by the interposition of the will of Heaven, preserved in her virginity. And so you come, like the Providence of God, to set the thing in order!"

My uncle looked up at the man, his hand covering the mutilated pawn, his face calm in reflection.

"You quote the tragic poets with much pedantry," he said. "Well, I will quote them too: 'Ofttimes, to win us to our harm, the instruments of darkness tell us truth!' How much truth, in all this discourse, have you told us?"

"Now, Abner," cried the man, "if it is truth you seek, and not the imaginations of a theory, how much could there be in it? If it were not for the granite ledges of reality, one might blow iris-colored bubbles of the fancy and watch them, in their beauty, journey to the stars! But alas, they collide with the hard edges of a fact and puff out. To begin with, the pistols have not been fired!"

"One could reload a pistol," replied my uncle.

"But one could not shoot a man, Abner, and leave no mark of the bullet on his body!"

He paused and addressed the old doctor.

"I sent for Storm, when I sent for Randolph, to rid me of every innuendo of a gossip. Ask him if there is a mark of violence on my brother's body."

The old man lifted his lined, withered face.

"There is no mark on him," the doctor said.

Vespatian Flornoy leaned across the table.

"Are you sure?" he said. "Perhaps, just possibly, you might be mistaken."

The words were in the taunting note of Elijah to the priests of Baal.

The old man made a decisive gesture. *"Voilà!"* he said, "I have handled a thousand dead men! I am not mistaken."

Vespatian Flornoy put up his hands as in a great, hopeless gesture.

"Alas, Abner," he said, "we must give up this pretty theory. It does honor to your creative instinct, and save for this trifle we might commend it to all men. But you see, Abner, Doctor Storm and the world will unreasonably insist that a bullet leaves a mark. I do not think we can persuade them against their experience in that belief. I am sorry for you, Abner. You have a reputation in Virginia to keep up. Let us think; perhaps there is a way around this disconcerting fact."

And he put his extended palm across his forehead in mock reflection.

It was at this moment, when for an instant the man's face was covered, that the girl standing before the door made a strange indicatory signal to my Uncle Abner.

Vespatian Flornoy, removing his hand, caught a glimpse of the girl's after-expression. And he burst out in a great laugh, striking the table with his clenched hand.

"Egad!" he cried. "By the soul of Satan! The coy little baggage is winking at Abner!"

He saw only the final composition of the girl's face. He did not see the stress and vigor of the indicatory sign. He roared in a pretension of jealous anger.

"I will not have my property ogle another in my house. You shall answer for this, Abner, on the field of honor. And I warn you, sir: I have the surest eye and the steadiest hand in the mountains of Virginia."

It was the truth. The man was the wonder of the countryside. He could cut a string with a pistol at ten paces; he could drive in a carpet tack with his bullet, across a room. With the weapon of the time, the creature was sure, accurate to a hair, and deadly.

"No man," he cried, "shall carry off this dainty baggage. Select your weapon, Abner—let us duel over this unguestly seduction!"

He spoke in the flippancies of jest. But my uncle's face was now alight with some great comprehensive purpose. It was like the face of one who begins to see the bulk and outlines of a thing that before this hour, in spite of every scrutiny, was formless.

And to Flornoy's surprise and wonder my uncle put out his hand, took up one of the pistols, and suddenly fired it into the wood of the mantelpiece beyond the table. He got up and looked at the mark. The bullet was hardly bedded in the veneer.

"You use a light charge of powder, Flornoy," said my uncle.

The man was puzzled at this act, but he answered at once.

"Abner," he said, "that is a secret I have learned. A pistol pivots on the grip. In firing, there are two things to avoid: a jerk on the trigger and the tendency of the muzzle to jump up, caused by the recoil of the charge. No man can control his weapon with a heavy charge of powder behind the bullet. If one would shoot true to a hair, one must load light."

It seemed a considerable explanation. And not one of the men who heard it ever knew whether it was, in fact, the controlling cause, or whether another and more subtle thing had inspired it.

"But, Flornoy," said my uncle, "if to kill were the object of a duelist, such a charge of powder might defeat the purpose."

"You are mistaken, Abner," he said. "The body of a man is soft. If one avoids the bony structure, a trifling charge of powder will carry one's bullet into a vital organ. There is no gain in shooting through a man as though one were going to string him on a thread. Powder enough to lodge the bullet in the vital organ is sufficient."

"There might be a point in not shooting through him," said Abner.

The man looked calmly at my uncle; then he made an irrelevant gesture.

"No object, Abner, but no use. The whole point is to shoot to a hair, to lodge the bullet precisely in the point selected. Look how a light charge of powder does it."

And taking up the other pistol, he steadied it a moment in his hand, then fired at Abner's bullet hole. No other mark appeared on the mantel board. One would have believed that the bullet, if the barrel held one, had wholly vanished. But when they looked closely, it was seen that my uncle's bullet, struck precisely, was driven a little deeper into the wood. It was amazing accuracy. No wonder the man's skill was a byword in the land.

My uncle made a single comment.

"You shoot like the slingers of Benjamin!" he said.

Then he came back to the table and stood looking down at the man. He held the mutilated ivory pawn in his closed left hand. The girl, like an appraised article, was in the doorway;

269

Storm and Randolph looked on, like men before the blind moving of events.

"Flornoy," said Abner, "you have told us more truth than you intended. How did your brother Sheppard die?"

The man's face changed. His fingers tightened on the pistol. His eyes became determined and alert.

"Damme, man," he cried, "do you return to that! Sheppard fell and died, where you stand, beside the table in this room. I am no surgeon to say what disorder killed him. I sent for Storm to determine that."

My uncle turned to the old eccentric doctor.

"Storm," he said, "how did Sheppard Flornoy die?"

The old man shrugged and put out his nervous hands.

"I do not know," he said, "the heart, maybe. There is no mark on him."

And here Randolph interrupted.

"Abner," he said, "you put a question that no man can answer: something snaps within the body, and we die. We have no hint at the cause of Sheppard's death."

"Why, yes," replied my uncle, "I think we have."

"What hint?" said Randolph.

"The hint, said Abner, "that the eloquent Vespatian gave us just now in his discourse. I think he set out the cause in his apt recollection from the Book of Samuel."

He paused and looked down at the man.

Vespatian Flornoy got on his feet. His face and manner changed. There was now decision and menace in his voice.

"Abner," he said, "there shall be an end to this. I have turned your ugly hint with pleasantry and met it squarely with indisputable facts. I shall not go any further on this way. I shall clear myself now, after the manner of a gentleman."

My uncle looked steadily at the man.

"Flornoy," he said, "if you would test your innocence by a device of the Middle Ages, I would suggest a simpler and swifter method of that time. Wager of battle is outlawed in Virginia. It is prohibited by statute, and we cannot use it. But the test I offer in its place is equally medieval. It is based on the same belief, old and persistent, that the Providence of God will indicate the guilty. And it is not against the law."

He paused.

"The same generation of men who believed in Wager of Battle, in the Morsel of Execration, in the red-hot plowshares, as a test of the guilt of murder, also believed that if the assassin touched his victim, the body of the murdered man would bleed!

"Flornoy," he said, "if you would have recourse to one of those medieval devices, let it be the last. . . . Go in with me and touch the body of your brother Sheppard and I give you my word of honor that I will accept the decision of the test."

It was impossible to believe that my Uncle Abner trifled, and yet the thing was beyond the soundings of all sense.

Storm and Randolph, and even the girl standing in the door, regarded him in wonder.

Vespatian Flornoy was amazed.

"Damme, man!" he cried, "superstitions have unhinged your mind. Would you believe in a thing like that?"

"I would rather believe it," replied my uncle, "than to believe that in a duel God would direct the assassin's bullet."

Then he added, with weight and decision in his voice, "If you would be clear of my suspicion, if you would be free to take and enjoy the lands and properties that you inherit, go in before these witnesses and touch the dead body of your brother Sheppard. There is no mark appearing on him. Storm has found no wound to bleed. You are innocent of any measure in his death, you tell us. There's no peril to you, and I shall ride away to assure every man that Sheppard Flornoy died, as Randolph has written, by the 'Providence of God.' "

He extended his arm toward the adjacent chamber, and across the table he looked Flornoy in the face.

"Go in before us and touch the dead man!"

"By the soul of Satan," cried the man, "if you hang on such a piece of foolery, you shall have it. The curse of superstition sticks in your fleece, Abner, like a burr."

He turned and flung open the door behind him and went in. The others followed—Storm and Randolph behind the man, the girl, shaken and fearful, and my Uncle Abner.

Sheppard Flornoy lay prepared for burial in the center of the room. The morning sun entering through the long windows flooded him with light; his features were sharply outlined in the mask of death, his eyelids closed.

They stood about the dead man, at peace in this glorious shroud of sun, and the living brother was about to touch him when my uncle put out his hand.

"Flornoy," he said, "the dead man ought to see who comes to touch him. I will open his eyes."

And at the words, for no cause or reason conceivable to the men looking on, Vespatian Flornoy shouted with an oath and ran in on my uncle.

He was big and mad with terror. But even in his youth and fury he was not a match for my Uncle Abner. Liquor and excess failed before wind and sun and the clean life of the hills. The man went down under my uncle's clenched hand, like an ox polled with a hammer.

It was Randolph who cried out, while the others crowded around the dead man and his brother unconscious on the floor.

"Abner, Abner," he said, "what is the answer to this ghastly riddle?"

For reply my uncle drew back the eyelids of the dead man. And stooping over, Randolph and old Storm saw that Sheppard Flornoy had been shot through the eye, and that the head of the ivory pawn had been forced into the bullet hole to round out the damaged eyeball under the closed lid.

The girl sobbed, clinging to my uncle's arm. Randolph tore the bill of sale into indistinguishable bits. And old Doctor Storm made a great gesture with his hands extended and crooked.

"*Mon Dieu!*" he cried, in a consuming revulsion of disgust. "My father was surgeon in the field for Napoleon, I was raised with dead men, and a drunken assassin fools me in the mountains of Virginia!"

THE LOCKED ROOM

BY JOHN DICKSON CARR

John Dickson Carr was born in 1906 in Uniontown, Pennsylvania. His earliest heroes included Sherlock Holmes and Father Brown. By the age of fourteen he was covering sports and murder trials for a newspaper. His first novel, *It Walks By Night*, was published in 1930. He married an Englishwoman, Clarice Cleaves, in 1932 and moved to England, where he began to write steadily under his own name and various pseudonyms. He collaborated with Adrian Conan Doyle on *The Life of Sir Arthur Conan Doyle* and a collection of Holmes pastiches, *The Exploits of Sherlock Holmes*. Carr died in 1977.

You may have read the facts.

Francis Seton was found lying on the floor behind his desk, near death from a fractured skull. He had been struck three times across the back of the head with a piece of lead-loaded broomhandle. His safe had been robbed. His body was found by his secretary-typist, Iris Lane, and his librarian, Harold Mills, who were, in the polite newspaper phrase, "being questioned."

So far, it seems commonplace. Nothing in that account shows why Superintendent Hadley of the C.I.D. nearly went mad, or why ten o'clock of a fine June morning found him punching at the doorbell of Dr. Gideon Fell's house in Chelsea.

Summer touched the old houses with grace. There was a smoky sparkle on the river, and on the flower-veined green of the Embankment gardens. Upstairs, in the library, with its long windows, Superintendent Hadley found the learned doctor smoking a cigar and reading a magazine.

Dr. Fell's bulk overflowed from a chair nearly large enough to accommodate him. A chuckle animated his several chins, and ran down over the ridges of his waistcoat. He peered up at Hadley over his eyeglasses; his cheeks shone, pinkly transparent, with warmth of welcome. But at Hadley's first words a disconsolate expression drew down the corners of his moustache.

"Seton's conscious," said Hadley. "I've just been talking to him."

Dr. Fell grunted. Reluctantly he put aside the magazine.

"Ah," he said. "And Seton denies the story told by the secretary and the librarian?"

"No. He confirms it."

"In every detail?"

"In every detail."

Dr. Fell puffed out his cheeks. He also took several violent puffs at the cigar, staring at it in a somewhat cross-eyed fashion. His big voice was subdued.

"Do you know, Hadley," he muttered, "I rather expected that."

"I didn't," snapped Hadley. "I didn't; and I don't. But that's why I'm here. You must have some theory about this impossible burglar who nearly bashed a man's head off and then disappeared like smoke. My forthright theory is that Iris Lane and Harold Mills are lying. If . . . hullo!"

Standing by the window, he broke off and glanced down into the street. His gesture was so urgent that Dr. Fell, with much labor, hoisted himself up wheezily from the chair and lumbered over to the window.

Clear in the strong sunshine, a girl in a white frock was standing on the opposite pavement, by the railings, and peering up at the window. As Dr. Fell threw back the curtains, she looked straight into their eyes.

She was what is called an outdoor girl, with a sturdy and well-shaped body, and a square but very attractive face. Her dark brown hair hung in a long bob. She had light hazel eyes in a tanned, earnest face. Her mouth might have been too broad, but she showed fine teeth when she laughed. If she was not exactly pretty, health and vigor gave her a strong attractiveness which was better than that.

"Iris Lane," said Hadley ventriloquially.

Dr. Fell, in an absent-minded way, was startled. He would have expected Francis Seton's secretary-typist to be either prim or mousy.

When she saw the two men at the window, Iris Lane's expressive face showed many things. Disappointment, surprise, even fear. Her knee moved as though she were about to stamp angrily on the pavement. For a second they thought she would turn and hurry away. Then she seemed to come to a decision. She almost ran across the street towards the house.

"Now what do you suppose—?" Hadley was speculating when the doctor cut him short.

"She wants to see me, confound you," he roared. "Or she did want to see me, until you nearly scared her off."

And the girl herself confirmed it a moment later. She was making an attempt to be calm and even jaunty, but her eyes always moved back to Hadley.

"It seems," she said, after a quick look round the room, "that I'm always trailing the superintendent. Or he's always trailing me. I don't know which."

Hadley nodded. He was noncommittal.

"It does seem like that, Miss Lane. Anything in particular on your mind now?"

275

"Yes. I—I wanted to talk to Dr. Fell. Alone."

"Oh? Why?"

"Because it's my last hope," answered the girl, raising her head. "Because they say nobody, not even a stray dog, is ever turned away from here."

"Nonsense!" said Dr. Fell, hugely delighted nevertheless. He covered this with deprecating noises which shook the chandelier, and an offer of refreshment. Hadley saw that the old man was half hooked already, and Hadley despaired.

Yet it seemed impossible to doubt this girl's sincerity. She sat bolt upright in the chair, opening and shutting the catch of a white handbag.

"It's quite simple," she explained, and hunched her shoulders. "Harold Mills and I were alone in the house with Mr. Seton. There was nearly three thousand pounds in the safe in his study."

Dr. Fell frowned.

"So? As much money as that?"

"Mr. Seton was leaving," said Iris Lane, with an effort. "He was going abroad, to spend a year in California. He always made his decisions suddenly—just like that." She snapped her fingers. "We didn't know anything about it, Harold and I, until he broke the news that morning. The man from the bank brought the money round; Mr. Seton put it into the safe, and told us why he had sent for it. That meant we were out of our jobs."

And she began to tell the story.

Of course (Iris admitted to herself), her nerves had been on edge that night. It was caused partly by losing a good job at a moment's notice, partly by the thick and thundery weather round the old house in Kensington, and partly by the personality of Francis Seton himself.

Francis Seton was a book collector. When Iris had first answered his advertisement for a secretary-typist, she had expected to find someone thin and ancient, with double-lensed spectacles. Instead she found a thickset bull of a man, with sandy hair and a blue guileless eye. His energy was prodigious. He animated the old house like a humming-top. He had the genuine collector's passion; he was generous, and considerate when it did not inconvenience him.

But he whirled off at a new tangent that morning, a hot

overcast day, when he called Iris Lane and Harold Mills into his study. They had been working in the long library on the first floor. The study, which opened out of it, was a large room with two windows overlooking a tangled back garden.

Seton stood by the big flat-topped desk in the middle of the study. Out of a canvas bag he was emptying thick packets of banknotes, one of which fell into the waste-paper basket.

"Look here," he said, with the confiding candor of a child. "I'm off to America. For a year at least."

(He seemed pleased at the way his hearers jumped.)

"But, sir—" began Harold Mills.

"Crisis!" said Seton, pointing to a newspaper. "Crisis!" he added, pointing to another. "I'm sick of crises. California's the place for me. Orange groves and sea breezes: at least, that's what the booklets say. Besides, I want to make old Isaacson sick with my 1593 *Venus and Adonis* and the 1623 folio."

His forehead grew lowering and embarrassed.

"I've got to let you both go," he growled. "I'd like to take you both with me. Can't afford it. Sorry; but there it is. I'll give you a month's salary in place of notice. Damn it, I'll give you *two* months' salary in place of notice. How's that?"

Beaming with relief now that this was off his chest, he dismissed the subject briskly. He gathered up the packets of banknotes, fishing the dropped one out of the wastepaper basket. It made his face crimson to bend over, since Dr. Woodall had warned him about high blood pressure; but he was all energy again.

A little iron safe stood against one wall. Seton opened it with his key, poured the money into a tin box, closed the safe, and locked it. In a vague way Iris noted the denominations on the paper bands round the packets of notes: £1, £5, £10, £20. A little treasure-trove. Almost a little fortune.

Perhaps because of the heat of the day, there was perspiration on Harold Mills's forehead.

"And when do you want to leave, sir?" he asked.

"Leave? Oh, ah." Seton considered. "Day after tomorrow," he decided.

"Day after tomorrow!"

"Saturday," Seton explained. "Always a good ship leaving. Yes, make it Saturday."

"But your passport—" protested Iris.

"That's completely in order," said Seton coolly.

The word which flashed through Iris Lane's mind just then was "robbed." She could not help it. There are times with everyone when the sight of so much money, all in a lump, makes the fingers itch and brings fantastic dreams of what might be.

She didn't mean it—as she was later to explain to the police. But there was a tantalizing quality in what had happened. Only yesterday she had been safe. Only a week ago she had returned from a holiday in Cornwall, where there had been little to do except lie on lemon-colored sands in a lemon-colored bathing-suit; or feel the contrast between sun on baking shoulders and salt water foaming and slipping past her body, in the cold invigoration of the sea. The future would take care of itself.

And more. There was a pleasant-looking man, just on the right side of middle age, who came to do sketches at the beach. They were such intolerably bad sketches that Iris was relieved to discover he was a doctor from London.

By coincidence, a breeze blew one of the sketches past her, and she retrieved it. So they fell into conversation. By coincidence, it developed that the man's name was Charles Woodhall; and that he was Francis Seton's doctor. It astounded Iris, who saw in this a good omen of summer magic. She liked Dr. Woodhall. He was as good a talker as Seton himself, without Seton's untiring bounce. And he knew when to be comfortably silent.

Dr. Woodhall would sit on a campstool, attired in ancient flannels, tennis-shoes, and shirt, and draw endless sketches of Iris. A cigarette would hang from the corner of his mouth. He would blink as smoke got into one eye, and amusement-wrinkles deepened from the corners of his eyes almost back to temples that were slightly gray. Meantime, he talked. He talked happily of all things in earth and sky and sea. He also offered a profound apology for the bad sketches. But Iris, though she secretly agreed with him, kept them all; and so passed the fortnight.

They would meet again in London.

And she had a good job to go back to there.

All the future looked pleasant—until Francis Seton exploded everything that morning.

The thunderstorm, which had been imminent all day, broke late in the afternoon.

278

It brought little relief to Iris. She and Harold Mills went on with their work and were still working long after dinner, in the library under the shaded lamps and the rows of books behind their wire cages. It was a rich room, deep-carpeted like every other room in the house; but it was tainted with damp. Iris's head ached. She had sent off two dozen letters, and arranged every detail of Seton's trip: all he had to do now was pack his bag. Seton himself was in the study, with the door closed between, cleaning out the litter in his desk.

Harold Mills put down his pen. "Iris," he said softly.

"Yes?"

Mills glanced towards the closed door of the study, and spoke still more softly.

"I want to ask you something."

"Of course."

She was surprised at his tone. He was sitting at his own writing table, some distance away from her, with a table-lamp burning at his left. The light of the lamp shone on his flat fair hair, brushed with great precision round his head, on his waxy-colored face, and on his pince-nez. Since he was very young, it was only this pince-nez which gave him the sedate and donnish appearance; this, or the occasional slight fidgeting of his hands.

He almost blurted out the next words.

"What I mean is: are you all right, Iris? All right financially, I mean?"

"Oh, yes."

She didn't know. She was not even thinking of this now. Dr. Woodhall had promised to drop in that evening, to see Seton. It was nearly eleven now. Seton, who always swore that his immense vitality was due to the regularity of his habits, was as regular as that clock over the mantelpiece. At eleven o'clock he would smoke the last of the ten cigarettes allowed him a day, drink his one whisky-and-soda, and be in bed by eleven-thirty sharp. If Dr. Woodhall didn't hurry . . .

Iris's head ached still more. Mills kept on talking, but she did not hear him. She awoke to this with a start.

"I'm sorry. I'm afraid I didn't catch—?"

"I said," repeated the other, somewhat jerkily, "that I'm sorry for more reasons than one that we're leaving."

"So am I, Harold."

"You don't understand. Mine is rather a specialized job. I'll not get another in a hurry." Color came up under his pince-nez.

"No, no, that isn't what I mean. I'm not complaining. It's very decent of Seton to provide two months' salary. But I'd hoped that this job would be more or less permanent. If it turned out to be that, there was something I wanted to do."

"What was that?"

"I wanted to ask you to marry me," said Mills.

There was a silence.

She stared back at him. She had never thought of him as awkward or tongue-tied, or anything like the man who now sat and cracked the joints of his knuckles as though he could not sit still. In fact, she had hardly ever thought of him at all. And his face showed that he knew it. "Please don't say anything." He got to his feet. "I don't want you to feel you've got to say anything." He began to pace the room with little short steps. "I haven't been exactly—attentive."

"You never even . . ."

He gestured.

"Yes, I know. I'm not like that. I can't be. I wish I could." He stopped his pacing. "This fellow Woodhall, now."

"What about Dr. Woodhall?"

He never got the opportunity to say. This was the point at which they heard, very distinctly, the noise from the next room.

When they tried to describe it afterwards, neither could be sure whether it was a yell, or a groan, or the beginning of incoherent words. It might have been a combination of all three. Then there were several soft little thuds, like the sound of a butcher's cleaver across meat on the chopping-block. Then silence, except for the distant whisper of the rain. . . .

That was the story which Iris Lane began to tell at Dr. Fell's flat. Both Dr. Fell and Superintendent Hadley listened with the closest attention, though they had heard it several times before.

"We didn't know what had happened," said Iris, moving her shoulders. "We called out to Mr. Seton, but he didn't answer. We tried the door, but it wouldn't open."

"Was it locked?"

"No; it was warped. The damp from the rain had swollen and warped the wood. Harold tried to get it open, but it wouldn't work until he finally took a run and jumped at it.

"There was nobody in the study except Mr. Seton," she went on. "I know, because I was afraid we should see someone. The place was brilliantly lighted. There's a big bronze chandelier, with electric candles, hanging over the flat-topped desk in the

280

middle. And there was even a light burning in the cloakroom—
it's hardly more than a cupboard for a washbasin, really—
which opens out of the study. You could see everything at a
glance. And there wasn't any possibility of anybody hiding in
the room."

She paused, visualizing the scene.

Francis Seton lay on the far side of the desk, between the
desk and the windows. He was unconscious, with blood coming
out of his nostrils.

His cigarette, put down on the edge of the desk, was now
scorching the mahogany with an acrid smell. The desk-chair
and a little table had been overturned. There was a stain on the
thick gray carpet where his glass had been upset, together with
a stoppered decanter which had not spilt, and a siphon enclosed in metal cross-bands. Seton was moaning. When they
turned him over on his side, they found the weapon.

"It was that hollow wooden thing with lead inside," said Iris.
She saw it as vividly as though it lay on the carpet now. "Only six
or seven inches long, but it weighed nearly a pound. Harold,
who'd started to study medicine once, put his fingers down and
felt round the back of Mr. Seton's head. Then he said I'd better
hurry and 'phone for a proper doctor.

"I had backed away against the windows—I remember that.
The curtains weren't quite drawn. I could hear the rain hitting
the window behind me. I looked round, because I was afraid
there might be somebody hiding in the curtains. We pulled the
curtains back on both windows. Then we saw the edge of the
ladder. It had been propped up against the right-hand window,
from the garden below. And I noticed something else that I'll
swear to, and swear to, and go on swearing to until you believe
me. But never mind what it was, for a minute.

"I ran out to 'phone for Dr. Woodhall, but it wasn't necessary.
I met him coming up the stairs in the front hall."

There were several things she did not tell here.

She did not say how heartening it was to see Dr. Woodhall's
shrewd, humorous face looking at her from under the brim of a
sodden hat. He wore a dripping mackintosh with the collar
turned up, and carried his medicine-case.

"I don't know how he got in," Iris went on. "Mr. Seton had
dismissed the servants after dinner. The front door must have
been unlocked. Anyway, he said, 'Hullo; is anything wrong?' I
think I said, 'Come up quickly; something terrible has hap-

pened.' He didn't make any comment. But when he had examined Mr. Seton he said it was concussion of the brain all right, from several powerful blows. I asked whether I should 'phone for an ambulance. He said Mr. Seton wasn't in shape to be moved, and that we should have to get him to bed in the house.

"When we were carrying him in to his bedroom, things started to fall out of his pockets. The key to the safe wasn't there: it had been torn loose from the other end of his watch-chain.

"You know the rest. The safe had been robbed, not only of the money, but of two valuable folios. Apparently it was all plain sailing. There was the ladder propped against the windowsill outside. There were scuffed footprints in a flower-bed below. It was a burglar. It must have been a burglar. Only—" She paused, clearing her throat. "Only," she went on, *"both those windows were locked on the inside."*

Dr. Fell grunted.

Something in this recital had interested him very much. He drew in several of his chins, and exchanged a glance with Superintendent Hadley.

"Both the windows," he rumbled, "were locked on the inside. You're quite sure of that? Hey?"

"I'm absolutely positive."

"You couldn't have been mistaken?"

"I only wish I could have," said Iris helplessly. "And you know what they think, don't you? They think Harold and I caught him and beat his head in.

"It's so awfully easy to think that. Harold and I were alone in the house. We were sitting outside the only door to the study. There was no intruder anywhere. Both the study windows were locked on the inside. It—well, it just couldn't have been anybody else but us. Only it wasn't. That's all I can tell."

Dr. Fell opened his eyes.

"But, my dear young lady," he protested, blowing sparks from his cigar like the Spirit of the Volcano, "whatever else they think about you, I presume they don't think you are raving mad? Suppose you had faked this burglary? Suppose you had planted the ladder against the window? Would you and Mills then go about swearing the windows were locked in order to prove that your story couldn't be true?"

"Just a moment," said Superintendent Hadley sharply.

282

Hadley was beaten, and he knew it. But he was fair.

"I'll be frank with you, Miss Lane," he went on. "Before you came in, I was telling Dr. Fell that Mr. Seton is conscious. He's talked to me. And—"

"And?"

"Mr. Seton," said Hadley, "confirms your story in every detail. His statement clears you and Mills of any complicity in the crime."

Iris said nothing. All the same, they saw her face grow white under its tan.

"He says," pursued Hadley, in the midst of a vast silence, "that he was sitting at his desk, facing the door to the library. He swears he could hear you and Mills talking in the library. His back, of course, was towards the windows. He agrees that the windows were locked, since he had just locked them himself. At a few minutes past eleven, he heard a footstep behind him. A 'shuffling' footstep. Just as he started to get up, something smashed him across the head, and that's all he remembers. So it seems you were telling the truth."

"H'mf," said Dr. Fell.

Iris stared at Hadley. "Then I'm not—you're not going to arrest me?"

"Frankly," snapped the superintendent, "no. I'm sorry to say I don't see how we can arrest anybody. The windows were locked. The door was watched. There was nobody hidden in the room. Yet someone, by the victim's own testimony, did get in and cosh Seton. We've got a blooming miracle, that's what we've got; and, if you don't believe me, come along and talk to Seton for yourself."

Francis Seton lived, and nearly died, in the grand manner. His bedroom was furnished in the heavy, dark, and florid style of the Second French Empire, with a four-poster bed. He lay propped up with his neck above the pillows, glowering out of a helmet of bandages.

"Time's nearly up," warned Dr. Charles Woodhall, who stood at one side of the bed. His fingers were on Seton's wrist, but Seton snatched the wrist away.

Hadley was patient.

"What I'm trying to get at, Mr. Seton, is this. When did you lock those two windows?"

"Told you that already," said Seton. "About ten minutes

283

before that fellow sneaked up and hit me on the head."

"But you didn't catch a glimpse of the person who hit you?"

"No, worse luck. Or I'd have—"

"Yes. But *why* did you lock the windows?"

"Because I'd noticed the ladder outside. Couldn't have burglars getting in, could I?"

"You didn't try to find out who put the ladder there?"

"No. I couldn't be bothered."

"At the same time, you were a little nervous?"

For some time Iris Lane had the impression that Seton, if it were not for his injury, would have rolled over on his side, buried his face in the pillows, and groaned with impatience. But the last question stung him to wrath.

"Who says I was nervous? Nervous! I'm the last man in the world to be nervous. I haven't got a nerve in my body." He appealed plaintively to Dr. Woodhall and to Harold Mills. "Have I?"

"You've got an exceptionally strong constitution," replied Dr. Woodhall blandly.

Seton appeared to scent evasion here. His bloodshot eyes rolled, without a turn of his neck, from Woodhall to Mills; but they came back to Hadley.

"Well? Anything else you want to know?"

"Just one more question, Mr. Seton. Are you sure there was nobody hidden in the study or the cloakroom before you were attacked?"

"Dead certain."

Hadley shut up his notebook.

"Then that's all, sir. Nobody hidden, before or after. Windows locked, before and after. I don't believe in ghosts, and so the thing's impossible." He spoke quietly. "Excuse me, Mr. Seton, but are you sure you were attacked after all?"

"And excuse *me*," interrupted a new voice, thunderous but apologetic.

Dr. Fell, whose presence was somewhat less conspicuous than a captive balloon, had not removed his disreputable slouch hat: a breach of good manners which ordinarily he would have deplored. But his manner had a vast eagerness, like Old King Cole in a hurry. Iris Lane could not remember having seen him for some minutes. He lumbered in at the doorway, with one hand holding an object wrapped in newspaper and the other supporting himself on his crutch-handled stick.

284

"Sir," he intoned, addressing Seton, "I should regret it very much if my friend Hadley gave you an apoplectic stroke. It is therefore only fair to tell you that you were attacked, and very thoroughly battered about the head, by one of the persons in this room. I am also glad the police have kept your study locked up since then."

There was a silence as sudden as that which follows a loud noise.

From the newspaper Dr. Fell took out a soda-water siphon, and put it down with a thump on the center table. It was a large siphon, bound round with metal bands.

And Dr. Fell reared up.

"Dash it, Hadley," he complained, "why couldn't you have told me about the siphon? Ten days in a spiritual abyss; and all because you couldn't tell me about the siphon! It took the young lady to do that."

"But I did tell you about a siphon," said Hadley. "I've told you about it a dozen times!"

"No, no, no," insisted Dr. Fell dismally. "You said 'a' siphon. Presumably an ordinary siphon, the unending white bulwark of the English pub. You didn't say it was this particular kind of siphon."

"But what the devil has the siphon got to do with it anyway?" demanded Hadley. "Mr. Seton wasn't knocked out with a siphon."

"Oh, yes, he was," said Dr. Fell. It was so quiet that they could hear a fly buzzing against one half-open window.

"You see," continued Dr. Fell, fiery with earnestness, "the ordinary siphon is of plain glass. It doesn't have these criss-cross metal bands, or that nickeled cap at the other side of the nozzle. In short, this is a 'Fountain-fill' siphon; the sort which you fill yourself with plain water, and turn into soda-water by means of compressed-air capsules."

Enlightenment came to Superintendent Hadley.

"Ah!" chortled Dr. Fell. "Got it, have you? The police, as a matter of ordinary routine, would closely examine the dregs of a whisky-glass or any decanter found at the scene of a crime. But they would never think twice about a siphon, because the ordinary soda-water siphon can't possibly be tampered with. And yet, by thunder, *this* one could be tampered with!"

Dr. Fell sniffed. He lumbered over to the bedside table, and picked up a tumbler. Returning with it to the center table, he squirted some of the soda into the glass. He touched his tongue to it.

"I think, Mr. Harold Mills," he said, "you had better give yourself up for theft and attempted murder."

Dr. Fell chuckled as he sat again in his own library at Chelsea.

"And you still don't see it?" he demanded.

"Yes," said Dr. Woodhall.

"No," cried Iris Lane.

"The whole trick," their host went on, "turns on the fact that the 'Mickey Finn' variety of knockout drops produces on the victim exactly the same sensation as being struck over the head: the sudden bursting explosion of pain, the roaring in the ears, and almost instant unconsciousness.

"Mills had a dozen opportunities that day to load the 'Fountain-fill' siphon with the drug. He knew, as you all knew, exactly when Francis Seton would drink his one whisky-and-soda of the day. Mills had already removed what he wanted from the safe. Finally, he had propped up a ladder outside the study window to make the crime seem the work of a burglar. All he had to do then was to wait for eleven o'clock.

"At eleven o'clock Seton drank the hocussed mixture, cried out, and fell, knocking over a number of objects on the carpet. Since the whole effect of this drug depends on a violent cerebral rush of blood, a man already suffering from high blood-pressure would be likely and even certain to bleed from the nostrils. It provided the last realistic touch."

Dr. Fell growled to himself, no longer seeming quite so cherubic. Then he looked at Iris.

"Mills," he went on, "deliberately fiddled with the door, pretending it was stuck: which it was not. He wanted to allow time for the imaginary burglar to loot the safe. Then he ran in with you. When he turned Seton over, he took that piece of lead-filled broom-handle out of his sleeve, slipped it under the body, and dramatically called your attention to it.

"Next, you remember, he felt at the base of Seton's skull in pretended horror, and told you to go out and 'phone for a doctor. As a result of this, you also recall, he was for several minutes completely alone in the study."

Iris was looking at the past, examining each move she herself had made.

"You mean," she muttered, "that was when he—?" She

286

brought up her arms in the gesture of one using a life-preserver.

"Yes," said Dr. Fell. "That was when he deliberately struck several blows on the head of an unconscious man to complete his plan.

"He removed the key to the safe from Seton's watch-chain. In case the police should be suspicious of any drinks found at the scene of a crime, he rinsed out the spilled whisky glass in that convenient cloakroom, and poured into the glass a few drops of harmless whisky from the decanter. He had no time to refill and recharge the siphon before you and Dr. Woodhall returned to the study; so he left it alone. A handkerchief round his hand prevented any fingerprints. Unfortunately, mischance tripped him up with a resounding wallop."

Dr. Woodhall nodded.

"You mean," he said, "that Seton noticed the ladder, and locked the windows?"

"Yes. And the unfortunate Mr. Mills never discovered the locked windows until it was too late. Miss Lane, as you have probably discovered, is a very positive young lady. She looked at the windows. She knew they were locked. She was prepared to swear it in any court. So Mills, floundering and drifting and never very determined except where it came to appropriating someone else's property, had to keep quiet. He could not even get at that betraying siphon afterwards, because the police kept the room locked up.

"He had one bit of luck, though. Francis Seton, of course, never heard any footsteps behind him just before the attack. Anybody who takes one look at the thick carpet of the study cannot fail to be convinced of that. I wondered whether the good Mr. Seton might be deliberately lying. But a little talk with Seton will show you the real reason. The man's boasted vitality is killing him: it has got him into such a state of nerves that he really does need a year in California. Once he saw that ladder outside the window, once he began to think of burglars, he was ready to imagine anything."

Iris was glancing sideways at Dr. Woodhall. Woodhall, a cigarette in the corner of his mouth, was glancing sideways at her.

"I—er—I don't like to bring it up," said Iris, carefully turning her glance away from the doctor, "But—"

"Mills's proposal?" inquired Dr. Fell affably.

"Well, yes."

287

"My dear young lady," intoned Dr. Fell, with all the gallantry of a load of bricks falling through a skylight, "there you mention the one point at which Mills really showed good taste. Discernment. *Raffinement.* It also probably occurred to him that a criminal who proposes marriage places the lady in a blind-eyed and sympathetic mood if the criminal should happen to make a slip in his game afterwards. But can you honestly say you are sorry it was Mills they took away in the Black Maria?"

Iris and Dr. Woodhall were not even listening.

THE BEARDED LADY

BY ROSS MACDONALD

Ross Macdonald is the pseudonym of Kenneth Millar, who was born in California on December 13, 1915, and raised in Ontario, Canada. He served in the Navy during World War II and received his doctorate from the University of Michigan in 1951 with a thesis on Coleridge. His first novel about Lew Archer, *The Moving Target,* was published in 1949. Archer has appeared in eighteen other novels, nine short stories, two movies (renamed "Harper"), and a television series. Kenneth Millar took his pseudonym in 1949 to avoid confusion between his books and those of his wife, mystery writer Margaret Millar.

THE UNLATCHED DOOR SWUNG inward when I knocked. I walked into the studio, which was as high and dim as a hayloft. The big north window in the opposite wall was hung with monk's-cloth drapes that shut out the morning light. I found the switch next to the door and snapped it on. Several fluorescent tubes suspended from the naked rafters flickered and burned blue-white.

A strange woman faced me under the cruel light. She was only a charcoal sketch on an easel, but she gave me a chill. Her nude body, posed casually on a chair, was slim and round and pleasant to look at. But her face wasn't pleasant at all. Bushy black eyebrows almost hid her eyes. A walrus mustache bracketed her mouth, and a thick beard fanned down over her torso.

The door creaked behind me. The girl who appeared in the doorway wore a starched white uniform. Her face had a little starch in it, too, though not enough to spoil her good looks. Her black hair was drawn back severely.

"May I ask what you're doing here?" she said brusquely.

"You may ask. I'm looking for Mr. Western."

"Really? Have you tried looking behind the picture?"

"Does he spend much of his time there?"

"No, and another thing he doesn't do—he doesn't receive visitors in his studio when he isn't here himself."

"Sorry. The door was open, so I walked in."

"You can now reverse the process."

"Just a minute. Hugh isn't sick?"

She glanced down at her uniform, then shook her head.

"Are you a friend of his?" I said.

"I try to be." She smiled slightly. "It isn't always easy, with a sib. I'm his sister."

"Not the one he was always talking about?"

"I'm the only one he has."

I reached back into my mental grab bag of war souvenirs. "Mary. The name was Mary."

"It still is Mary. Are *you* a friend of Hugh's?"

"I guess I qualify. I used to be."

"When?" The question was sharp. I got the impression she didn't approve of Hugh's friends, or some of them.

"In the Philippines. He was attached to my group as a combat artist. My name is Archer, by the way—Lew Archer."

"Oh. Of course."

Her disapproval didn't extend to me—at least, not yet. She gave me her hand. It was cool and firm, and went with her steady gaze.

"Hugh gave me the wrong impression of you," I said. "I thought you were still a kid in school."

"That was four years ago, remember. People grow up in four years. Anyway, some of them do."

She was a very serious girl for her age. I changed the subject. "I saw the announcement of his one-man show in the L.A. papers. I'm driving through to San Francisco, and I thought I'd look him up."

"I know he'll be glad to see you. I'll go and wake him. He keeps the most dreadful hours. Sit down, won't you, Mr. Archer?"

I had been standing with my back to the bearded nude, more or less consciously shielding her from it. When I moved aside and she saw it, she didn't turn a hair.

"What next?" was all she said.

But I couldn't help wondering what had happened to Hugh Western's sense of humor. I looked around the room for something that might explain the ugly sketch.

It was a typical working artist's studio. The tables and benches were cluttered with things that are used to make pictures: palettes and daubed sheets of glass, sketch pads, scratchboards, bleeding tubes of paint. Pictures in half a dozen mediums and half a dozen stages of completion hung on or leaned against the burlap-covered walls. Some of them looked wild and queer to me, but none so wild and queer as the sketch on the easel.

There was one puzzling thing in the room, besides the pictures. The wooden door frame was scarred with a row of deep round indentations, four of them. They were new, and about on a level with my eyes. They looked as if an incredible fist had struck the wood a superhuman blow.

"He isn't in his room," the girl said from the doorway. Her voice was very carefully controlled.

"Maybe he got up early."

"His bed hasn't been slept in. He's been out all night."

"I wouldn't worry. After all, he's an adult."

291

"Yes, but he doesn't always act like one." A deep feeling buzzed under her calm tone. I couldn't tell if it was fear or anger. "He's twelve years older than I am, and still a boy at heart. A middle-aging boy."

"I know what you mean. I was his unofficial keeper for a while. I guess he's a genius, or pretty close to it, but he needs somebody to tell him to come in out of the rain."

"Thank you for informing me. I didn't know."

"Now don't get peeved at me."

"I'm sorry. I suppose I'm a little upset."

"Has he been giving you a bad time?"

"Not really. Not lately, that is. He's come down to earth since he got engaged to Alice. But he still makes the weirdest friends. He can tell a fake Van Gogh with his eyes shut, literally, but he has no discrimination about people at all."

"You wouldn't be talking about me?"

"No." She smiled again. I liked her smile. "I guess I acted terribly suspicious when I walked in on you. Some pretty dubious characters come to see him."

"Anyone in particular?" I said it lightly. Just above her head I could see the giant fist-mark on the door frame.

Before she could answer, a siren bayed in the distance. She tilted her head. "Ten to one it's for me."

"Police?"

"Ambulance. The police sirens have a different tone. I am an x-ray technician at the hospital, so I've learned to listen for the ambulance. And I'm on call this morning."

I followed her into the hall. "Hugh's show opens tonight. He's bound to come back for that."

She turned at the opposite door, her face brightening. "You know, he may have spent the night working in the gallery. He's awfully fussy about how his pictures are hung."

"Why don't I phone the gallery?"

"There's never anybody in the office till nine." She looked at her unfeminine steel wrist watch. "It's twenty to."

"When did you last see him?"

"At dinner last night. We ate early. He went back to the gallery after dinner. He said he was only going to work a couple of hours."

"And you stayed here?"

"Until about eight, when I was called to the hospital. I didn't get home until quite late, and I thought he was in bed." She

292

looked at me uncertainly, with a little wrinkle of doubt between her straight eyebrows. "Could you be cross-questioning me?"

"Sorry. It's my occupational disease."

"What do you do in real life?"

"Isn't this real?"

"I mean now you're out of the Army. Are you a lawyer?"

"A private detective."

"Oh. I see." The wrinkle between her eyebrows deepened.

"But I'm on vacation," I said hopefully.

A phone burred behind her apartment door. She went to answer it, and came back wearing a coat. "It *was* for me. Somebody fell out of a loquat tree and broke a leg. You'll have to excuse me, Mr. Archer."

"Wait a second. If you'll tell me where the art gallery is, I'll see if Hugh's there now."

"Of course, you don't know San Marcos."

She led me to the French windows at the rear end of the hall. They opened on a blacktop parking space which was overshadowed on the far side by a large stucco building, the shape of a flattened cube. Outside the windows was a balcony from which a concrete staircase slanted down to the parking lot. She stepped outside and pointed to the stucco cube.

"That's the gallery. You can take a shortcut down the alley to the front."

A tall young man in a black leotard was polishing a red convertible in the parking lot. He struck a pose, in the fifth position, and waved his hand: *"Bon jour,* Marie."

"Bon jour, my phony Frenchman." There was an edge of contempt in her good humor. "Have you seen Hugh this morning?"

"Not I. Is the prodigal missing again?"

"I wouldn't say missing—"

"I was wondering where your car was. It's not in the garage." His voice was much too musical.

"Who's he?" I asked in an undertone.

"Hilary Todd. He runs the art shop downstairs. If the car's gone, Hugh can't be at the gallery. I'll have to take a taxi to the hospital."

"I'll drive you."

"I wouldn't think of it. There's a cabstand across the street." She added over her shoulder, "Call me at the hospital if you find Hugh."

I went down the stairs to the parking lot. Hilary Todd was still polishing the hood of his convertible, though it shone like a mirror. His shoulders were broad and packed with shifting muscle. Some of the ballet boys were strong and could be dangerous. Not that he was a boy, exactly. He had a little round bald spot that gleamed like a silver dollar on the top of his head.

"*Bon jour,*" I said to his back.

"Yes?"

My French appeared to offend his ears. He turned and straightened. I saw how tall he was—tall enough to make me feel squat, though I was over six feet. He had compensated for the bald spot by growing sideburns. In combination with his liquid eyes they gave him a sort of Latin look.

"Do you know Hugh Western pretty well?"

"If it's any concern of yours."

"It is."

"Now why would that be?"

"I asked the question, sonny. Answer it."

He blushed and lowered his eyes, as if I had been reading his evil thoughts. He stuttered a little. "I—well, I've lived below him for a couple of years. I've sold a few of his pictures. Why?"

"I thought you might know where he is, even if his sister doesn't."

"How should I know where he is? Are you a policeman?"

"Not exactly."

"Not at all, you mean?" He regained his poise. "Then you have no right to take this overbearing attitude. I know absolutely nothing about Hugh. And I'm very busy."

He turned abruptly and continued his polishing job, his fine useless muscles writhing under the leotard.

I walked down the narrow alley which led to the street. Through the cypress hedge on the left I caught a glimpse of umbrella-tables growing like giant multicolored mushrooms in a restaurant patio. On the other side was the wall of the gallery, its white blankness broken by a single iron-barred window above the level of my head.

The front of the gallery was Greek-masked by a high-pillared porch. A broad flight of concrete steps rose to it from the street. A girl was standing at the head of the steps, half leaning on one of the pillars.

She turned toward me, and the slanting sunlight aureoled her bare head. She had a startling kind of beauty: yellow hair, light hazel eyes, brown skin. She filled her tailored suit like sand in a sack—solidly.

"Good morning," I said.

She pretended not to hear. Her right foot was tapping the pavement impatiently. I crossed the porch to the high bronze door and pushed. It didn't give.

"There's nobody here yet," she said. "The gallery doesn't open until ten."

"Then what are you doing here?"

"I happen to work here."

"Why don't you open up?"

"I have no key. In any case," she added primly, "we don't allow visitors before ten."

"I'm not a tourist—at least, not at the moment. I came to see Mr. Western."

"Hugh?" She looked at me directly for the first time. "Hugh's not here. He lives around the corner from the gallery on Rubio Street."

"I just came from there."

"Well, he isn't here." She gave the word a curious emphasis. "There's nobody here but me. And I won't be here much longer if Dr. Silliman doesn't come."

"Silliman?"

"Dr. Silliman is our curator." She made it sound as if she owned the gallery. After a while she said in a softer voice, "Why are you looking for Hugh? Do you have some business with him?"

"Western's an old friend of mine."

"Really?"

She suddenly lost interest in the conversation. We stood together in silence for several minutes. I watched the Saturday-morning crowd on the street: women in slacks, women in shorts and dirndls, a few men in ten-gallon hats, a few in berets. Nearly half the cars in the road carried out-of-state licenses. San Marcos was a unique blend of western border town, ocean resort, and artists' colony.

A small man in a purple corduroy jacket detached himself from the crowd and bounded up the steps. His movements were quick as a monkey's. His lined face had a simian look, too. A brush of frizzled gray hair added about three inches to his height.

"I'm sorry if I kept you waiting, Alice."

She made a *nada* gesture. "It's perfectly all right. This gentleman is a friend of Hugh's."

He turned to me. His smile went on and off. "Good morning, sir. What was the name?"

I told him. He shook my hand. His fingers were like thin steel hooks.

"Western ought to be here at any minute. Have you tried his flat?"

"Yes. His sister thought he might have spent the night in the gallery."

"Oh, but that's impossible. You mean he didn't come home last night?"

"Apparently not."

"You didn't tell me that," the blonde girl said.

"I didn't know you were interested."

"Alice has every right to be interested." Silliman's eyes glowed with a gossip's second-hand pleasure. "She and Hugh are going to get married. Next month, isn't it, Alice? Do you know Miss Turner, by the way, Mr. Archer?"

"Hello, Mr. Archer." Her voice was shallow and hostile. I gathered that Silliman had somehow embarrassed her.

"I'm sure he'll be along shortly," he said reassuringly. "We still have some work to do on the program for the private showing tonight. Will you come in and wait?"

I said I would.

He took a heavy key ring out of his jacket pocket and unlocked the bronze door, relocking it behind us. Alice Turner touched a switch which lit up the high-ceilinged lobby and the Greek statues standing like frozen sentinels along the walls. There were several nymphs and Venuses in marble, but I was more interested in Alice. She had everything the Venuses had, and the added advantage of being alive. She also had Hugh Western, it seemed, and that surprised me. He was a little old for her, and a little used. She didn't look like one of those girls who'd have to settle for an aging bachelor. But then Hugh Western had talent.

She removed a bundle of letters from the mailbox and took them into the office which opened off the lobby. Silliman turned to me with another monkey grin.

"She's quite a girl, isn't she? And she comes from a very good family, an excellent family. Her father, the Admiral, is one of our trustees, you know, and Alice has inherited his interests in the arts. Of course she has a more personal interest now. Had you known of their engagement?"

"I haven't seen Hugh for years—not since the war."

"Then I should have held my tongue and let him tell you himself."

As we were talking he led me through the central gallery, which ran the length of the building like the nave of a church. To the left and right, in what would have been the aisles, the walls of smaller exhibition rooms rose halfway to the ceiling. Above them was a mezzanine reached by an open staircase.

He started up it, still talking. "If you haven't seen Hugh since the war, you'll be interested in the work he's been doing lately."

I was interested, though not for artistic reasons. The wall of the mezzanine was hung with twenty-odd paintings: landscapes, portraits, groups of semi-abstract figures, and more abstract still lifes. I recognized some of the scenes he had sketched in the Philippine jungle, transposed into the permanence of oil. In the central position there was a portrait of a bearded man whom I'd hardly have known without the label, *Self-Portrait*.

Hugh had changed. He had put on weight and lost his youth entirely. There were vertical lines in his forehead, gray flecks in his hair and beard. The light-colored eyes seemed to be smiling sardonically. But when I looked at them from another angle, they were bleak and somber. It was a face a man might see in his bathroom mirror on a cold gray hangover morning.

I turned to the curator hovering at my elbow. "When did he raise the beard?"

"A couple of years ago, I believe, shortly after he joined us as resident painter."

"Is he obsessed with beards?"

"I don't quite know what you mean."

"Neither do I. But I came across a funny thing in his studio this morning. A sketch of a woman, a nude, with a heavy black beard. Does that make any sense to you?"

The old man smiled. "I've long since given up trying to make sense out of Hugh. He has his own esthetic logic, I suppose. But I'd have to see this sketch before I could form an opinion. He may have simply been doodling."

"I doubt it. It was big, and carefully done." I brought out the question that had been nagging at the back of my mind. "Is there something the matter with him—I mean, emotionally?"

His answer was positive. "Certainly not! He's simply wrapped up in his work, and he lives by impulse. He's never on time for appointments." He looked at his watch. "He promised last night to meet me here this morning at nine and it's almost nine thirty."

"When did you see him last night?"

"I left the key of the gallery with him when I went home for dinner. He wanted to change some of the paintings. About eight or a little later he walked over to my house to return the key. We have only the one key, since we can't afford a watchman."

"Did he say where he was going after that?"

"He had an appointment, but he didn't say with whom. It seemed to be urgent, since he wouldn't stop for a drink. Well." He glanced at his watch again. "I suppose I'd better be getting down to work, Hugh Western or no Hugh Western."

Alice was waiting for us at the foot of the stairs. Both her hands gripped the wrought-iron banister as if she needed it to hold her up. Her voice was no more than a whisper, but it seemed to fill the great room with leaden echoes.

"Dr. Silliman. The Chardin's gone."

He stopped so suddenly I nearly ran him down. "That's impossible."

"I know. But it's gone, frame and all."

He bounded down the remaining steps and disappeared into one of the smaller rooms under the mezzanine. Alice followed him more slowly. I caught up with her.

"There's a picture missing?"

"Father's best picture, one of the best Chardins in the country. He lent it to the gallery for a month."

"Is it worth a lot of money?"

"Yes, it's very valuable. But it means a lot more to Father than the money—" She turned in the doorway and gave me a closed look, as if she'd realized she was telling her family secrets to a stranger.

Silliman was standing with his back to us, staring at a blank space on the opposite wall. He looked badly shaken when he turned around.

"I *told* the Board that we should install a burglar alarm—the insurance people recommended it. But Admiral Turner was the only one who supported me. Now of course they'll be blaming me." His nervous eyes roved around and paused on Alice. "And what is your father going to say?"

"He'll be sick." She looked sick herself.

They were getting nowhere, so I cut in, "When did you see it last?"

Silliman answered. "Yesterday afternoon, about five thirty. I showed it to a visitor just before we closed. We check the visitors very carefully from the office, since we have no guards."

"Who was the visitor?"

"A lady—an elderly lady from Pasadena. She's above suspicion, of course. I escorted her out myself, and she was the last one in. I know that for a fact."

"Aren't you forgetting Hugh?"

"By George, I was. He was here until eight last night. But you surely don't suggest that Western took it? He's our resident painter, he's devoted to the gallery."

"He might have been careless. If he was working on the mezzanine and left the door unlocked—"

"He always kept it locked," Alice said coldly. "Hugh isn't careless about the things that matter."

"Is there another entrance?"

"No," Silliman said. "The building was planned for security. There's only one window in my office, and it's heavily barred. We do have an air-conditioning system, but the inlets are much too small for anyone to get through."

"Let's have a look at the window."

The old man was too upset to question my authority. He led me through a storeroom stacked with old gilt-framed pictures whose painters deserved to be "hung," if the pictures didn't. The single casement in the office was shut and bolted behind a venetian blind. I pulled the cord and peered out through the dusty glass. The vertical bars outside the window were no more than three inches apart. None of them looked as if it had been tampered with. Across the alley I could see a few tourists eating breakfast behind the restaurant hedge.

Silliman was leaning on the desk, one hand on the cradle of the phone. Indecision was twisting his face. "I do hate to call the police in a matter like this. I suppose I must, though, mustn't I?"

Alice covered his hand with hers, the line of her back a taut curve across the desk. "Hadn't you better talk to Father first? He was here with Hugh last night—I should have remembered before. It's barely possible he took the Chardin home with him."

299

"Really? You really think so?" Silliman let go of the telephone and clasped his hands under his chin.

"It wouldn't be like Father to do that without letting you know. But the month is nearly up, isn't it?"

"Three more days." His hand returned to the phone. "Is the Admiral at home?"

"He'll be down at the club by now. Do you have your car?"

"Not this morning."

I made one of my famous quick decisions, the kind you wake up in the middle of the night regretting five years later. San Francisco could wait. My curiosity was touched, and something deeper than curiosity. Something of the responsibility I'd felt for Hugh in the Philippines, when I was the practical one and he was the evergreen adolescent who thought the jungle was as safe as a scene by Le Douanier Rousseau. Though we were nearly the same age, I'd felt like his elder brother. I still did.

"My car's around the corner," I said. "I'll be glad to drive you."

The San Marcos Beach Club was a long low building painted an unobtrusive green and standing well back from the road. Everything about it was unobtrusive, including the private policeman who stood inside the plate-glass doors and watched us come up the walk.

"Looking for the Admiral, Miss Turner? I think he's up on the north deck."

We crossed a tiled lanai shaded with potted palms, climbed a flight of stairs to a sun deck lined with cabanas. I could see the mountains that walled the city off from the desert in the northeast, and the sea below with its waves glinting like blue fish-scales. The swimming pool on the lee side of the deck was still and clear.

Admiral Turner was taking the sun in a canvas chair. He stood up when he saw us, a big old man in shorts and a sleeveless shirt. Sun and wind had reddened his face and crinkled the flesh around his eyes. Age had slackened his body, but there was nothing aged or infirm about his voice. It still held the brazen echo of command.

"What's this, Alice? I thought you were at work."

"We came to ask you a question, Admiral." Silliman hesitated, coughing behind his hand. He looked at Alice.

"Speak out, man. Why is everybody looking so green around the gills?"

300

Silliman forced the words out. "Did you take the Chardin home with you last night?"

"I did not. Is it gone?"

"It's missing from the gallery," Alice said. She held herself uncertainly, as though the old man frightened her a little. "We thought you might have taken it."

"Me take it? That's absurd! Absolutely absurd and preposterous! When was it taken?"

"We don't know exactly. It was gone when we opened the gallery."

"Damn it, what's going on?" He glared at her, then he glared at me from eyes like round blue gun muzzles. "And who the hell are you?"

He was only a retired admiral, and I'd been out of uniform for years; still he gave me a qualm.

Alice explained: "A friend of Hugh's, Father. Mr. Archer."

He didn't offer his hand. I looked away. A woman in a white bathing suit was poised on the ten-foot board at the end of the pool. She took three quick steps and a bounce. Her body hung jackknifed in the air, straightened and dropped, then cut the water with hardly a splash.

"Where is Hugh?" the Admiral said petulantly. "If this is some of his carelessness, I'll ream that son-of-a—"

"Father!"

"Don't father me. Where is he, Allie? You ought to know if anyone does."

"But I don't." She added in a small voice, "He's been gone all night."

"He has, has he?" The old man sat down suddenly, as if his legs were too weak to bear the weight of his emotions. "He didn't say anything to me about going away."

The woman in the white bathing suit came up the steps behind him. "Who's gone?" she said.

The Admiral craned his wattled neck to look at her. She was worth the effort from anyone, though she wouldn't see thirty again. Her dripping body was tanned and disciplined, full in the right places and narrow in the others. I didn't remember her face, but her shape seemed familiar. Silliman introduced her as Admiral Turner's wife. When she pulled off her rubber cap, her red hair flared like a minor conflagration.

"You won't believe what they've been telling me, Sara. My Chardin's been stolen."

301

"Which one?"

"I only have one. The *Apple on a Table*."

She turned on Silliman like a pouncing cat. "Is it insured?"

"For twenty-five thousand dollars. But I'm afraid it's irreplaceable."

"And who's gone?"

"Hugh," Alice said. "Of course it's nothing to do with the picture."

"You're sure?" She turned to her husband with an intensity that made her almost ungainly. "Hugh was at the gallery when you dropped in there last night. You told me so yourself. And hasn't he been trying to buy the Chardin?"

"I don't believe it," Alice said flatly. "He didn't have the money."

"I know that perfectly well," Sara said. "He was acting as agent for someone. Wasn't he, Johnston?"

"Yes," the old man admitted. "He wouldn't tell me who his principal was, which is one of the reasons I wouldn't listen to the offer. Still, it's foolish to jump to conclusions about Hugh. I was with him when he left the gallery, and I know for a fact he didn't have the Chardin then. It was the last thing I looked at before we left."

"What time did he leave you?"

"Some time around eight—I don't remember exactly." He seemed to be growing older and smaller under her questioning. "He walked with me as far as my car."

"There was nothing to prevent him from walking right back, was there?"

"I don't know what you're trying to prove," Alice said.

The older woman smiled poisonously. "I'm simply trying to bring out the facts, so we'll know what to do. I notice that no one has suggested calling the police." She looked at each of the others in turn. "Well? Do we call them? Or do we assume as a working hypothesis that dear Hugh took the picture?"

Nobody answered her for a while. The Admiral finally broke the ugly silence. "We can't bring in the authorities if Hugh's involved. He's virtually a member of the family."

Alice put a grateful hand on his shoulder, but Silliman said uneasily, "We'll have to take some steps. If we don't make an effort to recover it, we may not be able to collect the insurance."

"I realize that," the Admiral said. "But we'll have to take that chance."

302

Sara Turner smiled with tight-lipped complacency. She'd won her point, though I still wasn't sure what her point was. During the family argument I'd moved a few feet away, leaning on the railing at the head of the stairs.

She moved toward me now, her narrow eyes appraising me as if maleness was a commodity she prized.

"And who are you?" she said, her sharp smile widening.

I identified myself, but I didn't smile back. She came up very close to me. I could smell the chlorine on her, and under it the not so very subtle odor of sex.

"You look uncomfortable," she said. "Why don't you come swimming with me?"

"My hydrophobia won't let me. Sorry."

"What a pity. I hate to do things alone."

Silliman nudged me gently. He said in an undertone, "I really must be getting back to the gallery. I *can* call a cab. . . ."

"No, I'll drive you." I wanted a chance to talk to him in private.

There were quick footsteps in the patio below. I looked down and saw the partly naked crown of Hilary Todd's head. At almost the same instant he glanced up at us, turned abruptly, and started to walk away; then he changed his mind when Silliman called down:

"Hello there. Are you looking for the Turners?"

"As a matter of fact, I am."

From the corner of my eye I noticed Sara Turner's reaction to the sound of his voice. She stiffened, and her hand went up to her flaming hair.

"They're up here," Silliman said.

Todd climbed the stairs with obvious reluctance. We passed him going down. In a pastel shirt and matching tie under a bright tweed jacket he looked very elegant, and very self-conscious and tense. Sara Turner met him at the head of the stairs. I wanted to linger a bit, but Silliman hustled me out.

"Mrs. Turner seems very much aware of Todd," I said to him in the car. "Do they have things in common?"

He answered tartly, "I've never considered the question. They're no more than casual acquaintances, so far as I know."

"What about Hugh? Is he just a casual acquaintance of hers, too?"

He studied me for a minute as the convertible picked up speed. "You notice things, don't you?"

"Noticing things is my business."

"Just what is your business? You're not an artist?"

"Hardly. I'm a private detective."

"A detective?" He jumped in the seat, as if I had threatened to bite him. "You're not a friend of Western's then? Are you from the insurance company?"

"Not me. I'm a friend of Hugh's, and that's my only interest in this case. I more or less stumbled into it."

"I see." But he sounded a little dubious.

"Getting back to Mrs. Turner, she didn't make that scene with her husband for fun. She must have had reason. Love or hate?"

Silliman held his tongue for a minute, but he couldn't resist the chance to gossip. "I expect it's a mixture of love and hate. She's been interested in Hugh ever since the Admiral brought her here. She's not a San Marcos girl, you know." He seemed to take comfort from that. "She was a Wave officer in Washington during the war. The Admiral noticed her—Sara knows how to make herself conspicuous—and added her to his personal staff. When he retired he married her and came here to live in his family home. Alice's mother has been dead for many years. Well, Sara hadn't been here two months before she was making eyes at Hugh." He pressed his lips together in spinsterly disapproval. "The rest is local history."

"They had an affair?"

"A rather one-sided affair, so far as I could judge. She was quite insane about him. I don't believe he responded, except in the physical sense. Your friend is quite a demon with the ladies." There was a whisper of envy in Silliman's disapproval.

"But I understood he was going to marry Alice."

"Oh, he is, he is. At least he certainly was until this dreadful business came up. His—ah—involvement with Sara occurred before he knew Alice. She was away at art school until a few months ago."

"Does Alice know about this affair with her stepmother?" I asked.

"I suppose she does. I hear the two women don't get along at all well, though there may be other reasons for that. Alice refuses to live in the same house—she's moved into the gar-

304

dener's cottage behind the Turner house. I think her trouble with Sara is one reason why she came to work for me. Of course, there's the money consideration, too. The Turners aren't well off."

"I thought they were rolling in it," I said, "from the way he brushed off the matter of the insurance. Twenty-five thousand dollars, did you say?"

"Yes. He's quite fond of Hugh."

"If he's not well heeled, how does he happen to have such a valuable painting?"

"It was a gift, when he married his first wife. Her father was in the French Embassy in Washington, and he gave them the Chardin as a wedding present. You can understand the Admiral's attachment to it."

"Better than I can his decision not to call in the police. How do you feel about that, Doctor?"

He didn't answer for a while. We were nearing the center of the city and I had to watch the traffic. I couldn't keep track of what went on in his face.

"After all, it *is* his picture," he said carefully. "And his prospective son-in-law."

"You don't think Hugh's responsible, though?"

"I don't know what to think. I'm thoroughly confused. And I won't know what to think until I have a chance to talk to Western." He gave me a sharp look. "Are you going to make a search for him?"

"Somebody has to. I seem to be elected."

When I let him out in front of the gallery, I asked him where Mary Western worked.

"The City Hospital." He told me how to find it. "But you will be discreet, Mr. Archer? You won't do or say anything rash? I'm in a very delicate position."

"I'll be very suave and bland." But I slammed the door hard in his face.

There were several patients in the x-ray waiting room, in various stages of dilapidation and disrepair. The plump blonde at the reception desk told me Miss Western was in the darkroom. Would I wait? I sat down and admired the way her sunburned shoulders glowed through her nylon uniform. In a few minutes Mary came into the room, starched and controlled and efficient-looking. She blinked in the strong light from the

305

window. I got a quick impression that there was a lost child hidden within her.

"Have you seen Hugh?" she asked.

"No. Come out for a minute." I took her elbow and drew her into the corridor.

"What is it?" Her voice was quiet but it had risen in pitch. "Has something happened to him?"

"Not *to* him. Admiral Turner's picture's been stolen from the gallery. The one they all call the Chardin."

"But how does Hugh come into this?"

"Somebody seems to think he took it."

"Somebody?"

"Mrs. Turner, to be specific."

"Sara! She'd say anything to get back at him for ditching her."

I filed that one away. "Maybe so. The fact is, the Admiral seems to suspect him, too. So much so that he's keeping the police out of it."

"Admiral Turner is a senile fool. If Hugh were here to defend himself—"

"But that's the point. He isn't."

"I've got to find him." She turned toward the door.

"It may not be so easy."

She looked back in quick anger, her round chin prominent. "You suspect him, too."

"I do not. But a crime's been committed, remember. Crimes often come in pairs."

She turned, her eyes large and very dark. "You *do* think something has happened to my brother."

"I don't think anything. But if I was certain that he's all right, I'd be on my way to San Francisco now."

"You believe it's as bad as that," she said in a whisper. "I've got to go to the police."

"It's up to you. You'll want to keep them out of it, though, if there's the slightest chance—" I left the sentence unfinished.

She finished it: "That Hugh is a thief? There isn't. But I'll tell you what we'll do. He may be up at his shack in the mountains. He's gone off there before without telling anyone. Will you drive up with me?" She laid a light hand on my arm. "I can go myself if you have to get away."

"I'm sticking around," I said. "Can you get time off?"

"I'm taking it. All they can do is fire me, and there aren't enough good technicians to go around. Anyway, I put in three hours overtime last night. Be with you in two minutes."

I put the top of the convertible down. As we drove out of the city the wind blew away her smooth glaze of efficiency, colored her cheeks, and loosened her sleek hair.

"You should do this oftener," I said.

"Do what?"

"Get out in the country and relax."

"I'm not exactly relaxed, with my brother accused of theft—and missing."

"Anyway, you're not working. Has it ever occurred to you that perhaps you work too hard?"

"Has it ever occurred to you that somebody has to work or nothing will get done? You and Hugh are more alike than I thought."

"In some ways that's a compliment. But you make it sound like an insult."

"I didn't mean it that way. But Hugh and I are so different. I admit he works hard at his painting, but he's never tried to make a steady living. Since I left school, I've had to look after the bread and butter for both of us. His salary as resident painter keeps him in artist's supplies, and that's about all."

"I thought he was doing well. His show's had a big advance buildup in the L.A. papers."

"Critics don't buy pictures," she said bluntly. "He's having the show to try and sell some paintings, so he can afford to get married. Hugh has suddenly realized that money is one of the essentials." She added with some bitterness, "The realization came a little late."

"He's been doing some outside work, though, hasn't he? Isn't he a part-time agent or something?"

"For Hendryx, yes." She made the name sould like a dirty word. "I'd just as soon he didn't take any of that man's money."

"Who's Hendryx?"

"A man."

"I gathered that. What's the matter with his money?"

"I really don't know. I have no idea where it comes from. But he has it—plenty of it."

"You don't like him?"

"No. I don't like him and I don't like the men who work for him. They look like a gang of thugs to me. But Hugh wouldn't notice that. He's horribly dense where people are concerned. I don't mean that Hugh's done anything wrong," she added quickly. "He's bought a few paintings for Hendryx on commission."

"I see." But I didn't like what I saw. "The Admiral said something about Hugh trying to buy the Chardin for an unnamed purchaser. Would that be Hendryx?"

"It could be," she said.

"Tell me more about Hendryx."

"I don't know any more. I only met him once. That was enough. I know that he's an evil old man, and he has a bodyguard who carries him upstairs."

"Carries him upstairs?"

"Yes. He's crippled. As a matter of fact, he offered me a job."

"Carrying him upstairs?"

"He didn't specify my duties. He didn't get that far." Her voice was so chilly it quick-froze the conversation. "Now could we drop the subject, Mr. Archer?"

The road had begun to rise toward the mountains. Yellow and black Slide Area signs sprung up along the shoulders. By holding the gas pedal nearly to the floor, I kept our speed around fifty.

"You've had quite a busy morning," Mary said after a while, "meeting the Turners and all."

"Social mobility is my stock in trade."

"Did you meet Alice, too?"

I nodded.

"And what did you think of her?"

"I shouldn't say it to another girl, but she's a lovely one."

"Vanity isn't one of my vices," Mary said. "She's beautiful. And she's really devoted to Hugh."

"I gathered that."

"I don't think Alice has ever been in love before. And painting means almost as much to her as it does to him."

"He's a lucky man." I remembered the disillusioned eyes in Hugh's self-portrait, and hoped his luck was holding.

The road twisted and climbed through red clay cut banks and fields of dry chaparral.

"How long does this go on?" I asked.

"Another two miles."

We zigzagged up the mountainside for ten or twelve minutes more. Finally the road began to level out. I was watching its edge so closely that I didn't see the cabin until we were almost on top of it. It was a one-story frame building standing in a little hollow at the edge of the high mesa. Attached to one side was an open tarpaulin shelter from which the rear end of a gray coupe protruded. I looked at Mary.

She nodded. "It's our car." Her voice was bright with relief.

I stopped the convertible in the lane in front of the cabin. As soon as the engine died, the silence began. A single hawk high over our heads swung round and round on his invisible wire. Apart from that, the entire world seemed empty. As we walked down the ill-kept gravel drive, I was startled by the sound of my own footsteps.

The door was unlocked. The cabin had only one room. It was a bachelor hodgepodge, untouched by the human hand for months at a time. Cooking utensils, paint-stained dungarees, painter's tools, and soiled bedding were scattered on the floor and furniture. There was an open bottle of whiskey, half empty, on the kitchen table in the center of the room. It would have been just another mountain shack if it hadn't been for the watercolors on the walls, like brilliant little windows, and the one big window which opened on the sky.

Mary had crossed to the window and was looking out. I moved up to her shoulder. Blue space fell away in front of us all the way down to the sea, and beyond to the curved horizon. San Marcos and its suburbs were spread out like an air map between the sea and the mountains.

"I wonder where he can be," she said. "Perhaps he's gone for a walk. After all, he doesn't know we're looking for him."

I looked down the mountainside, which fell almost sheer from the window.

"No," I said. "He doesn't."

The red clay slope was sown with boulders. Nothing grew there except a few dust-colored mountain bushes ... and a foot, wearing a man's shoe, which projected from a cleft between two rocks.

I went out without a word. A path led round the cabin to the edge of the slope. Hugh Western was there, attached to the solitary foot. He was lying, or hanging, head down, with his face in the clay, about twenty feet below the edge. One of his legs was doubled under him. The other was caught between the boulders. I climbed around the rocks and bent down to look at his head.

The right temple was smashed. The face was smashed—I raised the rigid body to look at it. He had been dead for hours, but the sharp strong odor of whiskey still hung around him.

A tiny gravel avalanche rattled past me. Mary was at the top of the slope.

"Don't come down here."

She paid no attention to the warning. I stayed where I was, crouched over the body, trying to hide the ruined head from her. She leaned over the boulder and looked down, her eyes bright-black in her drained face. I moved to one side. She took her brother's head in her hands.

"If you pass out," I said, "I don't know whether I can carry you up."

"I won't pass out."

She lifted the body by the shoulders to look at the face. It was a little unsettling to see how strong she was. Her fingers moved gently over the wounded temple. "This is what killed him. It looks like a blow from a fist."

I kneeled down beside her and saw the row of rounded indentations in the skull.

"He must have fallen," she said, "and struck his head on the rocks. Nobody could have hit him that hard."

"I'm afraid somebody did, though." Somebody whose fist was hard enough to leave its mark in wood.

Two long hours later I parked my car in front of the art shop on Rubio Street. Its windows were jammed with Impressionist and Post-Impressionist reproductions, and one very bad original oil of surf as stiff and static as whipped cream. The sign above the windows was lettered in flowing script: *Chez Hilary*. The cardboard sign on the door was simpler and to the point. It said: *Closed*.

The stairs and hallway seemed dark, but it was good to get out of the sun. The sun reminded me of what I had found at high noon on the high mesa. It wasn't the middle of the afternoon yet, but my nerves felt stretched and scratchy, as though it were late at night. And my eyes were aching.

Mary unlocked the door of her apartment, stepped aside to let me pass. She paused at the door of her room to tell me there was whiskey on the sideboard. I offered to make her a drink. No, thanks, she never drank. The door shut behind her. I mixed a whiskey and water and tried to relax in an easy chair.

But I couldn't relax. My mind kept playing back the questions and the answers—and the questions that had no answers.

We had called the sheriff from the nearest fire warden's post, led him and his deputies back up the mountain to the body. Photographs were taken, the cabin and its surroundings searched, and many questions were asked. Mary didn't mention the Chardin. Neither did I.

Some of the questions were answered after the county coroner arrived. Hugh Western had been dead since eight or ten o'clock the previous night; the coroner couldn't place the time more definitely before analyzing the stomach contents. The blow on the temple had killed him. The injuries to his face, which had failed to bleed, had probably been inflicted after death. Which meant that he was dead when his body fell—or was thrown—down the mountainside.

His clothes had been soaked with whiskey to make it look like a drunken accident. But the murderer had gone too far in covering, and had outwitted himself. The whiskey bottle in the cabin showed no fingerprints, not even Western's. And there were no fingerprints on the steering wheel of his coupe. Bottle and wheel had been wiped clean.

I stood up when Mary came back into the room. She had brushed her black hair gleaming, and changed to a dress of soft black jersey which fitted her like skin. A thought raced through my mind like a nasty little rodent. I wondered what she would look like with a beard.

"Can I have another peek at the studio? I'm interested in that sketch."

She stared at me for a moment, frowning a little dazedly. "Sketch?"

"The one of the lady with the beard."

She crossed the hall ahead of me, walking slowly and carefully as if the floor was unsafe. The door of the studio was still unlocked. She held it open for me and pressed the light switch.

When the fluorescent lights blinked on, I saw that the picture of the bearded nude was gone. There was nothing left of her but four torn corners of drawing paper thumbtacked to the easel.

I turned to Mary. "Did you take it down?"

"No. I haven't been in the studio since this morning."

"Somebody's stolen it then. Is there anything else missing?"

"I can't be sure, it's such a mess in here." She moved around the room looking at the pictures on the walls and pausing finally by a table in the corner. "There was a bronze cast on this table. It isn't here now."

"What sort of cast?"

"The cast of a fist. Hugh made it from the fist of that man— that dreadful man I told you about."

"What dreadful man?"

"I think his name is Devlin. He's Hendryx' bodyguard. Hugh's always been interested in hands, and the man has enormous hands."

Her eyes unfocused suddenly. I guessed she was thinking of the same thing I was: the marks on the side of Hugh's head, which might have been made by a giant fist.

"Look." I pointed to the scars on the door frame. "Could the cast of Devlin's fist have made these marks?"

She felt the indentations with trembling fingers. "I think so." She turned to me with a dark question in her eyes.

"If that's what they are," I said, "it probably means that he was killed in this studio. You should tell the police about it. And I think it's time they knew about the Chardin."

She gave me a look of passive resistance. Then she gave in. "Yes, I'll have to tell them. They'll find out soon enough, anyway. But I'm surer now than ever that Hugh didn't take it."

"What does the picture look like? If we could find it, we might find the killer attached to it."

"You think so? Well, it's a picture of a little boy looking at an apple. Wait a minute—Hilary has a copy. It was painted by one of the students at the college, and it isn't very expert. It'll give you an idea, though, if you want to go down to his shop and look at it."

"The shop is closed."

"He may be there anyway. He has a little apartment at the back."

I started for the hall but turned before I got there. "Just who is Hilary Todd?"

"I don't know where he's from originally. He was stationed here during the war, and simply stayed on. His parents had money at one time, and he studied painting and ballet in Paris, or so he claims."

"Art seems to be the main industry in San Marcos."

"You've just been meeting the wrong people."

I went down the outside stairs to the parking lot. Todd's

convertible stood near the mouth of the alley. I knocked on the back door of the art shop. There was no answer, but behind the venetian-blinded door I heard a murmur of voices—a growling and a twittering. Todd had a woman with him. I knocked again.

After more delay the door was partly opened. Todd looked out through the crack. He was wiping his mouth with a red-stained handkerchief. The stains were too bright to be blood. Above the handkerchief his eyes were bright and narrow, like slivers of polished agate.

"Good afternoon."

I moved forward as though I fully expected to be let in. He opened the door reluctantly under the nudging pressure of my shoulder, backed into a narrow passage between two wallboard partitions.

"What can I do for you, Mr.—? I don't believe I know your name."

Before I could answer, a woman's voice said clearly, "It's Mr. Archer, isn't it?"

Sara Turner appeared in the doorway behind him, carrying a highball glass and looking freshly groomed. Her red hair was unruffled, her red mouth gleaming as if she had just finished painting it.

"Good afternoon, Mrs. Turner."

"Good afternoon, Mr. Archer." She leaned in the doorway, almost too much at ease. "Do you know Hilary, Mr. Archer? You should. Everybody should. Hilary's simply loaded and dripping with charm, aren't you dear?" Her mouth curled in a thin smile.

Todd looked at her with open hatred, then turned to me without changing his look. "Did you wish to speak to me?"

"I did. You have a copy of Admiral Turner's Chardin?"

"A copy, yes."

"Can I have a look at it?"

"What on earth for?"

"I want to be able to identify the original. It's probably connected with the murder."

I watched them both as I said the word. Neither showed surprise.

"We heard about it on the radio," the woman said. "It must have been dreadful for you."

"Dreadful," Todd echoed her, injecting synthetic sympathy into his dark eyes.

"Worse for Western," I said, "and for whoever did it. Do you still think he stole the picture, Mrs. Turner?"

Todd glanced at her sharply. She was embarrassed, as I'd intended her to be. She dunked her embarrassment in her highball glass, swallowing deeply from it and leaving a red half moon on its rim.

"I never thought he stole it," her wet mouth lied. "I merely suggested the possibility."

"I see. Didn't you say something about Western trying to buy the picture from your husband? That he was acting as agent for somebody else?"

"I wasn't the one who said that. I didn't know it."

"The Admiral said it then. It would be interesting to know who the other man was. He wanted the Chardin, and it looks to me as if Hugh Western died because somebody wanted the Chardin."

Todd had been listening hard and saying nothing. "I don't see any connection," he said. "But if you'll come in and sit down I'll show you my copy."

"You wouldn't know who it was that Western was acting for?"

He spread his palms outward in a Continental gesture. "How would I know?"

"You're in the picture business."

"I *was* in the picture business." He turned abruptly and left the room.

Sara Turner had crossed to a portable bar in the corner. She was splintering ice with a silver-handled ice pick. "May I make you one, Mr. Archer?"

"No, thanks." I sat down in a cubistic chair designed for people with square corners, and watched her take half of her fresh highball in a single gulp. "What did Todd mean when he said he *was* in the picture business? Doesn't he run this place?"

"He has to give it up. The *boutique*'s gone broke, and he's going around testing shoulders to cry on."

"Yours?" A queer kind of hostile intimacy had risen between us, and I tried to make the most of it.

"Where did you get that notion?"

"I thought he was a friend of yours."

"Did you?" Her laugh was too loud to be pleasant. "You ask a great many questions, Mr. Archer."

"They seem to be indicated. The cops in a town like this are pretty backward about stepping on people's toes."

"You're not."

"No. I'm just passing through. I can follow my hunches."

"What do you hope to gain?"

"Nothing for myself. I'd like to see justice done."

She sat down facing me, her knees almost touching mine. They were pretty knees, and uncovered. I felt crowded. Her voice, full of facile emotion, crowded me more.

"Were you terribly fond of Hugh?" she asked.

"I liked him." My answer was automatic. I was thinking of something else: the way she sat in her chair with her knees together, her body sloping backward, sure of its firm lines. I'd seen the same pose in charcoal that morning.

"I liked him too," she was saying. "Very much. And I've been thinking—I've remembered something. Something that Hilary mentioned a couple of weeks ago—about Walter Hendryx wanting to buy the Chardin. It seems Hugh and Walter Hendryx were talking in the shop—"

She broke off suddenly. She had looked up and seen Todd leaning through the doorway, his face alive with anger. His shoulders moved slightly in her direction. She recoiled, clutching her glass. If I hadn't been there, he would have hit her. As it was, he said in a monotone, "How cozy. Haven't you had quite a bit to drink, Sara, darling?"

She was afraid of him, but unwilling to admit it. "I have to do something to make present company bearable."

"You should be thoroughly anesthetized by now."

"If you say so, darling."

She hurled her half-empty glass at the wall beside the door. It shattered, denting the wallboard and splashing a photograph of Nijinsky as the Faun. Some of the liquid splattered on Todd's blue suede shoes.

"Very nice," he said. "I love your girlish antics, Sara. I also love the way you run at the mouth." He turned to me. "This is the copy, Mr. Archer. Don't mind her, she's just a weensy bit drunky."

He held it up for me to see, an oil painting about a yard square showing a small boy in a blue waistcoat sitting at a table. In the center of the linen tablecloth there was a blue dish containing a red apple as if he intended to eat it. The copyist had included the signature and date: *Chardin, 1744.*

"It's not very good," Todd said, "if you've ever seen the original. But of course you haven't?"

315

"No."

"That's too bad. You probably never will now, and it's really perfect. Perfect. It's the finest Chardin west of Chicago."

"I haven't given up hope of seeing it."

"You might as well, old boy. It'll be well on its way by now, to Europe or South America. Picture thieves move fast, before the news of the theft catches up with them and spoils the market. They'll sell the Chardin to a private buyer in Paris or Buenos Aires, and that'll be the end of it."

"Why 'they'?"

"Oh, they operate in gangs. One man can't handle the theft and disposal of a picture by himself. Division of labor is necessary, and specialization."

"You sound like a specialist yourself."

"I am in a way." He smiled obliquely. "Not in the way you mean. I was in museum work before the war."

He stopped and propped the picture against the wall. I glanced at Sara Turner. She was hunched forward in her chair, still and silent, her hands spread over her face.

"And now," he said to me, "I suppose you'd better go. I've done what I can for you. And I'll give you a tip if you like. Picture thieves don't commit murder—they're simply not the type. So I'm afraid your precious hypothesis is based on bad information."

"Thank you very much," I said. "I certainly appreciate that. Also your hospitality."

"Don't mention it."

He raised an ironic brow, and turned to the door. I followed him out through the deserted shop. Most of the stock seemed to be in the window. Its atmosphere was sad and broken-down— the atmosphere of an empty-hearted, unprosperous, second-rate Bohemia. Todd didn't look around like a proprietor. He had already abandoned the place in his mind, it seemed.

He unlocked the front door. The last thing he said before he shut it behind me was:

"I wouldn't go bothering Walter Hendryx about that story of Sara's. She's not a very trustworthy reporter, and Hendryx isn't as tolerant of intruders as I am."

So it was true.

I left my car where it was and crossed to a taxi stand on the opposite corner. There was a yellow cab at the stand, with a brown-faced driver reading a comic book behind the wheel.

The comic book had dead women on the cover. The driver detached his hot eyes from its interior, leaned wearily over the back of the seat, and opened the door for me. "Where to?"

"A man called Walter Hendryx—know where he lives?"

"Off of Foothill Drive. I been up there before. It's a two-fifty run—outside the city limits." His New Jersey accent didn't quite go with his Sicilian features.

"Newark?"

"Trenton." He showed bad teeth in a good smile. "Want to make something out of it?"

"Nope. Let's go."

He spoke to me over his shoulder when we were out of the heavy downtown traffic. "You got your passport?"

"What kind of place are you taking me to?"

"They don't like visitors. You got to have a visa to get in, and a writ of habeas corpus to get out. The old man's scared of burglars or something."

"Why?"

"He's got about ten million reasons, the way I hear it. Ten million bucks." He smacked his lips.

"Where did he get it?"

"You tell me. I'll drop everything and take off for the same place."

"You and me both."

"I heard he's a big contractor in L.A.," the driver said. "I drove a reporter up here a couple of months ago, from one of the L.A. papers. He was after an interview with the old guy— about a tax case."

"A corporate tax?"

"I wouldn't know. It's way over my head, friend, all that tax business. I have enough trouble with my own forms."

"What happened to the reporter?

"I drove him right back down. The old man wouldn't see him. He likes his privacy."

"I'm beginning to get the idea."

"You a reporter, too, by any chance?"

"No."

We left the city limits. The mountains rose ahead, violet and unshadowed in the sun's lengthening rays. Foothill Drive wound through a canyon, across a high-level bridge, up the side of a hill from which the sea was visible like a low blue cloud on the horizon. We turned off the road through an open gate

317

on which a sign was posted: *Trespassers Will Be Prosecuted.*

A second gate closed the road at the top of the hill. It was a double gate of wrought iron hung between a stone gatepost and a stone gatehouse. A heavy wire fence stretched out from it on both sides, following the contours of the hills as far as I could see. The Hendryx estate was about the size of a small European principality.

The driver honked his horn. A thick-waisted man in a Panama hat came out of the stone cottage. He waddled up to the cab and snapped, "Well?"

"I came to see Mr. Hendryx about a picture."

He opened the cab door and looked me over, from eyes that were heavily shuttered with old scar tissue. "You ain't the one that was here this morning."

I had my first good idea of the day. "You mean the tall fellow with the sideburns?"

"Yeah."

"I just came from him."

He rubbed his heavy chin with his knuckles, making a rasping noise. The knuckles were jammed.

"I guess it's all right," he said finally. "Give me your name and I'll phone it down to the house. You can drive down."

He opened the gate and let us through into a shallow valley. Below, in a maze of shrubbery, a long low house was flanked by tennis courts and stables. Sunk in the terraced lawn behind the house was an oval pool like a wide green eye staring at the sky. A short man in bathing trunks was sitting in a Thinker pose on the diving board at one end.

He and the pool dropped out of sight as the cab slid down the eucalyptus-lined road. It stopped under a portico at the side of the house. A uniformed maid was waiting at the door.

"This is farther than that reporter got," the driver said in an undertone. "You got connections?"

"The best people in town."

"Mr. Archer?" the maid said. "Mr. Hendryx is having his swim. I'll show you the way."

I told the driver to wait, and followed her through the house. I saw when I stepped outside that the man on the diving board wasn't short at all. He only seemed to be short because he was so wide. Muscle bulged out of his neck, clustered on his shoulders and chest, encased his arms and legs. He looked like a graduate of Muscle Beach, a subman trying hard to be a superman.

There was another man floating in the water, the blotched brown swell of his stomach breaking the surface like the shell-back of a Galapagos tortoise. Thinker stood up, accompanied by his muscles, and called to him, "Mr. Hendryx!"

The man in the water rolled over lazily and paddled to the side of the pool. Even his head was tortoiselike, seamed and bald and impervious-looking. He stood up in the waist-deep water and raised his thin brown arms. The other man bent over him. He drew him out of the water and steadied him on his feet, rubbing him with a towel.

"Thank you, Devlin."

"Yessir."

Leaning far forward with his arms dangling like a withered hairless ape, Hendryx shuffled toward me. The joints of his knees and ankles were knobbed and stiffened by what looked like arthritis. He peered up at me from his permanent crouch.

"You want to see me?" The voice that came out of his crippled body was surprisingly rich and deep. He wasn't as old as he looked. "What is it?"

"A painting was stolen last night from the San Marcos gallery—Chardin's *Apple on a Table*. I've heard that you were interested in it."

"You've been misinformed. Good afternoon." His face closed like a fist.

"You haven't heard all of it."

Disregarding me, he called to the maid who was waiting at a distance. "Show this man out."

Devlin came up beside me, strutting like a wrestler, his great curved hands conspicuous.

"The rest of it," I said, "is that Hugh Western was murdered at the same time. I think you knew him?"

"I knew him, yes. His death is unfortunate. Regrettable. But so far as I know, it has nothing to do with the Chardin and nothing to do with me. Will you go now, or do I have to have you removed?"

He raised his cold eyes to mine. I stared him down, but there wasn't much satisfaction in that.

"You take murder pretty lightly, Hendryx."

"Mr. Hendryx to you," Devlin said in my ear. "Come on now, bud. You heard what Mr. Hendryx said."

"I don't take orders from him."

"I do," he said with a lopsided grin like a heat-split in a

319

melon. His small eyes shifted to Hendryx. "You want for me to throw him out?"

Hendryx nodded, backing away. His eyes were heating up, as if the prospect of violence excited him. Devlin's hand took my wrist. His fingers closed around it and overlapped.

"What is this, Devlin?" I said. "I thought Hugh Western was a pal of yours."

"Sure thing."

"I'm trying to find who killed him. Aren't you interested? Or did you slap him down yourself?"

Devlin blinked stupidly.

Hendryx said from a safe distance, "Don't talk. Just give him a going-over and toss him out."

Devlin looked at Hendryx. His grip was like a thick handcuff on my wrist. I jerked his arm up and ducked under it, breaking the hold, and chopped at his nape. The bulging back of his neck was hard as a redwood bole.

He wheeled, then reached for me again. The muscles in his arms moved like drugged serpents. He was slow. My right fist found his chin and snapped it back on his neck. He recovered, and swung at me. I stepped inside his roundhouse and hammered his ridged stomach, twice, four times. It was like knocking my fists against the side of a corrugated iron building. His great arms closed on me. I slipped down and away.

When he came after me, I shifted my attack to his head, jabbing with the left until he was off-balance on his heels. Then I pivoted and threw a long right hook which changed to an uppercut. An electric shock surged my arm. Devlin lay down on the green tiles, chilled like a side of beef.

I looked across him at Hendryx. There was no fear in his eyes, only calculation. He backed into a canvas chair and sat down clumsily.

"You're fairly tough, it seems. Perhaps you used to be a fighter? I've owned a few fighters in my time. You might have a future at it, if you were younger."

"It's a sucker's game. So is larceny."

"Larceny-farceny," he said surprisingly. "What did you say you do?"

"I'm a private detective."

"Private, eh?" His mouth curved in a lipless tortoise grin. "You interest me, Mr. Archer. I could find a use for you—a place in my organization."

"What kind of organization?"

"I'm a builder, a mass-producer of houses. Like most success-ful entrepreneurs, I make enemies: cranks and bleeding hearts and psychopathic veterans who think the world owes them something. Devlin here isn't quite the man I thought he was. But you—"

"Forget it. I'm pretty choosy about the people I work for."

"An idealist, eh? A clean-cut young American idealist." The smile was still on his mouth; it was saturnine. "Well, Mr. Ideal-ist, you're wasting your time. I know nothing about this picture or anything connected with it. You're also wasting my time."

"It seems to be expendable. I think you're lying, in-cidentally."

Hendryx didn't answer me directly. He called to the maid, "Telephone the gate. Tell Shaw we're having a little trouble with a guest. Then you can come back and look after this." He jerked a thumb at muscle-boy, who was showing signs of life.

I said to the maid, "Don't bother telephoning. I'm leaving now."

She shrugged and looked at Hendryx. He nodded. I fol-lowed her out.

"You didn't stay long," the cab driver said.

"No. Do you know where Admiral Turner lives?"

"Curiously enough, I do. I should charge extra for the in-formation."

"Take me there."

He let me out in a street of big old houses set far back from the sidewalk behind sandstone walls and high eugenia hedges. I paid him off and climbed the sloping walk to the Turner house. It was a weathered frame building, gabled and turreted in the style of the nineties. A gray-haired housekeeper who had sur-vived from the same period answered my knock.

"The Admiral's in the garden," she said. "Will you come out?"

The garden was massed with many-colored begonias, sur-rounded by a wine-covered wall. The Admiral, in stained and faded khakis, was chopping weeds in a flower bed with furious concentration. When he saw me he leaned on his hoe and wiped his wet forehead with the back of his hand.

"You should come in out of the sun," the housekeeper said in a nagging way. "A man of your age—"

321

"Nonsense. Go away, Mrs. Harris." She went. "What can I do for you, Mr.—?"

"Archer. I guess you've heard that we found Hugh Western's body."

"Sara came home and told me half an hour ago. It's a foul thing, and completely mystifying. He was to have married—"

His voice broke off. He glanced toward the stone cottage at the rear of the garden. Alice Turner was there at an open window. She wasn't looking in our direction. She had a tiny paint brush in her hand, and she was working at an easel.

"It's not as mystifying as it was. I'm starting to put the pieces together, Admiral."

He turned back to me quickly. His eyes became hard and empty and again they reminded me of gun muzzles.

"Just who are you? What's your interest in this case?"

"I'm a friend of Hugh Western's. I stopped off here to see him, and found him dead. I hardly think my interest is out of place."

"No, of course not," he growled. "On the other hand, I don't believe in amateur detectives running around like chickens with their heads cut off, fouling up the authorities."

"I'm not exactly an amateur. I used to be a cop. And any fouling up there's been has been done by other people."

"Are you accusing me?"

"If the shoe fits."

He met my eyes for a time, trying to master me and the situation. But he was old and bewildered. Slowly the aggressive ego faded from his gaze. He became almost querulous.

"You'll excuse me. I don't know what it's all about. I've been rather upset by everything that's happened."

"What about your daughter?" Alice was still at the window, working at her picture and paying no attention to our voices. "Doesn't she know Hugh is dead?"

"Yes. She knows. You mustn't misunderstand what Alice is doing. There are many ways of enduring grief, and we have a custom in the Turner family of working it out of our system. Hard work is the cure for a great many evils." He changed the subject, and his tone, abruptly. "And what is your idea of what's happened?"

"It's no more than a suspicion right now. I'm not sure who stole your picture, but I think I know where it is."

"Well?"

"There's a man named Walter Hendryx who lives in the foothills outside the city. You know him?"

"Slightly."

"He probably has the Chardin. I'm morally certain he has it, as a matter of fact, though I don't know how he got it."

The Admiral tried to smile, and made a dismal failure of it. "You're not suggesting that Hendryx took it? He's not exactly mobile, you know."

"Hilary Todd is very mobile," I said. "Todd visited Hendryx this morning. I'd be willing to bet even money he had the Chardin."

"You didn't see it, however?"

"I didn't have to. I've seen Todd."

A woman's voice said from the shadow of the back porch, "The man is right, Johnston."

Sara Turner came down the path toward us, her high heels spiking the flagstones angrily.

"Hilary did it!" she cried. "He stole the picture and murdered Hugh. I saw him last night at midnight. He had red mountain clay on his clothes."

"It's strange you didn't mention it before," the Admiral said dryly.

I looked into her face. Her eyes were bloodshot, and eyelids were swollen with weeping. Her mouth was swollen, too. When she opened it to reply, I could see that the lower lip was split.

"I just remembered."

I wondered if the blow that split her lip had reminded her.

"And where did you see Hilary Tod last night at midnight?"

"Where?"

In the instant of silence that followed, I heard footsteps behind me. Alice had come out of her cottage. She walked like a sleepwalker dreaming a bad dream, and stopped beside her father without a word to any of us.

Sara's face had been twisting in search of an answer, and finally found it. "I met him at the Presidio. I dropped in there for a cup of coffee after the show."

"You are a liar, Sara," the Admiral said. "The Presidio closes at ten o'clock."

"It wasn't the Presidio," she said rapidly. "It was the bar across the street, the Club Fourteen. I had dinner at the Presidio, and I confused them—"

The Admiral brushed past her without waiting to hear more,

323

and started for the house. Alice went with him. The old man walked unsteadily, leaning on her arm.

"Did you really see Hilary last night?" I asked her.

She stood there for a minute, looking at me. Her face was disorganized, raddled with passion. "Yes, I saw him. I had a date with him at ten o'clock. I waited in his flat for over two hours. He didn't show up until after midnight. I couldn't tell *him* that." She jerked one shoulder contemptuously toward the house.

"And he had red clay on his clothes?"

"Yes. It took me a while to connect it with Hugh."

"Are you going to tell the police?"

She smiled a secret and unpleasant smile. "How can I? I've got a marriage to go on with, such as it is."

"You told me."

"I like you." Without moving, she gave the impression of leaning toward me. "I'm fed up with all the little stinkers that populate this town!"

I kept it cool and clean, but very nasty. "Were you fed up with Hugh Western, Mrs. Turner?"

"What do you mean?"

"I heard that he dropped you hard a couple of months ago. Somebody dropped him hard last night in his studio."

"I haven't been near his studio for weeks."

"Never did any posing for him?"

Her face seemed to grow smaller and sharper. She laid one narrow taloned hand on my arm. "Can I trust you?"

"Not if you murdered Hugh."

"I didn't—I swear I didn't! Hilary did!"

"But you were there last night."

"No."

"I think you were. There was a charcoal sketch on the easel, and you posed for it, didn't you?"

Her nerves were badly strained, but she tried to be coquettish. "How would you know?"

"The way you carry your body. It reminds me of the picture."

"Do you approve?"

"Listen, Mrs. Turner. You don't seem to realize that that sketch is evidence, and destroying it is a crime."

"I didn't destroy it."

"Then where did you put it?"

"I haven't said I took it."

324

"But you did."

"Yes, I did," she admitted finally. "But it isn't evidence in this case. I posed for it six months ago, and Hugh had it in his studio. When I heard he was dead this afternoon, I went to get it, just to be sure it wouldn't turn up in the newspapers. He had it on the easel for some reason, and had ruined it with a beard. I don't know why."

"The beard would make sense if your story was changed a little. If you quarreled while Hugh was sketching you last night, and you hit him over the head with a metal fist. You might have drawn the beard yourself, to cover up."

"Don't be ridiculous. If I had anything to cover up I would have destroyed the sketch. Anyway, I can't draw."

"Hilary can."

"Go to hell," she said between her teeth. "You're just another stinker like the rest of them."

She walked emphatically to the house. I followed her into the long, dim hallway. Halfway up the stairs to the second floor she turned and flung down to me, "I hadn't destroyed it, but I'm going to now."

There was nothing I could do about that, and I started out. When I passed the door of the living-room, the Admiral called out, "Is that you, Archer? Come here a minute, eh?"

He was sitting with Alice on a semicircular leather lounge, set into a huge bay window at the front of the room. He got up and moved toward me ponderously, his head down like a charging bull's. His face was a jaundiced yellow, bloodless under the tan.

"You're entirely wrong about the Chardin," he said. "Hilary Todd had nothing to do with stealing it. In fact, it wasn't stolen. I removed it from the gallery myself."

"You denied that this morning."

"I do as I please with my own possessions. I'm accountable to no one, certainly not to you."

"Dr. Silliman might like to know," I said with irony.

"I'll tell him in my own good time."

"Will you tell him why you took it?"

"Certainly. Now, if you've made yourself sufficiently obnoxious, I'll ask you to leave my house."

"Father." Alice came up to him and placed a hand on his arm. "Mr. Archer has only been trying to help."

"And getting nowhere," I said. "I made the mistake of assuming that some of Hugh's friends were honest."

"That's enough!" he roared. "Get out!"

Alice caught up with me on the veranda. "Don't go away angry. Father can be terribly childish, but he means well."

"I don't get it. He lied this morning, or else he's lying now."

"He isn't lying," she said earnestly. "He was simply playing a trick on Dr. Silliman and the trustees. It's what happened to Hugh afterwards that made it seem important."

"Did you know that he took the picture himself?"

"He told me just now, before you came into the house. I made him tell you."

"You'd better let Silliman in on the joke," I said unpleasantly. "He's probably going crazy."

"He is," she said. "I saw him at the gallery this afternoon, and he was tearing his hair. Do you have your car?"

"I came up here in a taxi."

"I'll drive you down."

"Are you sure you feel up to it?"

"It's better when I'm doing something," she said.

An old black sedan was standing in the drive beside the house. We got in, and she backed it into the street, then turned downhill toward the center of town.

Watching her face I said, "Of course you realize I don't believe his story."

"Father's, you mean?" She didn't seem surprised. "I don't know what to believe, myself."

"When did he say he took the Chardin?"

"Last night. Hugh was working on the mezzanine. Father slipped away and took the picture out to the car."

"Didn't Hugh keep the door locked?"

"Apparently not. Father said not."

"But what possible reason could he have for stealing his own picture?"

"To prove a point. Father's been arguing for a long time that it would be easy to steal a picture from the gallery. He's been trying to get the board of trustees to install a burglar alarm. He's really hipped on the subject. He wouldn't lend his Chardin to the gallery until they agreed to insure it."

"For twenty-five thousand dollars," I said, half to myself. Twenty-five thousand dollars was motive enough for a man to steal his own picture. And if Hugh Western witnessed the theft, there was motive for murder. "Your father's made a pretty good story out of it. But where's the picture now?"

"He didn't tell me. It's probably hidden in the house some-where."

"I doubt it. It's more likely somewhere in Walter Hendryx' house."

She let out a little gasp. "What makes you say that? Do you know Walter Hendryx?"

"I've met him. Do you know him?"

"He's a horrible man," she said. "I can't imagine why you think he has it."

"It's pure hunch."

"Where would he get it? Father wouldn't dream of selling it to him."

"Hilary Todd would."

"Hilary? You think Hilary stole it?"

"I'm going to ask him. Let me off at his shop, will you? I'll see you at the gallery later."

The *Closed* sign was still hanging inside the plate glass, and the front door was locked. I went around to the back of the shop by the alley. The door under the stairs was standing partly open. I went in without knocking.

The living-room was empty. The smell of alcohol rose from the stain on the wall where Sara had smashed her glass. I crossed the passage to the door on the other side. It, too, was partly open. I pushed it wider and went in.

Hilary Todd was sprawled face down on the bed, with an open suitcase crushed under the weight of his body. The silver handle of his ice pick stood up between his shoulder blades in the center of a wet, dark stain. The silver glinted coldly in a ray of light which found its way through the half-closed venetian blinds.

I felt for his pulse and couldn't find it. His head was twisted sideways, and his empty dark eyes stared unblinking at the wall. A slight breeze from the open window at the foot of the bed ruffled the hair along the side of his head.

I burrowed under the heavy body and went through the pockets. In the inside breast pocket of the coat I found what I was looking for: a plain white business envelope, unsealed, containing $15,000 in large bills.

I was standing over the bed with the money in my hand when I heard someone in the hallway. A moment later Mary appeared at the door.

"I saw you come in," she said. "I thought—" Then she saw the body.

"Someone killed Hilary," I said quietly.

"Killed Hilary?" She looked at the body on the bed and then at me. I realized that I was holding the money in plain view.

"What are you doing with that?"

I folded the bills and tucked them into my inside pocket. "I'm going to try an experiment. Be a good girl and call the police for me."

"Where did you get that money?"

"From someone it didn't belong to. Don't tell the sheriff about it. Just say that I'll be back in half an hour."

"They'll want to know where you went."

"And if you don't know, you won't be able to tell them. Now do as I say."

She looked into my face wondering if she could trust me. Her voice was uncertain. "If you're sure you're doing the right thing."

"Nobody ever is."

I went out to my car and drove to Foothill Drive. The sun had dipped low over the sea, and the air was turning colder. By the time I reached the iron gates that cut off Walter Hendryx from ordinary mortals, the valley beyond them was in shadow.

The burly man came out of the gatehouse as if I had pressed a button. He recognized me, then pushed his face up to the window of the car. "Beat it, chum. I got orders to keep you away from here."

I restrained an impulse to push the face away, and tried diplomacy. "I came here to do your boss a favor."

"That's not the way he feels. Now blow."

"Look here." I brought the wad of bills out of my pocket, and passed them back and forth under his nose. "There's big money involved."

His eyes followed the moving bills as if they were hypnotized. "I don't take bribes," he said in a hoarse and passionate whisper.

"I'm not offering you one. But you should phone down to Hendryx, before you do anything rash, and tell him there's money in it."

"Money for him?" There was a wistful note in his voice. "How much?"

"Fifteen thousand, tell him."

328

"Some bonus." He whistled. "What kind of a house is he building for you, bud, that you should give him an extra fifteen grand?"

I didn't answer. His question gave me too much to think about. He went back into the gatehouse.

Two minutes later he came out and opened the gates. "Mr. Hendryx'll see you. But don't try any funny stuff or you won't come out on your own power."

The same maid was waiting at the door. She took me into a big rectangular room with French windows on one side, opening on the terrace. The rest of the walls were lined with books from floor to ceiling—the kind of books that are bought by the set and never read. In front of the fireplace, at the far end, Hendryx was sitting half submerged in an overstuffed armchair, with a blanket over his knees.

He looked up when I entered the room. The fireplace danced on his scalp and lit his face with an angry glow. "What's this? Come here and sit down."

The maid left silently. I walked the length of the room and sat down in an armchair facing him. "I always bring bad news, Mr. Hendryx. Murder and such things. This time it's Hilary Todd."

The turtle-face didn't change, but his head made a movement of withdrawal into the shawl collar of his robe. "I'm exceedingly sorry to hear it. But my gatekeeper mentioned a matter of money. That interests me more."

"Good." I produced the bills and spread them fanwise on my knee.

"Do you recognize these?"

"Should I?"

"For a man who's interested in money, you're acting very coy."

"I'm interested in its source."

"I had an idea that *you* were the source of this particular money. I have some other ideas. For instance, that Hilary Todd stole the Chardin and sold it to you. One thing I have no idea about is why you would buy a stolen picture and pay for it in cash."

His false teeth glistened coldly in the firelight. Like the man at the gate, he kept his eyes on the money. "The picture wasn't stolen. I bought it legally from its rightful owner."

329

"I might believe you if you hadn't denied any knowledge of it this afternoon. I think you knew it was stolen."

His voice took on a cutting edge. "It was not." He slipped his blue-veined hand inside his robe and brought out a folded sheet of paper, which he handed me.

It was a bill of sale for the picture, informal but legal, written in longhand on the stationery of the San Marcos Beach Club, signed by Admiral Johnston Turner, and dated that day.

"Now may I ask you where you got hold of that money?"

"I'll be frank with you, Mr. Hendryx. I took it from the body of Hilary Todd, when he had no further use for it."

"That's a criminal act, I believe."

My brain was racing, trying to organize a mass of contradictory facts. "I have a notion that you're not going to talk to anyone about it."

He shrugged. "You seem to be full of notions."

"I have another. Whether or not you're grateful to me for bringing you this money, I think you should be."

"Have you any reason for saying that?" He had shifted his eyes from the money on my knee to my face.

"You're in the building business, Mr. Hendryx?"

"Yes." His voice was flat.

"I don't know exactly how you got this money. My guess is that you gouged it out of home buyers, by demanding a cash bonus in addition to the appraised value of the houses you've been selling to veterans."

"That's a pretty comprehensive piece of guesswork, isn't it?"

"I don't expect you to admit it. On the other hand, you probably wouldn't want this money traced to you. The fact that you haven't banked it is an indication of that. That's why Todd could count on you to keep this picture deal quiet. And that's why you should be grateful to me."

The turtle-eyes stared into mine, and admitted nothing. "If I *were* grateful, what form do you suggest my gratitude should take?"

"I want the picture. I've sort of set my heart on it."

"Keep the money instead."

"This money is no good to me. Dirty money never is."

He threw the blanket off and levered himself out of the chair. "You're somewhat more honest than I'd supposed. You're offering, then, to buy the picture back from me with that money?"

330

"Exactly."

"And if I don't agree?"

"The money goes to the Intelligence Unit of the Internal Revenue Bureau."

There was silence for a while, broken by the fire hissing and sputtering in an irritable undertone.

"Very well," he said at length. "Give me the money."

"Give me the picture."

He waded across the heavy rug, moving his feet a few inches at a time, and pressed a corner of one of the bookcases. It swung open like a door. Behind it was the face of a large wall safe. I waited uncomfortably while he twirled the double dials.

A minute later he shuffled back to me with the picture in his hands. The boy in the blue waistcoat was there in the frame, still watching the apple, which looked good enough to eat after more than two hundred years.

Hendryx's withered face had settled into a kind of malevolent resignation. "You realize that this is no better than blackmail."

"On the contrary, I'm saving you from the consequences of your own poor judgment. You shouldn't do business with thieves and murderers."

"You still insist the picture was stolen?"

"I think it was. You probably know it was. Will you answer one question?"

"Perhaps."

"When Hilary Todd approached you about buying this picture, did he claim to represent Admiral Turner?"

"Of course. You have the bill of sale in your hand. It's signed by the Admiral."

"I see that, but I don't know his signature."

"I do. Now, if you have no further questions, may I have my money?"

"Just one more: who killed Hugh Western?"

"I don't know," he said heavily.

He held out his brown hand with the palm upward. I gave him the sheaf of bills.

"And the bill of sale, if you please."

"It wasn't part of the bargain."

"It has to be."

"I suppose you're right." I handed it to him.

"Please don't come back a third time," he said as he rang for

331

the maid. "I find your visits tiring and annoying."

"I won't come back," I said. I didn't need to.

In the early evening traffic lull I made good time back to the center of town. I drove automatically, thinking of other things: the dead man on the mountain, the other dead man in the bedroom, the twenty-five thousand dollars' worth of canvas and pigment on the seat beside me. Hendryx had answered one question, but he had raised ten more. The questions and the facts that failed to answer them swarmed in my head like bees.

I parked in the alley beside the art gallery and got out of the car with the Chardin under my arm. There was talk and laughter and the tinny din of cutlery in the restaurant patio beyond the hedge. On the other side of the alley a light was shining behind the barred window of Silliman's office. I reached up between the bars and tapped on the window. I couldn't see beyond the closed venetian blinds.

Someone opened the casement. It was Alice, her blonde head aureoled against the light. "Who is it?" she said in a frightened whisper.

"Archer," I had a sudden, rather theatrical impulse. I held up the Chardin and passed it to her edgewise between the bars. She took it from my hands and let out a sudden little yelp of surprise.

"It was where I thought it would be," I said.

Silliman appeared at her shoulder, squeaking, "What is it? What is it?"

My brain was doing a double take on the action I'd just performed. *I had returned the Chardin to the gallery without using the door!* It could have been stolen the same way, by Hilary Todd or anyone else who had access to the building. No human being could pass through the bars—but a picture could!

Silliam's head came out the window like a gray mop being shaken. "Where on earth did you find it?" I had no story ready, so I said nothing.

A gentle hand touched my arm and stayed, like a bird alighting. It was Mary.

"I've been watching for you," she said. "The sheriff's in Hilary's shop, and he's raving mad. He said he's going to put you in jail, as a material witness."

"You didn't tell him about the money?" I said in an undertone.

332

"No. Did you really get the picture?"

"Come inside and see."

As we turned the corner of the building, a car left the curb in front of it, and started up the street with a roar. It was Admiral Turner's black sedan.

"It looks like Alice driving," Mary said.

"She's gone to tell her father, probably."

I made a sudden decision, and headed back to my car.

"Where are you going?"

"I want to see the Admiral's reaction to the news."

She followed me to the car. "Take me."

"You'd better stay here. There's no telling what might happen."

I tried to shut the door, but she held on to it. "You're always running off and leaving me to make your explanations."

"All right, get in. I don't have time to argue."

I drove straight up the alley and across the parking lot to Rubio Street. There was a uniformed policeman standing at the back door of Hilary's shop, but he didn't try to stop us.

"What did the police have to say about Hilary?" I asked her.

"Not much. The ice pick had been wiped clean of finger-prints, and they had no idea who did it."

I went through a yellow light and left a chorus of indignant honkings at the intersection behind me.

"You said you didn't know what would happen when you got there. Do you think the Admiral—?" She left the sentence unfinished.

"I don't know. I have a feeling we soon will, though."

Finally I asked, "Is this the street?"

"Yes."

My tires shrieked on the corner, and again in front of the house. She was out of the car before I was.

"Stay back," I told her. "This may be dangerous."

She let me go up the walk ahead of her. The black sedan was in the drive with the headlights burning and the left front door of the house was closed but there was a light behind it. I went in without knocking.

Sara came out of the living room. All day her face had been going to pieces, and now it was old and slack and ugly. Her bright hair was ragged at the edges, and her voice was ragged. "What do you think you're doing?"

"I want to see the Admiral. Where is he?"

"How should I know? I can't keep track of any of my men." She took a step toward me, staggered, and almost fell.

Mary took hold of her and eased her into a chair. Her head leaned limply against the wall, and her mouth hung open. The lipstick on her mouth was like a rim of cracked dry blood.

"They must be here."

The single shot that we heard then was an exclamation point at the end of my sentence. It came from somewhere back of the house, muffled by walls and distance.

I went through and into the garden. There were lights in the gardener's cottage, and a man's shadow moved across the window. I ran up the path to the cottage's open door, and froze there.

Admiral Turner was facing me with a gun in his hand. It was a heavy-caliber automatic, the kind the Navy issued. From its round, questioning mouth a wisp of blue smoke trailed. Alice lay face down on the carpeted floor between us.

I looked into the mouth of the gun, then into Turner's granite face. "You killed her."

But Alice was the one who answered. "Go away," she said. The words came out in a rush of sobbing that racked her prostrate body.

"This is a private matter, Archer." The gun stirred slightly in the Admiral's hand. I could feel its pressure across the width of the room. "Do as she says."

"I heard a shot. Murder is a public matter."

"There has been no murder, as you can see."

"You don't remember well."

"I have nothing to do with that," he said, "I was cleaning my gun, and forgot that it was loaded."

"So Alice lay down and cried? You'll have to do better than that, Admiral."

"Her nerves are shaken. But I assure you that mine are not." He took three slow steps toward me, and paused by the girl on the floor. The gun was very steady in his hand. "Now go, or I'll have to use this."

The pressure of the gun was increasing. I put my hands on the door frame and held myself still. "You seem to be sure it's loaded now," I said.

Between my words I heard the faint, harsh whispering of shifting gravel on the garden path behind me. I spoke up loudly, to drown out the sound.

"Admiral, you say that you had nothing to do with the murder. Then why did Todd come to the beach club this morning? Why did you change your story about the Chardin?"

He looked down at his daughter as if she could answer the questions. She made no sound, but her shoulders were shaking with internal sobbing.

As I watched the two of them, father and daughter, the pattern of the day finally came into focus. As its center was the muzzle of the Admiral's gun, the round blue mouth of death.

I said, very carefully, to gain time, "I can guess what Todd said to you this morning. Do you want me to dub in the dialogue?"

He glanced up sharply, and the gun glanced up. There were no more sounds in the garden. If Mary was as quick as I thought, she'd be at the telephone.

"He told you he'd stolen your picture and had a buyer for it. But Hendryx was cautious. Todd needed proof that he had a right to sell it. You gave him the proof. And when Todd completed the transaction, you let him keep the money."

"Nonsense! Bloody nonsense." But he was a poor actor, and a worse liar.

"I've seen the bill of sale, Admiral. The only question left is why you gave it to Todd."

His lips moved as if he was going to speak. No words came out.

"And I'll answer that one, too. Todd knew you killed Hugh Western. So did you. You had to keep him quiet, even if it meant conniving at the theft of your own picture."

"I connived at nothing." His voice was losing its strength, but his gun was as potent as ever.

"Alice did," I said. "She helped Todd steal it this morning. She passed it out the window to him when Silliman and I were on the mezzanine. Which is one of the things he told you at the beach club, isn't it?"

"Todd has been feeding you lies. Unless you give me your word that you won't repeat those lies, not to anyone, I'm going to have to shoot you."

His hand contracted, squeezing off the automatic's safety. The tiny noise it made seemed very significant in the silence. It echoed from the walls.

"Todd will soon be feeding worms," I said. "He's dead, Admiral."

335

"Dead?" His voice had sunk to an old man's quaver, rustling in his throat.

"Stabbed with an ice pick in his apartment."

"When?"

"This afternoon. Do you still see any point in trying to shoot me?"

"You're lying, Archer."

"No. There's been a second murder—Todd's."

He looked down at the girl at his feet. His eyes were bewildered. There was danger in his pain and confusion. I was the source of his pain, and he might strike out blindly at me. I watched the gun in his hand, waiting for a chance to move in on it. My arms were rigid, braced against the door frame.

Mary Western ducked under my left arm and stepped into the room in front of me. She had no weapon, except her courage.

"He's telling the truth," she said. "Hilary Todd was stabbed to death today."

"Put down the gun," I said. "There's nothing left to save. You thought you were protecting an unfortunate girl. She's turned out to be a double murderess."

He was watching the girl on the floor. "If this is true, Allie, I wash my hands of you."

No sound came from her. Her face was hidden by her yellow sheaf of hair. The old man groaned. The gun sagged in his hand. I moved, pushing Mary to one side, and snatched it away from him. He didn't resist, but my forehead was suddenly streaming with sweat.

"You were probably next on her list," I said.

"No."

The muffled word came from his daughter. She began to get up, rising laboriously from her hands and knees like a hurt fighter. She flung her hair back. Her face had hardly changed. It was as lovely as ever, on the surface, but empty of meaning—like a doll's plastic face.

"I was next on my list," she said dully. "I tried to shoot myself when I realized you knew about me. Father stopped me."

"I didn't know about you until now."

"You did. You must have. When you were talking to Father in the garden, you meant me to hear it all—everything you said about Hilary."

"Did I?"

The Admiral said with a kind of awe, "You killed him, Allie. Why did you want his blood on your hands? Why?" His own hand paused in mid-air. He looked at her as if he had fathered a strange and evil thing.

She bowed her head in silence. I answered for her. "She'd stolen the Chardin for Todd and met his conditions. But then she saw that he couldn't get away, or if he did he'd be brought back, and questioned. She couldn't be sure he'd keep quiet about Hugh. This afternoon she made sure. The second murder always comes easier."

"No!" She shook her blonde head violently. "I didn't murder Hugh. I hit him with something, but I didn't intend to kill him. He struck me first—he *struck* me, and then I hit him back."

"With a deadly weapon, a metal fist. You hit at him twice with it. The second blow didn't miss."

"But I didn't *mean* to kill him. Hilary knew I didn't mean to kill him."

"How would he know? Was he there?"

"He was downstairs in his flat. When he heard Hugh fall, he came up. Hugh was still alive. He died in Hilary's car, when we were starting for the hospital. Hilary said he'd help me cover up. He took that horrible fist and threw it into the sea.

"I hardly knew what I was doing by that time. Hilary did it all. He put the body in Hugh's car and drove it up the mountain. I followed in his car and brought him back. On the way back he told me why he was helping me. He needed money. He knew we had no money, but he had a chance to sell the Chardin. I took it for him this morning. *I had to!* Everything I did, I did because I had to."

She looked from me to her father. He averted his face from her.

"You didn't have to smash Hugh's skull," I said. "Why did you do that?"

Her doll's eyes rolled in her head, then came back to me, glinting with a cold and deathly coquetry. "If I tell you, will you do one thing for me? One favor? Give me Father's gun for just a second?"

"And let you kill us all?"

"Only myself," she said. "Just leave one shell in it."

"Don't give it to her," the Admiral said. "She's done enough to disgrace us."

"I have no intention of giving it to her. And I don't have to be

337

told why she killed Hugh. While she was waiting in his studio last night, she found a sketch of his. It was an old sketch, but she didn't know that. She'd never seen it before, for obvious reasons."

"What kind of sketch?"

"A portrait of a nude woman. She tacked it up on the easel and decorated it with a beard. When Hugh came home he saw what she'd done. He didn't like to have his pictures spoiled, and he probably slapped her face."

"He hit me with his fist," Alice said. "I killed him in self-defense."

"That may be the way you've rationalized it. Actually, you killed him out of jealousy."

She laughed. It was a cruel sound, like vital tissue being ruptured. "Jealous of *her?*"

"The same jealousy that made you ruin the sketch."

Her eyes widened, but they were blind, looking into herself. "Jealousy? I don't know. I felt so lonely, so all alone in the world. I had nobody to love me—not since my mother died."

"It isn't true, Alice. You had me." The Admiral's tentative hand came out and paused again in the air, as though there was an invisible wall between them.

"I never had you. I hardly saw you. Then Sara took you. I had no one—no one until Hugh. I thought at last that I had someone to love me, someone I could count on—"

Her voice broke off. The Admiral looked everywhere but at his daughter. The room was like a cubicle in hell where lost souls suffered under the silent treatment. The silence was finally broken by the sound of a distant siren. It rose and expanded until its lamentation filled the night.

Alice was crying, with her face uncovered. Mary Western came forward and put her arm around her. "Don't cry." Her voice was warm. Her face had a grave beauty.

"You hate me, too."

"No. I'm sorry for you, Alice. Sorrier than I am for Hugh."

The Admiral touched my arm. "Who was the woman in the sketch?" he said in a trembling voice.

I looked into his tired old face and decided that he had suffered enough.

"I don't know," I said.

But I could see the knowledge in his eyes.

MURDER UNDER THE MISTLETOE

BY MARGERY ALLINGHAM

Margery Allingham was born in London on May 20, 1904, to a family prominent in English literary circles. Her novel about smuggling and piracy, *Blackerchief Dick*, was published when she was a teenager. In 1927 she married Philip Youngman Carter, who, when he was only seventeen, had designed the jacket for the book. Her detective Albert Campion was introduced in 1929 in *The Crime at Back Dudley*. Besides mysteries, she wrote works of English social history. Her most highly praised book, *The Tiger in the Smoke* (1952), was made into a film in 1956. Miss Allingham died in 1966.

"MURDER UNDER THE MISTLETOE—and the man who must have done it couldn't have done it. That's my Christmas and I don't feel merry, thank you very much all the same." Superintendent Stanislaus Oates favored his old friend Mr. Albert Campion with a pained smile and sat down in the chair indicated.

It was the afternoon of Christmas Day and Mr. Campion, only a trifle more owlish than usual behind his horn rims, had been fetched down from the children's party which he was attending at his brother-in-law's house in Knightsbridge to meet the Superintendent, who had moved heaven and earth to find him.

"What do you want?" Mr. Campion inquired facetiously. "A little armchair miracle?"

"I don't care if you do it swinging from a trapeze. I just want a reasonable explanation." Oates was rattled. His dyspeptic face with the perpetually sad expression was slightly flushed and not with festivity. He plunged into his story.

"About eleven last night a crook called Sampson was found shot dead in the back of a car in a garage under a small drinking club in Alcatraz Mews—the club is named The Humdinger. A large bunch of mistletoe which had been lying on the front seat ready to be driven home had been placed on top of the body, partially hiding it—which was why it hadn't been found before. The gun, fitted with a silencer, but wiped of prints, was found under the front seat. The dead man was recognized at once by the owner of the car who is also the owner of the club. He was the owner's current boyfriend. She is quite a well-known West End character called 'Girlski.' What did you say?"

"I said 'Oo-er'," murmured Mr. Campion. "One of the Eumenides, no doubt?"

"No." Oates spoke innocently. "She's not a Greek. Don't worry about her. Just keep your mind on the facts. She knows, as we do, that the only person who wanted to kill Sampson is a nasty little snake called Kroll. He has been out of circulation for the best of reasons. Sampson turned Queen's evidence against him in a matter concerning a conspiracy to rob Her Majesty's mails and when he was released last Tuesday Kroll came out breathing retribution."

"Not the Christmas spirit," said Mr. Campion inanely.

"That is exactly what *we* thought," Oates agreed. "So about five o'clock yesterday afternoon two of our chaps, hearing that Kroll was at the Humdinger, where he might have been expected to make trouble, dropped along there and brought him in for questioning and he's been in custody ever since.

"Well, now. We have at least a dozen reasonably sober witnesses to prove that Kroll did not meet Sampson at the club. Sampson had been there earlier in the afternoon but he left about a quarter to four saying he'd got to do some Christmas shopping but promising to return. Fifteen minutes or so later Kroll came in and stayed there in full view of Girlski and the customers until our men turned up and collected him. *Now* what do you say?"

"Too easy!" Mr. Campion was suspicious. "Kroll killed Sampson just before he came in himself. The two met in the dusk outside the club. Kroll forced Sampson into the garage and possibly into the car and shot him. With the way the traffic has been lately, he'd hardly have attracted attention had he used a mortar, let alone a gun with a silencer. He wiped the weapon, chucked it in the car, threw the mistletoe over the corpse, and went up to Girlski to renew old acquaintance and establish an alibi. Your chaps, arriving when they did, must have appeared welcome."

Oates nodded. "We thought that. *That is what happened.* That is why this morning's development has set me gibbering. We now have two unimpeachable witnesses who swear that the dead man was in Chipperwood West at six last evening delivering some Christmas purchases he had made on behalf of a neighbor. That is *a whole hour* after Kroll was pulled in.

"The assumption is that Sampson returned to Alcatraz Mews sometime later in the evening and was killed by someone else—which we know is not true. Unfortunately the Chipperwood West witnesses are not the kind of people we are going to shake. One of them is a friend of yours. She asked our Inspector if he knew you because you were 'so good at crime and all that nonsense.' "

"Good heavens!" Mr. Campion spoke piously as the explanation of the Superintendent's unlikely visitation was made plain to him. "I don't think I know Chipperwood West."

"It's a suburb which is becoming fashionable. Have you ever heard of Lady Larradine?"

"Old Lady 'ell?" Mr. Campion let the joke of his salad days escape without its being noticed by either of them. "I don't believe it. She must be dead by this time!"

"There's a type of woman who never dies before you do," said Oates with apparent sincerity. "She's quite a dragon, I understand from our Inspector. However, she isn't the actual witness. There are two of them. Brigadier Brose is one. Ever heard of *him?*"

"I don't think I have."

"My information is that you'd remember him if you'd met him. Well, we'll find out. I'm taking you with me, Campion. I hope you don't mind?"

"My sister will hate it. I'm due to be Santa Claus in about an hour."

"I can't help that." Oates was adamant. "If a bunch of silly crooks want to get spiteful at the festive season, someone must do the homework. Come and play Santa Claus with me. It's your last chance. I'm retiring in the summer."

Oates continued in the same vein as he and Mr. Campion sat in the back of a police car threading their way through the deserted Christmas streets where the lamps were growing bright in the dusk.

"I've had bad luck lately," the Superintendent said seriously. "Too much. It won't help my memoirs if I go out in a blaze of no-enthusiasm."

"You're thinking of the Phaeton Robbery," Mr. Campion suggested. "What are you calling the memoirs? *Man-Eaters of the Yard?*"

Oates's mild old eyes brightened, but not greatly and he grimaced as he spoke to his companion.

"Something of the kind," he admitted. "But no one could be blamed for not solving that blessed Phaeton business. Everyone concerned was bonkers. A silly old musical star, for thirty years the widow of an eccentric Duke, steps out into her London garden one autumn morning leaving the street door wide open and all her most valuable jewelry collected from strongrooms all over the country lying in a brown paper parcel on her bureau in the first room off the hall. Her excuse was that she was just going to take it to the Bond Street auctioneers and was

342

carrying it herself for safety! The thief was equally mental to lift it."

"It wasn't salable?"

"Salable! It couldn't even be broken up. The stuff is just about as well-known as the Crown Jewels. Great big enamels which the old Duke had collected at great expense. No fence would stay in the same room with them, yet, of course, they are worth the earth as every newspaper has told us at length ever since they were pinched!"

"He didn't get anything else either, did he?"

"He was a madman." Oates dismissed him with contempt. "All he gained was the old lady's housekeeping money for a couple of months which was in her handbag—about a hundred and fifty quid—and the other two items which were on the same shelf, a soapstone monkey and a plated paperknife. He simply wandered in, took the first things he happened to see and wandered out again. Any sneakthief, tramp, or casual snapper-upper could have done it and who gets blamed? *Me!*"

He looked so woebegone that Mr. Campion hastily changed the subject. "Where are we going?" he inquired. "To call on her ladyship? Do I understand that at the age of one-hundred and forty-six or whatever it is she is cohabiting with a Brig? Which war?"

"I can't tell you." Oates was literal as usual. "It could be the South African. They're all in a nice residential hotel—the sort of place that is very popular with the older members of the landed gentry just now."

"When you say landed, you mean as in Fish?"

"Roughly, yes. Elderly people living on capital. About forty of them. This place used to be called The Haven and has now been taken over by two ex-society widows and renamed The CCraven—with two Cs. It's a select hotel-cum-Old Ducks' Home for Mother's Friends. You know the sort of place?"

"I can envisage it. Don't say your murdered chum from The Humdinger lived there too?"

"No, he lived in a more modest place whose garden backs on the CCraven's grounds. The Brigadier and one of the other residents, a Mr. Charlie Taunton, who has become a bosom friend of his, were in the habit of talking to Sampson over the wall. Taunton is a lazy man who seldom goes out and has little money but he very much wanted to get some gifts for his fellow guests—something in the nature of little jokes from the chain stores, I understand; but he dreaded the exertion of shopping for them and Sampson appears to have offered to get him some little items wholesale and to deliver them by six o'clock on Christmas Eve—in time for him to package them up and hand them to Lady Larradine who was dressing the tree at seven."

"And you say Sampson actually did this?" Mr. Campion sounded bewildered.

"Both old gentlemen—the Brigadier and Taunton—swear to it. They insist they went down to the wall at six and Sampson handed the parcel over as arranged. My Inspector is an experienced man and he doesn't think we'll be able to shake either of them."

"That leaves Kroll with a complete alibi. How did these Chipperwood witnesses hear of Sampson's death?"

"Routine. The local police called at Sampson's home address this morning to report the death, only to discover the place closed. The landlady and her family are away for the holiday and Sampson himself was due to spend it with Girlski. The police stamped about a bit, making sure of all this, and in the course of their investigations they were seen and hailed by the two old boys in the adjoining garden. The two were shocked to hear that their kind acquaintance was dead and volunteered the information that he had been with them at six."

Mr. Campion looked blank. "Perhaps they don't keep the same hours as anybody else," he suggested. "Old people can be highly eccentric."

Oates shook his head. "We thought of that. My Inspector, who came down the moment the local police reported, insists that they are perfectly normal and quite positive. Moreover, they had the purchases. He saw the packages already on the tree. Lady Larradine pointed them out to him when she asked after you. She'll be delighted to see you, Campion."

"I can hardly wait!"

"You don't have to," said Oates grimly as they pulled up before a huge Edwardian villa. "It's all yours."

"My dear Boy! You haven't aged any more than I have!"

Lady Larradine's tremendous voice—one of her chief terrors, Mr. Campion recollected—echoed over the crowded first-floor room where she received them. There she stood in an outmoded but glittering evening gown looking, as always, exactly like a spray-flecked seal.

344

"I *knew* you'd come," she bellowed. "As soon as you got my oblique little S.O.S. How do you like our little hideout? Isn't it *fun!* Moira Spryg-Fysher and Janice Poole-Poole wanted something to do, so we all put our pennies in it and here we are!"

"Almost too marvelous," murmured Mr. Campion in all sincerity. "We really want a word with Brigadier Brose and Mr. Taunton."

"Of course you do and so you shall! We're all waiting for the Christmas tree. Everybody will be there for that in about ten minutes in the drawing room. My dear, when *we* came they were calling it the Residents' Lounge!"

Superintendent Oates remained grave. He was startled to discover that the dragon was not only fierce but also wily. The news that her apparently casual mention of Mr. Campion to the Inspector had been a ruse to get hold of him shocked the innocent Superintendent. He retaliated by insisting that he must see the witnesses at once.

Lady Larradine silenced him with a friendly roar. "My dear man, you can't! They've gone for a walk. I always turn men out of the house after Christmas luncheon. They'll soon be back. The Brigadier won't miss his Tree! Ah. Here's Fiona. This is Janice Poole-Poole's daughter, Albert. Isn't she a pretty girl?"

Mr. Campion saw Miss Poole-Poole with relief, knowing of old that Oates was susceptible to the type. The newcomer was young and lovely and even her beehive hair and the fact that she appeared to have painted herself with two black eyes failed to spoil the exquisite smile she bestowed on the helpless officer.

"Fabulous to have you really here," she said and sounded as if she meant it. While he was still recovering, Lady Larradine led Oates to the window.

"You can't see it because it's pitch-dark," she said, "but out there, down in the garden, there's a wall and it was over it that the Brigadier and Mr. Taunton spoke to Mr. Sampson at six o'clock last night. No one liked the man Sampson—I think Mr. Taunton was almost afraid of him. Certainly he seems to have died very untidily!"

"But he *did* buy Mr. Taunton's Christmas gifts for him?"

The dragon lifted a webby eyelid. "You have already been told that. At six last night Mr. Taunton and the Brigadier went to meet him to get the box. I got them into their mufflers so I know! I had the packing paper ready, too, for Mr. Taunton to take up to his room . . . rather a small one on the third floor."

She lowered her voice to reduce it to the volume of distant traffic. "Not many pennies, but a dear little man!"

"Did you *see* these presents, Ma'am?"

"Not before they were wrapped! That would have spoiled the surprise!"

"I shall have to see them." There was a mulish note in the Superintendent's voice which the lady was too experienced to ignore.

"I've thought how to do that without upsetting anybody," she said briskly. "The Brigadier and I will cut the presents from the Tree and Fiona will be handing them round. All Mr. Taunton's little gifts are in the very distinctive black and gold paper I bought from Millie's Boutique and so, Fiona, you must give every package in black and gold paper not to the person to whom it is addressed but to the Superintendent. Can you do that, dear?

Miss Poole-Poole seemed to feel the task difficult but not impossible and the trusting smile she gave Oates cut short his objections like the sun melting frost.

"Splendid!" The dragon's roar was hearty. "Give me your arm, Superintendent. You shall take me down."

As the procession reached the hall, it ran into the Brigadier himself. He was a large, pink man, affable enough, but of a martial type and he bristled at the Superintendent. "Extraordinary time to do your business—middle of Christmas Day!" he said after acknowledging the introductions.

Oates inquired if he had enjoyed his walk.

"Talk?" said the Brigadier. "I've not been talking. I've been asleep in the card room. Where's old Taunton?"

"He went for a walk, Athole dear," bellowed the dragon gaily.

"So he did. You sent him! Poor feller."

As the old soldier led the way to the open door of the drawing room, it occurred to both the Superintendent and Mr. Campion that the secret of Lady Larradine's undoubted attraction for the Brigadier lay in the fact that he could hear *her* if no one else. The discovery cast a new light altogether on the story of the encounter with Sampson in the garden.

Meanwhile, they had entered the drawing room and the party had begun. As Mr. Campion glanced at the company, ranged in a full circle round a magnificent tree loaded with gifts and sparkling like a waterfall, he saw face after familiar face. They were elder acquaintances of the dizzy 1930s whom he had

346

mourned as gone forever, when he thought of them at all. Yet here they all were, not only alive but released by great age from many of the restraints of convention.

He noticed that every type of headgear from night-cap to tiara was being sported with fine individualistic enthusiasm. But Lady Larradine gave him little time to look about. She proceeded with her task immediately.

Each guest had been provided with a small invalid table beside his armchair, and Oates, reluctant, but wax in Fiona's hands, was no exception. The Superintendent found himself seated between a mountain in flannel and a wraith in mauve mink, waiting his turn with the same beady-eyed avidity.

Christmas Tree procedure at the CCraven proved to be well organized. The dragon did little work herself. Armed with a swagger stick, she merely prodded parcel after parcel hanging amid the boughs while the task of detaching them was performed by the Brigadier who handed them to Fiona. Either to add to the excitement or perhaps to muffle any unfortunate comment on gifts received by the uninhibited company, jolly Christmas music was played throughout, and under cover of the noise Mr. Campion was able after a while to tackle his hostess.

"Where is Taunton?" he whispered.

"Such a nice little man. Most presentable, but just a little tecny-weeny bit dishonest."

Lady Larradine ignored the question in his eyes and continued to put him in the picture at great speed, while supervising the Tree at the same time. "Fifty-seven convictions, I believe, but only small ones. I only got it all out of him last week. Shattering! He'd been so *useful,* amusing the Brigadier. When he came, he looked like a lost soul with no luggage, but after no time at all he settled in perfectly."

She paused and stabbed at a ball of colored cellophane with her stick before returning to her startled guest.

"Albert, I am terribly afraid that it was poor Mr. Taunton who took that dreadful jewelry of Maisie Phaeton's. It appears to have been entirely her fault. He was merely wandering past her house, feeling in need of care and attention. The door was wide open and Mr. Taunton suddenly found himself inside, picking up a few odds and ends. When he discovered from all that fuss in the newspapers what he had got hold of—how well-known it was, I mean—he was quite horrified and had to

347

hide. And where better place than here with us where he never had to go out?"

"Where indeed!" Mr. Campion dared not glance across the room at the Superintendent unwrapping his black and gold parcels. "Where is he now? Poor Mr. Taunton, I mean."

"Of course I hadn't the faintest idea what was worrying the man until he confessed," the dragon went on stonily. "Then I realized that something would have to be done at once to protect everybody. The wretch had hidden all that frightful stuff in our toolshed for three months, not daring to keep it in the house; and to make matters worse, the impossible person at the end of the garden, Mr. Sampson, had recognized him and *would* keep speaking. Apparently people in the—er—underworld all know each other just like those of us in—er—other closed circles do."

Mr. Campion, whose hair was standing on end, had a moment of inspiration. "This absurd rigmarole about Taunton getting Sampson to buy him some Christmas gifts wholesale was *your* idea!" he said accusingly.

The dragon stared. "It seemed the best way of getting Maisie's jewelry back to her without any *one* person being involved," she said frankly. "I knew we should all recognize the things the moment we saw them and I was certain that after a lot of argument we should decide to pack them up and send them round to her. But, if there *were* any repercussions, we should *all* be in it—quite a formidable array, dear Boy—and the blame could be traced to Mr. Sampson if absolutely necessary. You see, the Brigadier is convinced that Sampson *was* there last night. Mr. Taunton very cleverly left him on the lawn and went behind the toolshed and came back with the box."

"How completely immoral!" Mr. Campion couldn't restrain himself.

The dragon had the grace to look embarrassed.

"I don't think the Sampson angle would ever have arisen," she said. "But if it had, Sampson was quite a terrible person. Almost a blackmailer. Utterly dishonest and inconsiderate. Think how he has spoiled everything and endangered us all by getting himself killed on the *one* afternoon when we said he was here, so that the police were brought in. Just the *one* thing I was trying to avoid. When the Inspector appeared this morning I was so upset I thought of you!"

In his not unnatural alarm Mr. Campion so far forgot him-

348

self as to touch her sleeve. "Where is Taunton now?"

The dragon threshed her train. "Really, Boy! What a fidget you are! If you must know, I gave him his Christmas present—every penny I had in cash for he was broke again, he told me—and sent him for a nice long walk after lunch. Having seen the Inspector here this morning he was glad to go."

She paused and a granite gleam came into her hooded eyes. "If that Superintendent friend of yours has the stupidity to try to find him once Maisie has her monstrosities back, none of us will be able to identify him, I'm afraid. And there's another thing. If the Brigadier should be *forced* to give evidence, I am sure he will stick to his guns about Mr. Sampson being down in the garden here at six o'clock last night. That would mean that the man Kroll would have to go unpunished for his revenge murder, wouldn't it? Sampson was a terrible person—but *no one* should have killed him."

Mr. Campion was silenced. He glanced fearfully across the room.

The Superintendent was seated at his table wearing the strained yet slap-happy expression of a man with concussion. On his left was a pile of black and gilt wrappings, on his right a rajah's ransom in somewhat specialized form.

From where he stood, Mr. Campion could see two examples amid the rest—a breastplate in gold, pearl, and enamel in the shape of a unicorn and an item which looked like a plover's egg in tourmaline encased in a ducal coronet. There was also a soapstone monkey and a solid-silver paperknife.

Much later that evening Mr. Campion and the Superintendent drove quietly back to headquarters. Oates had a large cardboard box on his knee. He clasped it tenderly with both hands.

He had been silent for a long time when a thought occurred to him. "Why did they take him into the house in the first place?" he said. "An elderly crook looking lost! And no luggage!"

Mr. Campion's pale eyes flickered behind his spectacles.

"Don't forget the Duchess' housekeeping money," he murmured. "I should think he offered one of the widows who really run that place the first three months' payment in cash, wouldn't you? That must be an impressive phenomenon in that sort of business, I fancy."

Oates caught his breath and fell silent once more. Presently he burst out again.

"Those people! That woman!" he exploded. "When they were younger they led me a pretty dance—losing things or getting themselves swindled. But now they're old they take the blessed biscuit! Do you see how she's tied my hands, Campion?"

Mr. Campion tried not to grin.

"Snapdragons are just permissible at Christmas," he said. "Handled with extreme caution they burn very few fingers, it seems to me."

Mr. Campion tapped the cardboard box. "And some of them provide a few plums for retiring coppers, don't they, Superintendent?"